Seven

TRISTAN K. HODGES

Seven BY TRISTAN K. HODGES

This is a work of fiction. Although based on historical stories found in the Bible, the events and characters described here are products of the author's imagination.

ISBN 13: 978-168419316-5

DPP Double Portion Publishing
1053 Eldridge Loop
Crossville, TN 38571
www.doubleportionpublishing.com

Cover image: "Flaming June" by Sir Frederic Leighton, 1895, Museo de Arte de Ponce, Ponce, Puerto Rico. This work is in the public domain in the United States.

Dedicated to the Lord

"...so that they may know the truth, and that they may come to their senses and escape the snare of the devil, having been taken captive by him to do his will."
2 Timothy 2:25-26

Seven

PROLOGUE

WHERE IT ALL began she fights to forget. Somewhere within her a door had been unlocked, and the first of many spirits eased open the entryway leading to her soul. What she chooses to remember, however, gives her immeasurable peace. She has survived the unthinkable. Like two shadows that walk beside her, memories both to forget and to remember demonstrate their allegiance. Though they are silent she can still feel them calling to her.

Miriam...

The earth's heat radiates from its surface, warming feet and hooves alike in the early days of autumn. Miriam travels with a convoy from Jerusalem to Galilee, donkeys weighed down with provisions and camels loaded with possessions. The caravan inches along the well-worn road like ants advancing in single file, moving north at a steady pace. They travel through wilderness, a place of vipers and scorpions. As soon as the shelter—coppery and golden in the late afternoon sun—comes into sight Miriam lets out a sigh of relief. Her tired body aches to rest. Throughout the day she had envisioned a calm and peaceful evening, enjoying a modest meal over a simple fire, where her mind and limbs would release their laden loads.

Upon arriving, she dips a piece of cloth into one of the water troughs, using it to wipe away the grime and sweat stuck on her skin. The coolness of the water refreshes her in a powerful way, giving her the energy to finish the day's tasks. With the help of Susanna and Joanna, she prepares for their group a light supper of dried fish, dates, and olives, accompanied by some day-old wine. They sit around the fire eating with mountainous hunger.

Once satisfied, Miriam reclines, allowing the quietness to flood over her. For such a large lodging, the caravansary comprises only a single story limestone building, a walled courtyard, and a well. The rooms open out into the courtyard, where the animals and travelers draw fresh water from a well that seems to have an endless supply. Activities trickle to a slow pace. Only a handful of others mingle throughout the caravansary as night begins to fall.

On that clear, starlit night, she is drawn into the warmth of the saffron flickers that seem to entrance her like a charmed snake. Miriam allows her body to ease under its soft light after many parched and baked hours of travel. She can hardly recall how long they had been on the road that day. Now at a place where water, coolness, and rest serve her like dutiful servants, she begins to move towards sweet slumber. With preparations for the next day completed, she turns with exhaustion upon her blankets and permits her eyes to close. The heat has at last given way to a pleasant temperature, and Miriam—lulled by the nocturnal insects playing their timeless music—drifts off into a comfortable sleep.

"Open the gate! Quickly, this man needs help!" The voice is authoritative and strong, dashing the tranquility.

Miriam emerges from her sleep with a jolt as a great disturbance fills the courtyard. The sharp and sudden words ring out through the caravansary, containing great urgency. Confusion fills both her mind and the camp as she and the other travelers attempt to discover the meaning of the cries. With men shouting and animals bleating, clouds of dust rise up from under all of the moving feet. Miriam tries to focus her eyes on the unfolding commotion.

"What's wrong?" someone says.

"What happened?" says another.

Miriam begins to formulate questions of her own, but her voice is drowned out by the various sounds of a campsite abruptly coming to life in the darkness of night.

"This man was left for dead," the Samaritan says.

"He looks dead," the innkeeper says. "Is he alive?"

"Yes."

"Is he Judean? Greek?"

"I don't know."

"Where did you find him?" someone says.

"I found him beside the road, stripped of clothes, beaten, and lying half dead."

"Bandits," says the innkeeper with disdain. "Did you see what happened?"

"Not the assault." The crowd looks intently as the Samaritan explains. "I saw a priest ahead of me on the road, but when he saw the man lying there he crossed to the other side of the road and passed him by, not giving a second glance."

"Won't risk becoming unclean," a voice whispers.

"But then another man—a temple assistant—saw him and walked over to him. I thought he was going to help, but he just looked at him lying there, and then passed by on the other side as well."

Miriam's mind begins to race. From the look of it, the man appears to be holding death's hand. It will truly be a miracle if he lives, Miriam thinks. But such things are not uncommon to her anymore.

"I thought he was dead, as the others did, but I wanted to make sure," said the Samaritan. "I put some olive oil and wine on his wounds and bandaged them as best I could."

"You are a good man to bring a beaten stranger to shelter," the innkeeper says.

Susanna whispers to Miriam, "A good Samaritan *is* hard to find."

Miriam shoots her a stern look. "We will help care for him," she says. Beside her, Susanna and Joanna nod in agreement.

Handing the innkeeper a bag of money, the Samaritan says, "This should be enough to allow him time to stay and heal."

"More than enough," he says, the silver coins jingling in his hand.

Miriam and Susanna exchange glances, both recalling a similar scene. Chills scamper across her body.

"If his bill runs higher, I will pay you the next time I'm here."

"Where do you want to put him?" the innkeeper asks Miriam.

Pointing, she indicates a room on the ground floor that opens out into the courtyard. They quickly move the injured man from the Samaritan's donkey to the sheltered area. Not wasting any time, the women begin tending to him. A single oil lamp sits on the ground, illuminating the small room. Though it seems that he isn't breathing, Miriam can hear little rasps of air coming from his chest now and again. The caravansary quiets down to sleep once again, and she is thankful for the stillness. With great care and focus she cools his head with damp rags. Joanna applies aloe to his burned skin, and Susanna bandages his wounds. Their touch is gentle and warm. Miriam then washes his hands and feet. Her hands move with measured tenderness, her lips whisper prayers on his behalf. In an effort to combat the dehydration that has ravaged his body, Miriam takes a rag soaked in water and presses it against his mouth. Some of the liquid seeps in, sliding down his throat, but most runs down the sides of his face and neck. When they have done all that they can, they sit in silence, waiting to see if he will live or die.

At that moment, the innkeeper enters the room. "Will he live?"

"I'm not sure," Miriam answers. "We are doing everything we know how."

Staring at the beaten man, he says, "If my wife were here she would know what to do. She always knew how to handle situations like this."

"What happened to her?" Joanna asks cautiously. "Where is she?"

Sighing deeply, he says, "She left me for another man. He was a guest here once, many years ago."

"I am sorry to hear that."

"They say that her marriage to him didn't last long either. Seems her lust has gotten beyond her control."

"What do you mean?" Miriam says.

"I hear that she has had *five* husbands, and now lives with a man who is *not* her husband."

Susanna's face registers surprise, and Miriam lowers her head, smiling at the realization. She had heard of this woman from her traveling companions. Only yesterday as they'd passed to the west of Sychar were they talking about this sinful Samaritan woman and her marital experiences.

"Perhaps she has mended her ways," Miriam offers.

"Impossible," he says, snorting.

"With God *all* things are possible. Even for your wife... and this man here," Miriam says, looking back at the dying stranger.

Not understanding, the owner gives Miriam a look of suspicion and then departs.

Moments later Susanna says, "Samaria... the sooner we get out of here the better."

"Seems like everyone here is connected to each other somehow," Joanna answers.

"If the owner's wife doesn't stop sinning, she's going to have to move to

Judea because there won't be anyone left for her to marry," says Susanna.

Miriam laughs under her breath.

"At least *he's* not an option," Joanna says, nodding at their patient.

"He's going to need constant care and supervision," Miriam says.

The women agree to watch him throughout the night, taking turns so they can each get some sleep. Miriam volunteers to go first and promises to wake them when she gets tired.

When Joanna and Susanna settle down on their pallets, Miriam truly sees him for the first time. Like a pile of crumbled stones, he lays broken and unmoving on the makeshift bed. Bald, thin, and ragged looking, he has lines of deep creases on his face and hands, each one seeming to disclose a story. His only identification comes from the torn bits of clothing that reflect different regions and styles. Weathered from the baking sun, the man carries an internal emptiness that echoes loud enough for her to hear. In utter compassion Miriam's heart goes out to him, and she hopes that God will use her to keep him alive. The prospect of that, however, doesn't look promising.

For a while Miriam just stares at him, wondering all sorts of things. In her mind she runs though different scenarios, trying to guess how he ended up in this condition. But then she tries another approach.

"Can you hear me?" she says softly. No response or movement. "You were found on the road and have been brought to this shelter in Sebaste. You're beaten and bleeding..."

Silence.

"But I'm here to take care of you."

Miriam hopes that he will respond in some way, to give a signal that he can hear what she is saying. She hopes that her voice will lure him out like the warmth of the sun on a cold day. But her efforts at engaging him fall to the ground like heavy raindrops, their lifespan short-lived and bursting upon impact. In the end, Miriam accepts the fact that he is incoherent and unresponsive. Her attention shifts to the shadows that loom in the room, and she recalls her own shadows. She isn't prepared, however, for the deluge of emotions that wash over her.

So much has happened and yet there is still so much to process. The past few years seem somewhat surreal even though the memories run through her head with regularity. Before her that night, memories mingle with the shadows, and Miriam realizes that she needs to vocalize the things that swirl about inside her, to give words to her experiences. And since the patient lying beside her is comatose, she feels safe to disclose it all. She does not, nevertheless, desire to spew it all out as if confessing sins before a priest; that will not suffice. Just as she escorts that thought from her mind, another one enters. It's the perfect method, one as ancient as her heritage. As the primary means for passing on information to generations of people, it is not only a crucial part of her culture, it is a part of her very being.

Within moments she hears her voice transform into that of a storyteller. Inside herself she also hears the echoes of her mother and sister and other women who have taught her the importance of this sacred art. Through various inflections and tones, in both Greek and Hebrew, she creates an atmosphere ruled by animation, reverence and mystery. Surprised at how uninhibited the words are, Miriam feels a growing excitement as she listens to what pours forth from her own lips. On a base level the story keeps her awake and helps pass the time, but on a deeper and more entrenched level it serves as a therapeutic balm. What unfolds in the silence—what only the stars overhear—is the account that has brought her to that very room.

PART ONE

1

It ALL STARTED when seven wicked spirits wanted to have fun one late full-mooned night as they roamed like hungry, wild animals throughout the Galilean town of Magdala, seeking something to devour. After all, they were always on some sort of assignment from their evil master. Looking around, one of the creatures suggested with great excitement that they seize the lone nomad who was emerging from the valley and coming toward the town.

The man chosen had been wandering from town to town, from one odd job to another, working only to feed himself. In fact, he lived without purpose as much as the desert lives without rain. The spirits would use this to accomplish their unrighteous goals in the same way that *Melek Dâvîd*, King David, used the battle against the Ammonites to kill *Ûwrîyâhûw*, or Uriah, so he could marry the man's wife. And so, the seven spirits all agreed to possess the nomad, and on they jumped. In an instant, they transformed the man into a prowler seeking a prey.

Creeping around the roadways of *Migdâl*, or Magdala, in the still of night, the man saw few things other than common animals for prey opportunity, that is, until a young girl was spotted sitting by herself. In that moment one wicked spirit led the charge, and the remaining spirits agreed to attack. They, of course, didn't care that she was frail and powerless. They existed solely to steal, kill, and destroy. To them it would be just another satisfying conquest and victory.

But I'm jumping ahead of myself. The story actually begins a bit further back.

As a girl of twelve *Miryâm*, Miriam, lived a simple life. Her hometown of Magdala was modest in size and filled with Jewish families as it sat perched in the northern portion of the land of *Yisrâ'êl*, Israel, otherwise known as the *Gâlîyl*, or Galilee, region. Galilee was a beautiful land as colorful as a painter's work of art: vibrant hills decorated with fragrant flowers, snow-tipped mountains, green valleys that guided streams of water, and the only living sea in the country. Because most of the surrounding areas—like Judea, Samaria and Idumea—offered a dry and barren landscape, Galilee stood distinct from them, as though it had been misplaced somehow.

Seated at the base of *Har Ârvêl*, Mount Arvel—a mountain that towered like a giant over the city and its people— Magdala nestled snugly next to the waters of *Yâm Gâlîyl*, the Sea of Galilee. In that part of the land the fishermen lined the coastline the way rocks lined the shallow areas of the sea floor. As the main focus of the town, the waters served as a source of trade for thousands of people, specifically those who made their home on the shores.

A lovely body of water, the sea resided in a long, slender rift of land that extended down from its northern neighbor of Syria and up from its southern neighbors in eastern Africa. Two major trade routes sat on either side of the rift, just as a rider's legs flanked each side of a horse's body, with the King's Highway on the east and the Way of the Sea on the west. Hundreds of thousands of feet, hooves, chariots and caravans left their imprints, trade goods, histories, cultures and languages along the those roads, creating a mosaic as colorful and bright as *Nôach's*, Noah's, rainbow. These avenues connected Greece to Egypt, Asia to Africa, and Germania to Arabia. That was why the land resembled a cooking pot of nationalities and cultures, and earned the name Galilee of the Gentiles.

In spite of all they brought to the land these Gentiles, or *Gôyim*, had been labeled outsiders from the general Jewish way of thinking. As an *Y'hûwdîy*, or Jew, Miriam flourished in a family who operated under the commandments given by *Môsheh*, Moses, who had received the law thousands of years before that time. Though the God of Israel had many names, such as *Elôhîm* or *Adônâi*, the one used most often was *Yâhwêh*, Yahweh. Not unlike some other cultures, the Jewish race set themselves apart from all other peoples in worship, customs, and diet. For them it wasn't just a religion, it was a standard of living. Even though it seemed like an odd and constricting way of life from a Gentile perspective, the Jews viewed it as blessed. And so, for the most part, these two entities of people kept their interactions with one another to a minimum, in the same way that camels and snakes do.

As it happened, on a hot, late summer night a *gêyr*, foreign man, traveled through Galilee by the Way of the Sea and split off down a narrow well-worn path, heading towards the sea from the countryside. Like water funneled downhill through the crevices of rocks, he was guided—or pulled as if by an unseen force—to the end of the road where he was spit out at the hem of Magdala. The dangerous path he'd taken, known as the Valley of Robbers, was home to scores of roaming bandits and nomads. With craggy coves and dark corners, it offered areas of protective covering for the bandits who waited for unsuspecting tribesmen and caravans to pass through. These outlaws, as thirsty for blood as the Philistines or Ammonites, created their own law of thievery and brute force, which is to say their operations of business took on a violent nature. While not everyone who passed through this valley encountered them, most everyone knew the dangers involved in traversing the path and traveled at their own risk.

Just as the nomad made his way toward the seaside town Miriam stirred in her bed. She was restless in her sleep that night, due in part to the nagging summer heat. In the same manner that cats creep around in silence, she made her way through the stale air of the dark house toward the outdoors, hoping that the sounds of nature and the stars would soothe her restlessness. At once she felt the night confront the thin layer of sweat that coated her body and caused her hair to stick to her neck and temples. In one long inhalation Miriam breathed in the Galilee air, warm yet fresh. It calmed and soothed her just the way her mother's songs did as a young child. Fragrances of honeysuckle and hyacinth gently greeted her, like soft and tender kisses.

"I love nights like this," she whispered.

Miriam stood there a moment, enjoying her surroundings before deciding to venture out further into the night. Right then only one thing could've felt better to her skin...the cool waters of the sea. Barefoot, she walked on her toes without a sound through the courtyard behind her home, around a handful of her neighbors' homes, and out onto the road that led to the sea.

She could feel the water beckoning her, calling her by name. Jewish custom, though, didn't approve of women, and especially girls, traveling alone during daylight hours, even more so after dark. But that regulation didn't prevent her journey that night, or on other nights, for that matter. Though it was a secret she kept with more care than *Râchêl*, Rachel, hiding pagan idols from her husband *Yaʿăqôv*, or Jacob, she had cooled her feet in the water on many hot summer nights. As she made her way toward the water, Miriam looked around making sure no one would spot her, especially the overabundance of men who fished the fruitful waters. To her delight, all was quiet and peaceful. Sounds of wind and lapping water caressed her ears. The moon, distant in the sky, shined a path of light for her steps, though she knew the way by heart and could find her destination even if her eyes were covered.

After creeping to the coastline, which looked to her like a mosaic of small brown and gray and black stones, Miriam's feet soon found the cool liquid. Once there, she slowly pulled up her nightclothes—with caution and uncertainty, of course—then eased into the water. Gliding in between her toes, over the tops of her feet, and climbing her thin legs above her bony knees, the sea enveloped her. In silence she thanked it for the soothing licks of the tiny waves. Throughout the years and varying temperaments, she could count on the water to befriend her. On a certain, perhaps childish, level Miriam felt companionship.

After the water had cooled her well enough she began to make her exit. The longer she stayed the greater her chances of being seen, so Miriam bid the sea farewell. But before returning home her legs needed time to dry off. Then she eyed her special spot on the hill that overlooked the water, as if it was a guard protecting the harbor.

Within minutes Miriam found her favorite place—a small, grassy table that sat half way up a small hill, with remarkable views. Raised above the seaside homes, she observed the town made by human hands that huddled inside the cloak of Yahweh's creation. A few oil lamps dotted the cityscape, but mostly the light came from the twinkling sky above. It seemed to Miriam that the tall, thick grass beneath her tried to hide her from the world, even for a moment. As she rested there with her knees pulled to her chest and her thin arms wrapped around her legs, she embraced the warm night air that gave way to occasional soft breezes. Her long, dark hair fell in loose curls over her shoulders and down her back, swaying with each wave of wind. Her almond-shaped eyes gazed up into the depths of the universe. Once again she marveled at having been born in such a majestic place.

Miriam carried an amenable quality that ushered her through life with a joyful heart and a profound sense of ease. She displayed a carefree nature to everyone around her, like a butterfly that fluttered through the air without a care in the world. What's more, she'd been given a love for singing, and a voice to match. Her father used to say that her voice rivaled the sounds of the seraphim angels. Almost every day of Miriam's life she and her mother, *Channâh*, Hannah, had sung a particular song called the Shepherd's Psalm. A psalm of David—the greatest king in the history of Israel—it was Miriam's favorite. Softly, she hummed the familiar tune with its lovely language, and counted her many blessings.

Enraptured in her thoughts and praises to Yahweh who made the wonders of heaven and earth, Miriam didn't hear the man approach her from behind until she felt his tight grip over her mouth.

"Don't say a word," he whispered into her ear. Making sure she wasn't going to scream, he then spoke in his distant accent. "You remind me of a daughter I once had."

With his left hand clutched firmly on her mouth, the stranger managed to pin her back against the soft, green ground and then crawl atop her. The man, propelled by the seven raging spirits, aimed to take from her the fragile things that belonged to someone else, which is to say her purity and innocence.

Overcome with panic and acting on instinct, Miriam struggled against the forces seen and unseen in what was, in essence, a fight for her life. But her limbs were no match against his. The man, who smelled worse than a beast covered in filth, let her struggle as much as she could without fighting back. He merely held her in a tight grip, allowing her energy to escape into the night air just as smoke from incense drifts up and disappears. For a while all she heard was the sound of air being sucked into her nose, which felt to her like too many people trying to fight their way through a small door. When she stopped struggling from weariness she heard his thick voice.

"Now, that is better."

With his matted hair hanging in her face and his sulfurous breath burning her nostrils, she turned her head to the right as best as she could in order to escape his evil, possessed eyes. She chose to look at the stars instead. They were her only peace that night. Tears ran down the sides of her face and small whimpers seeped through his fat, grimy hand. And with every sound that she made he gripped her tighter, reinforcing his control. To his satisfaction, her noises were instantly muffled. As he had predicted, no one down in the city heard a thing.

The man wasn't all that big, in fact, just overweight and surprisingly strong. He reminded her of those average looking men who could lift an object three times their size. Beginning with her face, the man began to sweep over her skin with his coarse paw, for indeed it felt like an animal's. He moved slowly down her neck, managing to touch almost every part of her exposed skin.

Why is he doing this? She begged someone to hear her thoughts. *Doesn't anyone know what is happening? Somebody help me!*

Taking his time and eyeing his treasure, the man inched his way down with his free hand. Panic surged again through her body, and Miriam began to fight anew. Even though he expected it his patience was thinning and his loins were ready.

"It won't be long now," he said under his breath.

Suddenly, there was a noise—faint but unmistakable. He stopped and glanced quickly toward the direction where he thought it had originated. Looking around the dark, he scanned the horizon. Even though he saw nothing, he waited and watched. Miriam didn't hear it, but she knew that something had altered his attention away from her. She too perked her ears for a sign, praying that someone was there to rescue her. It was then that she noticed how hard and loudly her heart pounded against its tiny cage, as if trying to break free from the boundary placed around it. But other than her heart, Miriam heard nothing.

The attacker reached the same conclusion after a few moments. "Nothing. I am hearing things."

As fast as lightning, the seven spirits brought his attention back to Miriam. Focusing him, they were the driving force behind the frightful event, not leaving him any room to think about the wickedness of his actions. Like a rudder that controlled a boat, the spirits guided his every move. Once again, the man faced Miriam and smiled with an evil so forceful that she thought her heart would stop. She feared that his irritation at being disturbed would cause him to inflict unbearable violence, so she braced herself as much as she could.

"Please stop, please!" she cried in a muffled whimper.

But as they both knew, he had no intention of stopping. Just as he started to touch her again he noticed something strange.

"Look at me," he demanded.

Miriam kept her head turned in spite of his command. She couldn't bear to look into those eyes burning with the fires of *sh'ôl*, or hell. Angry, he yanked her head until they were face-to-face, noses mere inches apart. What the nomad saw changed everything.

"Diabolos! Your eyes!" he cried.

As if she had leprosy, he jumped up and disappeared in the same fashion as he'd appeared, which is to say without a sound. As she later learned, only the spirits stayed behind. After that Miriam found herself hearing over and over his parting words. Even though they came from his mouth it sounded like an unearthly voice. *You WILL NOT tell anyone about this or I will kill you. I will come back and find you again.*

Despite the fact that she'd never seen him before, she had no doubt that he would indeed come back for her if she spoke up. Foreigners traversed Magdala on a frequent basis; he would stand out no more than all the others. She guessed that he was a bandit, spewed from the mouth of the Valley of Robbers like *Yôwnâh*, Jonah, from the great fish. Miriam knew, of course, that lawless bandits roamed the Galilee region, and she knew about the famous legend. The events of the legend—which had taken place only a few years prior to her birth—told of the capture and execution of the most gruesome bandit leader by Herod Antipas, the Roman governor of Galilee. It had been a significant victory for Herod as well as the people of northern Galilee, but sadly there were always more waiting to take the fallen leader's place.

At that point Miriam picked herself up off the ground and ran home where she crawled into bed, crying until she fell into a fitful sleep. For hours her mind wrestled, like Jacob with the angel of the Lord, over the night's events—the place where she had been saved by the fact that Yahweh had given her one eye as green as emeralds and the other as brown as tawny soil.

When she woke an hour after dawn, the exhaustion she felt encompassed every part of her. Her eyes were puffy and her face was hardened from the rivers of burning tears that had trekked over it during the night. Not wanting to get out of bed and face her family, Miriam remained curled up under the blankets, hiding from the world and her memories. Even though she hadn't been ravaged, she might as well have been. It was, in essence, the same thing. She'd been touched in places that were supposed to be reserved for her husband alone. In other words, the situation left her every bit as impure as muddy water. If she told the truth, she would be stained, the way henna stains the hands. *I will be marked for life.* With that thought, a hope and a future vanished before her eyes.

"Miriam!" she heard a familiar voice cry out.

Once again her mother ordered her to get up and do her chores. Water had to be drawn from the well, bread had to be baked, and her father needed help in the olive grove. There was no time for lounging in bed during a workday. Too many tasks had to be accomplished to assure that the household ran smoothly; Miriam was well aware of that. But getting up meant addressing what had happened a few hours before. Her face would surely betray her. Staying in bed meant she could avoid the questions her mother would ask after looking into her eyes. To tell the truth, Miriam didn't know what to do with her distress. Perhaps she should trust someone to help her, or perhaps she should keep it a secret. In her mind, talking about it seemed unbearable. On the other hand, ignoring the problem seemed just as impossible. Either way, it would affect the course of her life. She felt like a tunic torn in two; no matter what she decided, she'd never be whole again.

"Miriam, is there something wrong?" her mother finally inquired. Hannah's tone carried a great deal of impatience.

After a long pause she responded, "No. I just had bad dreams."

Her experience and the weight of her thoughts led her to make a decision as big as the wilderness. She would try with all her might to bury it deeper than a well of fresh water.

Seven

And so, the door to her soul had been cracked open. As a result of her lie the seven spirits had entrance into her inner sanctuary. Lies were familiar territory for them; that was what they knew. Truth was the only force that kept them away. But lies had replaced the truth. The signal had been given.

2

ONCE MIRIAM HAD indicated that she would rather lie than tell the truth, the spirits began formulating a long-term plan. It was a job for the seven of them. They could each possess her separately, but destruction was always more fun when the seven worked as a team. For them, the experience would be more destructive and more devastating, or in other words just more enjoyable.

Sitting around like a brood of vipers, the spirits chattered about and drooled at the opportunity that stood before them. They each shouted out ideas for ultimate destruction, their vileness unrestrained. More and more the seven spirits grew enthused as they stirred each other up, bantering back and forth and flaunting their tools of wickedness. And they cackled with fierce laughter, sounding like a pack of wild dogs, as they plotted to unravel another life.

Determining the order of entrance into Miriam's life was a fierce process because all seven spirits wanted to be first. None wanted to be submissive to the others; after all, they viewed themselves as equally evil, even though ranks existed within their kingdom. So they drew lots. That method proved to be the only one suitable to lessen the amount of nasty bickering. And despite the order that fell, they respected one another's position. Frequent competition existed between the seven, to be sure, as to which one could perform the best, but in the end they cheered each other on in their unified pursuit of possession.

The first lot drawn belonged to the Spirit of Fear. Dark and ugly, Fear slinked around with a mysterious aura, seeping—undetected, of course—into people's lives like smoke absorbs into clothing. With heavy, penetrating eyes, the evil spirit exuded control, not afraid to stand its ground in fierce aggression. The spirit gave meaning to the word sinister. In an instant, Fear's power could be felt by anyone, for it was a power that mimicked the speed, force, and uncertainty of lightning.

As the first spirit, Fear smiled at the fact that it would take Miriam's hand and lead her into the kingdom of darkness. In order to make false evidence appear real, the Spirit of Fear would use its powers of persuasion along side its threatening presence. The first spirit to enter always held the position of being the gateway spirit, which allowed all others to gain access. It alone had the responsibility to bring her into a place of submission so that the other six spirits could follow with ease. As it turned out, Fear was an excellent gateway.

* * *

Before talking to her, the Spirit of Fear followed Miriam everywhere for three days. It wanted to watch her for a while in order to determine the best avenue of attack. Sitting in the corner of her room at night while she slept, the spirit had examined its target in the same way that a hunter scopes a grazing animal. During the day it had watched her body language, her interactions with others, her moments alone—when she worked, when she ate, when she avoided her family and friends. The spirit waited with eagerness and then stepped into her life as if crossing the threshold of a home.

Miriam was helping her father in their olive grove one balmy day, the light illuminating the silvery-green leaves of the trees, catching her eye. Miriam rubbed the long, slender leaves between her fingers, noticing how they contrasted sharply with the dark brown branches and trunk. Green and brown. Like her eyes. All her life she hated the fact that she had eyes in different colors. She had endured for twelve years the looks of fear from adults, the teasing of cruel children, and the unanswered questions to Yahweh. But the truth was they had saved her that night. Her eyes had scared the nomad with a power greater than the earth shaking. And for the first time, Miriam thanked Yahweh for her mismatched eyes.

It was late afternoon that day, but she felt as if the sun had suddenly disappeared. Looking around, Miriam saw nothing out of place. Butterflies chased one another between the rows of trees. Songbirds whistled sweet melodies back and forth. Her brothers were watering the tree roots to battle the hot summer temperature. She bent down to remove some weeds growing by the gnarled truck of a tree, and when she stood up she heard it.

"Next time you won't escape."

The invisible voice was as clear as the sky overhead. Miriam dropped her basin and walked away, leaving the weeds scattered on the ground. She found a jug of water a few trees over and attempted to relieve her suddenly parched throat. Shaking with fright, she felt a wave of queasiness rise up in her belly.

To tell the truth, Fear's strategy wasn't complicated: it attacked the weak spot within her. It began with a simple lie. And she believed it, maybe because she was only twelve years old or maybe because it wasn't inconceivable for him to return. At that point, and without her permission of course, Fear latched on with forceful talons like a hawk on its prey.

"What if he really comes back?" Miriam whispered. "What if he tries to kill me anyway even though I haven't told anyone?"

More lies waited. "Of course he'll show up again. He's probably watching your every move, waiting for the right time," Fear mocked. The spirit's voice sounded in her mind like a *shôphâr*, or ram's horn, signaling battle.

Miriam spun around expecting the nomad to be nearby. She felt her head spin with dizziness. It took only a few seconds for the thought of her attacker to produce a spasm of fear within her. The image brought fear and fear brought more terrifying images. To the spirit's delight, it was a trap of gladiatorial proportions. She was pitted, in essence, against a force a thousand times stronger and more committed on being victorious. Truth be told, she didn't stand a chance.

Minutes later after regaining her physical and mental balance, Miriam paced around the grove the same way that young David had when fearing for his life at the hand of *Melek Shâ'ûwl*, King Saul. Without her knowledge, the Spirit of Fear watched her blurt out a confession of dread.

"What am I going to do? I'm afraid that he'll find me... I'm afraid that the next time will be worse... I'm afraid that something will happen while I'm sleeping... or when I least expect it. I'm just so afraid of what could happen!" Miriam seemed to be holding her breath in concentration. She exhaled heavily. "I can't be a fool and believe that I'll live to be Methuselah's age—I could die tomorrow. He could come and kill me tomorrow!"

Pleased, the Spirit of Fear applauded Miriam. "You *should* be afraid! You never know what's going to happen—what tomorrow holds. Always keep the worst in mind so you'll be ready for it."

"Maybe if I stay close to my family everything will be fine. He wouldn't attack me with other people around." She looked at her father and brothers.

"The truth is your family was unable to protect you before, and they won't be able to in the future either," Fear lied.

"Oh, Yahweh help me!"

Miriam heard a wicked cackle that turned her skin into ripples that looked like the flesh on a chicken. Unable to find stable ground, she faltered as though walking on fields soaked with too much rain.

"Miriam!" Benjamin yelled as he approached her.

For the second time in ten minutes she almost jumped out of her skin. "What?" she said, tensely.

"What are you doing? Who are you talking to?"

"Nothing. Nobody. Just myself."

"Are you all right? You look as pale as the moon," he told her.

"I do? Yes, I'm fine," she said, glancing at the olive trees around them.

"Is there something going on?" Concern filled his voice.

"Just the heat, I think." Rubbing her eyes, she said, "Let's get back to work."

But Miriam couldn't concentrate. Her thoughts, in fact, were almost worse than the actual event. Every time she envisioned herself in a dangerous situation her pulse quickened and all the muscles in her body tensed in response. Her imagination was not only running away with her, it was dragging her through the mud like a chariot pulling a tortured body at the arena games.

Thanks to the thread of lies that Fear strung along before her, Miriam found herself in such a state of confusion that she didn't know what to believe, her common sense or her nerves. Everything had become unclear and clouded. She had lost her innocence of youth. She had lost the security for her future. She had lost confidence in herself as well as in the safety of her home. Worst of all, she had lost her dreams. Lost not in the sense of misplaced but of robbed as if by bandits.

As Miriam later learned, the secret to the spirits' control could be found in their weapons. Each demonic spirit carried weapons that were used to assert control, like a bag of magic tricks that fooled the spectator. Never did they operate without them, nor did they want to. These weapons, formed with purpose against the victims, were deliberate, and they prospered more than the riches of the Roman Empire.

For Fear—and all evil spirits, in fact—lies were essential. Over and over, lies proved to be the strongest weapons available to achieve destructive results. And so, they were used again and again, without measure. Fear knew that truth brought freedom and that, in contrast, lies brought captivity. In light of that, its goal was clear, which is to say it would keep her believing lies, no matter what it took.

After weeks of festering, Miriam felt that she needed to confide in someone. She rocked back and forth like a vessel on choppy water, trying to decide if the idea was sound or flawed.

"I'm afraid to tell someone, but I want to. Can I really keep this a secret forever?" she asked herself.

"You should *always* keep this a secret," the Spirit of Fear said. "It will only make things worse if you confess."

"Who would I be able to tell?"

"Certainly not your father or brothers."

"No, definitely not. I can hardly even imagine how they'd react."

"And not your friends," said Fear.

"They would just tell their parents..."

"Who would probably tell the Pharisees. Then you'd be dragged into the center of town and stoned to death! Is that what you want?"

"There must be someone who would understand... But who?"

"Exactly! There is no one. Even if you did tell someone they wouldn't believe you." Without hesitation, Fear kept the deception moving right along. "They'll think you're making it up to get attention."

"But I don't do things like that."

"Maybe, but think. Can you really tell someone all of the dreadful details that would be necessary to make the story believable?"

Miriam let a long pause fill the air as she considered the spirit's question. Her soft voice ended the silence. "No, probably not. It's just too painful! I can hardly think about it much less talk about it."

Seven

The Spirit of Fear allowed Miriam some time with these freshly brewed untruths, letting her feel that her conclusion was the only way. Because Miriam agreed with Fear, she, in essence, secured her mind to a false line of thinking like a boat tied to a dock. Knowing that the tactic had succeeded, the spirit gave her another idea for good measure.

"Besides, your father would punish you for wandering out of the house in the middle of the night."

"That's true, he would," she said. "The last thing that I need is Abba's wrath. On top of everything, that would be too much to bear."

"Better to keep it all to yourself."

Miriam nodded in silent agreement. And with that understanding, the relationship between Miriam and the Spirit of Fear became fortified. The spirit fed her thoughts that dripped of dread, and she consumed them, succumbing day after day to their demands just as her stomach submitted to the persistent demands of hunger. In turn, she created a suitable place for the spirit to dwell, much like an internal city fortress guarded by high walls. The arrangement, which the spirit savored, was perfect.

From summer to fall Fear resided with her, and Miriam began to see glimpses of her bondage, though she would never admit it. She believed in a realm where spirits roamed as well as in the existence of good and evil. But beyond that she hadn't given much thought to unclean spirits. She assumed wrongly, of course, that those kinds of spirits controlled only unrighteous people, or rather people who were plainly wicked. She'd been raised, after all, in a family that feared Yahweh. Miriam couldn't imagine why an evil spirit would want to afflict her. And so, the Spirit of Fear came to her in a voice that sounded like her own, tickling her ears with more lies.

"You're right; there are no evil spirits around you. Nothing is haunting you."

"Maybe I'm imagining things," she said.

"That's right, it's only your imagination! You're making it all up."

"I must be."

Just as lying was easier than telling the truth, denial was easier than acceptance. The spirit knew that she couldn't confront it unless she believed it was real. The Spirit of Fear, as clever as the serpent in *Gan Êden*, the Garden

23

of Eden, told Miriam what she wanted to hear. By lying and twisting the truth Fear made things that were true seem false and things that were false seem true. Because Miriam didn't believe that the truth would free her, she accepted the fear and confusion that swaddled her tighter than an infant in fresh linens.

* * *

By the middle of fall it seemed to Miriam that she'd been saddled with a harness of fear, in the same way that oxen carried a yoke. The more that she gave in to the Spirit of Fear, the tighter the harness grew. The plan, as Fear had intended, was working beautifully.

Without apology, Fear brought torment. Working from within Miriam, the Spirit of Fear extended its arms into every part of her being in the same way that sickness spreads into each limb and organ. Fear manifested itself during the day, throughout her chores, in her thoughts and conversations, and always at night. She lived in a state of tension for the most part, unable to breathe freely, suffering under the invisible cloak of heaviness that robed her. Despite the fact that she was more terrified than *Hâmân*, Haman, when his plan to kill the Jews was discovered by *Melek Ăchashvêrôwsh*, King Ahasuerus, Miriam tried to keep on a veil of normalcy, to keep all of the madness and disgrace inside. But more and more she found it difficult to keep up the outward show, especially to her family.

If things had been different, Miriam's older sister, *Hădaççâh*, would've noticed right away; but as chance would have it, Hadassah had recently gotten married and moved to Chorazin. So instead, the first person to confront Miriam was her eldest brother *Binyâmîyn*, Benjamin. With dark curly hair and dark brown eyes he bore a greater resemblance to Miriam than *Lêvîy*, Levi, her other brother. Benjamin—stocky like a wine cask and as perceptive as an eagle—was the most outspoken of them all. He never hesitated to confront family members when he thought problems existed. For Miriam, she both loved and hated that part of her brother.

One afternoon while she was mending the hems of her tunics in a corner of their house, Benjamin snuck up behind her and placed a hand on her shoulder. Miriam jumped and fell off the stool. Her heart pounded harder than *Âdâm's*, Adam's, in the Garden of Eden when, naked and afraid, he heard the voice of Yahweh calling him.

"Miriam, why are you so tense?" he asked.

"I'm not; you scared me, that's all. Don't sneak up on me, Benjamin."

"I didn't—you were deep in thought and didn't hear me come in. What were you thinking about?"

"Nothing, just this hem."

"I need to bring some tools over to Seth's house, do you want to walk there with me?" he asked. He would, of course, try to get her to talk as they went.

"No thanks," she replied. Her quick refusal concerned him all the more.

"Why not?"

"I need to finish this."

"But it's a gorgeous day. You never turn down an excuse to get out of the house on a day like today," Benjamin pointed out.

"I'd rather stay here."

"What's wrong with you lately? You never want to go outside anymore. You're always inside... like you're hiding from something or someone," he said. "Is one of your friends bothering you?"

Miriam shook her head while continuing to keep her hands busy. He didn't comment on the fact that they were shaking.

"Then what?"

"Nothing, Benjamin. There's nothing wrong," she lied.

He watched her for a moment, trying to find the best way to get her talking. He kneeled down beside her and spoke in a tone as sweet as fresh honey. "Okay, Miri, but still, you don't seem like yourself these days. Are you all right?"

"Yes, I'm... fair."

"To be honest, I don't believe you," he said. "Look me in the eyes and say that again."

Hesitating, Miriam gathered her strength and set her eyes in a glaze so as to pass his test. "I'm all right," she said, quickly looking away. She hoped against hope that he didn't see the fear lurking behind her eyes. She couldn't imagine trying to explain everything that had happened.

Benjamin let out a big sigh. "Miriam, whatever is the matter—and there *is* something the matter—you're not letting me help you or protect you."

"It's too late for your protection," Miriam whispered. Tears began to form in the corners of her eyes.

"What did you say?"

Afraid of where the conversation was headed, Miriam pressed her fingers against her eyes to halt the tears. "Nothing."

"Are you sure you don't want to go with me? Come on, it'll be fun, just the two of us."

"I can't," she answered, shaking her head and keeping her eyes on her task.

In the end, her brother conceded and departed in total confusion. The whole way over to *Shêth's*, Seth's, he attempted to figure out why Miriam had refused him. It was so unlike her. She seemed to be more and more of a mystery, and that bothered him to his core. Miriam knew, of course, that her brother would continue to probe until he got answers. But her resolve would have to be stronger than his curiosity.

"Nicely done," the Spirit of Fear said to Miriam when they were alone.

"I feel like he saw straight through my lies," she said in a voice that could hardly be heard.

"Even if he suspects that you're lying, which he probably doesn't, you made a smart decision by shutting him out."

"I wonder how long I can keep this up."

"Don't worry; it will just get easier and easier. Once people understand that you have nothing to disclose they will respect your privacy."

"I hope so."

"It's really none of their business anyway, remember that."

"I know." Her voice, though, betrayed her.

"Be sure about it. You're doing the right thing," Fear said.

* * *

"Wake up, Miriam," her mother said softly. "It's time."

Noises filled the dark, pre-dawn house. More than any other day, Miriam loved the morning of the first olive harvest. She could hear her father and brothers buzzing around the house in preparation for the day. She jumped up and threw on her clothes, joining the others for a breakfast of bread, tomatoes, cheese, and fruit. Anticipation and excitement bounced around the room, everyone eager to acquire the bountiful harvest.

"Let's finish up," her father said. "It's almost sunrise."

For the next few weeks, every day would be focused on harvesting the olives from the grove from sun up to sun down. They always began with the olives that were still green, as the un-ripened ones produced a strong, bitter flavor when pressed. A week later, the olives turning from green to black would be harvested, slightly bitter with hints of sweetness. Lastly, the week following, the black olives remaining would conclude the harvest—olives full of smooth, briny flavor.

As the sky grew brighter and more colorful, the grove filled up with men, women, and children. Thousands upon thousands of olives waited to be gleaned. Her father had hired extra hands to pick the bountiful harvest, as was common in years of abundance. The women clustered together with their children underfoot, while the men spread out, covering a larger area. Everyone, children included, picked the olives and collected them in large baskets. The men used long rakes to shake the top branches, letting the olives rain down onto large nets spread below each tree.

After an hour or so, the morning conversations settled down and singing began. One voice, then two. Melodies floated through the air, weaving in and out of branches, around the olives and into the baskets, which just about every woman claimed made them taste better. The men contributed here and there, not to be left out. Laughter from the children, now running and playing, created a harmony that rose up to the heavens. Soon the wooden carts pulled by donkeys filled up, laden with heaps of olives. They were taken to the mill, where oxen turned the grinding stone around and around to press out the fragrant essence of the fruit. Olive oil flowed as swiftly as water from the rock that Moses struck at the camp of *Rephîydîym*, Rephidim. The scent of crushed olives permeated the air, celebrating community, praising harvest. And for a few weeks Miriam forgot all her worries.

Worry, after some time, became the filter through which all her decisions and opinions passed, like a guard that regulated the passage of travel through the city gates. For instance, she grew anxious when thinking about her bodily development, afraid that the arrival of her breasts and the expansion of her hips would lure the nomad out of the valley once again. Fear caused Miriam to focus her attention on these types of assumed misconceptions. It seemed like she lived in a churning cycle of anxiety, tumbling head over feet without a horizon line to steady her.

The idea of being anxious for nothing—something she would've once believed in—seemed, at that point, illogical and impossible. The worries of her soul would not allow the sensations of fear to slip away, as water disappeared from a cracked urn. Though she wanted to ignore the harsh truths of her life, Miriam understood that she would never be allowed to return to a place of sweet innocence, where life and light danced together in perfect rhythm and unity. To her dismay, darkness and uncertainty were the only things found moving around her.

All at once, Miriam's tears arrived with savage force, but hours of crying out of emotional distress brought no relief. The peace that she desired remained out of her reach, unable to replace the viscous anxiety that clung to her.

During those days with the Spirit of Fear, Miriam remained quiet and withdrawn from everyone. The slow days after harvest time gave her a cover to retreat. Afraid that her family members would discover the truth, she spent most of her time hiding in her small room, giving in to the voice that nagged her. As alone as baby Moses had been in the basket floating on the Egyptian waters, she drifted further and further down a river of seclusion. She no longer sang or played with friends or tagged along behind her older brothers. Because it contrasted so greatly with her prior nature, her family took notice, and she overheard them trying to figure it out.

"It's just not right. She's acting so strange," her father *Zevûwlûn*, Zebulun, said.

"Something must have happened," Levi suggested.

"Has she confessed anything to you, Benjamin?" Hannah asked.

"No, nothing. I tried talking to her, but she said everything was all right."

"And you believed her?" Levi asked.

"At the time she was very convincing, though I did have some doubt. When I think about it now, I probably should've done something else."

Zebulun listened to his sons and then spoke. "I'm concerned about her. What do you think is going on?"

Seven

"Maybe one of her friends is giving her trouble," Benjamin said.

"Maybe she did something foolish and is hiding from embarrassment," Levi said.

"And maybe she's just growing out of childhood into womanhood," Hannah suggested. "She's at that age where things change a lot, and what makes sense one day doesn't the next."

"But this never happened to our other daughter."

"True, but you can't compare our children like that. Hadassah went through her changes as if nothing was happening. It could be the opposite for Miriam. But it does seem strange, I admit."

Each questioned her in a variety of ways, though to no reward. Miriam's lips remained as tight as a sealed jar of oil against their persistent efforts. She kept her secrets and lies alive, letting them grow. She felt the Spirit of Fear breathing down her neck, making sure she said the right things. The hairs on the back of her neck came to attention while shivers crisscrossed her body. The yoke of despair and oppression that weighed her down showed up even in her walk, which is to say the cheerfulness of tip toes had been replaced by the soberness of flat feet.

* * *

"Hello, again," the slimy voice whispered in her ear.

Gasping with fright, Miriam woke up from her dream. She froze with fear in the same way that the Israelites did when the giant *Golyath*, Goliath, arrived at the battle sight. Panic ran through her thin veins, feeling as liquid fire might. For months terrifying dreams had infiltrated her sleep. Sometimes they replicated the night of the attack; sometimes they were full of wicked, grotesque creatures. But the one that night—the recurring dream that she hated most—was the one with his voice.

Dream after dream, moment after moment, the Spirit of Fear haunted her with its persistence. Momentum played a large role in the spirit's strategy, where the different forms of torment used stacked upon one other like large stones of a temple. Only the temple that the spirit was building existed as a shrine to itself. Miriam could feel Fear's grip increasing, tightening a little bit more each day. The balance of power had shifted slowly yet noticeably. Even though she didn't want to admit it, she realized the power controlling her life belonged to someone else.

Then it happened one night as the dry fall changed into a wet winter. She awoke deep in the night, many hours before sunrise, to find herself sitting straight up, her heart trying to pound its way out of her chest. Feeling as though something was trying to pull her spirit out from her body, to drag her to the abode of the dead, Miriam screamed a single word over and over. Consumed with terror and panic, she clawed at the air, trying to break out of sleep's heavy covering that felt like layers of blankets on top of her. She pulled and yanked at covers and sleep clothes, responding to forces unseen. Cold sweat dripped down her body like oil used for anointing. The sound of her heart raced against the sound of her panting. Whipping her head around, Miriam expected to see someone in her room. She saw nothing, but knew she wasn't alone. Fear embraced her as she sat on her bed, draping itself across her body. Breathless as if she had just run from Magdala to *Kefâr Nâchûm*, Capernaum, Miriam understood.

Later on, Miriam thought that the same kind of gripping fear that rushed through her must have surged through *Yitschâq*, Isaac, upon the altar of sacrifice, and with the same violence. Isaac, the only son of *Avrâhâm*, Abraham, suffered under the visible hand of his father who held a knife over his body, whereas Miriam suffered under the invisible hand of the spirit. Though their circumstances differed as night and day she understood with great clarity the depths to which fear penetrated the heart and the mind, regardless of time or situation. Perhaps she was experiencing a test just as her ancestor had; yet she didn't truly believe that. Instead, she felt disconnected from everything and everyone, left to fend against something as forceful and unexpected as the earth trembling.

After hearing the scream, Miriam's mother appeared at her side. She brushed back her daughter's hair from her face and wiped the sweat from her brow.

"Shh, Miriam, it's all over now," Hannah said. "What were you dreaming about?"

Miriam didn't answer and kept her eyes down, even in the dark. "I don't know," she said.

"You were screaming."

"I was?"

"Yes, you kept saying the word *no* over and over."

All Miriam could do was shake her head. She put her hands over her eyes and fought the urge to cry.

"Miriam, you're shaking. Can't you remember anything?"

"No, I can't. I'm sure it was nothing." She couldn't seem to control her body from trembling.

"Of course it was something, sweet child, or else you wouldn't have been startled like this out of sleep. You see, the thoughts and feelings that we have during the day are stored away in our minds, and at night they all come out in one way or another. Sometimes the dreams are pleasant and sometimes they are frightening." Hannah paused, then asked, "Are you scared of something, Miriam?"

She took a deep breath and tried to keep the lie believable. "No, Ima, I'm not scared."

"We all get scared at one time or another, even your father and I, so it helps to talk about what scares us. That way it doesn't seem too bad." Hannah waited for her daughter to respond. It was clear that something had been bothering her. So Hannah waited some more, but nothing. It was too late to be honest now, Miriam reasoned. Too much time had elapsed. It was far easier to continue stringing the lies together than to announce the truth. Confessing would bring only more anxiety, not to mention humiliation. The Spirit of Fear kept a tight grip over her mouth the same way the nomad did that night.

"How about I sing to you? To calm you down and help you fall back to sleep."

"Yes," Miriam said, lying back down.

With the silkiness of oil, Hannah's voice began to pour out the shepherd's psalm. *"The Lord is my shepherd, I shall not want—"*

"Stop!" Miriam cried. The last time she sang that song the nomad had attacked her moments later. "Not that song."

"But you love that song; it's your favorite."

Shaking her head, Miriam said, "Something else. Please."

"All right," said Hannah. Thinking for a moment, she then started singing the *berâkâh*, or blessing, from the book of *Devarîm*, Deuteronomy. *"The Lord bless you and keep you, the Lord make His face to shine upon you. The*

Lord bless you and keep you, the Lord make His face to shine upon you. And be gracious unto you, and be gracious unto you. The Lord lift up His countenance upon you and give you rest."

It looked as if Miriam had drifted off. Kissing her forehead, Hannah whispered, "Rest now and be at peace."

As soon as Miriam was alone again she opened her eyes. Right away she sensed again a distinct presence lurking around. Feelings of distress swelled inside her. Further sleep for the night would be impossible. So she remained awake on her bed, thinking about the fear that wrapped itself around her heart in the same way that a turban wrapped around the head. To tell the truth, Miriam was frightened beyond all comprehension. Her thoughts resounded in her ears and emerged as a desperate cry.

"What is going on? Why can't I get control of this? What's the matter with me? Why does it keep coming back to haunt me?"

Fear howled with laughter at her questions. After a few moments of amusement, Fear hissed into Miriam's ear with fierce wickedness, in a voice that sounded exactly like the nomad's. *"BECAUSE I REMAIN IN CONTROL!"* It let out a roar of satisfaction that rippled through the air and hit her with incredible force.

Shivers ran all over her body and her insides shook violently. She closed her eyes only to see images of a hideous face seething with determination to torment her. Though she couldn't see the spirit with her natural eye, she knew it was real. No amount of Miriam's might could free her from the forces of Fear. They outmatched her every time. The spirit had swung Miriam from one end of fear to the other, whispering to screaming, back and forth. She wasn't aware, however, that such dominion would become permanent, promising to remain throughout the next decade of her life.

* * *

The next day, Miriam couldn't seem to get enough fresh air outside. As she pulled water up from the courtyard well, she heard the shouts of fishermen. The sea must have given them a plentiful catch, their voices full of excitement and urgency carrying up and down the streets of the village. Truth be told, Miriam longed to go back, to draw near to the water. From the time of their last encounter, the Sea of Galilee had called out to Miriam, sometimes during the day and sometimes at night. The sweet invitations floated to her in the same way that the fresh springtime fragrances drifted in the air after a lengthy winter. Their strength and allure reached the very core of her being.

"Come! Drench yourself in my comfort," the waters seemed to say. "Let me soothe you once again, just like old times."

But Miriam couldn't summon the courage to go back to the water's edge. The memory of her last visit was still too raw, too painful. After all, it had occurred a little more than six months ago. She assumed that returning to the sea would feel like pouring salt onto her wounds. In order to feel safe she needed to keep her distance. Shaking her head, she turned back to her chores. But as she did, visions danced before her eyes. She saw herself greeting the water with her feet and then falling into its outstretched arms—escaping the continual presence of Fear and pretending that the last handful of months hadn't existed.

3

AFTER WHAT SEEMED like an endless winter of rain and cold, spring began to take over. Miriam celebrated her thirteenth year with every bit of enthusiasm as *Ezrâ*, Ezra, had concerning the intermarriage of the Israelites with the Canaanites, which is to say with none at all. Whereas Miriam once resembled a bright flower whose face beamed toward the sun, her posture now drooped. Trying to make sense of the shameful events that took place on the hillside, she attempted to find a logical reason.

"It wasn't my fault; he attacked me. What did I do to deserve that?"

The Spirit of Rejection—the second spirit—offered to help. With a slinking gait and an appearance that had a filmy quality to it, as if it were wasting away, the spirit glided up beside her the way a faint wind does. Rejection hooked its arm around Miriam's shoulder. From this position it could whisper numerous lies into her ear, depositing them one after another just like drops of ointment that appear harmless but in the end are deadly.

"Ah, but maybe you *did* deserve it. Maybe it really *was* your fault. You did, after all, pull up your night clothes." The spirit saw Miriam think about this like a fish eyeing bait, unsure whether or not to take it.

"I probably shouldn't have pulled up my clothes," Miriam responded, "but I was just so hot—I needed to cool down... and I didn't see anyone there."

"If you had only stayed inside, none of this would have ever happened." The spirit's words seared her heart. "You're really the one to blame."

Covering her eyes with her hands, Miriam began to cry. "I can't believe I was so careless. I shouldn't have left the house. I guess it is partly my fault. He couldn't have attacked me if I wasn't sitting there like a bird bathing in the sun. I wish I could take back that whole night."

"But you can't. What's done is done."

Using the power of regret, the Spirit of Rejection convinced her to bear all of the responsibility. Quietly, she waved her flag of surrender. Even though she shouldn't have, Miriam accepted the blame. Because she took on the responsibility that belonged, of course, to the nomad, she compounded her misery. Truth be told, the violence, the improper touching, and the evil visible in the man's eyes were enough to bear. But when she took on the fault as her own everything changed. In the same way that a master lashes his slave for a wrong doing, Miriam began to beat herself with the rod of blame. Perhaps she had made a selfish decision, creating an opportunity for disaster. The guilt was heavier than a slab of marble in *Sh'lômôh's*, Solomon's, temple, yet the Spirit of Rejection compelled her to carry it.

* * *

One day in the second month of spring, Miriam's family awoke to a clear morning. Soft clouds dotted the crisp blue sky. They planned on fertilizing the olive grove—a process that ensured an abundance of fruit. The trees had begun to blossom, the small flowers white, delicate, and gently fragrant. Soon, tiny olive buds would appear as if by magic. Second only to harvest, spring was Miriam's favorite season in the grove. Her father and brothers headed out after a quick breakfast, her mother cleaned and prepared for the afternoon meal before joining them.

"Miriam, I have started making the bread," Hannah said, wiping her hands of flour. "Stay here while it bakes and then come up to the grove."

"Yes, Ima."

Moments later Hannah departed leaving Miriam alone. With the spirits of Fear and Rejection close by she forced herself to focus on her mother's instructions. Taking care not to burn the bread, she watched it rise then turn golden brown. Then she removed it from the fire and set it aside to cool. As Miriam looked back at the flames, she wished she could burn away the haunting memories.

"I can't burn the past, but maybe I can wash it away," she said with an idea.

Getting up, she made sure no one was around and then moved to the back of the house to a small room that held the sunken stone *mikvêh*, or immersion bath. Miriam quickly removed her clothes—with much apprehension, to tell the truth—and stepped down the three stairs. The cool water quickened her breath so the prayers of repentance came faster than normal. She knew she was ceremonially and lawfully unclean, the *Tôrâh*, Torah—otherwise known as the five books of Moses—explained that in precise terms. Every word of solemn, ritualistic prayer she spoke seemed to offer hope. Perhaps she would emerge clean and set free. Three times she dipped herself in the water, three times saying prayers, hoping to be as clean as *Na'amân*, Naaman, after plunging in the Jordan river seven times to rid himself of leprosy. Coming up the last time she heard a familiar voice.

"You know this won't work," the Spirit of Rejection said.

"It has to," Miriam whispered.

"Do you really think three dips in some water will wash away your defilement?"

Miriam began to scrub her skin, using her fingernails. Red marks developed on her arms and legs and belly. Her skin reacted to the aggressive cleaning, as if to say: *Look at your skin—it's bright red, stained with sin and shame.* Miriam looked at her body. Her skin throbbed and seemed to glow, making her feel worse than before. The marks and redness didn't dissipate but appeared to intensify, to her dismay.

"It's not going away. Nor will it ever," lied Rejection.

Frustrated and disappointed, Miriam dried herself and quickly redressed, covering her bare arms and legs as well as the shame that swelled like *Bath-Shêba's*, Bathsheba's, belly carrying an unlawful child.

"You are permanently damaged, and as unclean as the goat used on the Day of Atonement," the spirit said.

"I still feel so impure. I was hoping..." Miriam said.

"You'll never be able to wash the defilement away. It's with you for life."

"Always unclean..."

"And only unclean men will desire you. Watch, you'll see. Men know when a woman isn't pure—the righteous ones will refuse you, but the unrighteous ones will be attracted to you."

Tears formed in her eyes and grief poured out from them. "For the rest of my life I will belong with disgraceful and corrupt people. A leper must live among other lepers. Even though they aren't aware of it, I have brought dishonor to my family. I never thought that something like this could happen to me."

"You brought it upon yourself."

"I'm so ashamed." Miriam's confession felt as bitter and sweet as bread dipped in vinegar and honey. "I'm ashamed of what happened, of how I feel, of who I am."

"Shame keeps you honest," the spirit lied.

Just as the moon passes over the sun, causing an uneasy and eerie darkness, day became night in her world. She trusted in lying words that could not profit her. Miriam assumed that guilt would be the toughest emotion to tolerate, that is, until Rejection introduced her to guilt's partner, shame. To tell the truth, she felt every bit as ashamed as *Tâmâr*, Tamar, after being raped by her half-brother *Amnôwn*, Amnon, and then sent away in disgrace. Overwhelmed, she vowed again to keep her secrets locked in her inner chamber as if they were fine gold. Her tears dried up in time and shame settled into her heart and into her soul, just as dust settles upon household objects, noiselessly yet noticeably. And there it remained, draping Miriam with an invisible layer of grime.

"You are not lovable anymore."

The matter-of-fact tone in the spirit's voice shocked her system. She felt as if someone had run into her at full speed, slamming her onto the ground and knocking the wind from her chest. The spirit couldn't have delivered a better hit. Without a doubt, it was the most destructive and devastating lie, which was the reason Rejection cherished it. Like a worm eating through an apple, this lie ate to the core of her being.

"You are no longer worthy of affection—to receive or give love," Rejection said, savoring the effect.

Miriam sighed so deeply that she thought her lungs might collapse. "It's true—nobody will love me because of my shameful secret."

"That's right. Your secret and your shame make you who you are. They define you—the new you."

The loss of her purity had marred her like scars from a bad burn, yet they remained internal and invisible to the untrained eye. Miriam understood, as did the Spirit of Rejection, that physical impurity made her as blemished as a rejected *Peçach*, or Passover, lamb, despite her status as a good Jewish daughter from a solid and respectable home.

"At least I still have my family."

"The only reason your family still loves you is because they're ignorant of the past. If they knew what happened their love for you would definitely change," Rejection proclaimed.

It was the one flaw that cut through her belief. The wicked spirit counted on the fact that Miriam wouldn't dissect truth from lie. Taking the lies with both hands, Miriam tried them on like a new head covering, and believed that they somehow suited her. She was foolish enough to think that her family would give her love based only on certain conditions. Miriam now had her mind turned toward the unreasonable.

"They probably *wouldn't* love me the same if they knew. Nothing would ever be the same. How could I live with that?"

"Make your vow again," Rejection told her.

"I cannot let them find out. I will not."

Inside her head, Miriam could trust only herself with the secret information that would change her life if discovered. She protected the lies that she'd accumulated as a collector of fine jewels protects his diamonds, emeralds, and rubies. Miriam worked hard at keeping her secrets, and the Spirit of Rejection worked harder at keeping Miriam in a place of separation. When she remained lonely and secluded, like a prisoner confined to a small cell, the spirit's ploys did the most damage.

An entire year had passed since the nefarious incident. It was summer again, the season that seemed to escalate her tension. One morning as she was bringing water back from the well Miriam heard her brothers talking in lowered voices. What were they saying? Was it about her? Why were they whispering? She crept closer and hid behind a wall in the courtyard to listen to them. Levi's voice reached her first.

"I still can't figure out what's wrong with her."

"Me either. It's almost as if she has become a completely different person," Benjamin said.

"I agree, and I don't like it."

"I hate to admit this but I don't want to be in the same room with her anymore. Her moods are more unpredictable than this spring weather. I don't like her right now."

"True, but we should keep trying, don't you think?" Levi said.

"Yes, but I don't think I can."

"What do you mean? Why not?"

"Because I'm afraid of what I might do. I just want to shake some sense into her."

"I don't think that will help, Benjamin."

"You do something then."

"Why me?"

"You're always the one to keep the peace in our house. That comes easy to you."

"Let's just leave her alone. Give her some space like Ima suggested. It will pass, I'm sure. Besides, we have plenty of things to do to keep us busy from now until the feasts," said Levi.

Suddenly, their voices grew louder and Miriam held her breath. They were leaving through the courtyard on their way to the olive grove, but to her relief they were engrossed in their plans for the upcoming festivals. Soon they were out of sight, their voices fading into the air. She could hardly believe what she'd just heard. In all honesty, it felt as though she'd been seared with a hot coal, such was the pain.

"You see?" whispered the Spirit of Rejection. "They want to keep their distance from you. They don't like you."

"I know," Miriam said sadly.

"They seem to be ignoring you, don't they?"

"Yes," she said. "Maybe they just want to be rid of me..."

Despite the fact that the unclean spirit knew the truth, which is to say that her parents and brothers were allowing her some breathing room, it misled her by weaving the situation into a cloak of deception more colorful than the one Rachel made for her son *Yôwçêph*, Joseph. Miriam's mind and emotions listened to the lies of the Spirit of Rejection, making her a slave in the same way that the Israelites had served the Egyptians. Even though she sometimes found comfort in being isolated from family and friends, it was, to tell the truth, painful. She chose to hide, wrestling not against flesh and blood but against the powers of darkness. Just as the spirits intended, Miriam traveled down a pathway of seclusion, as if pulled by a team of oxen. And the more she gave into it, the stronger it became.

Harvest season had come and gone, and the time for pruning had arrived. Once Miriam's family had climbed the hill to the olive grove, her father directed everyone to a specific area to prune the trees. Miriam normally helped one of her brothers since she was young and unable to handle the larger branches on her own. That day, however, things turned out differently.

"Miriam, you take the north section, Benjamin the south, Levi the west. Your mother and I will take the east."

"But Abba, I can't do it by myself," said Miriam.

"You are old enough now, Miriam. You've helped us prune these trees since you learned how to walk. Today, you do the hard work on your own."

Frustrated, she said, "Fine." She turned north toward her quadrant, walking alone, feeling pushed away.

Just a few steps later she heard her mother say, "Do you think she's all right up there alone? Maybe you're being too hard on her."

"Miriam has been asking to be alone for weeks, and now she wants some company? I don't like how she's manipulating this family. She will be fine."

Miriam ascended the hilly grove to her section. Shadows spread out beneath each tree, looking like round blankets. She wove in and out among them, dried leaves crunching under her feet. The gnarled trunks—as knobby as Miriam's adolescent knees—twisted up toward the sky, revealing a history of weather, insects, drought, and prosperity. For hours she pruned the north area tree by tree, branch by branch. Beginning with the lowest branches, she gently clipped the ends of each one, moving in a circle around the tree. Miriam continued this pattern until she could reach no higher, knowing that her father or brothers would come later and climb up to reach the top limbs. While her hands worked rhythmically, her mind began simmering on past conversations with her family as well as the lies from the Spirit of Rejection. Truth be told, she worked up a mental stew as seductive as the one *Êsâv*, Esau, sold his birthright for.

Abruptly, Miriam turned and walked over to Levi in the west section of the grove. Considering the severity of Rejection's words, it wasn't surprising that Miriam wanted to verify them for herself. She knew, without having to think twice, that the best person in her family to assess was Levi. Soft-spoken and composed, Levi was the younger of her two brothers. With light brown hair and stunning blue eyes he was the complete opposite of Benjamin. Tall and lean, Levi was as charming as King Solomon with his hundreds of wives, and as humorous as a performer in the king's court. Miriam hoped to find the truth through him.

Spotting her brother through several trees, Miriam watched him for a moment. He would welcome her company, right? Surely he would be honest and kind? She hoped they would connect somehow, to put her mind at ease. The cracking of branches under foot let Levi know she was approaching. He looked in her direction but didn't smile.

"Hi, Levi."

Gathering branches for the cart, he replied, "Hello, Miriam."

"Can I help you?"

Unsure and wary, Levi considered how to respond. "Actually, I don't need any right now. Does father know you're over here?" Though motivated by pure intentions, he failed to help the situation. From Miriam's point of view he was indeed making matters worse.

"No," she replied tensely.

"Maybe you should go back. You know how he feels about being disobeyed."

Sensing the pangs of rejection, Miriam tried another approach. "How about taking me down to the marketplace later to watch the turban maker? We haven't been in so long!" Visiting the strange man who made exotic turbans was one of their favorite excursions. Surely he wouldn't say no to that.

Smiling at the image of the turban maker's monkey—his way to increase sales—Levi considered the idea. "As fun as that would be, there won't be any time. I have to finish this section of the grove today." He noticed that the expression on Miriam's face changed at lightning speed. It was clear that she was testing him, but he couldn't determine why. "Maybe some other time."

"Of course, some other time," Miriam responded in frustration. Turning and walking back, she mumbled to herself the same way that Jacob had on his deathbed.

Levi watched her depart, wondering if he had said and done the right thing. He was so uncertain those days of how to interact with his sister because one wrong word could produce the wrong results, as seen just moments ago. Miriam, on the other hand, focused on the lies that danced like flames from polished oil lamps.

"They really are scorning me," she said.

"You can't deny it. The proof is right there in front of you," the Spirit of Rejection replied.

"I can hardly believe it! They're supposed to accept me and love me."

"It's clear that they don't. Apparently you aren't as good as they thought. You're a disappointment for them. The truth is difficult to believe, but it's staring you in the face."

"Well, if that's the way they want to treat me then that's the way I'll treat them."

"Perfect! Reject them back! Show them how it feels. They deserve it, you know."

As faulty as it was, the logic didn't keep Miriam from grasping at Rejection's lies, like a starving man who grasps at discarded food. The evil spirit succeeded in clouding not only her mind but her heart as well. And as Miriam's sense of rejection grew, so did the spirit's delight at watching her suffer. For Rejection, it was exhilarating to heap emotional pain upon her with no end in sight.

At that moment Miriam thought back to a time when all was right with her family. She'd always been loved and adored by them, and life had been every bit as carefree as a bird in the warmth of summer. Even their neighbors had cherished sweet little Miriam. In some respect, Miriam knew that her family still cared for her, yet her thoughts, feelings, and emotions all cried the opposite. She felt, in essence, completely rejected. It reminded her of *Mîykâl*, or Michal, who rejected and condemned her husband, David, when she saw him dancing and playing music before the Lord. Everything had changed in the blink of an eye. Whatever praises and places of sanctuary she had held onto before drained out from her. She held only a sense of emptiness. Although her thoughts didn't make complete sense, they were still her thoughts. As a result, Miriam turned even on herself.

Time worked against her. The spring feasts of *Peçach* and *Shâvuôt*, also known as the feasts of Passover and Weeks, came and went, and Miriam felt worse with each passing day. Because she allowed rejection to settle in like a long lost relative, her demeanor changed. Once, her personality had possessed a sweet sincerity—delightful and charming. Now, having accepted the lie that she was unlovable, Miriam gave off a fragrance of rejection to others and withdrew deeper into herself, shutting out all voices except that of the spirit. Without any awareness, she repelled people. And because she surrendered her sense of value as well as her confidence, she lost the appeal of her youth that once attracted people to her in the same way that Torah drew men to study. Feeling rejected led to being rejected. Around and around, Miriam performed an ancient dance of ceremony with the Spirit of Rejection.

A few months later, with summer only days away, she came to the conclusion that her situation was hopeless. Yet in that moment of utter despair a faint glimmer of hope appeared. There was one person she could always count on to love her, someone who couldn't possibly let her down.

He had been smitten with her since the age of five. A neighborhood friend as well as a descendant from an honorable Jewish family, *L'mûw'êl*, Lemuel, embodied everything that Miriam's parents could want for their youngest daughter. Intelligent, athletic, sensible, and somewhat handsome, he seemed to have it all. And Miriam agreed. Yet she wasn't attracted to him. Truth be told, she liked him well enough, but he didn't capture her heart. Lemuel always knew that Miriam viewed him as a friend only, refusing to allow their friendship to become anything else. Though he never understood why she held him at a distance, he remained hopeful that she would have a change of heart and want to marry him someday. Silently she ached for him because she knew he would wait for something that would never arrive.

Growing up in the shadow of Levi and Benjamin, Miriam felt at ease spending time with boys. In a way, they expected less of her than the women in her community, and so she felt free to be herself. Miriam supposed that her easy nature seemed inviting to Lemuel. With each passing year of their youth, his affection for her had increased, yet she never outwardly acknowledged his adoration.

In spite of their differences of heart, Miriam and Lemuel, only two and a half years apart in age, had spent as much time together as their culture and families would allow. One of their favorite activities was to sneak out of their homes, which were practically connected, late at night and meet on the roof of her house. Accessible by a staircase, the flat rooftop was empty at night, but during the day clothes dried there in the sun, meals were consumed, prayers recited, and rest enjoyed from work on *Shabbât*, or the Sabbath. There Lemuel and Miriam had spent countless hours lying on their backs, gazing at the stars. On those nights, Miriam could hardly fathom how Yahweh, the God of her ancestors, would care to know each star by name. Admiring the handiwork of the heavens, she had felt like a pebble on the sea's floor in comparison. She had also felt that the heavens were spread out like a stage, the shooting stars and rising moon moving gracefully before her as their audience. In hushed voices Miriam and Lemuel had talked about everything from Judaic law to family secrets to personal dreams and goals, and it all stayed between them and the stars. For them both, those times of peaceful conversation were, in their innocence, sweeter than honey in the honeycomb.

Recalling all of those wonderful moments, Miriam determined to set everything aright. To tell the truth, she felt that she was sinking in a pool of rejection that the spirit had filled, but certainly Lemuel could pull her out.

"Why didn't I think of this sooner? Of course Lemuel is the answer. Finally, those years of his adoration for me will count for something!" she said to herself.

But as she walked to find him she realized that over the past year his attitude had changed. He had not reminded her over and over again that he cared for her. Startled by this thought, Miriam feared that he too didn't love her anymore. Fighting against the mockery of it all, she began to run in the hopes of finding welcoming arms.

"I need to talk to you, Lemuel," Miriam said as she tried to regain her breath. The Spirit of Rejection traveled right along side her, the other six spirits following as well behind them.

"Miriam, I have work to do right now," he explained. He hardly looked up from molding the clay, a basic task in his family's pottery business.

"I know, but it's almost sundown, and this is really important. Please?" she pleaded, touching his hand lightly.

"Why? What is it?"

Seven

"Let's go up to the roof and talk there."

They both knew she meant to have a serious conversation. His eyes locked onto hers and filled with questions. They hadn't spent much time talking in the last few months, much less talking alone. It seemed to Lemuel that their friendship had been let out to dry like clothes in the afternoon sun, where it had become stiff and unyielding. Perhaps today they would start on the road to recovery. Her urgency gave him hope, which felt like the first rays of the morning sun on his face.

After moving two steps at a time in order to keep up with Miriam's pace, Lemuel could feel his heart racing faster than his feet. Once they arrived at the rooftop they sat down opposite one another, close enough so they did not have to speak loudly but not close enough to touch. Realizing that she was struggling over how to begin, Lemuel offered to speak first.

"What's going on, Miri?" Only a handful of people called her by her childhood nickname, in particular those in her immediate family.

Pulling her knees to her chest—a symbol that was once endearing but now guarded—she dove straight in. "Do you still love me?" She could hear Rejection snickering. Her hopes seemed pathetic.

Lemuel furrowed his brow. "What?"

"I need to know. I need to know if you still truly care for me."

After a moment of looking at her, stricken and embarrassed, Lemuel felt a touch of embarrassment as well. "Sure, I still do. Why?"

"No, I mean, do you *really* care about me? Are you still hoping to marry me?"

"Oh," he said softly, looking away. It was apparent to them both that he was unsure of how to answer. In fact, he was unsure of her motives, of his true feelings, of what had come between them. How was he supposed to react to her when she sent his emotions flipping and flopping like a fish out of water? "Miriam, you have always been who I want for my wife, and probably will be as long as I live, but..."

"But what?" she demanded.

"But something is different with you lately. You're not the same anymore. You've changed."

"How? What's different?" *Tell me, please! I need to know what you see!* The thoughts in her head screamed so loudly that she wondered if he could hear them also. It reminded her of thunder cracking, resounding from a blackened sky.

"I'm not quite sure; it's difficult to say. It's more of a feeling that I get from you. You seem distracted and uninterested in anything or anyone these days. Like you'd always rather be alone. Unhappy, I guess."

After some moments of silence he said, "Are you?"

Miriam released a heavy sigh and thought about his words as she stared out into the distance of the approaching evening. *I'm so much more than unhappy*, she wanted to say. *I'm tired, I'm scared, I'm alone—fighting things that I cannot even name. I feel overwhelmed. Lost.* Miriam looked at him with heavy eyes, longing for him to say, "It doesn't matter what it is; I will always accept you for who you are. Even love you for it." But those words never came.

At that point—after she offered no response to his questions—Lemuel said, "So I guess people are leaving you alone. Like me."

Closing her eyes, she contemplated his honesty. In essence, it echoed back to her what she already knew, like a voice resounding off the hills. And the space between them grew every bit as large as the sky overhead.

I wish that I could tell you what's been happening to me. But I'm not sure that even you would understand. She wanted to tell him about her thoughts and the voices, but she knew the words would stick in her throat like old, dry bread. Refusing to submit to the tears that she felt rising, Miriam found her voice again. "Are you saying that you don't want to be around me anymore? That you aren't interested in spending time with me at all?"

His voice was kind and gentle, like a peacemaker's trying to diffuse an altercation. "Sort of...you're not exactly fun to be with right now."

"That's just great. I cannot believe that *you* are rejecting me too," she sneered as she stood to leave. She could feel the mocking smile of the Spirit of Rejection.

"What? Miri...wait..." he called after her.

As quickly as she had come, she departed. In confusion, Lemuel watched as his beloved friend, murmuring to herself under her breath, vanished in the town as quickly as *Hâgâr*, Hagar, and her son *Yishmâ'êl*, Ishmael, fled into the wilderness of *Be'êr Sheba*, or Beersheba.

Seven

Hagar, the Egyptian maidservant of Abraham's wife *Sârâh*, Sarah, had been dealt with harshly after being used in a failed attempt to fulfill Yahweh's promise to them. Without a doubt, Hagar suffered deep stabs of rejection at the hand of Sarah, and as a result, fled in an effort to escape Sarah's voice. Miriam too stormed away from a voice—the voice of the Spirit of Rejection. Relentless and nagging, it refused to leave her alone. The weary, according to the seven spirits, were not to receive rest.

"I told you," she heard Rejection say. "You're not lovable anymore. Even Lemuel thinks so."

The Spirit of Rejection emptied all of the truth out of the situation like wringing out water from saturated cloth. Drop by drop the truth dripped out, falling to the earth until all that remained was a damp fabric. Loneliness and despair shrouded her mind. She could feel herself shrinking farther and farther back into a cave of isolation. The goal of deceiving and ensnaring Miriam had been as enjoyable as watching the cities of *Ç'dôm* and *Ămôrâh,* otherwise known as Sodom and Gomorrah, burn to the ground.

In all honesty, Miriam's conversation with Lemuel made her more restless and unsettled. What she needed was someone to embrace her, secrets and all, even for a moment. What she wanted was something to dull the pain and quiet the turbulence within her. But she couldn't think of anyone. With all of her might she wished that it were possible to let it all go! And yet, her wishes were as impossible to grasp as the wind.

Though she didn't realize where her footsteps were leading her, Miriam ended up at the shore of the sea. All of the feelings of fear that had kept her away for so long now yielded to the feelings of rejection. As she approached the water, Miriam felt tears rising up through her chest, climbing her throat, moving into her eyes. She fought them back, that is, until she stepped foot into the sea. And then she could hold them no longer. In a great rush they fell faster than the parted walls of water after Moses and the Israelites had passed through. The open arms of the sea took every drop that escaped from her eyes, joining water with water. She desperately wanted to set her burdens upon the surface and send them adrift, never to return.

She craved for the water to grant her freedom from the pain. Though the sea offered a momentary reprieve, it could not save her. Something had changed, something was different. Even the forces of nature were weaker than the forces controlling her.

4

WATCHING CLOSELY, THE Spirit of Bitterness waited for its turn, seething with excitement. The evil spirit brimmed with anticipation the same way a pot of liquid over a flame bubbled up to the edge, threatening to spill its contents. Bitterness, of course, didn't want to disappoint the other spirits as each set of eyes focused in its direction. The preparation by Rejection and Fear had been executed flawlessly, and Bitterness was ready to join in the wicked delight. Complimenting them on a job well done, the Spirit of Bitterness took its first step toward their captive, lips pulled tight in a taut smile.

* * *

Now fourteen, Miriam felt like she'd been basted with a coat of anguish. Her thoughts spun around and around with questions that seemingly couldn't be answered. Why was everyone against her? Why did Yahweh allow the brutal attack years ago? Why didn't anyone understand her? She had been hurt: by the nomad, by her family, by Lemuel. Nursing those hurts grew the angst inside her. After a while, the pain and pity she felt for herself turned into anger, the opening that led her directly to the doorstep of Bitterness. The door was unlocked. In fact, Spirit of Bitterness didn't have a lock on its door; it was always ready for company. And in she marched.

From the first night that the sun had set on her anger Miriam had offered the Spirit of Bitterness a place in her heart. As she went about her daily routines, still keeping quiet and to herself, Bitterness nudged her deeper into an arena of hostility. The spirit coaxed her with continual messages and ideas, telling her that she was misunderstood and that everything was unjust. These thoughts oozed down toward her heart and gut. Almost immediately they began to turn her rancid like old goat's milk curdling in a jug. The process was a steady yet effective one, where her insides changed at the hands of superior force.

To make matters worse, Miriam realized that in the depths of her being she held a special reserve of anger for the wicked nomad who had changed her life. No amount of ire that she held onto compared with the animosity for *him*. Truth be told, she nurtured it in the same way that a farmer nurtured and grew his crops day after day. Stemming from burning hatred against the thief who stole her purity, the resentment she held created the stronghold for Bitterness. It vowed to keep her in that place of resentment because it knew that in the spiritual realm un-forgiveness brought torturing spirits. And just like the other six spirits, Bitterness enjoyed torturing people.

The Spirit of Bitterness certainly didn't develop its system of controlling people overnight. Centuries of observation and practice enabled it to establish a doctrine of lies so destructive that even the strongest of character could succumb to it. King Saul, for example, suffered great bitterness against David for years, and sought to kill the former shepherd boy because his resentment had grown out of control. The Spirit of Bitterness had perfected and maintained a certain method throughout the ages, and was quite proud of its accomplishments. In fact, the spirit—through its doctrine—had an amazing number of devoted followers from kings to average citizens to children, in all countries and all religions. Yet to tell the truth, they were all as blind to bitterness as they were devoted to their religions.

The doctrine of this wicked spirit relied upon a system of principles that drew its captives into an internal poverty. What the Spirit of Bitterness offered, of course, didn't reveal its true nature—hostile, resenting, unforgiving, stubborn—for that would be defeating its purpose. Instead, an opposite nature was presented—one that was logical, attractive, comforting, and safe. And because it was disgraceful, wretched, and profane, the Spirit of Bitterness enjoyed it beyond measure.

To no surprise the unclean spirit used the same creed for Miriam. Tearing up any roots of peace and kindness, Bitterness aimed to replace them with roots of its own as strong as the cedars of *L'bânôwn*, Lebanon. Each root of bitterness was based on part of the doctrine, and in turn contributed to the doctrine as a whole, like separate sections of hair that formed a braid. The stronger and deeper the roots, the stronger and deeper the bitterness. And so, using language as smooth as freshly churned cream, the Spirit of Bitterness presented Miriam with its sensible yet defiling doctrine.

* * *

Pruning season had arrived once again. Day after day Miriam's family carefully pared the branches on each olive tree, ensuring good growth for the following season. Miriam, craving seclusion, planted herself on the far border of the grove, up the hill and out of sight. She could hear the voices of her family drifting toward her, but truth be told, she enjoyed entertaining the voices in her head more.

The winter sky was overcast—high clouds stretched thin like spun wool. The ground, still damp from last week's rain, gave off a chill that seeped in through her sandals. Earthy fragrances floated up from the watered soil. A cold, steady wind wove its way through the trees, causing the half-bare branches to seem like arms reaching out for her. They swayed and creaked, as if speaking a warning of something. Suddenly, out of nowhere, a flock of more than fifty crows raced toward the grove from the north, landing in the trees surrounding her. Black as night, the birds cawed and squawked, louder and louder. Miriam felt the hairs on her body leap to attention. The black, beady eyes and sharp, black beaks made her feel as though they were about to eat her flesh just as *Yechezqêl*, or Ezekiel, had prophesied to the ancient enemies of Yahweh. She stood frozen in place, listening to the shrill cries, watching their movements among the trees. Then all at once the birds stopped cawing. Silence filled the grove as well as an eerie presence Miriam hadn't felt before. The Spirit of Bitterness stepped closer to Miriam, eyes locked on her every bit as much as the crows'.

"He has no right to be forgiven."

The spirit told Miriam the first doctrine as it circled around her, like a legal advocate pacing the courts. Initial contact was always the most important; it could make the relationship easy or challenging. So with forceful yet veiled devices—woven, like beautiful lace, with hints of seduction—Bitterness presented a sound and reasonable proposition.

"The man is sheep dung, and he deserves your hatred."

Absolutely, she thought. "What a Goliath he was! The very thought of him makes my stomach twist in knots and my hair stand on end."

"Don't be afraid to curse him for what he did to you. Proclaim curses upon him and every aspect of his life—his body, his mode of living, his future. Curse him with as much vengeance as Yahweh curses those who disobey Him," Bitterness demanded.

At once, as if listening to one of Magdala's seamen, she heard herself produce a string of profanity suitable for the lowest of low. Even though she'd never used such language before, Miriam spoke easily and naturally. The cold, tense atmosphere seemed to permeate her. The crows continued to eye her, the Spirit of Bitterness as well.

A corner of the spirit's mouth elevated. The strategy was working. As the spirit knew, momentum was crucial to the task at hand.

"You, on the other hand, have all the rights."

"I do?"

"Yes!" it said in a piercing voice. "You have a right to be angry and hateful; you have a right to wish him harm; you have a right to hold a grudge; you have a right to be bitter and resentful; you have a right to want him dead..."

Nodding in agreement, Miriam said, "I do have the right to feel the way I do."

Hearing that she had a right to this and a right to that, over and over again, made Miriam think of her orthodox countrymen who repeated the same short prayer hour after hour as they swayed forward and back on their knees. But whereas their prayers honored and glorified Yahweh, the mantra of Bitterness honored and glorified selfish ambition and discord.

To tell the truth, Miriam found some comfort in believing these rights. She felt entitled to her new feelings of bitterness and self-protection. And just as the *Mishlê*, or book of Proverbs, declared, out of the abundance of her heart her mouth spoke.

"If you forgive him you will be condoning his actions."

After lying to her with the second doctrine, the spirit surveyed her face for consent. With every lie that spewed out of the mouth of Bitterness, its strength grew with as much persistence as weeds overtaking a garden.

"There is no way that I can forgive him. Not ever. It's beyond human reason to forgive what he did to me. It's impossible! And I don't *want* to! He doesn't *deserve* forgiveness!" She worked herself up and watered the bitter roots. By this point she needed only a suggestion before she galloped off into a burst of emotion.

"You shouldn't forgive him," Bitterness asserted. "He doesn't deserve it. That would be the same as approval."

"Pardoning his actions would mean being weak, and I need to be strong. I have to hold onto my feelings. They are my only protection against the memories."

"You are doing the right thing. If you forgive the savage brute you are applauding him—maybe even encouraging him to strike again, whether it's you or some other woman."

The Spirit of Bitterness' words secured her belief that she was, indeed, doing the right thing. She took the ideologies and wrapped herself in them, creating a barrier against what she perceived to be evil forces at work in the world around her. And yet, she had no idea that she was draping herself in a coat of wickedness.

"You just can't pretend that it never happened," said the Spirit of Bitterness.

Like adding yeast to flour in order for it to rise up, Bitterness added the third doctrine as an extra measure. Full of negative authority, the wicked spirit enjoyed watching Miriam become more and more like itself, which is to say hard, sour, and spiteful.

"Why would you ignore the fact that someone meant to hurt you? That's ridiculous! You can't simply move on as if it's not a big deal. You have to keep your spite alive!"

Not realizing that by holding onto the bitterness and resentment of the man who wronged her, Miriam allowed him to continue harming her, which in turn kept her in a cycle of unhappiness. Bitterness' grip tightened further.

"I hate that man!" Together, the statement brought relief and rage like sweet and sour flavors on the tongue. "Men like that should be dismembered and given a slow, torturous death," Miriam said. "A Roman death."

With wicked amusement, Bitterness smiled as it watched all its poisonous arrows lodge into Miriam, piercing her soul and bleeding her spirit. The more that she confessed her hardness of heart, the more she believed the lies to be truth. The steady wind whipped up again, sending the crows into a commotion. Flapping their wings wildly, they launched into the air as quickly as they had descended, their piercing cries reverberating throughout the grove. Circling and diving amongst the trees, the black birds swarmed around Miriam. She watched them with trepidation yet comprehension. Slowly, as if forming a funnel over her, the crows gathered and ascended higher and higher into the bleak sky. Miriam stood transfixed, listening to their screams, staring as they grew smaller and smaller until they flew off toward the four corners of the earth. Bitterness looked on as well, grinning at the fowl under his control. The cold she felt penetrated deeper than the weather. Hearing a branch snap, Miriam looked around but found herself still alone. She sensed that she wasn't unaccompanied, yet she forced the thought from her head. Gathering the dead branches, she loaded the cart, bringing them home for the fire.

Like the changing of the seasons, Miriam's life had progressed from days of warmth to months of cold. Nothing could be viewed with the same eyes. As proof of that the very shade of her eyes seemed to darken a hue, as if an oil lantern had been turned down or the sun had shaded itself with a film of haze. Life had given her a vicious experience, making her as bitter as the herbs eaten on Passover. And because she couldn't control such external factors, she determined to control the internal ones. Indeed, she had become deceived inside and out, led astray by the one who intended to harm her far more than the nomad. The torment that roared within her grew like a ferocious storm on the sea, and her confessions held more bitterness than the complaints of *Îyôv*, or Job.

Lying in bed one cold night, Miriam could feel the company of evil occupying her room. The same darkness that blanketed the night had crept into her heart, her confidence in Yahweh a troubling memory.

"Revenge is better than forgiveness."

With as much intention as *Yârob'âm*, Jeroboam, who set up golden calves to worship at Dan and Bethel, the Spirit of Bitterness saved its favorite and best lie for last. The fourth doctrine intensified Miriam's defilement. Whereas the concept of revenge before held no ground, it now seemed appropriate.

Seven

"Get revenge by hating him with your entire being!" the Spirit of Bitterness cried, swirling, and dancing about her. "Imagine yourself enacting moments of revenge—it bestows such sweet satisfaction! You're certain to love it and how it makes you feel. Just try it and see."

During those winter days acts of rage previously unimaginable to Miriam were all of a sudden taking shape in her mind. Without much effort, scenes of revenge played over and over in her mind just like the ceaseless lapping of waves at Magdala's shore.

"How am I able to dream up such gruesome images?" she said.

"It's all coming from within your mind and your heart. You're simply allowing your emotions to take physical shape. There's nothing wrong with that," Bitterness lied. "And this is what it looks like. You're just being honest!"

For example, Miriam's favorite plot of revenge was one that she developed over the course of several months, adapting and adjusting bits and pieces along the way. It began with a setting quite similar to the fateful summer night. She imagined herself to be the one looking for *him* in the dark shadows, small sword in hand that she'd taken from her father's hidden chest. The nomad would, of course, be traveling through the Valley of Robbers again; finding him wouldn't be too difficult. Armed and ready, she would wait patiently for hours, seeking just the right moment to thrust the weapon into his skull or neck or heart or wherever she could in the heat of the moment.

"Remember me?" she imagined asking with gritted teeth. She would take pleasure watching him writhe in unspeakable pain. "I'm the one you attacked in the middle of the night... the one who reminds you of your daughter."

She imagined moans of agony seeping from his lips. His blood would crawl from under its fleshy covering and paint the hard ground. This time every second of enjoyment would derive from her and every second of agony would take place in him. Miriam visualized herself circling the man, without touching him, allowing the sweetness of revenge to linger in her mouth.

"It's not fun being the one in *that* position, is it? Not knowing whether you will live or die... not knowing how much more pain is coming...."

"What...what is happening?" he would answer with slowed, belabored breath.

"I'm taking an eye for an eye. Only your situation will be a bit more permanent. Don't you know that I *hate you* with all that is within me? With all that I can gather? Surely you have felt my revulsion for you over the past few years?! No? Well, since wishing you dead didn't work, I'm now taking matters into my own hands. Not so unlike your intent to ravage me—an innocent girl!"

In her imagined story, Miriam had no hesitation about seeing the nomad die slowly. She would allow her anticipation to grow with each remaining breath, hoping that it would end sooner than later. And with his last breaths, she would turn and walk away leaving that section of her past to return to the dust from which it came. She imagined herself, after the distance between them reached a length of two men, hearing the final seep of air leak from his bloody body. Stopping to absorb the moment—an exchange of life: his to replace her old one—she would close her eyes and exhale firmly, letting herself feel the hungered freedom. Though it was just a fantasy, it felt every bit as real to Miriam as the harsh winds of winter on her face.

The Spirit of Bitterness cheered Miriam on as she created these passionate plays of revenge. It encouraged her to create more and more mental dramas in hopes that they might evolve into actual realities—if Bitterness could accomplish *that* the other six spirits would certainly be envious. Dancing around her on tiptoes with uncontained enthusiasm, Bitterness squealed in sinful delight as it assisted in giving her hostility a specific shape.

"What FUN this is!" Bitterness cooed, clapping its hands.

"If only I had the opportunity to see him again," Miriam said. "No one would have to know—I could kill him and make it look like his fellow bandits were responsible."

"Maybe someday you'll get your chance."

"He should pay for what he did to me. Just thinking about it gets me upset."

"But don't you feel better now?" the spirit said.

And for the most part, Miriam did, for revenge—even imagined revenge—contained an element of pleasure. The spirit knew that keeping Miriam occupied with her feelings of bitterness and revenge would prevent her from forgiving. It would keep her suspended as though she was a tunic left hanging on a clothesline.

Again and again Miriam replayed the scenes in her mind, swinging from emotional relief to rampant anger. In all honesty, she believed that given the opportunity it would be a justifiable murder, and that afterward she could finally rest at night. But in the meantime, her mental plays consoled her bitterness and angst over an eight-month period. They weren't enough, however, to quench the vicious fire that had ignited internally. No matter how much she pretended otherwise, the fantasies remained imaginative, and Miriam often cried to be set free from it all. Even so, the bitterness settled deeper and deeper into her soul, not unlike No'ômîy, or Naomi.

According to *Rûwth*, Ruth, a book in the Hebrew Scriptures, Naomi had turned severely bitter after burying her husband and the only two sons she birthed. Whereas Naomi had lost her family, Miriam lost her childhood innocence, yet together they shared both grief and bitterness. And like Naomi, Miriam often dreamed that her name had been changed to *Mara*, meaning bitter.

After every dream, whether in the day or night, Miriam would open her eyes only to find the harsh truth of the world looking her in the face. It seemed to her that the weight of bitterness loaded her down like a camel traveling for days through the low desert. There was no relief in sight. Little did she know that the same spirits who afflicted the nomad were now afflicting her.

Within almost a year's time Miriam had become, with the Spirit of Bitterness, intolerable. There was no other word for it. More and more, she disliked people and circumstances that occurred in her everyday life, all for no apparent reason. Yet, in her mind, there *were* reasons, and they made perfect sense. She believed she was justified in her action and attitudes, to tell the truth.

Miriam climbed the invisible ladder of bitterness that the wicked spirit set up for her. Higher and higher she ascended alongside the mounds of resentment that had accumulated in her life month after month, grumbling as she went. After reaching the top, she sat down on the sour layers, feeling reasonably content. Underneath it all, somewhere near the bottom, the sweet little Miriam from years ago was buried.

Once a kind, adoring and polite child, Miriam had always been a delight to her mother. After clinging to her mother's legs like most young children, Miriam had switched her focus to her father. Because Miriam found new attention in her father's eyes the relationship with her mother seemed to wane like the tide under the pull of a full moon. Miriam chose to confide in her father more because she had felt that her *âbba*, or father, didn't judge her the way her *ima*, or mother, did. Regardless of the error of that assumption, Miriam perceived it as the truth. Hannah wished they were more intimate, but she was content to educate Miriam in the duties of wife and mother in their Jewish culture. In her mother's eyes, it was a cherished training that produced an excellent wife—something that neither her father nor her brothers could provide.

On a late-spring morning they sat together in the large storage room of their house where hundreds of jars sat waiting to be filled with the olive oil from their grove. After pressing the olives taken at harvest, Miriam's family stored the oil in large barrels and then poured it into smaller vessels for the marketplace. The vast majority would be sold at the market throughout the year. While most of the oil was sold in its pure, unaltered form, a small portion was combined with fragrances such as spikenard, myrrh, or cassia, and sold as costly perfumes. Hannah carefully added the oil and fragrance together in delicate milky-white alabaster jars, mixing and swirling the two as if in a dance. Miriam poured oil from the heavy containers into less substantial ones—some wood, some glass, some clay—of various size, sealing each one with cork. Their hands worked rhythmically side by side, the only ones talking as Miriam and Hannah operated in silence. The strong scent of spikenard filled the room in the same way that the *Shêkinâh*, Shekinah, glory filled the holy of holies in Solomon's Temple. As if on cue, Hannah began singing, her voice light and ethereal. Miriam rolled her eyes and gave a slight moan, which Hannah promptly ignored.

Truth be told, Hannah had given Miriam a love for singing at an early age. Whether humming, whistling, or singing, Miriam's mother always carried a tune, especially as she went about her daily routine. Her beautiful voice resonated throughout their house, landing on everything in sight and giving ordinary things a simple radiance. It sounded every bit as lovely as the voice of *Ahărôwn's*, Aaron's, prophetess sister who sang and made music with timbrels after Yahweh saved the Israelites from the Egyptians. Miriam had always admired the way that she sang wherever and whenever, without shyness or embarrassment. In her eyes, the pure, heartfelt joy that had emerged in Hannah's songs seemed like one of the hot springs that bubbled up, flowed out, and warmed people with a simple touch. Truly, Hannah's voice—a rare and passionate sound—was haunting and smooth and deeply Hebraic, carrying echoes of centuries past.

Miriam had followed Hannah's lead for so many years, yet lately she refrained from anything that resembled music. It was as if the source had been shut off and boarded up. Worse still, Miriam couldn't tolerate her mother's consistent, passionate singing. She wanted others, especially her mother, to suffer as she was suffering, in the strange and unknown abyss of musical silence. It would be years later before Miriam understood the reasons behind her irrational thinking. Hearing people sing to their heart's content drove Miriam further into the outstretched arms of Bitterness. For the unclean spirit, it was progress in the right direction.

Miriam huffed and turned away on her stool.

"Miriam, what is troubling you, my sweet daughter?" she said, using words coated in honey.

"Nothing, I'm all right." Miriam said, annoyed.

"You don't seem that way."

"How do I seem then?"

"Angry and afraid—of what I can't figure out—and sour."

"I'm no more sour than the grapes used for our wine."

"I disagree. You're worse than rotten olives. Are you sure that you don't want to tell me anything?"

"There's nothing to tell. Nothing is wrong. *I am fine.*"

"I just don't believe that anymore, Miriam."

"What *do* you believe, Ima?" Miriam's tone sent a ripple of distress through the room.

"That you've become someone else in the last few years. Try and imagine it from my point of view. Life is normal until one day everything flips around, but you don't know why. There are no explanations or reasons, just dramatic change. And not a good change, I might add." Getting no response, she continued, "I don't like watching this change in you. In fact, I've hated it from the beginning. Despite what others might say, I can sense something isn't right. I know you too well."

"You don't know *me* anymore," Miriam said bitterly.

"Why? Why is that? Tell me what is happening to you; what *has* happened to you."

"Nothing. Just let me be."

And with that Miriam walked out of the house, leaving her mother to sit there confused and hurt. Hannah exhaled a long sigh of frustration and bewilderment as the lack of answers and explanations hung in the air like thick fog. Closing her eyes, Hannah tried to make sense of their unproductive conversation by replaying it over and over. But it led her only in circles. She wondered how Miriam could be as angry and bitter as the children of Israel under the hard bondage of Egypt. There must be something behind it all, she reasoned. But nothing—no memories or clues or thread of connection— emerged that could lead to the source. All that kept reappearing was Miriam's behavior, which was worse than carrion. Hannah had to leave her questions resting in time's balancing scales, like a handful of grains at the market.

Because Miriam pushed her mother away and chose to walk alone, the bells of isolation, as if in confirmation, rang out once again. Like the walking staff of Moses, the Spirit of Bitterness guided Miriam along her path of isolation, driving further internal seclusion. Whereas before Miriam had once been able to confide in her mother, she now recoiled at the idea of doing so; she would rather keep her thoughts to herself. Dwelling on her reasons for being bitter, Miriam created a dangerous environment for her mind. The mental dramas of revenge served only to remind her of her wounds. With no outside voice of reason—a direct result of Bitterness' deception as well as of her choosing—she listened to the advise of Bitterness, which felt to her like a rescue boat as she raged against the rising waves of the sea that surrounded her on all sides.

Walking toward the blossoming grove, Miriam pulled her head covering tighter and cursed everyone—her parents, brothers, the nomad, even Yahweh—for not loving her the way she wanted. Simultaneously, a string of curses soared out from the Spirit of Bitterness' mouth like bats out of a desert cave. Scowling from the tops of its eyes, the hostile Spirit of Bitterness—as sacrilegious as it was short—made a twisted face that could mean only true satisfaction. Together they walked side by side wrapped in an apron of blasphemies.

5

FOR THE PAST three years, the three previous spirits had been as much a part of Miriam's life as her Jewish heritage. To tell the truth, she felt that her life was more crooked than the roots of an olive tree. Relationships seemed to take more effort, decisions seemed to contain more heaviness, and thoughts seemed to trap her in a valley of insecurity. Not wanting her to come to her senses and escape the snare of the spirits, the next spirit held the pivotal position among the seven as the one central in changing her outward course of direction. With depths of evil that unraveled the human spirit, the Spirit of Rebellion took its job with the utmost seriousness.

Whereas Fear, Rejection, and Bitterness had approached Miriam in gradual measure with their deception, the Spirit of Rebellion approached her in the opposite manner, which is to say abruptly and without warning. All at once, the spirit began to entice her with thoughts and ideas that previously held no bearing. With an eternal obligation to wickedness, the spirit sought to lower her down to its kingdom, where offensiveness and witchcraft were inscribed on the gateposts.

* * *

Just like the snake in Eden's garden, the Spirit of Rebellion had perfected the art of being sly. Getting humans to rebel wasn't terribly difficult since it was engrained in their fallen nature. After *Chavvâh*, Eve, had disobeyed Yahweh by eating of the fruit on the forbidden tree and had given Adam, her mate, some to share, rebellion had been passed down from parent to child like a generational curse. The Spirit of Rebellion slithered up to her one day and began offering Miriam some fruit.

"You know, Miriam, you have been good all of your life. You never get into trouble, you never disobey your parents, and you always do what you're asked."

"Yes, that's true."

"But what has that gotten you? What do you have to show for all those years of being good?" Rebellion lured her further.

She thought for a few moments. "I don't know. Not much, I suppose."

"Well isn't it time that you do something about that? All children rebel—it's part of their nature. After all, aren't you tired of always being good? Surely there is a part of you that wants to experience the thrill of being bad. You really don't know what you're missing!"

"In a way I *am* tired of always being a good daughter, always obedient, always compliant. Now that I think about it, they don't expect anything different from me. They just assume I'll always be that way."

"You are different now. You have to be more assertive in making choices that are right for you! No one should tell you what you can and cannot do, say, or think."

"Exactly. I'm old enough to take care of myself and do what I want, no matter what my parents—or anyone else for that matter—says."

"There is a world of pleasure awaiting you out there—the kind of fun that lasts forever. You won't regret it," Rebellion lied.

Her mind, having been spun like a child's toy, continued to turn around and around on its own. She viewed the ideas from different angles and positions. She wasn't aware, however, that thoughts left unchecked would lead to beliefs, and beliefs would lead to actions. This, of course, was what Rebellion counted on.

At that moment, with her thoughts skipping around as though on hot coals, Miriam felt the sudden urge to skip rocks. The rhythmic activity always helped her to think. Making her way down to the water's edge after her morning chores, Miriam picked up all of the small, flat stones that she could find and carried them in the fold of her dark brown tunic. Her father would be expecting her to help sell oil at the marketplace, but she purposefully headed the opposite direction.

Once she arrived at the sea, she wasted no time lining up the stones, preparing them for their brief journey across the smooth surface. Levi and Benjamin had shown her how to skip rocks as soon as she was old enough to grasp the concept. At first she was uncoordinated and awkward, but soon Miriam blossomed into a talented stone thrower.

Tzip, tzip, tzip, plunk. She loved the sound of the abrupt contact of the rock meeting the water—that quick slap of surfaces in rapid succession. And then, as fast as a toad snatches a fly, the water swallowed the rock with a gulp. Again and again Miriam sent a rock out as she worked through her thoughts.

Growing up I always wanted to be good. But after years of doing things the right way and being obedient I can't really see the benefits of it all. What was it all for anyway? Is my life better because of it? Certainly not! Look at where I am today. Alone and hungry for something else. All of the effort and willingness to do what I was told seems wasted somehow. Shouldn't I see the fruits of being good? Otherwise, I don't see the point.

With that thought still lingering, Miriam skipped her last rock, sending it further out into the sea than any other rocks she'd skipped. Even though she didn't recognize it, the imagery of her decision to move outside the boundaries of her childhood stared her in the face. Just like the Spirit of Rebellion. From its point of view, the wicked spirit sneered at the ease of carrying out its responsibilities. Rebellion kept with the momentum and took advantage of the present situation.

Nearby a young man was busy unloading merchandise from his boat. As soon as Miriam, now fifteen, caught sight of him—his lighter skin, his muscular body, his handsome features—she found herself staring. His sand-colored hair looked to her like waves of wheat in the harvest hills; his brown eyes like an auburn stone found at the water's edge. The other two people in the boat—his older cousin and his cousin's mistress, as she later learned—flagged his attention, letting him know that he had an admirer. Looking up, he paused from his work and gave a friendly smile. Under normal circumstances Miriam would have looked away and then departed the scene; under normal circumstances she would never have considered approaching a strange man, in particular a strange Gentile man; under normal circumstances she would be hesitant to partake in any activity that smelled of risk. But something told her to stay.

"Go ahead. Take a chance. Nobody is watching. Remember, your days of following the rules are over," the Spirit of Rebellion prodded. "Go have some fun!"

Smiling to herself, Miriam walked over to the boat, feeling as excited and unsure as Ruth had been going into *Bô'az's*, Boaz's, tent.

"Hello," she said.

"Hello." His heavy Greek accent took her by surprise.

The other man and woman in the boat greeted her as well. Their smiles were polite yet inquisitive.

"Where is your home?" she asked the handsome man.

"Tiberias. Have you been there?"

"No, I have only heard about it. But I would like to," she quickly added.

Nodding his head the man replied, "I think that I could probably arrange that."

With her wide grin and dancing eyes Miriam thanked him. The older man in the boat—heavy set and dark skinned—whispered something to him in Greek, and they both nodded in agreement.

"In fact," he said in his practiced Aramaic, "we are returning there tomorrow morning. Would you like to come along?"

Sucking in a sharp breath, Miriam blurted, "Yes!"

"All right then. Meet us here at sunrise tomorrow and we will go."

"Yes. I will."

So great was the exhilaration that ran through her body as she walked away from the shoreline that Miriam felt as though she was a shooting star, soaring through the night sky. Truth be told, there wasn't a sound reason why she had agreed with such haste, or why she trusted the group of strangers, specifically the young Greek. Every part was contrary to what she knew was right and safe—contrary to her religion, contrary to her family, contrary to common sense. But temptation overtook her. The Spirit of Rebellion, escorting her home the way the Romans escorted a felon to his death, grinned with satisfaction.

"It feels good to be daring, doesn't it? Don't worry about what anyone will say, you can deal with that later—just do what you want. Live in the moment!"

"I am so excited! My first trip to Tiberias! And with three people that I don't even know. It's probably foolish… but I can't wait to go!" Miriam practically bounced the whole way home, as if she had just found an abandoned stash of gold.

Seven

When she walked in, her father stood glowering. "You were supposed to help at the market today."

Miriam looked away, trying to formulate a response.

"We needed you there, Miriam. The oil doesn't just sell itself. Harvest is almost upon us."

"I know."

"What was more important?" he asked.

She thought of her time at the shoreline, away from her family. Then she thought of the three visitors from Tiberias. All of that seemed more important to her. But confessing her heart would lead to more rift, more punishment.

"I just needed..." she began.

"What?"

"Never mind."

"What, Miriam? What are your needs? Are they greater than the needs of this family? Are your needs greater than the need for you to obey me?"

She heard the Spirit of Rebellion telling her to say, "Yes! Yes, they are!" But she bit her lip, frustration mounting inside her. Her lack of apology slapped Zebulun in the face.

"Miriam," he said, voice stern, "you have disappointed me."

She closed her eyes and Zebulun took that as a sign of remorse. Yet, truth be told, Miriam was shutting out his face, his voice. If he was this upset about missing work in the olive grove, how would he respond to her going to Tiberias with strangers? She thought about changing her plans but decided, in the end, to go. Her heart was set on it.

The fourteen hours between their meetings seemed to disappear without a trace. She hardly slept that night as she stretched out on her bed, envisioning what the next day would offer. As soon as the dim glow of dawn arrived—the signal for her to slip out of the house unnoticed—she walked to the shore with as much restraint as she could gather, in order to mask the bubbling anticipation that crouched directly beneath the surface. It was a warm fall day, the magnificent kind before the chill sets in. With a fresh tunic and combed hair peeking out from under her head covering, Miriam approached the boat as though she were a child eagerly reaching for a priceless gift.

"I don't even know your name," she said. The sweet tone of her voice grabbed his attention in the same way that flowers enticed bees. "I forgot to ask last time."

"Dagon. Named after the Philistine god."

The story of *Dâgôwn* and *Šimšon*, or Dagon and Samson, was one that Miriam knew well. Samson, a mighty warrior who had delivered Israel out of the hands of the Philistines, possessed a secret strength from Yahweh, which could be found in the seven locks of hair on his head. In all of his life no razor had ever touched his head because he was a *Nâzîyr*, or Nazarite—a man who consecrated himself unto Yahweh by taking a vow, separating himself as an offering, and abstaining from wine or strong drink. But when Samson fell in love with a Philistine woman named *Delîylâh*, Delilah, he revealed the secret of his great strength to her, after persistent coercion and prodding. She in turn had revealed the secret to her people, and they captured Samson, cut his hair, gouged out his eyes, bound him with bronze chains, and left him in prison.

While Samson was suffering the results of breaking his holy vow, the Philistines celebrated with great jubilation. They gathered together to offer a sacrifice to their god, Dagon, and to rejoice that Samson, their enemy, had been delivered into their hands. They ate and drank until they could hardly stand up. To make matters worse, they then called for Samson to perform in their temple. Blind and humiliated, his hands groped around and discovered that he stood between the pillars supporting the temple. At that moment, with his arms stretched wide, Samson cried out to Yahweh, asking for vengeance on the Philistines for his two eyes. And in one final feat of strength, he pushed against the pillars with all his might, causing the temple to completely collapse. Everyone, including Samson, was killed. In that one event, more Philistines had been killed than during his entire lifetime. The Philistines lost thousands of men and women, yet the Israelites lost just one man. Unfortunately, he was one of their greatest heroes. Miriam could only guess which group—the Israelites or the Philistines—had felt the loss more.

"My name is Miriam. It's Hebrew."

"It is lovely," Dagon said with a grin.

"My name is Lydia, and this is Brutus," said the woman next to Dagon.

Seven

Lydia had long red hair that fell perfectly straight half way down her arms, and big blue eyes surrounded by dark, inky lashes. She reminded Miriam of a beautiful flower whose colorful petals circled around a contrasting center. She figured that Lydia was not too much younger than her mother, and that Brutus—dark skinned and as hairy as Esau—was a generation older than her father.

Miriam smiled at them both, forcing herself to deny the nervousness and fear that bounded around her insides.

"Let us head on over to Tiberias then," Dagon said.

So far, everything had gone smoothly, and she smiled as she took Dagon's hand while stepping into the boat. The ride across the Galilean waves couldn't have been more fun for Miriam. She gazed over the landscape from the side of the small boat, soaking in the moist air and smiling with satisfaction. With eyes closed, she breathed the assortment of fragrances deep into her chest, hoping to somehow capture them all. The smell of the sea, the mountains, the damp air, and the plants was, in her opinion, the distinct aroma of coastal Galilee, as if it were a fragrance that Yahweh had poured out from heaven. The warm breeze brushed against her face and lifted the ends of her hair in ripples. At first she tried to keep her head covering on, but she soon decided that exposing her head to the sun and sea was part of the overall experience. In the same way, the unseen force of the wind and of the Spirit of Rebellion caused Miriam to lower her standards, affecting her rituals of dress and Jewish conduct.

Along the way to Tiberias, Miriam's senses—heightened by the fact that morning was her favorite time of the day—danced as though they were alive. The anticipation of what the city and the people would be like was almost too much to endure. Though the possibility existed, she couldn't imagine Tiberias being undesirable; it held too great a mystery, too great an appeal. No matter how strange, Miriam knew she would take pleasure in every sight and sound of the Roman city. Despite the fact that Magdala was within a day's walk to Tiberias, she felt as if she were traveling to a distant country. Along the way she wondered if she could, in fact, break from the Jewish way of life. And if so, would she have the resolve to follow through with it? Truth be told, Miriam knew no other way of living. Judaism was the only lifestyle she'd ever experienced. Though it provided comfort—as do all things that are familiar—she didn't want to pass up a chance to walk a different road for the sake of being comfortable. The closer they came to the docks, the faster her heart beat until she felt that it might stop from being overworked.

Once they arrived, Miriam followed her new friends up and down the streets of their hometown, where people buzzed with activity the way that the temple courtyards buzzed with moneychangers and sacrificial animals on a high holy day. Every sound, every sight seemed to tell how different Tiberias—a Hellenistic city among Jewish communities—was from its northern neighbors. Sitting south on the coast from Magdala like a Gentile orphan, Tiberias had all the characteristics that her hometown did not. It possessed a unique and magical allure in Miriam's eyes.

As they walked into the center of town, Dagon explained to Miriam that it was a newly built homage fashioned by the hands of Herod Antipas who, as she knew, was the governing authority in the Galilee region. The Romans created great cities with the highest cultural splendor in mind, and Tiberias was no different. In fact, it couldn't be more unlike a typical Galilean village. Red tiles covered the roofs and frescoes decorated the walls. The buildings were more than basic, practical structures; rather, they sparkled with color and design, making them seem like jewels set into a king's robe.

Tiberias was a feast of Hellenistic culture, sophisticated and worldly. They left the harbor and arrived at the marketplace. Carpenters, basket weavers, tailors, butchers, and farmers all displayed their commodities in the road, and for every one of those merchants there were two or three buyers haggling prices with them. Grains from Egypt and Africa; fabrics from Greece, Spain, China, and Syria; ivory from Africa and India; glass from Rome; and foods from Germania, Spain, and Arabia cried out to be purchased. Each item was more beautiful than the next. Feeling as if the goods had actual hands pulling her toward them, Miriam wanted to sample it all! Dagon watched her out of the corner of his eye and saw her raw interest. He introduced her to a variety of foods that were strictly forbidden in her own culture, such as boars cured with honey, sea scallops in cream, and red meats dripping with pink blood.

"Here, taste this. It's a Greek favorite," Dagon said. He handed her a piece of soft, flat bread with meat, cucumbers and onions covered by a white sauce. As soon as her mind sounded the alarm of the unlawful food—the combination of meat and milk—she dismissed it, and took a bite.

Seven

"That's wonderful," she said, wiping the sauce from her mouth.

"I used to eat these every day in Greece. Finish it—there's always more."

"What else do you like?"

In her mind nothing seemed too formidable to try. It didn't take long before Miriam switched the way she thought from being sheltered to being permissive. Her ears had tasted the words of the Spirit of Rebellion just as her tongue had tasted the forbidden foods of the Gentiles. She was in full control, making her own decisions. Or at least she thought she was.

All during this time, the Spirit of Rebellion walked along with them, guiding them to certain sights and sounds as if it were the host at a celebration. The spirit knew that Magdala remained mostly free from the pagan ideals that defined the Hellenistic way of life; and for that reason Rebellion played upon Miriam's natural weakness. Where Magdala thrived as a Jewish community, Tiberias thrived as a Roman one. The people of Magdala worshipped one god to the same extent that the people of Tiberias worshipped many. While Magdala stood for integrity and simplicity and tradition, Tiberias valued power and wealth and fame. Opposite in their approach to living, each city believed their own methods to be the best. And just as *R'ûwbên*, Reuben, had been lured by the forbidden beauty of his father's concubine *Bilhâh*, Bilhah, Miriam fell prey to the charms of Tiberias.

Throughout the day Dagon taught Miriam some basic Greco-Roman values of his seaside town, which, logically, had been named in honor of the Roman Emperor Tiberias. For example, he explained the importance of enjoying the fruits of life in food, drink and physical pleasure; of worshipping a variety of gods; and of using slaves for any requests, in order to be served at all times. This pagan approach to being served, fornication, gluttony, and greed opposed Jewish sages every bit as much as winter sat opposite summer. Initially speaking his second language of Aramaic, which was an essential tool in the Galilee region, Dagon then began to familiarize Miriam with his first, and preferred, language of Greek. (In his opinion, Greek went hand in hand with the civilization of Tiberias, even though Latin took its place as the official language of the Romans.) His hope, as it turned out, was that she'd be lured into staying longer than one day. Though she didn't know it at the time, the Spirit of Rebellion guided Dagon who in turn guided her.

The most outstanding moment for Miriam that day happened when Dagon escorted her to one of the Roman bathhouses for which the city was famous. With seventeen hot springs near the south end, Tiberias had incredible bathhouses, which in a way reminded Miriam of the Jewish bath—a pool of water to cleanse the lawfully unclean. The Romans, on the other hand, used bathhouses for both recreational and social purposes. As soon as they entered, Miriam soaked in every detail from top to bottom. Colorful mosaics covered the walls and pools in various shapes and temperatures adorned the rooms like wives and concubines adorned the arms of King Solomon. Her eyes bounced from the beautiful marble floors to the serene waterfalls to the windows set high in the walls that let light bathe each room. Never had she seen anything like it! At that moment Miriam hoped that she too would be able to enjoy the atmosphere of the bathhouse someday, as more than an observer, that is.

As they were walking out, Dagon bumped into someone he knew, an instrument in the hands of the Spirit of Rebellion.

"Dagon! Where have you been?"

"Working, Oreb, working," Dagon said.

"Too much work! You need to play more," said Oreb, laughing. "Life is short, my friend."

"Yes, but you may spend all your money and be left with nothing one day."

"Impossible! My inheritance stretches as far as the sky. In fact, I am throwing another party tomorrow, and I want you there," Oreb said with a huge grin. "And bring this beautiful young woman."

"Miriam," Dagon said, pointing to his friend, "Oreb." Miriam could only infer what they were saying as she, at that point, knew no Greek.

Miriam smiled at the handsome, stout Greek man. His tanned skin, dark hair, and amber eyes drew her in like a warm blanket.

"Those eyes!" he exclaimed. "She would be the sensation of my party!"

"Fascinating, yes, but I'm taking her back to the north shore today."

"Syrian?" Oreb asked Dagon.

"Hebrew. Doesn't speak Greek."

"Expanding your horizons, then, my friend?" laughed Oreb. "Excellent. Tomorrow night, I expect you there!"

Seven

"All right," Dagon said with a chuckle. "Your parties are always the envy of Tiberias."

"One day they will write stories about them! Like none other in all the land," Oreb said. "See you tomorrow!" He nodded his head to Miriam and entered the bowels of the bathhouse.

"Who was that?" Miriam asked Dagon.

"A friend. A very rich, jovial friend."

"What were you talking about?"

"He is throwing another one of his lavish parties tomorrow."

"Sounds exciting," she said.

"He does know how to throw an entertaining festivity. Oreb doesn't do much of anything in moderation. Everything is always extravagant. He enjoys being at the center of abundant attention."

Miriam smiled, enraptured in thought of what the party would be like.

"We need to go now," Dagon said.

"All right." Though she wanted to stay, she followed Dagon back into town.

"I think it's time to return to Mig-dala."

Miriam nodded, but her thoughts were far from home. "I wish that we could stay longer. There's still so much more to see and do here." With the taste of pork lingering in her mouth and the images of the bathhouse dancing in her mind, Miriam was overwhelmed by Gentile pleasures. If only she could have them every day! But in truth, she was stuck at home with her family and the Jewish law.

Throughout the entire voyage back to Magdala, Dagon watched Miriam, wondering what she was thinking. The day spent in Tiberias had been blissful for them both. Reflecting on it all, Miriam sat in the boat with sheer contentment. Lost in a state of dreaming, she didn't notice the lengths at which Dagon stared at her until they were almost to Magdala. Though at first caught off guard, Miriam enjoyed the attention that he showered on her. Her broad smile said as much.

"I can't thank you enough for today."

"You are welcome. I enjoyed it too."

"Maybe we can go again sometime."

"I visit Mig-dala once or twice a month, so perhaps in a few weeks,"

Dagon said.

"I'll look for you," Miriam promised. She smiled at the way he pronounced Magdala with his Greek accent, for it sounded to her as sensual as soft caresses.

"Good."

A spark had caught fire, and Rebellion was fanning the flame.

On the short journey from the harbor to her home Miriam's feet hardly touched the ground. Her cheeks actually hurt from smiling so much. But as soon as arrived and saw her mother, she swallowed her smile. She felt as if a dark cloud had covered up the warmth of the sun.

"Where have you been?"

"I was with some friends."

"Which friends? Because I asked all over town and none of your current friends knew, so don't lie to me, Miriam."

"I made some new friends." Her tone crept around with as much caution as a new mother around a sleeping baby.

"Who? And when?"

Hannah threw question after question at her so that she wouldn't have time to ponder the answers. It was a tactic she'd seen used on her father numerous times.

"Recently," Miriam answered.

"Who are they?"

"Some people from Tiberias."

"What?!" This clearly wasn't the answer she was expecting. "Did you *go* to Tiberias, Miriam?"

"No."

"With strangers?!" she continued.

"Ima—"

"Bad things could've happened to you!"

"Bad things can happen to me in Magdala too." Her tone caught Hannah off guard.

"What does that mean? What happened?"

"Forget I said anything. It was only a comment," she lied.

"Where did you meet them?"

"Down by the harbor. They are sophisticated and smart."

"Worldly!" Hannah said with disgust.

"There are Gentiles all over Magdala too! We pass them on the way to synagogue, we see them in fishing boats...we even sell oil to them at the market!"

"But we don't make friends with them!" Hannah retorted.

"They are not lepers, Ima," said Miriam snidely.

"They are *not* trustworthy, Miriam."

"Ima, just let me—"

"So what did you do all day besides *risk your life* for a little fun?"

Hannah's voice was getting more severe, backing her into a corner. Miriam debated how to respond. Then the Spirit of Rebellion whispered in her ear.

"If you want the truth, here it is," she said with a touch of arrogance. "We did sail to Tiberias, and then we walked around the city. Dagon, Lydia, and Brutus—my new friends—took me to the harbor, the marketplace, and a Roman bathhouse. They all live there. Dagon, the youngest, sells pagan merchandise, and comes into Magdala once or twice every month, depending on his sales. Brutus, Dagon's cousin, has an endless supply of money from his Roman side of the family, so he doesn't work, but instead travels around and collects writings of all languages. And Lydia, Brutus' mistress, likes to mix colorful powders and unguents to wear on her face, like Egyptian women. None of them are married, and all of them are gracious."

Just as Miriam had counted on, giving her mother more information than she really wanted threw her into stunned silence. At that moment, though no one saw it, the Spirit of Rebellion placed a thick, leathery hand on Miriam's shoulder and smiled with approval.

"First, let me say that you won't *ever* be seeing these Gentiles again," Hannah said after a few moments. "But more than that, you will wash yourself in the mikveh seven times for being unclean in more ways than I'd like to think. Then, you will repent for the fifty laws you disobeyed. Finally, you will stay within my sight for the next two months, doing everything asked of you."

As much as Miriam yearned to rebel against the things her mother said, she bit her tongue and lowered her eyes so as to hide her growing frustration. With a great rush she felt heat rising throughout her body like waves rising in a storm.

"You have brought dishonor to this family, Miriam. I can only imagine how your father will respond."

* * *

During the upcoming weeks her family would be consumed with the fall feasts as well as the olive harvest. Preparations were being made daily, the anticipation in the air growing alongside the excitement. Everyone was eager for the activities of autumn—everyone but Miriam, that is. Comparing her day with Dagon to her structured and religious days at home, she craved a change from Jewish life and law. Established by Yahweh through Moses, the Hebraic law—outlined in the sacred Scriptures known as the Torah—demanded obedience in a variety of forms: no worship of idols, dietary restrictions, sacrificial systems, festivals and feasts, cleansing rituals, and commandments. In all, six hundred and thirteen commandments governed the Jewish people! No matter how hard she—or anyone else for that matter—tried to follow that many rules, she always failed. Miriam felt, in all honesty, that it was an impossible expectation. The laws—and Yahweh for enforcing them—were simply impossible. But on the other hand, what else was there? Worship of pagan idols? In essence, Miriam couldn't see how that would be any better.

"There is another option, you know," the Spirit of Rebellion said.

"What other option?"

"Freedom from all worship."

"Worship nothing at all?" Miriam said in confusion.

"Think about it," the spirit suggested. "You would answer to yourself only. No rituals to obey, no guidelines to commit to memory, no punishment to fear, no wrath to endure. You would make your own rules—however many or few you desire."

Miriam had never heard of such an idea, because everyone she knew worshipped something. At first, the idea of worshipping nothing seemed as improbable to her as the sunken ax head floating back to the surface at *Ĕlîyshâ's*, Elisha's, doing. Yet in an instant the veil of uncertainty lifted.

"What a great idea!" she whispered with eyes wide.

"Truly, it's the only way to live," mocked Rebellion. "Why not give it a try?"

"Yes, of course! This may just be the answer I'm looking for. Not Judaism, not paganism; just nothing."

Smirking, the Spirit of Rebellion took satisfaction in the fact that her mind was welcoming, which is to say open and ready for change. Miriam steered her thoughts around like a shepherd guiding sheep, sending the old ones out and bringing the new ones in. And Rebellion served as her staff.

"The more that I think about doing things my way, the more sense it makes. After all that has happened, I need to be in a position to take care of myself, regardless of what anyone else thinks. I'm tired of trying to please everyone. I just can't do it anymore."

"Absolutely! You need to be the one in control of your life. Don't submit to anyone or anything—that only causes problems. Be assertive and stand up for what you want. Enjoy living however you'd like. Do whatever feels right for you, and don't restrict yourself to the law—man's or any god's."

"I want to be free from all the restrictions—my parents, this ancient society, the Law!"

"Living by the Law is a waste of your time," Rebellion mocked in blasphemy.

The rebellion that wrapped itself around Miriam's heart mimicked a vine that in the end choked the life out of whatever it touched. Throughout that season and into the next, Miriam's thoughts watered the vine's roots, making it stronger and sending it higher. According to the Scriptures, rebellion was the same as the sin of witchcraft. Even with that serious warning, she acted as the Israelites had done for thousands of years as told by the prophets *Hôwshêä, Mîykâh,* and *Yôw'êl*—Hosea, Micah, and Joel—defying obedience, defying Yahweh. To make matters worse, the Spirit of Rebellion made sure she had plenty of opportunities to demonstrate her stubbornness.

* * *

After their heated confrontation regarding Miriam's trip to Tiberias, her father watched her with a hawk's eye. A full year came and went where she spent almost all of her time in and around the house. That isn't to say that Miriam had changed her mind as to her rebellious attitude. Instead, she found little ways to press against the restrictions placed upon her without causing too much friction. Certainly her heart hadn't grown any more remorseful, for she could feel it getting harder month by month, in the same way that the heart of *Par'ōh*, or Pharaoh, had been hardened against Moses and the Israelites.

For more than a dozen years Miriam had been an ideal child. As the youngest, she naturally inherited mounds of adoration from her older brothers and sister as well as from her parents. From the time she was a baby, Zebulun had lavished his love on Miriam—the apple of his eye. For years he thought that she could do no wrong. She had existed as a fountain of endless joy, and her father had drunk as deeply of those refreshing waters as Noah had drunk of strong wine upon finally setting foot on solid ground. Indeed, Miriam had been intoxicating for so many people, not because of external beauty but because of an internal gift of grace that emanated without effort.

Zebulun, like most fathers, wanted only the best for his daughter, which is to say a life filled with promise and purpose. Though she wasn't permitted to be formally educated by the Jewish rabbis, her education covered a broader scope. She learned the honorable ways of being a devoted wife and mother; she learned to play the lyre, just as the psalmists had; she learned the heritage of her people, in order to pass down to future generations the glories of being among Yahweh's chosen ones. Zebulun knew beyond a shadow of a doubt that Miriam would have a great influence on people's lives. But Yahweh alone was to determine that, as long as she trusted in the Lord with all her heart and leaned not on her own understanding. If she acknowledged Yahweh in all her ways, then He would surely direct her path, as David declared in his *Tehillīm*, or Psalms. In the meantime, Zebulun continued to guide and instruct her as best he could, in whatever ways he could. And as Miriam had grown older, her father brought out the best in her personality as well as her abilities. She, in turn, had the same effect on him.

All throughout her childhood Miriam had loved her father with abandon. In fact, she'd revered him almost to the point of idolatry, since he embodied total perfection in her eyes. Caring, gentle and wise, her father had strengthened her nature as if he was a carpenter building a house. She had desired to be like him, for his character and outstanding reputation in their community rang as loud as the market bells. The fact that she was built just like him—in physique, in imagination, in speech—only added to their harmony. It seemed to her that their souls danced together in a lovely rhythm.

Seven

But then everything had changed. Without warning, without explanation, the current Miriam was no longer *his* Miriam. Sweetness had been replaced by ugliness; peace by foul temperaments. She'd become someone foreign to him, and that pierced his heart and twisted his gut as if he'd been attacked by a Roman soldier. No one seemed to know the cause of the noticeable transformation that had taken place in his daughter, especially him. And yet, of all the people who were aware of what was happening, he'd been affected the hardest. Though it wasn't his fault, Zebulun felt that he was somehow, someway ultimately responsible for Miriam's drastic downturn. Speculations naturally ran wild among their family and friends throughout the neighborhood.

Just like everyone else, Zebulun and Hannah wondered why Miriam had openly rebelled against them. They had raised her up in the fear—or reverent awe—and admonition of Yahweh. The commandments were to be taken seriously: having no other god before the Holy One of Israel, keeping the Sabbath, honoring father and mother, and a host of others. Despite their efforts, Miriam continued to challenge them on the law. Although her father had continually warned Miriam about her attitude and obedience, she didn't believe, in essence, that he would do anything about it. Once again he found himself staring into the eyes of her disobedience. Little did he know that he was attempting to control a force greater than a flood.

One afternoon between fall and winter, Zebulun found his daughter alone in her small and sparse room. He watched her for a few moments before speaking.

"Avoiding everyone on purpose?"

Miriam looked up at him with a defensive glare. "What, Abba?"

The Spirit of Rebellion who stood nearby felt invigorated by the tone of her voice. The conversation promised to be good!

"We need to talk, Miriam," her father said, offended at her tone.

She rolled her eyes and sighed deeply. "About what?"

"About why you've been as stubborn and wayward as a donkey."

"Abba—"

"Just listen for a minute, Miriam. You need to hear what I have to say."

With venom in her eyes she sat in silence, letting him talk. *Here he goes. I wonder how long this one will last. I just hate these talks! Why can't he leave me alone?* As if reading her thoughts, her father stood there looking at her. Feeling the heavy silence between them was enough to make her want to scream. *This is worse than his rambling.*

"Just say what you have to say and go."

"You are treading on dangerous ground, Miriam," he cautioned. "You may not think that your actions or your decisions are wrong, but let me tell you why they are." Knowing that the usual methods of persuasion, such as bringing dishonor or disappointing the family, wouldn't have an affect on his daughter, he created an illustration that she would remember for the rest of her life. "As members of Yahweh's chosen people, we have the choice to obey or to rebel, reaping the consequences of either decision. He has provided for us a spiritual tent—an enormous covering. As long as you, Miriam, obey the commandments and do what is right, you live under the tent in complete safety. But as soon as you choose to rebel and venture out from underneath the tent, you are exposed and can no longer expect to receive His protection."

Miriam remained quiet, hating his instruction, now more than ever. *This is a new lesson.* Full of spite, her eyes seemed to bore holes into his flesh. Meeting her father's face, Miriam answered with obvious disgust, "Yes, Abba."

"Your attitude is unacceptable, Miriam!" he said with far less patience and far more provocation.

"I don't care! I don't *want* Yahweh's protection! I don't want *your* protection either. I am old enough to make decisions and face the responsibilities that come with that. I'm willing to take chances. I *want* to take risks! I can't stand living by your rules and the law anymore!"

Rebellion cackled with delight. The conversation smelled as strongly of fervent defiance as the synagogue smelled of incense. In all honesty, nothing could've been better for the unclean spirit.

"Torah says that 'rebellion is as the sin of *witchcraft*, and stubbornness is as iniquity and *idolatry*.' You're testing Yahweh, Miriam, and that is unwise. Torah says, 'Yahweh will not be mocked.'"

The Torah says this, the Torah says that. Ach, the Torah! But her eyes had been blinded to the truth. All she could see was the glorious side of evil.

"Just as Yahweh warned Cain, I am telling you now: 'Sin crouches at your door and its desire is for you, but you should master over it.'" He recited from the book of *B'êrêshîth*, or Genesis.

"Maybe I want to sin."

"You don't mean that, Miriam."

"Yes I *do*!" She felt as though the veins in her forehead would explode with determination. "I make better decisions for myself than you make for me—you're an unjust father!"

At that moment her words sounded like the hissing of a snake. Bearing the markings of the Spirit of Rebellion, they echoed throughout the room. The spirit swelled with triumph.

Miriam's father struggled between righteous indignation and obvious heartache for his beloved daughter. Tears that burned with love for her threatened to run down his cheeks, yet he held them back as he shook with determination to stay in control. With sudden clarity, Zebulun felt the force of evil every bit as much as he'd felt the wind's chill earlier that day. Rather than pursue that line of thinking, he turned to his undisclosed plan.

"Miriam, you have given me no choice."

After a moment she said, "What does that mean?"

"I've arranged for your marriage."

Her mouth went dry and the Spirit of Rebellion shrieked for her in disgust. Whereas she sat frozen in place, the spirit bounced around the room offering Miriam disrespectful responses to her father's declaration.

"No!"

Zebulun nodded his head, never taking his eyes off her.

"Hadassah didn't have an arranged marriage."

"Unlike you, Hadassah earned the rewards of obedience."

This isn't happening!

"In the end, you'll be as happy as your sister is in her marriage," he said.

This really can't be happening!

"Who?" Miriam whispered the one word in a shaky voice, afraid of the answer.

"Lemuel."

As if the skies had opened up and dumped rain on her, Miriam felt panic soaking every thread of her being. The heat of anger welled up in her and sent her heart beating as fast as a horse's sprint. "But I don't love him."

"Lemuel is good for you, Miriam. I could've chosen someone worse."

That, of course, was true, yet it didn't seem to lessen the dread she felt. "I don't want to marry him!"

"I've been warning you for months now, but you've continued to defy me worse than the Israelites defied the Lord in the time of the prophets."

"You can't do this to me—I want to choose whom I'll marry!"

"It's too late. It's already been arranged. One month from today."

In that instant, Miriam knew that nothing would ever be the same.

"One more thing, Miriam," her father said. "Until then keep this in mind: Be sure your sins will find you out."

And with that he departed, all the while trying to shake the feeling that something suspicious controlled his daughter. Zebulun knew that Miriam was going to reap what she was sowing, but he prayed that the Lord would have mercy on her. His eyes showed how much he ached for his daughter. Without a doubt, they both knew that if she determined in her heart to rebel then she'd find a way. Though her father had hopes that Miriam would refuse a lifestyle of rebellion, he could see how his warnings hadn't deterred her obvious objective to sin and disobey. *Sin is fun for a season, but it always leads to death and destruction*, he had said countless times. But Zebulun felt he had reached an end with his warnings. Just like Yahweh had to deal with the Israelites' continued disobedience, he too had to take action. Which was why he had arranged Miriam's marriage, and in miraculous time, as a matter of fact.

"He's not in control of your life anymore—you are! Curse him!" the Spirit of Rebellion said.

"I hate him!" Cursing words writhed up from her belly, protruding into the air as if they were poisonous fumes. These fumes, these words—originating from the Spirit of Rebellion—lingered in the air around Miriam in the same way that beggars hung around the city gates of *Y'rûwshâlayim*, or Jerusalem.

"He can't do this to me. I refuse to marry Lemuel! But how can I avoid it? There must be some way," Miriam said to herself. Who could help her out? Not her mother, of course. Her brothers were of no use either, since they would never oppose their father on an issue such as this. She couldn't ask Lemuel, as he would be excited about the arrangement. Growing desperate, Miriam ran through a list of other names, each one worse than the next.

"Aren't you forgetting someone?" the Spirit of Rebellion asked.

"Who?"

"Your Tiberian friend..."

"Dagon! Of course! He's the perfect answer."

In an act of rebellion as great as King Saul's when he consulted the medium of *Êyn-Dôr*, En-Dor, after Yahweh told him to banish all psychics from the land, Miriam left for Tiberias without telling anyone. Her missing clothes and her father's missing money would give her away soon enough. Tiberias, among other cities, was the logical place to look, but without knowing for sure they'd be searching for months. To make matters worse, Tiberias had been built on the site of a cemetery, which meant nothing to Gentiles but serious uncleanness to observant Jews. This, naturally, prevented her father and brothers from stepping foot in the city. Unlike them, Miriam regarded the ban on visiting a city built upon graves as mere superstition, which happened to be another forbidden feature of the Jewish faith, yet many followed them like pigs to a feeding trough. In her mind it didn't matter where people were buried because death was a part of the life cycle, after all. Leading her in the same way that the North Star led sailors, the Spirit of Rebellion laughed at the image that Miriam was physically heading toward the graves with her soul not far behind. She, however, couldn't see it.

After arriving in Tiberias by foot Miriam found Dagon in the marketplace urging some travelers to purchase his goods. Though surprised to see her so unexpectedly, he smiled as wide as the Sea of Galilee and kissed her hand in greeting.

"What are you doing here?" he asked.

"I'm here to see you again."

"But it has been such a long time—I thought you had forgotten about me."

"I could never forget. I'm sorry that I was unable to meet you again, but my family forbade me. For months they watched me with a hawk's eye, and I hated every minute of it. But I'm here now, and I'm happy to see you again," said Miriam.

"I am glad you are here, Miriam. Are you planning on staying?"

"I'm not going back."

"Won't they come looking for you?"

"Probably. But I will avoid the obvious places," said Miriam.

"Even so, you will need to blend in more," Dagon explained.

Miriam looked down at her clothes and sandals, then at the resident Gentiles. Understanding, she nodded.

"Lydia has things you can borrow."

"Thank you, that is very kind."

"I assume you also need a place to sleep?" he asked.

Miriam smiled shyly. "I don't have much money..."

"Don't worry. We have separate quarters available for you. Our house is plenty big, as Brutus firmly believes in overindulging," Dagon laughed.

Only twenty-two, he owned, with Brutus, a large and well-decorated villa in the wealthier side of town toward the hot springs. He had paid for the villa with his profitable earnings from his merchandise business, where he sold an assortment of things he'd purchased for a mite's worth during his travels. Dagon's favorite items to sell were ornaments and objects that claimed to have a connection with the spirit world, such as crystals beads that dangled from a string, wind chimes, and charms for good luck, to name a few. Though he didn't believe that the articles he sold held any significance, that fact never prevented him from lying in order to make a sale. In fact, he told people whatever they needed to hear, and they in return lapped up the exotic stories as if dying from thirst. Dagon created stories of how his magic charms connected them with the gods, and how they ensured favoritism and benevolence from the myriad of idols, whether Greek, Roman or Egyptian. So, with a clever tongue and handsome features, Dagon gathered the money up faster than a dog licked up its own vomit, as the book of Proverbs put it.

Always watching for a sale, Dagon tried to sell his misinformation to Miriam using the same tactics. But Miriam wasn't interested. For the first time in her life she was living without the rules of an established system of worship. She wasn't about to trade that in for the shackles of pagan gods. While she at first thought Gentiles were foolish for putting their faith in tangible objects, she soon came to the conclusion—thanks in part to Dagon and Lydia—that people should believe in whatever they wanted, no matter how strange. Dagon stopped persuading her and affirmed her decision to stay away from the gods and the dutiful practices required by them, just as he had. What's more, he believed religion was a big curse, passed down throughout each generation by parents and priests. But truth be told, Miriam and Dagon—in their desire to avoid getting tangled in the nets of religion—served the same master that the pagans served, which is to say *ha-Sâtân*, or Satan. Only they didn't know it.

The Spirit of Rebellion laughed at the mockery of it all. One way or another, either through the worship of Greek and Roman idols or through the worship of themselves, the spirit owned them. Both pathways led to destruction and were as dependable as a camel on a long trek through the desert.

Three weeks in Tiberias went by faster than Miriam had expected. She had avoided the areas of town where she might be discovered. She made every effort to blend in as much as possible, wearing Lydia's tunics of fine linen, decorated sandals, and earrings that swayed in the breeze whenever she ventured outside the villa. Every once in a while Miriam heard rumors of men paid to hunt down a Jewish girl hiding within the city walls, but Rebellion quickly steered her to safety.

Day by day and piece by piece, she traded the memory and security of her home for a life of supposed freedom. Once she chose to pursue her own way instead of her father's, she made the rift between them as wide as the Great Sea to the west of Israel. But Miriam, in taking on the lifestyle of a Gentile, isolated herself not only from her family but also from her heritage and religious culture. As if it was an unappetizing meal, she declined the spiritual inheritance of her ancestors, which in turn excluded her from almost everyone she knew. But to tell the truth, she didn't care. Miriam preferred to stand apart from them, alone and withdrawn. Her isolation begat more isolation. Her defiance grew as large as the list of generational tribes listed in *Lêvîyŷ* and *Micpâr*, otherwise known as the books of Leviticus and Numbers.

The Spirit of Rebellion radiated with satisfaction. Like animal fat falling on a fire, Rebellion sent the flames that roared within her upward and outward, lashing against everything in its reach—singeing, charring and burning whatever it touched. The spirit received wild praise from the others for its talent at spiritual destruction. And Rebellion absorbed all the proffered glory.

6

THE SPIRIT OF LUST licked its lips in seductive fashion, eyeing Miriam with desire. The time had come at last. Gazing from behind heavy eyelids, Lust formed lewd gestures with its claws. The unclean spirit, girded with weapons of corruption and iniquity, knew that promiscuity offered passion and excitement. Opportunity for depravity soared as limitless as the sky above Galilee, and everything had the Spirit of Lust's approval. Using the path that the Spirit of Rebellion had carved, Lust took the enticement of Tiberias to lure Miriam as if she was a dog after meaty bones. It couldn't wait to add another layer of bondage to her soul. The spirit sauntered up to Miriam, carrying its two most charming forms of seduction. And they were impossible to refuse.

* * *

Once she had settled in to living with Dagon and Brutus in their Roman-style home, Miriam took to walking the roads of town. By the time the Spirit of Lust entered Miriam's life, she had lived with the first four spirits for quite some time—more than five years to be exact—growing used to their voices, their directions, and their control. So strong were the voices of the unclean spirits that they drowned out the whispers of her sense of right and wrong. Instead, she heard the beckoning of the Roman world with its exotic foods and beautiful garments. Her heart was filled with hunger and rebellion, ready for the Spirit of Lust to enslave her to a lifestyle of immorality in both body and mind. At that point, Miriam didn't know what simmered beneath the surface, only that something within her was changing once again.

One day as she followed Dagon around the city, he lured Miriam into confessing the truth that she'd kept secret from him.

"How long will you stay in Tiberias?"

"For a while," she said, looking at him with hopeful eyes.

"Will your family not continue to look for you?"

"Not here. This city is built on a cemetery, as you know, so they won't step foot on it. In Jewish custom it's unclean to walk on graves."

"Oh," he said. "But I have seen Jews walking in Tiberias."

Nodding, she said, "Some, unlike my family, are not concerned about the law and uncleanness. They are, of course, looked down upon by the 'righteous' ones, but they don't seem to care too much."

"And you left Mig-dala to get away from your family or from these Jewish customs?"

"Both. I didn't want to live under the strict ways of our faith—that faith, I mean. It demands too much."

Dagon looked at her as she spoke, but Miriam kept her eyes on the lush palaces and Roman statues that decorated the city, which seemed as assorted as one of *Dâniyê'l's*, Daniel's, visions.

"In fact," Miriam said, "My father, in his strict way of doing things, had arranged my marriage right before I left."

"In truth? Who were you to marry?"

"His name is Lemuel. I've known him since birth."

"And you do not want to marry him?" Dagon said.

"Absolutely not."

"You do not love him?"

"No, I don't love him, and I certainly don't want to live with him until I die." After a moment she added, "I'd rather live with you."

Miriam's eyes took on a glow like the morning sun, and Dagon answered with a confident and charming smile. Walking behind them, the Spirit of Lust placed a hand on each of their shoulders and gently pushed them together until they were touching like a pair of gazelles headed toward the ark.

Dagon took her hand and they made their way down to the marketplace where they indulged in a variety of foods. Now that she had overcome the obstacle of eating unclean things, her appetite roared louder than lions in the Roman coliseum. Miriam permitted herself to feast on all of the fruits of the sea—shrimp, scallops, and mussels—and beasts of the land—deer, pig, rabbit—in order to satisfy her impatient lust, not unlike the all-consuming desire that turned Lot's wife into a pillar of salt upon feasting her eyes on a burning Sodom and Gomorrah. For weeks and weeks Miriam gorged on tastes as numerous as the stars, becoming more and more familiar with the Tiberian lifestyle. At that time food—and the endless variety of choices— seemed to be the only thing other than Dagon to hold her full attention. But, wanting her to expand her lust of the eyes, the Spirit of Lust guided her in another direction.

Then it happened that Miriam was walking through the market on a cool and cloudless late-fall day when she noticed with more than a casual interest the clothing that danced before her eyes. Never before feeling the pull of material possessions—her family having money but never showing their wealth—she discovered a desire to completely alter her attire. Boasting colors and fabrics and styles from Egypt to Greece to India, the selection of garments made her head spin as if she'd had too much wine. Here and there she'd seen beautiful tunics and cloaks, much like the one Lydia had loaned her, but hadn't coveted them. Overall her clothes were made with good materials, yet they were simple, purposeful, and bland. She looked down at her tunic the color of a camel's hide and furrowed her brow.

"I will never wear plain clothes again. There are far too many pretty fabrics to have," Miriam vowed as she walked by the merchants, fingering the cloth goods.

"Owning these beautiful garments will make you more attractive," the Spirit of Lust said. "You'll feel better about yourself if you wear expensive, nice-looking things. You'll fit in here better, and the people will accept you as one of their own."

"I do want to look like them and have what they have."

"Having material possessions will satisfy you in ways you can't imagine." The lie, delivered in a seductive tone, was as straight and pointed as a warrior's arrow.

And so, Miriam decided that there was no better person to help her dress in the latest fashions than Lydia. She always wore tunics of fine-woven cloth, where color and texture blended together like leaves and grapes on a vineyard trellis. Since Lydia held the position as Brutus' mistress, she inherited—with great pleasure, to tell the truth—his generosity, which is to say his boundless money. This enabled her to buy whatever she wanted. With her bright red hair and freckled skin tone, Lydia never looked anything less than lovely, no matter what she wore.

Miriam found her sitting before the reflecting glass, where she applied several shades of powder to her face. For a few moments Miriam just stood there entranced. She reminded Miriam of the Queens of Egypt who were displayed in mosaics around the city.

"Hi, Miriam," Lydia said, turning around.

Pulling herself out of the trance, Miriam said, "Hi." Touches of red sprouted in her cheeks from mild embarrassment.

"Come, sit next to me." Miriam obeyed with a smile. "Do you want to try some of my powders?"

"Yes." Miriam's ability to converse in Greek had multiplied day by day like the widow of *Tsârephath's*, Zarephath's, oil.

"Let's see, with your skin the color of dark olives, you will need these shades of green and earth brown accented by a little charcoal for your eyes."

Miriam turned her face away and looked in the small mirror, feeling the fingers of insecurity. Gently, Lydia touched her chin, bringing her face back around.

"Your eyes, Miriam, are the most unusual thing I have ever seen."

"I wish they were different."

"But they are so beautiful," said Lydia.

"More like a curse."

"I can see how people might be afraid or confused…"

"Or think I'm possessed by evil spirits," Miriam said.

Lydia laughed and shook her head. "People can be so ignorant! Can you imagine? Sweet little Miriam possessed by spirits?" And they both laughed until their cheeks hurt.

"But watch, we can turn your eyes into something magical." Lydia lined her eyes, blending and shading powders and inky pastes until the composition stood out more than the colors of her eyes. She turned Miriam toward the mirror.

"By the gods!" she exclaimed, using a well-worn Tiberian expression.

"Now they are your best feature," Lydia declared.

"That is miraculous. It changes the whole look of my face."

"Do you like it?"

"So much that I will always wear it!"

Lydia smiled, "And now for your cheeks and lips, warm colors of apricot and wine. You have to balance everything—too much will make you look like a harlot. We will find colors that best match your clothes each day."

At the same time they both glanced at Miriam's plain tunic, and giggles escaped out of their mouths, making them sound like two little girls.

"I guess there is not much to work with here," Miriam said.

"Well, we can either make you look like a desert princess in shades of tan and brown, or we can get you some new clothes."

"I want to have clothes like yours," she confessed. "But I don't know where to find them or how to have them made."

"I know just the place."

"I thought you might. I want to look like a Tiberian woman."

"Even better—like a Greek goddess. Come!"

Grabbing her hand, Lydia jumped up from her cushion and led Miriam out the door. They spent the rest of the day, and many days throughout the season, buying all manner of tunics and clothes and accessories. Both of them felt such satisfaction, Lydia for helping Miriam, and Miriam for stepping into another world. She had hung up her old Jewish lifestyle for a new Gentile one.

Hours later they walked back into the villa, looking radiantly beautiful in their new adornments. Miriam's hair was pulled high, a crowd of curls held by shimmering gold bands. Slender tapestry earrings fell gracefully toward her shoulders; a lavender tunic draped her body, emphasizing her emerging curves; gold bracelets laced her arms, glowing against her smooth olive skin. A long necklace lay on her chest, the pink stone resting softly among folds of skin. Lydia had just commented on how many men had eyed Miriam throughout the town when Dagon bumped into them in the anteroom. He stopped, arrested.

"By the gods," he said under his breath.

Lydia laughed. "Doesn't she look stunning?"

"A goddess," Dagon replied.

"I told you," Lydia whispered to Miriam.

"I would not have recognized you on the street," said Dagon.

"Lydia did it all," Miriam admitted.

"We both knew it was time for a change," Lydia replied. "I think it befits you rather well. Wouldn't you agree, Dagon?"

"Entirely," he said, grinning. "I have to go to the market for a few hours, but I want to take you out for some wine—"

"And some scallops?" Miriam asked, hopeful for her new favorite food.

"Of course," Dagon promised. "I have the perfect place to go."

"All right."

"I'll be back soon," he said, departing and grabbing one last look.

When they were alone again Lydia said, "I haven't seen him that excited in a long time. He was interested in you before, Miriam, but now he might be fixated."

"I have never had someone look at me like that," Miriam confessed.

"Well, my former daughter of the Hebrews, you have stepped into a sophisticated world, and you are most alluring. Now, I am going upstairs to take a nap. Your evening sounds promising..."

"Thank you, Lydia. I am so grateful to you."

"My pleasure, beautiful one," Lydia said, kissing her cheek.

Entering her room, Miriam stood before the small mirror marveling at Lydia's handiwork. The change was remarkable.

"It really is miraculous," she said, running her hands down the expensive gown. Turning her head side to side, she admired the way Lydia had arranged her hair. "I never thought I could look like this."

The Spirit of Lust responded, "Now you are truly beautiful."

"I look like one of Solomon's wives."

"Without all of the accessories you are just ordinary. You have value now because of the fine clothes—they have made you into something desirable. And it feels wonderful, doesn't it?" the spirit continued.

"Yes, in all my life I have never felt so good about myself."

Biting its lips, the Spirit of Lust eyed Miriam with lewd intentions. It would be rather easy to lure her into more dangerous forms of lust now, and the spirit anxiously awaited that day.

"I'm creating a new me. I am no longer a girl of Magdala but am now a woman of Tiberias. I shall have whatever satisfies me and deny myself nothing."

Breathing in the aroma exuded from her lust, the spirit leaned in and whispered in her ear with heavy breath. "Your life will be better for it. You need these worldly goods; they bring happiness and fulfillment like nothing can."

Because Dagon loved beautiful women the way that Jews loved festival feasts, he found himself showering Miriam with more attention than she knew what to do with. That night, and many nights in the future, he spoiled her with mounds of attention and affection. This, in turn, kept her focused on looking exquisite. She spent untold amounts of time searching for the right garments and accessories such as pearl necklaces, gold earrings, ruby rings, and ankle bracelets that chimed. In essence, Miriam's obsession emerged from the desire to create a new future as well as to forget her tiresome past.

Without a doubt, the Spirit of Lust drove her endless desires. It enjoyed getting Miriam to covet almost everything she saw. Though it was engraved upon the stone tablets of Moses, the commandment against coveting went ignored. The allure of having everything she desired gave her such immediate pleasure. There was no end to the craving to buy and to have. Whatever was the latest import or the rarest item, that's what she wanted. Truth be told, material possessions mastered her life in the same way that rage overtook the sons of Jacob when they murdered the men of *Sh'kem*, Shechem, to avenge their sister *Dîynâh*, Dinah.

Using Dagon's riches, Lust ensured that she received whatever her heart and flesh desired, refusing nothing that struck her liking. He enjoyed lavishing gifts on Miriam, and with every ounce of adoration that she gave him in return, it filled him with a hunger for more. She too hungered for Dagon and the belongings that seemed important. Adornments and oils coated her hair, her face, her skin; jewelry dangled from her body; tailored sandals protected her feet; and imported linens covered her bed. Dagon bought, in essence, Miriam's affection and devotion with purchase after purchase. Possessions began controlling Miriam. Subtle though it was, the transition of power strengthened the Spirit of Lust's domination.

For weeks Miriam felt as if she floated on air. Life in Tiberias couldn't have been better. The remarkable city provided her with endless tangible objects on which she could project her fondness and attach her sense of worth. With every craving, whether it was eaten or worn, Miriam sought satisfaction. But, of course, it lasted only as long as the changing wind. She merely swung like a chime in the breeze from one pleasure to another, enjoying the thrills of her supposed freedom. By all appearances the commodities she coveted were essential, yet underneath their glistening exteriors emptiness glared forth. And as soon as Miriam glimpsed the hollowness of one object she moved on to the next. The fulfillment she sought didn't exist. By feeding her endless desires, Miriam gave permission to the Spirit of Lust to rule over her. And rule it did.

* * *

With a sharp click, the Spirit of Lust affixed the second invisible shackle to Miriam. If the lust of the eyes was the chain that confined her arms then the lust of the flesh confined her feet. Together they completed the wicked spirit's agenda, which is to say enslavement to all things physical.

Once winter had settled upon Tiberias, Miriam traded her daily outings around the city for the comfort of a cozy fire. Though Dagon still spent part of the day making sales in the marketplace, he more often than not settled in beside Miriam, warming himself against the chill in the air. Several times he sat close enough to her to feel the heat coming from her body, which seemed to him to produce more warmth than the fire. And so, with eyes more inviting than the harlot spoken of in Proverbs, Miriam lured him without words. She had wrestled for years with the lie that had been whispered in her ear by the Spirit of Rejection: *You will never be loved by a man.* Now, reminding her of that statement, the Spirit of Lust poked at the embers burning in Miriam's heart. She wanted to prove Rejection wrong, so she responded to the opportunity sitting next to her. Miriam hungered for love and thirsted for justification like someone who just ended a month of fasting longs for bread and water.

One night around the turn of her sixteenth year, as rain fell on the tiled rooftop and cold temperatures seeped into the marble corridors of the villa, Dagon saw Miriam shivering under a wool cloak. He approached her as she huddled near the fire. All at once Miriam felt Dagon's arms wrap around her, pulling her into his body. Closing her eyes, she shuddered with gratitude and excitement. To tell the truth, both Miriam and Dagon had released signals of desire to one another, yet neither of them had altogether acted on it. There had been plenty of hand holding and casual embraces, but until that moment nothing sinful had taken place. Then, as suddenly as the wind changed direction, they threw their arms around each other and pressed themselves together with wild passion.

Dagon swept her up in his arms. He brought her the few steps into his bedroom chamber, the wool blanket left in a heap by the fire, a picture of her covering shed for the excitement of forbidden transgression. The silk linens on Dagon's bed felt as lustrous as fresh-pressed olive oil, the pillows as soft as fleecy feathers. Faint aromas of incense floated around them, their own scents of lust folding in. Enjoying each other's caresses, they drank their fill of love until morning. Only David and Bathsheba knew more unlawful obsession.

Miriam had always assumed that she would soil her marital linens with her husband, but that idea was now completely abandoned. Life for her had changed, and she responded accordingly. In the few hours after she crossed the licentious boundary, Miriam had mixed emotions about giving herself to Dagon. For days afterward, she wrestled between the two extremes of feeling satisfied that she had actively pursued physical love, and feeling remorseful about sacrificing her original intentions. However, the Spirit of Lust didn't allow Miriam to wobble in a state of discomfort. Instead, it praised her decision.

"You see? That wasn't such a big deal," the spirit lied. "You should be happy with yourself for finally taking that step! You've crossed over the threshold, entering into the realm of true womanhood."

"I have, yes."

"All the formality about physical union for marriage alone is a bunch of lies."

"There was always such a heavy burden to keep myself pure until marriage, especially in light of Moses' law. But now I'm free of that."

"There's no turning back now."

"That's right, there's nowhere to go but forward. Even though it was different than I had imagined, I don't regret it. Actually, it was a rather nice experience considering the fact that I didn't know what I was doing. I'm sure it will get better."

"Practice makes perfect."

All throughout that winter and into the next spring Miriam and Dagon lived from one day to the next, from one passionate session to the next, where they burned in their lust for one another just as the wife of *Pôwtîyphar*, Potiphar, lusted after Joseph. Their emotional highs matched their physical highs, where everything seemed to flow without effort, or as naturally as water traveling downhill. Miriam learned a great deal about passion and the lust that drove her into Dagon's arms each night. During those days she viewed their time together as educational as well as passionate, for Dagon's experience in matters of heated intimacy far exceeded her imagination. In the same way that a potter molded his clay, he taught her how to achieve the most out of every encounter, showing her that her needs and wants were important.

But despite her initial excitement, Miriam learned, with time, the ruthless truth of her intimate relationship, which is to say that it was based on selfish motives. Selfishly, Dagon used Miriam to fulfill his flesh-driven and immediate desires. Selfishly, Miriam responded to him, attempting to fill the void within her. The true, honest love she sought in her relationship with Dagon wasn't to be found. That, of course, didn't prevent her from trying. Fogging her eyes like a room filled with steam, the Spirit of Lust—her spirit of harlotry—blinded Miriam to the truth.

To make matters worse, Dagon began demanding with subtle hints that Miriam cater to his needs and his wants. Having been through this routine before with other women—the ones he'd seduced during his travels to all sides of the sea—Dagon knew a few conventional methods that would produce the results he craved. He played upon her emotions and insecurities rather than embracing her genuine feelings of affection. His affections oozed like an aloe plant with false devotion. His cunning manipulations, his questionable expressions, his slithering advances all carried an air of supposed adoration, backed only by deep, selfish motives. Dagon caressed his way around her with his words, creating a mixture of feelings that bellowed of obsession yet emptiness. In the end, all of it reduced to the base of primal lust, nothing more, nothing less.

For the Spirit of Lust, bringing Miriam to a place where she presented the members of her body again and again as instruments of unrighteousness to sin was of great importance. Like a building's cornerstone, it was the foundation of its mission. Once there, she walked according to her flesh in the lust of uncleanness, and lived in a vicious cycle of desire. Only the spirit understood that the desires were in the end insatiable.

The most challenging part for the Spirit of Lust had been pushing Miriam over the edge of purity. As it turned out, even that wasn't too difficult. After that, maintaining immorality required far less effort. The world offered endless opportunities for corruption, as ancient cities such as *Nîyn'vêh* and *Bâbêl,* otherwise known as Ninevah and Babylon, had shown. And Tiberias was just as rich in wickedness. In order to get Miriam to participate in additional methods of lust, the unclean spirit built her up with as much effort as the people of *Y'rîychôw,* or Jericho, had built their walls.

"Be secure in your sensuality; you have a beautiful body, so use it!" Lust said. "Men want you, Miriam. You are irresistible—a source of constant distraction. Don't refuse the love they want to give you."

"I do want them to love me."

"Your confidence will attract them and your charm will cause them to fall at your feet."

"Like slaves before their master," Miriam said, laughing.

"Exactly."

And so, after sharing intimacies with Dagon alone for a year—through the warmth of spring days and the heat of summer nights—Miriam opened herself up to other means of carnal sin. She permitted herself, for example, to be seduced by married men while Dagon traveled away from Tiberias. Surprised at how little adultery bothered her, Miriam repeatedly broke the seventh commandment, much to Yahweh's dismay. In all honesty, the proverb that warned men to avoid immoral women seemed to describe Miriam down to her toes, with her lips as sweet as honey and her mouth smoother than oil. Her steps headed straight to the grave, for she didn't care about the path to life. She staggered down a crooked trail, not realizing where it led.

Just like the adulterous woman that Solomon described, Miriam spread out on her bed colored sheets of the finest linen from Egypt and perfume of myrrh, aloes, and cinnamon. With each man she drank her fill of love while

Dagon journeyed to the other cities of Galilee, one after another almost as if she were trying on different tunics. She didn't worry about being stoned to death since she lived in a Gentile world of pleasure. But, of course, all of these meetings—passionate though they were—contained nothing of substance and nothing lasting. Even so, the truth of the matter didn't discourage her as the Spirit of Lust persisted on making lies her only basis of reality.

Truth be told, her lust of the flesh was forming a noticeable addiction. At least to the Spirit of Lust it was noticeable. Fornication and adultery didn't equate to love, but Miriam journeyed in vain otherwise. Like dangling a diamond in front of her eyes, Lust used the false promise of finding love in a man's bed to string her along. And with each encounter Miriam formed another soul tie. Spiritually speaking, all of her intimate unions formed soul ties, or in other words an unseen transformation of two people becoming one, yoked together like oxen. From the days of Adam and Eve, when a man joined a woman they became one flesh. Inside of marriage the yoke was a blessing; outside of marriage it was bondage. That was the Spirit of Lust's purpose. Working with great diligence to get Miriam obeying her flesh, Lust led her further and further away from liberty.

One afternoon Miriam decided to visit a well-known Roman bathhouse without the company of Dagon or Lydia. The local Tiberians loved their bathhouses, which dotted the city landscape as stars did the night sky. Some were designed for bathing only, some for socializing, and some for conducting business. But all standard bathhouses included a warm room, a hot room, a cold room, and a room for oiling. Most of the public baths separated the women from the men. Certain smaller baths existed, though, for joint bathing, where activities of wickedness paraded around.

Miriam, as always, bathed and socialized only with other women, learning the language and practices of Romans and Greeks. This particular bathhouse offered an array of treatments including massages, mud baths, facial cleansers, and salt scrubs. The scrub, which happened to be Miriam's favorite, renewed and refreshed her skin from head to toe. Healing, mineral-rich salts from the Dead Sea were blended with fragrant oils, such as hyssop, almond, and rosehip. Relaxing on a table as an attendant rubbed her body with the sweet-smelling salts, Miriam felt every bit as indulged as *Eçtêr*, Esther, did during her months of beauty preparations before seeing King Ahasuerus. When that was complete, Miriam rinsed off the crystals in a tepid pool of water, leaving the oils to remain on her skin to be absorbed. She smelled for days afterward like a handful of wild flowers.

That day Miriam felt a strong sudden urge as she was leaving to visit the unorthodox bathhouse. It seemed to beckon her audibly. She knew that the people and activities differed greatly from her usual one, but it still remained somewhat of a mystery.

"Aren't you at all interested to know what goes on inside?" Lust said.

"Of course."

"Go ahead then; see for yourself what it's really like. It's just harmless fun—men and women celebrating their bodies and instinctual desires. You were made to enjoy these kinds of things!"

"Visiting one time won't hurt," Miriam agreed. "I've heard about the things that happen there...but I'd like to see for myself."

"Naturally. And if you don't like it then you don't have to go back."

Lust's flagrant lie enticed her further. The spirit knew that such places and visions of lustful flesh formed a sticky web that made escape difficult. Indeed, following the initial visit Miriam discovered that the sultry atmosphere possessed a certain lure. She didn't understand why she was drawn to the bawdy scenes that occurred there, but she knew that she would, in fact, return again. And every time she went, Miriam witnessed a variety of practices that would make Solomon blush.

On her way out of the provocative bathhouse Miriam heard a voice behind her and felt a small tap on her shoulder.

"Excuse me?"

She turned around to see Oreb, Dagon's friend.

"Aren't you the woman I saw with Dagon a long time ago?"

Miriam nodded and smiled.

"I almost didn't recognize you. You have really changed!" Oreb said with a jovial laugh.

"Yes, I decided that if I was going to live in Tiberias then I should look like a Tiberian," she replied. Miriam didn't need to ask him what he thought of her transformation as his eyes told her everything. She could feel desire oozing from his body. The power she felt pulsed through her blood. Without any doubt, Miriam knew she could fully seduce Oreb if she desired.

"Do you want to come to my house tonight? For a party?" he asked. "Come and meet my friends."

"That sounds tempting."

"We will have music and food and wine, and even some entertainment if you're interested."

The mystery intrigued Miriam even more. "When?"

"Sunset," Oreb answered. "And bring Dagon!"

"Of course."

Oreb took Miriam's hand and kissed it, looking up at her through thick, dark lashes. His swarthy skin and light brown eyes exuded warmth, and his smile a genuine invitation for company.

That evening Miriam and Dagon walked through the city, weaving a path to Oreb's house. She wore a long raspberry-colored tunic embroidered with intricate flowers of purples and reds. Her braided hair hung long down her back, wisps of curls breaking free and framing her face gently. Gold and silver bracelets chimed rhythmically on her slender arms in cadence with their sandals clapping against the stone streets.

"Sometimes the festivities at Oreb's parties can get...graphic," Dagon warned her.

"Don't worry," she replied, "it won't bother me."

"Maybe, but don't be alarmed by the brazenness—most of his friends have no sense of shame."

"I will be fine, Dagon."

"I'm just warning you," he said. "Some activities can be pretty shocking for a Hebrew girl from Mig-dala."

"For the old Miriam, yes. But the one on your arm can abide anything." His laugh made her smile and surge with self-confidence.

As they approached the villa, the music and laughter grew louder and more inviting. Opening the massive wood door, Dagon ushered Miriam into the entrance hall where a man overcome by drunkenness hung sloppily on a woman who laughed at her companion. Her glass of wine sloshed back and forth like the waves of the sea, though she managed to keep it from spilling over. They hardly noticed Dagon and Miriam as they staggered through to the next room, barely missing the costumed juggler throwing alabaster jars into the air.

Looking at Miriam, Dagon said, "It's always entertaining." He grabbed her hand and said, "Come on."

In each room they passed Miriam saw all manner of sights: people lounging and feasting on rich foods, people dancing, dogs running here and there, eating the fallen morsels. When they entered the main open room, they saw Oreb at the center of attention, reciting passages of poetry to the beautiful women who looked at him longingly. Miriam had to admit that Oreb had a gift for caressing a woman without even touching her. When he finished the women clapped wildly, alternating giving him kisses and caresses of their own. Drinking it up like a man dying of thirst, Oreb exulted in their praise, fleeting though it was. Just then he caught sight of Miriam and Dagon, and broke free from the harem.

"Friends! So happy you could join us tonight!" he said with arms outstretched. He kissed them both and slapped Dagon on the back. He wore a thick velvet robe in midnight blue, gold chains around his neck, and rings of silver stacked like firewood.

As Miriam looked around she noticed that drapes the color of blood hung from the walls, covering the windows, and that furniture of gold tapestries lined the perimeter of the room. Even the decorative colors seemed to cry of passion and greed. Long tables bulging with food offered a centerpiece for continual feasting. Wine seemed to flow like the river *Yardên*, Jordan, making sure everyone who partook was pleasantly drunk. Musicians, like the juggler, moved from room to room, lyres and harps and cymbals ringing out.

"Eat! Drink! There's plenty," said Oreb. "Help yourself to whatever you like." He leaned over to Dagon and whispered, "And don't limit yourself to just food." They laughed, pretending to spare Miriam though she overheard. Oreb introduced her to some people walking by. She recognized a few from the marketplace but most she had never seen before.

"My house is yours," Oreb said. "Look around and mingle. Nothing is off limits! Enjoy yourselves, the night is just beginning!"

A large woman draped in transparent linens grabbed Oreb's hand. "Come with me," she purred.

Smiling at them, he said, "Excuse me, love beckons."

Dagon turned to Miriam and said, "I see some acquaintances in the next room. Get some food while I go say hello."

Miriam ate, watching with curiosity like a child visiting the Temple during Passover for the first time. She seemed to melt into the atmosphere feeling more aroused by the minute. She couldn't decide which was more sensual, the people or the food. A servant girl—tall, thin, and Egyptian looking—offered Miriam some wine.

"Thank you," she said.

With curiosity growing, Miriam took Oreb's offer to look around his villa. She walked toward the back of the estate and passed through heavy, dark drapes.

"You'll enjoy this, I promise," the Spirit of Lust whispered in her ear, each word dripping with dirtiness.

"I wonder what's happening back here," she whispered.

"This is where ultimate desires are fulfilled," it said. "You will feel as high as the clouds. There's nothing like it."

Immediately she thought of the bathhouse and how it had prepared her for the things in front of her. In truth, the bathhouse was mild compared to what she saw there. Walls displayed mosaics of provocative acts, such as men with women, men with men, women with women, people in groups, people with animals, objects used for pleasure and pain, to name a few. It was a staggering amount of fornication, the likes of which Miriam never dreamed possible. A subtle gasp escaped from her mouth as if she'd been startled. Her hand went up to cover the sound of her surprise. Miriam felt her face flush with the heat of embarrassment, but she refused to peel her eyes away. She stood there for a few minutes, staring at it all. Then she felt a smile of wonder replace the uneasiness, so she lowered her hand. The Spirit of Lust smiled with her as it watched her switch from being uncomfortable to being delighted in an inquisitive way. She even went so far as to imagine herself engaging in the lewdness.

Eyes wide, Miriam walked by open rooms and witnessed a variety of acts too sinful to mention. Full of adultery, fornication, and lewdness, Oreb's friends couldn't cease from feasting on one another's flesh. To tell the truth, the people were more obscene than the crowds of men that demanded Lot to bring out the angels sent to save him. Each partaker of pleasure knew how to possess his own vessel in the passion of lust. For Miriam, the carnal desires were as colorful as idolatrous temples. People moved around in a way that mimicked snakes slithering over the floor and furniture. What Miriam didn't see, however, was the group of unclean spirits, all of whom controlled their victims, just as the Spirit of Lust was doing to her.

Overrun with vulgarity from every angle, Miriam realized that the images would stay with her forever. They would become a part of her like a scar on her skin. Though she experienced moments of disgust and repulsion, overall she felt drawn into the fornicating group of men and women, if only through her eyes. Without a doubt the Spirit of Lust had achieved victory, invigorated for more. When Miriam left the villa she felt the taste of lust—a sensation that the spirit knew too well—coat the inside of her mouth in the same way that strong garlic and onions did.

It wasn't long before the Tiberian women and men enfolded Miriam into their circle of sin. Once she grew accustomed to their pagan rituals she visited again and again. Having bought the lies and having compromised her values, Miriam secured for herself an oppression of untold heaviness. Between the bathhouses, the parties, and intermittent time with Dagon, she spent her days and nights playing the harlot. But she naturally believed otherwise.

"You are getting love and physical devotion from so many people," the Spirit of Lust said, slithering around her.

"They really do love me, don't they?!"

"Their actions speak louder than words; they shower you with attention because they love and need you."

"It's remarkable! I'm so glad that they love me."

"It feels wonderful, doesn't it?"

"Better than anything," Miriam said.

Under the impression that she was making progress along her path of life, Miriam didn't recognize the fact that she was, instead, wandering through a deep maze. Every lie that she believed led to another arm of the maze through which she struggled to find an end. But her spirits were not foolish; they created the maze without a door. The only way out was to find truth, but at that time truth was nowhere in sight.

* * *

Even though the Spirit of Lust showered Miriam with fresh lies, they didn't take the place of the lies she'd been told beforehand. As she later learned, the wicked spirits worked together side by side for the same goal, which is to say compounded bondage. Each of the seven spirits built upon the work of the others. Lust and its lies operated with Rejection and its lies, which tied in with the lies of Rebellion, Bitterness and Fear. All seven would have their turn to control, but they didn't perform independently of one another. They were, in essence, stronger than a team of horses pulling a Roman chariot. The process of bringing about Miriam's personal destruction would continue as long as the sun rose up each morning.

As promised, both the lust of the eyes and lust of the flesh formed the two reins with which Miriam was harnessed. She lusted but didn't have anything to show for it. Sinking further down into the abyss of corruption, she lived in a dark underworld, much like the dungeons of an arena that offered no way back to the surface. She had made certain choices, of course, but she often times felt as if someone or something else controlled her, allowing her to think that she was truly in charge. Knowing no other means to address the alarming feeling, Miriam turned a cold shoulder and tried to ignore it.

Then, after almost three years of carousing in her own deceptions with the Spirit of Lust, Miriam caught a glimpse of her folly. For a brief moment she understood that her longings and lust wouldn't secure ultimate contentment. Time had proven that. Yet she continued to strive otherwise, feeling disconnected even as people gave her physical attention. Surrounded by friends but completely alone.

Without a doubt the isolation that Miriam felt stemmed from her lifestyle of sin. Because this awareness within her rose up like leavened bread she felt more and more powerless as she struggled against its prevailing force. Over time Miriam had become cut off from all things pure, all things virtuous, and all things righteous. The carnal bondage that the Spirit of Lust had produced rang out louder then the sound of fishing boats colliding. Feeling smug, the spirit took pleasure in the fact that it had compelled Miriam to willingly degrade herself in both physical and spiritual form. The flames of lust burned hotter than the sun that stood still in *Gib'ôwn*, Gibeon, at *Y'hôwshû'a's*, or Joshua's, command. An excitement of inhuman proportions gripped the wicked spirit as it let out a laugh that stabbed the air like lightning, thundering against the kingdom of darkness.

7

It seemed as if it was floating upwards like incense toward the sky. The Spirit of Pride, more talkative than a herd of bleating sheep, reveled in raising others up to its level of haughtiness—the higher the better, of course. The magnificent high that the spirit offered resembled nothing else, a feeling quite unto its own. Certain that it was going to offer the best feat of bondage of the seven spirits, Pride flaunted its power, for it was brash, arrogant, and domineering.

* * *

Though it appeared as if Miriam surrendered one entity for another (rebellion for lust, lust for pride), in truth she added them one on top of another in the same way that heavy stones had been stacked to create the walls for the Temple in Jerusalem. She carried each spirit around with her, and they used her surroundings to shape the events of her life. Just as the great river in Egypt had many branches of water at the mouth of the large sea to its north, Miriam had many spirits imposing their individual wickedness upon her. They all merged together at the core of her being, or her heart. The spirits' objectives could be reduced to one summation, which is to say lies, sweet and fragrant. Only there was nothing sweet about them.

The Spirit of Pride, subtle and skillful, planted thoughts in her mind without a trace. Its strategy needed to be as straightforward and convincing as Jacob's plan to be his twin brother, Esau, in order to obtain the birthright from their blind father, Isaac.

"You should be proud of yourself! Look at what you've done lately: you have moved to a new city and established yourself knowing only three people. You've made handfuls of friends; you contribute to society; and you've made your own choices for your life and created a better, more enjoyable existence," the spirit said.

"I have done all of those things, haven't I? And with very little help," said Miriam. "I am resourceful and independent—more so than any other woman my age that I know." She could feel her ego swell like Adam's son *Qayin*, Cain, when the Lord told him that his offering wasn't as righteous as the one of his older brother *Hebel*, Abel.

"It's all about *your* strengths and *your* merits."

"Yes, but I don't want to come across as too boastful. That would repel people."

"Being proud of yourself is a good thing," Pride said. "If you don't exude pride and respect for yourself, nobody else will give it to you. You have to be assertive on this."

On the one hand, being proud of someone or something—or being *pleased*, as it more accurately meant—seemed to cause little problems. On the other hand, a person's pride was a dangerous possession, for it more often than not was a stumbling block. The unclean spirit had changed the meaning of pride, as colors changed under morning and evening light, so that it was acceptable and even expected. It was a deception as large as the giants of Gath. But Magdala rabbis neglected to mention—perhaps because they too reasoned that pride possessed certain merits—that in the Scriptures Yahweh didn't condone pride. Not one biblical passage spoke of pride as good and beneficial. In fact, as stated in the book of Proverbs, Yahweh hates pride, arrogance, corruption, and perverted speech every bit as much as fishermen hate tangled nets. The reason for this, as Miriam would learn later, was because pride left unchecked consumed a person's character.

During the winter months of Miriam's eighteenth year the Spirit of Pride used Brutus to pull her into its den of deception. She still spent time with Dagon of course, playing the harlot, and with Lydia, storing up treasures where moths and rust ate away. After a while Miriam turned her attention to the activities that Brutus consumed himself with. She knew from the first day that she'd met him long ago that he enjoyed reading. More than that, Brutus collected manuscripts and scrolls on various topics, in various languages, with as much enthusiasm as a bee collecting pollen in springtime. In fact, there was an entire room full of them at the villa. For years Brutus had worked on his library, creating and fashioning it. Each wall held a system of shelves and compartments into which the scrolls were placed. It reminded Miriam of a honeycomb, as the wood reflected a rich golden color in the morning sun. Brutus had organized all of the scrolls and manuscripts by language and category, so that he could find a particular one in less time than it takes a jumping fish to show its head and disappear again. There, in his library, Miriam's eyes were opened to a whole new world.

"How many scrolls do you own?" she asked as she entered his library one morning. To Miriam, Brutus looked more content with his nose pressed to a scroll than *P'rûshîm*, or Pharisees, reading Torah in a synagogue.

"Five hundred and seventy-two," he said with a big grin.

"You've read them all?"

"Of course! Most of them I've read two or three times."

Miriam raised her eyebrows in surprise. She wondered how many years that had taken him.

As if he could read her thoughts he said, "I began collecting manuscripts and scrolls as a young man, so what you see here is more than twenty years worth of time and money. I have traveled all over, to nations farther than you could dream of, and looked for valuable works written by diligent men, some formally educated and some not."

"But why? What do you do with them all?"

"One very simple reason: for knowledge. You see, scrolls and manuscripts and documents are more than information in written form. They are power, as all knowledge is."

All at once Miriam thought of the tree of the knowledge of good and evil that had been placed in the middle of Eden's garden. Its only residents were content in their state of simple happiness, that is, until the serpent explained to them that having knowledge would improve their lives in a powerful way. Miriam knew Brutus was right. For better or for worse, knowledge and power were joined together as if in a marital union.

"Are these the same types of documents that are kept by the Roman government?" Miriam said as she lightly touched them.

"Some, yes. Duplicates are made in case the originals get lost or stolen. But that is the way it is for most things written by scribes, whether or not they belong to governing officials. As you know, we have a small but good selection of materials to read at the communal library here in Tiberias, even though a good portion of the population can't read. The materials used by the public are mostly for finding references to something or someone."

"Do you go there?"

"Not any more. I've been there, of course, but why should I now? I own a wider selection of books than the library, so I have no more need of it. One day I predict that owning manuscripts and books will be common, where everyone will have them in their homes."

Miriam couldn't imagine such a thing. She walked around the room, looking at the individual manuscripts and noticing the smooth papyrus papers used. It crossed her mind that her father and brothers might be envious of her at that moment, standing before such an imposing collection of writings.

"The ones you're touching there are from Rome. On this wall over here are ones from Alexandria in Egypt. Even though Rome likes to believe it produces the most and best manuscripts, Egypt surpasses them by a thousand chariot lengths."

"Why is that?" Miriam said.

"The country's language and natural resources. Egypt has as many types of papyrus papers as birds have feathers because of the great fertile river that runs through it. That alone enables the Egyptians to produce the greatest number of books, manuscripts, and documentations in this part of the world. But added to that is the Greek language, which is considered the most civilized in countries surrounding the great sea."

She smiled as she thought of her own language, Aramaic. Now that she'd been exposed to a greater understanding of the world from living in Tiberias, she knew Brutus spoke the truth. "Does that mean that most of your scrolls and books are from Egypt?"

Brutus nodded. "I would like to expand my collection to have more items in languages other than Greek. Perhaps some in Aramaic, your native tongue."

"Not if I were you. Do not bother too much with Aramaic. Nothing of real significance is written in it, and what is only the Jews find interesting and important. It certainly is not as fascinating and widespread as Greek or Latin."

"I hate Latin," Brutus replied. "I suppose it's useful on some level, but I think one day it will die and be forgotten."

"I thought you could speak and read Latin."

"Well, yes, of course I can speak it, read it, and write it. But that doesn't mean I enjoy it," he said, laughing in that arrogant way of his.

"I would like to learn it," Miriam said.

Brutus raised an eyebrow and looked at her curiously. "Whatever for?"

"To have more knowledge, just as you said." Her smile and clever answer took him by surprise.

"You did pick up Greek with remarkable ease. Maybe you have a gift for learning languages. You never spoke anything else in Magdala?"

"Never. My family used Aramaic only. My father and brothers did study Hebrew—for reading Torah—but nothing more than that entered our house. I was not allowed to read or speak Hebrew formally, but my brothers spoke phrases to me and I devoured them like apples covered in honey. Most of the time I listened closely as they recited passages and prayers, saying them over and over to myself. They would all be surprised at how much Hebrew I know."

"Well, there's only one thing to do then. You teach me what you know in Hebrew and I shall do the same for you in Latin and Greek."

And so, in a manner of speaking, Miriam and Brutus exchanged languages. As with Greek, Latin seemed to Miriam a language of excitement and adventure. In a few short months she was able to converse in either language as if she'd been speaking it all her life.

While winter turned over its reins to spring, Miriam sat in Brutus's library, reading as much as her mind could absorb, which turned out to be great deal more than either of them expected. Though he didn't show it, Brutus seemed mildly jealous of Miriam's natural talent. Yet she chose not to focus on that. Instead, she immersed herself in writings with more dedication than an orthodox Jew submerged himself in prayer three times a day. Whatever Brutus handed her she read. Month after month her stimulation and enthusiasm grew, leaping about inside her, causing her to crave more.

Seven

With each new manuscript or scroll that she mastered Miriam could feel the pride within her swell. And what Yahweh had intended for good—her natural ability to understand diverse languages—the Spirit of Pride used for evil.

"Look at how easily you understand these languages and ideas," the spirit said.

"My mind does work well in that area, I must admit."

"Just like the people who built the tower that reached to the sky in Babylonia, it will be your monument to your greatness!"

Miriam smiled, feeling the delightful pull of pride, as it most often feels. Instead of praising Yahweh for blessing her with the gift of tongues, with the turn of her eyes she praised herself.

"Men of all nations would pay great money to have your ability," Pride said.

"I suppose it's as rare as snow in southern Judea."

"Just think of all the things you can do with knowledge of many languages. People would accommodate you—need you even—and you could demand what you wanted from them. After all, the more languages you speak the more control you'll have."

"I'd like that. To have people crave my knowledge more than fine gold, to recognize me for my achievements and abilities that far surpass most others. I could charge a high sum of money for my services and become wealthy!"

Miriam's mounting arrogance pleased the unclean spirit. Indeed, her strengths had been used against her in the name of goodness. She didn't feel the creeping vines of pride rising up from the darkness as the Spirit of Pride purposely kept her distracted.

* * *

In some form or another Miriam knew that people from every nation felt pride. Jews, of course, were not above wearing their pride like a head covering. Because Yahweh called them the chosen ones they deemed themselves, quite naturally, as more important and valuable than Gentiles. What's more, the laws of cleanliness and purity lifted them higher and separated them further. But pride snuck into the Jewish people's faith and traditions, which were intended originally to be a blessing to them. As it turned out, they were no better than Gentiles who prided themselves over their achievements and power. Pride was no respecter of persons.

Once Miriam appreciated the extent of her superior skill for literature and languages, she sold her services to Roman rulers and Greek officials with the same self-satisfaction that Dagon sold his trinkets in the marketplace. With each passing week her accomplishments expanded with greater speed than *Nechemyâh*, Nehemiah, rebuilding the city walls of Jerusalem. More and more she was sought after for her ideas and insight. More and more she puffed up with pride. She had climbed, quite happily, into a world where such pride was celebrated with passion.

Miriam read about many philosophies, such as worshipping multiple gods or promoting women into traditional male roles, and politics, but one particular idea resonated within her. The system of praising man's wide range of accomplishments was, to her, practical and not at all mythical. When she discovered, with Brutus' help, that this specific practice existed as a sort of belief system, Miriam jumped on board faster than *Yôwnâh*, Jonah, jumped aboard the boat to *Tarshîysh*, or Tarshish. More and more she exposed herself to as much information as she could, listening to lectures by Romans (men and women alike, but mostly men) and attending meetings where the latest and greatest of man's achievements dominated all conversation. Taking one idea at a time, she knit them all together like an embroidered tunic. Her all-consuming focus rested on the contributions, culture, and spirit of human beings.

Though it wasn't the most popular choice, many Romans worshipped the feats and intelligence of man as well as the gods. With a myriad of Roman gods to placate, the majority of people spent their time and energy kneeling before stone images set in elaborate temples. But Miriam was more interested in worshipping man than any god, including the one of her ancestors. To tell the truth, she thought she was abstaining from worship, in the traditional sense of the word. Without a temple or sacrificial system the Romans or Jews didn't see it as a true form of worship. But Miriam chose to view it as a celebration of human intellect and capacity, or in other words who man was and could be. The triumphs of man were tangible and visible, and so she grasped onto that as tightly as *Mal'âkîy*, or Malachi, had with his prophesies for Israel.

"The reason you're attracted to this type of information is because you belong with these types of people—the unrivaled both in mind and body," the Spirit of Pride said.

"It does speak to me more than anything else ever has. It feels like who I truly am. At last! I wish I'd discovered this before!"

"Your mind operates in ways that confuse and intimidate most people."

"Even Brutus and Dagon aren't as insightful as I am."

"You are an intelligent and discerning person; you should take credit for who you are and what you do. The praise belongs to you. Receive what is rightfully yours." The Spirit of Pride voiced its subtle lies.

"I love who I am and who I'm becoming; I'm *worthy* of being admired."

Because she identified with the worship of man, Pride flourished in her heart. The spirit understood that pride was a natural, inborn condition within her, as well as within all humanity. The fallen nature of man promised as much. Every now and then Miriam would remember a verse from the writings of David and Solomon, among others, about the folly of pride, such as how it led to disgrace and destruction or how it brought a person to humiliation. But she dismissed them as soon as they entered her mind, in the same way that Job dismissed the council of his three friends after losing all of his possessions. The Spirit of Pride, in essence, guaranteed that man chose himself. Pride and worship of one's self interlaced fingers, walking hand in hand.

To make matters worse, Miriam began to take her earthly standpoint and apply it to her eternal future. The Spirit of Pride was all too eager to assist her in voicing thoughts as haughty as most Roman rulers.

"If I meet a divine being when I die, I will not fall on my knees in supreme humility as most people would..." she said.

"Why *should* you bow your knee? Be different! Be bold!"

"Instead, I will stand before him with my shoulders thrown back and my head upright and my eyes on his eyes. I shall then say, 'I am an intelligent and beautiful person, so I shall stand, not bow, before you with confidence and boldness.'"

"It's who you are!"

"Yes, that is the posture I would choose to represent who I am."

"Brilliant," said Pride.

Choosing to ignore the truth that Yahweh resisted the proud but gave grace to the humble, Miriam created a false physical as well as spiritual existence. She devoured the lies uttered by Pride as if they were shellfish soaked in sweet cream.

After a year of wading in the pools of human adoration, Miriam reached the basis of all that she was embracing, which is to say worship of self. The Spirit of Pride was pleased with her self-focus, yet it pushed her further still.

"There is no need for the idea of a more intelligent being," the spirit said. "In fact, not many people know this, but gods and goddesses don't exist. It's just a myth designed by people who cannot reason intelligently."

"How can that be?"

"Thousands of years ago one person said that there must be a god, and someone else believed it. Now many different gods 'exist', both male and female, with every nation on earth worshipping them."

"All this time I've believed otherwise..."

"But today you've seen the light of truth."

"So many people in this culture, especially women, believe in the divine female. Goddesses everywhere. People can be so deceived... I'm thankful I *now* know the truth."

Because Pride posed as an angel of light and truth, its lies seemed every bit as majestic as a blue sky after a storm. "Everything that you need is contained within you. All you have to do is unlock it."

"Yes, looking inside of me does make more sense than looking to a higher being."

"Look to yourself to find divineness of being," the Spirit of Pride said.

"There is nothing greater than myself. There is only me—everything circles back to me."

"Your present and future lie solely in your hands, as it should."

"I will no longer depend on anyone or anything, or even the idea of something. I've been fooled long enough, so it's time to start over. What's inside me is as good as any deity can offer. I don't need a divine being anymore than I need leprosy. I'll answer only to myself and believe in my instincts for all things."

Miriam's arrogance was as genuine as her ignorance. She raised herself, in other words, above the role of a god or goddess, or any deity at all for that matter—whatever the name, whatever the power. Unlike other people, such as her family or Lydia and Brutus, Miriam saw the need for a higher power as foolishness. The Spirit of Pride rejoiced in the blasphemy.

The words of her mouth spoke great swelling messages of emptiness, as hollow as desert caves. Since so few others around her believed exactly as she did, she often felt out of place or time. But Miriam believed that she lived on a higher plane than everyone else, which allowed her to justify her actions in the same way that *Îyzebel*, Jezebel, had when she ordered *Nâbôwth*, Naboth, to be stoned to death because he refused to give his vineyard to her husband *Melek Ach'âb*, or King Ahab. As though she was looking in a pool of clear water, Miriam saw her image and the pearls of pride that served as her necklace sparkling with deceptive beauty. Miriam, adorned in arrogance, smiled at the thought of her insight.

* * *

Whereas once Miriam had lived in a state of humility (before the spirits entered her life), now she lived as a woman whose arrogance over her own intelligence drove her away from people. Miriam had evolved into a higher state of being, or so she thought. She claimed people's intolerance of her to be the direct result of their inferior natures. Plain and simple she considered herself better than them, or in other words more intelligent, deeper in emotion, stronger in mind.

Early one evening Miriam walked into the room for dining to join Brutus, Lydia and Dagon for supper. But before she made it to the table, she stopped cold.

"Not again…" she said under her breath.

"What?" Brutus said.

Miriam sighed. "Politics, business, and gossip."

"Miriam, these topics are important," Dagon said.

"Well, maybe not gossip," Brutus replied.

"Of course gossip is important," Lydia said with all seriousness.

"Not to me," Miriam answered.

"So you're above that now, are you? You and I used to gossip like old women not too long ago."

"A waste of time." Miriam sighed again and sat down.

"What *is* important to you these days?" Dagon asked.

"Ideas or theories or concepts. Things of true, lasting importance."

"That would be a matter of opinion, don't you think?" he challenged again.

"What about the languages we've been studying together?" asked Brutus.

"Yes, of course that. But not the speculated conquests of Rome or the ever-changing tax laws or who is having an affair with whom."

"What a shame. Those are the things that keep the world turning," Lydia said. Her smile was as equally sarcastic as it was sincere.

Miriam just shook her head. It seemed that the last remaining threads of connection between them all were unraveling before her eyes. Not even colorful robes worn by a king's virgin daughter could last forever. "No Lydia, what is shameful is how you waste your intelligence on such trivial things. Have some pride and leave the gossip to the people in the marketplace. You really should respect yourself more."

Dagon laughed. "Miriam—

"And as for you, Dagon, do you honestly think you're fooling people with the magic you sell? Anyone with common sense can see straight through your act."

"Then why do I have so many customers?"

"It's difficult to believe, I know, but some people are as brainless as sheep."

"Are you putting me in that category?" Dagon asked with an edge to his voice.

"Sounds like it," Brutus said.

"All I'm saying is that you could do something or sell something that is actually useful to society. Instead, all you offer is useless items."

"Useful to some, Miriam." The tone of Dagon's tone took on a sudden hardness.

"In no way does it sustain life. You offer nothing that contributes to the growth, education or security of our city. With all of the money that you've inherited from your family, you'd think that you could come up with something better, something worthwhile. But apparently not."

"You're just too blind to see that I'm doing good for some people."

"The only person you serve, Dagon, is yourself," said Miriam.

"And how are you any different?" Lydia challenged.

"Unlike you three," she said, looking intently at them each for a moment, "I don't pretend to serve others. What I do, I do for myself, and other people are just fortunate to reap the rewards of my knowledge. Maybe you all could learn something from my approach to living, and become better for it."

"You have really changed, Miriam," Lydia said.

Dagon added, "And not for the better."

"I have evolved into someone stronger," Miriam replied. "More educated, more sophisticated, more admired."

"If you keep talking like that you might find yourself without any friends," said Lydia.

Miriam, in exasperation, stood up and walked out. By pride came nothing but strife. Like a horse's bit, Miriam clenched onto the rod of pride that rested in her mouth. She was blind to the sheer ugliness of her heart.

During the following weeks the three people with whom Miriam shared a house attempted to reveal the truth of the matter to her, which is to say that she was exalting herself at the expense of others. But she wouldn't compromise her new values, even with—especially with—her friends. After all, if she couldn't be honest with them, she didn't need or want them. Miriam refused to see any folly or faultiness in her logic. Worse still, she blamed them for disapproving.

"They are unqualified to make any accusations against you. What do they know?" the Spirit of Pride said. "They worship Roman gods, having no interest in anything else."

"They *are* blind to higher ways of thinking."

Truth be told, she wondered what they all still had in common. They wanted to discuss politics and business and gossip, and she wanted to discuss ideas and values. She felt that she wasn't one of them any more, that she'd risen above the masses. At the risk of alienating everyone, Miriam—as stubborn as *Bil'ām's*, Balaam's, donkey—refused to believe that she'd be lonely at the top.

"You've done nothing wrong," Pride said. "Don't give into their reasoning. Be strong and stand firm in what you believe!"

"Why can't they see that I'm becoming a stronger, more confident person? I certainly like myself better."

"They just don't understand. You're a better person now than you were just a few years ago. You can't expect people with small reasoning capacity to recognize your advancement." The condescending chuckle reverberated in her head.

"That's true."

"The best you can do is pity them."

In all honesty Miriam saw the distortions that the unclean spirit told her as helpful and encouraging. Her false confidence invited more lies. And around and around they spun; yet Miriam had no idea that she was twirling with the enemy of her soul.

One by one Miriam memorized all of the lies that the Spirit of Pride had given her. She replayed them over and over in her mind, sometimes voicing them aloud. With each confession she strengthened the pride in her heart. Miriam stood in agreement with Pride just like *Melek Uzzîyâhûw*, King Uzziah, who illegally walked into the Temple sanctuary, subsequently bringing leprosy upon him. Pride had wormed its way into the tiniest crevices of Miriam's heart, eating at her character. And every day her old nature died a little bit more and a little bit more. Everyone saw it but her.

"I made you who you are," Dagon said. "You'd still be in Mig-dala if not for me."

"You're wrong, Dagon, I have done it all on my own. *I* approached *you*. *I* was the one to initiate conversation. You were just a vessel to get me from there to here. But I don't need you anymore."

"I don't tell many women this, Miriam, but sometimes I wish I'd never met you."

"Well, on that we agree."

At that point Miriam didn't see eye to eye with many people. Rather than finding common ground with Dagon, Lydia, and Brutus, she felt that her friendship with them had been severed as swiftly as Goliath's head under David's sword. Without a word Miriam left the villa one afternoon to establish a place for herself, where she could tend and grow her garden of pride. Miriam found another living arrangement through a local teacher of Greek philosophy.

Seven

"The guest quarters are the only space available here," the widow said. She was short, frail, and hardened. Her white hair held onto a few streaks of black, giving it the appearance of stripes on an animal's fur. Her fingernails had turned yellow, matching her teeth. Worst of all, she carried an aroma that forced Miriam to hold her breath.

"That will be fine," Miriam replied.

"They need a good cleaning, don't they?"

"I can take care of that."

"You're alone, right?"

"Yes. No one will be moving in with me, if that is what you are asking."

"Good. You can move in as soon as you like...after paying me, that is."

"Here you are," Miriam said as she handed her the money. Having stashed away a fund for such a time as this, Miriam praised herself again for rising above it all.

"Well, you must be eager to move in."

"More eager to leave where I am now."

The widow raised her eyebrows and waited for Miriam to explain, but she did not. So the owner turned toward the door, back to the main villa. "I forgot to mention the only rule I have here."

"What is that?"

"Don't ever step foot inside the villa. I like my space and I don't want any intruders. I stopped inviting guests long ago." Miriam furrowed her brow and opened her mouth to ask the obvious question, but the woman answered her thoughts. "Because I'm getting old, and I just want someone to know when I die."

"What do you mean?"

"At the end of every week I will pay you a visit and collect money from you. When I stop coming you'll know that I'm dead."

"And then what?"

"Then you find another place to live."

Her bluntness took Miriam by surprise. "Do you have any family members I should tell?"

"No. Even if I did I wouldn't want them to help. Tell the authorities; that will be enough. I will leave instructions for them in my room. I don't

117

plan on dying any time soon, but you never know when death will take you by the hand and lead you from this life."

"Like a thief in the night."

"Do we have an agreement, then?" the widow asked.

"Of course, yes, we have an agreement."

"Good."

In an instant the widow disappeared faster than *Êlîyâhûw*, or Elijah, being taken up into the clouds. Miriam stood alone in her new home and smiled. Like the widow she welcomed solitude. Aside from the grounds, that was the only thing they would share.

As Miriam looked around the living space she wondered who last occupied it. She couldn't tell the exact color of the tiled floor underneath the dirt and dust, or the actual shade of the gauze curtains hanging over the two windows. Pulling them aside, Miriam opened the shutters for fresh air and caught a glimpse of a friend she once knew. The sea, beautiful and sprawling, sat there gleaming in the sunlight with a peacefulness Miriam coveted. Unlike other times in her life, it didn't beckon her. Or perhaps she just couldn't feel the lure anymore. With that thought Miriam turned her attention to cleaning and settling into the quarters, leaving the past to dwell outside the walls that now enclosed her.

Each day after that Miriam spent time developing her knowledge of languages, translating manuscripts for paying government officials, and pouring over writings of various topics. Months passed by with hardly a notice, and the long days of late summer waned into the shorter days of fall. When winter arrived Miriam seemed to notice for the first time that she had become cut off from society. At twenty-one, stubborn and isolated, she bore a greater resemblance to the widow than anyone close to her age.

On some level Miriam enjoyed the indulgence of being alone, but to tell the truth she suffered her isolation now more than ever. A pang of remorse moved through her as fast as lightning, appearing and disappearing almost at the same time.

"Lydia and Dagon are probably wondering where I am, what I'm doing. Maybe I should go back and explain why I left in such a hurry. But, oh, I can't imagine going back and facing them again!"

"Forget about going back there," the Spirit of Pride said. "You're better off without them."

"I don't *want* to, but *should* I?"

"No! You have nothing to apologize for. They're just as set in their beliefs and ways as you are. You're entitled to feel how you feel."

"I really *haven't* done anything wrong," Miriam said. "I'm not going back. If they want to see me then they can find me."

Though she couldn't feel it, the spirit turned her back against everyone, focusing all attention on herself. The only thing facing her was lies. With as much dedication as *Sh'mûw'êl*, Samuel, had serving *Êlîy*, Eli, the priest, she resolved to believe only in herself for all things. And like the sacred tools and rituals of the Temple that assisted the priests, the arms of Pride supported Miriam by embracing her.

Over the months Miriam became thinner than a person on an extended fast. The thought of bumping into Brutus, Dagon or Lydia in the marketplace or around town kept her eating meals created from almost nothing. The Spirit of Pride was, of course, pleased beyond measure. To someone outside the villa it looked like Miriam and the widow were in a race toward death. But that force, unknown to Miriam, was soon to arrive.

At that point, if Miriam's character could have been defined in one word it would be defilement. She stubbornly held her ground, thinking herself justified in every way. She became a lover of herself, a boaster, headstrong and haughty. She embodied pride. In essence, she became her own false idol to the same degree as the people of Yahweh in the time of the later prophets, *Âmôwç, Nachûwm, Ôbadyâh*, otherwise known as Amos, Nahum, and Obadiah. As Scripture said, pride preceded destruction, and a haughty spirit ushered in stumbling. That was the nature of the indulgence. The Spirit of Pride could count on it.

8

THE LAST OF the seven spirits hovered, ready to pounce on Miriam. All of the others had carried out their responsibilities in deception and destruction with confidence and skill. Nothing less would take place with the final spirit. The Spirit of Death rejoiced in its position as the one to finish the job. With the stench of sulfur draped like a cloak around its shoulders, the spirit breathed heavily and deeply of its own aroma. The others watched the smoke flow out of Death's nostrils, curling downward in the air, two columns of ferocity. Red, fiery eyes burned with fury and determination. Bringing with it the powers from the depths of hell, Death embraced its authority and completed the circle that was seven spirits strong.

* * *

One evening as Miriam was studying and writing in her room a strange thing happened. The curtains that had not moved all day suddenly waved wildly like a sailboat's mast in high wind. She looked up from her table to see if a storm was approaching the city, but the skies were clear and colorful. The papers shifted around and fell onto the floor, yet not a single tree outside blew in the wind. Gathering the items together, Miriam had the unmistakable sense that something had entered her room through the window. In that brief moment the Spirit of Death arrived. Miriam's body shivered. When she looked up everything was still once again, as if nothing had happened. She wondered about it for a minute, but then dismissed all thoughts concerning what she couldn't see. Instead, she returned to what lay in front of her, picking up where she left off.

Fierce and spiteful, the Spirit of Death had operated with a vengeance against the human race since day one. Mankind was created to have fellow-ship with Yahweh, and so the unclean spirit had a deep desire to kill and destroy that fellowship. The spirit's goal was to exist as a wedge, separating man from Yahweh in life and in death. Going to and fro on the earth, walking back and forth on it, the Spirit of Death was never without a mission. In the same way, the spirit now paced in Miriam's room, focusing on the task that sat before it.

Standing behind her and looking over her shoulder, Death began its planned attack against Miriam. Miriam had to participate in her own decline. In fact, it was crucial. Just as she was writing some notes on a Latin manuscript, the unclean spirit tipped over the jar of ink, spilling dark liquid everywhere.

"Son of a goat," she said in frustration.

Rather than handing her an easy means for cleaning up, Death handed her more profane words, which she repeated right away. "Makes you feel better to say those things, doesn't it?"

"I'm not sure why, but it does."

"Foul words carry more meaning and more power."

My father once said that foul words were used only by fools, she thought.

"That's a lie. Everyone uses them because they're the best way to express feelings!"

"I must admit that they give a certain satisfaction," said Miriam, "though they offend others, no doubt."

"Don't be concerned with the way other people feel. It's their problem if they can't accept that some expressive words are a necessary part of life. Don't change who you are to suit their preferences," Death demanded.

"Of course not. Why should I accommodate them?"

"You shouldn't. And don't think for a moment that they don't curse either under their breath or in private. Because they do!" The spirit's tone of finality gave Miriam no room for response.

A few curses and blasphemous phrases quickly turned into a quiver full. Whereas before that sort of language rarely touched her tongue, it now flowed in and out of her mouth like mere breaths of air. From one evil word to another she cursed like the people of Jericho, when their walls suddenly came down, forming a habit as unclean as the spirit directing her. Like the ruined manuscript, the spirit stained her with darkness.

Just then Miriam heard the familiar sound of footsteps. The widow was making her way to the guest quarters to collect money. Although from week to week the changes in her face were subtle, the wrinkles that crossed back and forth on her brown skin like the streets of Tiberias had seemed to deepen. Everything else, including her faded olive-green tunic and bare feet, remained unchanged.

"Still alive, I see," Miriam said.

"Unfortunately, yes."

Miriam laughed. "It will come, sooner or later."

"Yes, though I've been thinking of helping it along."

"Killing yourself is foolish." The pride in her voice was as hard as the widow's feet on the tile floor.

"Perhaps," the widow replied. "But that doesn't matter to me. Miriam, when I depart this earth will you return to where you were living before?"

"I would rather die than go back there!"

The widow laughed, showing a space of missing teeth. It was the first and last time Miriam saw her smile. "I know how that is." She took a long look at Miriam, trying to assess her.

"What about getting married?" she asked Miriam. "You're young and attractive, and there are plenty of men in this city."

"That's the reason I left my home in Magdala. My parents had arranged my marriage—against my wishes, of course."

"One day you might change your mind."

"There are other things besides a husband that I can't live without."

The widow nodded. After a moment she said, "Have you considered buying your own place to live?

"I'll never live long enough for that."

"Ah, I understand now."

"What?" Miriam said with suspicion.

"Why you're hiding here. It sounds to me like you too are waiting for someone from the unseen world to deliver you from unhappiness."

Miriam glared at her. "Here's your money."

"Don't worry, Miriam, wanting death isn't the same as helping it along."

Once the widow had departed, the curses flew through the air in the same way that a flock of bats rushes out from a dark cave. "You don't know me! I'm not asking for death to come. Curses on you! Cursed be your body and your wealth and your dead husband!"

Taking what seemed to be a harmless feature, which is to say her tongue, the spirit encouraged Miriam to speak words of death. The wicked spirit knew that death and life rested in the power of the tongue, and those who loved the power would eat of its fruit. Death taught Miriam how to invite destruction with her own lips, condemning herself with her words. And words held enormous power.

Miriam, of course, didn't believe that they held any lasting power. To her the phrases were empty expressions, a companion to emotion. But by speaking words of negativity over and over Miriam closed the window of life and propped open the door for Death. Using Death's language, she uttered words that decomposed her bit by bit from within. These words stuck to and picked at her flesh, as if they were insects sucking the blood from her veins. Her vocabulary became a pattern of hopeless attitudes, negative reactions, and destructive desires. In essence, Miriam began digging up the earth of her own grave, which her seventh spirit planned on filling.

As an extra measure, the Spirit of Death gave Miriam other things to think about in addition to cursing whatever displeased her. It offered her, for example, various ways in which she could die. Though the imaginative scenes of death were as varied as the twelve tribes of Jacob, there was one idea that haunted her the most. And so the unclean spirit lied to her with more confidence than Abraham when he told *Ăbíymelek*, or Abimelech, that Sarah was his sister.

"Even though you grew up playing in it, the Sea of Galilee will be your future grave."

"But I know how to swim," she protested.

"When the time comes not even your best efforts will uphold you."

"That can't be!"

"It's true."

"Of all the ways to die that would be the worst!"

"And because you hate the idea of drowning, it's sure to happen. There's truth in believing what you fear most."

"Then I won't go anywhere near the water from now on."

"You cannot change the course of events for your life."

"But there must be a way to avoid that," she said, thinking as hard as she could.

"You can try, but you will fail," Death promised.

Knowing that such statements would cause Miriam to envision herself drowning again and again, the spirit rejoiced. It changed the focus on how she spent her time and energy—she was consumed with dying. No matter how much she hated pondering her own death, she couldn't stop her mind from pursuing it. In the same way that the anointing oil ran over the head and beard of the first priest, Aaron, the Spirit of Death's silt covered Miriam from her head down.

"But what would I do? Fight until all of my strength was gone? Relax and just die peacefully? Or would I close my eyes to escape the face of death or maybe keep them open until the last second? Curses! There's no easy way!"

"Think about it some more..."

"No matter how many ways I imagine it happening, I'll never be prepared," she said. "I hope that death will be quick and somewhat painless."

Staring at her coldly from an arm's length away, the Spirit of Death ridiculed her. "Don't worry."

After a while, Death increased its opposition and influence over Miriam. In addition to her own death she began to imagine the deaths of other people as well. In reality, the act was more important than the victim, just as the wicked spirit had intended.

On the one hand, she pictured people she knew meeting their deaths in any number of ways. She saw the widow falling down the marble stairs after collecting her money, or choking on a piece of dried pork. She imagined that Dagon had been hunted down by an angry customer who discovered that he'd been deceived; or that he'd caught a fatal disease from a harlot while visiting a bathhouse. For Lydia, she thought about a possible deadly reaction to one of her many potions; or getting trampled in a mad rush of zealots in the marketplace; or being struck with the flesh eating disease of leprosy because of her endless gossiping just like Moses' sister, Miriam. And Brutus she envisioned being murdered for his collection of writings.

On the other hand, she saw images of death in perfect strangers, such as a tax collector being crushed by a falling stone block, or a fisherman getting tangled in his net and drowning, or a young girl stumbling upon a poisonous snake. Accidents, murders and acts of nature could be found all around her. Miriam saw the hand of Death everywhere, able to do whatever it wished.

When it came to ending life, the Spirit of Death was resourceful. As the Scriptures showed, Cain killed Abel; the sons of Jacob murdered the men of Shechem; *Yā'ēl*, Jael, drove a tent peg through *Çîyçerā's*, Sisera's, head; Eli fell backwards and broke his neck; and *Ăchîythôphel*, Ahithophel, hanged himself. Miriam knew that Death would be equally as inspired for her. But instead of releasing the thoughts that haunted her, she held onto them as if they were keeping her alive. She was, in all honesty, consumed with death. Or rather, the Spirit of Death consumed her, leaving a barren feeling to linger in her bones.

"Today is the last day that you will live."

In the midst of the busy springtime marketplace she froze. Within seconds Miriam was covered with cold, damp sensations. Her face turned the color of a lifeless fish. She watched everything around her as if looking for a face that matched the voice. No one paid her any attention as they went about their ways. But for Miriam, it seemed that the people around her moved with exaggerated motions, mocking her. All at once she felt the force of darkness surround her. Then more words.

"You will not make it through the night to see another day," the calm voice of Death resonated in her ear. "There's nothing that you can do about it. Just accept this as your time." Though spoken calmly the words struck her like the deadly teeth of a bear, tearing at her soul.

"No! Not now! But it's unmistakable—I can feel it in the air!" Miriam said, her voice and body shaking.

Staring into the crowd, Miriam believed that Death was trying to grab her hand, as the widow would say. Fear too was there, yet Miriam felt more hopeless than afraid. She didn't want to die, of course, but she felt she had no control. Like a donkey covered with flies, Miriam tried to shake the horrible feeling off her, but it kept coming back. She started walking with a hurried pace toward the villa, and more importantly, away from the Sea of Galilee. During those few minutes Miriam wondered if she should tell someone.

"But who would understand? Who would believe me? After all, it's just a feeling—a strong one, but still a premonition. How could I possibly describe it to someone?" She thought about it some more. "Maybe if I tell the widow... Of all people she might recognize what's happening to me."

"No, she'll just laugh at your imagination," the spirit said. "She doesn't have the answers you're looking for."

"Who *does*?"

The question was, of course, unanswerable. Shutting her eyes, she tried to make sense of the voice as well as her emotions raining down harder than the waters that flooded the earth and every living thing on it. Miriam turned back to the villa in an attempt to leave it all in the marketplace. Just as she was departing the busy street she caught a glimpse of Dagon entering from the other end. If the sound of an invisible voice made her retreat quickly, then seeing Dagon made her run.

"Not today! Of all the times to catch sight of him.... *Curses!*"

Fortunately for her, Dagon was focused on jingling the moneybags of Tiberias' visitors. Like Miriam, he operated under the influence of unclean spirits, some the same as hers, but mostly different. To her satisfaction their paths didn't cross that day.

As she hurried back, Miriam thought about the presence of things unseen. No matter how much she desired to be free from this latest wickedness, the desire within the Spirit of Death overshadowed her. In other words, it was a David and Goliath battle with the exception that Miriam had no stones to throw. Death fed on Miriam's helplessness with an insatiable appetite.

Miriam dreaded death, like so many others, because of the uncertainty of what awaited her. Egyptians believed in an afterlife, so they mummified their dead and surrounded them with gold and jewels to take to the next place. Her family believed that when a man died he "slept" in the earth, returning to the dust out of which he came, awaiting resurrection from the long-awaited *Mâshîyach*, or Messiah. Some eastern traditions believed in the return of a soul as another life, whether human or animal. But Miriam didn't know what she believed. In all honesty, all of those ideas frightened her.

Back in her room that day Miriam waited and waited for her last breath, wondering how it would feel. She realized now that the assurance of drowning had been a lie. She was nowhere near the water and yet the feeling was growing stronger with each passing hour. That night she dreaded falling asleep. Yet, the harder she tried to stay awake, the quicker she slipped into the clutch of sleep and into the grip of Death.

Before long she lost the battle against her tiredness. With eyelids heavier than a sack of grain she murmured, "I know that as soon as I fall asleep death will come. I can feel it waiting for me. But I can't fight it anymore..."

Chuckling with pleasure, the Spirit of Death watched as Miriam drifted off to sleep. Unlike her, the wicked spirit knew with certainty what would happen next. Death was only a matter of time, as its fellow spirits of darkness liked to say.

When she awoke the following morning relief set in. Miriam looked around, caught between gratitude and confusion. Death, however, wasn't confused. It knew exactly what it was doing, which is to say harassing her with threats and lies. Because Death had refrained from taking her life that night didn't mean it lacked power or authority. In fact, the opposite was true. Taking a life instantly was a great feat, to be sure, but reducing a life to the shreds of a quivering existence—a living death—was an even greater feat.

For six months these experiences plagued Miriam worse than the locusts and boils on Pharaoh and the Egyptians. One after another she lived through them. Never once did she grow accustomed to them. No two experiences were alike, just as the spirit wanted. Death enjoyed keeping her guessing as much as it enjoyed lying to her.

Truth be told, Miriam simply could not see. Without any defenses she remained in the dark, unable to fight against the warfare of the wicked spirit. She had no protection, and the spirit possessed ground on which to prevail. The emotional and mental affliction that Miriam felt was deeper than the waters that had drowned the Egyptians on their way to re-capture Moses and the children of Israel who had left in a mass exodus.

Even though her eyes were unable to see the Spirit of Death, her nose was a different matter. Whether in her room or sneaking around town, Miriam often breathed in a certain smell that was unlike anything else she'd ever encountered. To her it resembled the stench of sulfur mixed with the decay of rotting fruit.

"What is that *awful* smell?" she said while looking around her. "Where is it coming from? It's disgusting! It makes me want to be sick!"

Always, she clapped a hand over her mouth and nose, in an attempt to keep her stomach from lurching upward. In her room she would pull back the curtain and throw open the shutters for fresh air. In town she would run to a side street that had few people on it, hoping to escape the overpowering smell. But every time, Death stood beside her, amused that its aroma could cause such a strong and immediate reaction. With more purpose than a man blowing air on a spark to light a fire, the unclean spirit breathed in her face the fumes from the bowels of the dead.

* * *

Then, one late-summer night when she was twenty-two years old her life took a turn for the worse. Outside her bedroom the mild air and clear sky declared the beauties of creation. Inside she sat on her bed reading her muddled reflections on life and death, but mostly death. Whereas once she'd read material that focused on living and the promise of a future, she now consumed herself with the opposite. Death, and how it affected the living, was as much a mystery to her as Greek was to her family in Magdala. She couldn't pull herself away from it; but more truthfully, it pulled her with a force greater than that which shook the ground.

All at once her room turned frigid. It seemed to her that the air, so pleasant and so calm, had been sucked out within a matter of seconds. Alarmed, Miriam looked around, trying to identify the reason for the drastic change. But nothing seemed out of place or unusual. Then the Spirit of Death passed before her face; every hair on her body leapt up in response. Her limbs began to shake and her mouth went as dry as the desert sand. The spirit stood in front of her, but Miriam couldn't see what she sensed.

And then it hit her.

Without warning, Miriam was thrust back flat against her bed. With one hand the Spirit of Death held onto her throat and with the other it pushed against her abdomen. Unable to speak or to move, Miriam choked for air and tried lifting her arms to fight for her life, but she couldn't move. Her eyes bulged, her fingers clutched the bed, and her feet arched painfully backward. Those were the only indications that she was feeling the literal hand of Death. Staring deeply into her eyes, the spirit grinned with mocking fury as it felt Miriam's natural plea for survival.

A voice roared with violence. "YOUR FOUNDATION IS IN THE DUST, AND TO IT YOU SHALL RETURN. YOU SHALL PERISH FOR-EVER, WITH NO ONE REGARDING."

Just as the force had attacked without warning, the weight lifted from her. Choking on air, Miriam rolled to her side and put her hands to her neck. She then fell off the bed onto the floor, landing on her hands and knees. Heaving with sobs and cries of pain, she unleashed everything within her. Her hair hung in her face, mixing with the mucus and the drool and the tears. Every part of her quivered, but she could not move any farther. Instead, she rested her forehead on the floor and let the emotions pour out. Great weeping came forth, the volume scaring her even more. Miriam felt like an animal at the mercy of a bowman. Nothing within her could challenge the force of the unseen spirit. And nothing could save her.

Like a layer of clouds that sometimes hung over the sea, the spirit hovered in the room. If Miriam had looked over her shoulder she would've seen the Spirit of Death floating above her bed like a giant black mass. But all she saw at that moment was the pattern in the tile that lined the floor, blurred by the tears streaming from her eyes. She cried until they were swollen shut and her head throbbed with the pain of too much pressure. Her mouth lost its moisture and her lips cracked from continual sobbing. In all honesty, she now welcomed death. She had no more strength, no more will. The spirit had taken everything from her and left her to die alone. And so, with a final breath she closed her eyes and fell into a peaceful state.

Hours later when she awoke, Miriam had to remember why she was lying face down on the hard floor. The memories sent shivers throughout her body. Even though it had lasted only a few moments, the length of the dreadful experience seemed to defy time. What she'd barely survived in those minutes felt like eternity crammed into a few moments. Miriam had been given a glimpse into ageless condemnation, or so it seemed.

At that point it didn't matter that she couldn't feel the presence of Death because she knew—with as much certainty as *Hôwshêä*, Hosea, had that his wife *Gômer*, Gomer, would return to a life of harlotry—that it was still in her room. The furniture didn't even seem as real as the unseen spirit. But more than that, Miriam was struck with a sense of utter despair. There was absolutely nothing she could do. Fighting, much less surviving, against that kind of force was more futile than wishing she'd never been born. The wicked spirit seemed every bit as determined as Jezebel's daughter *Ăthalyâh*, Athaliah, had been on killing all of the heirs to the throne of *Y'hûwdâh*, Judah, during her reign.

As an extra measure, the words of Death, the promise that it had given her, echoed in her ears. While others lay in deep sleep, she got up and moved toward the window. Staring out into the dark night with vacant eyes and a wounded soul, she heard over and over again the whispers left from a visitor in the night.

As it turned out, her brush with death was just another lie. While the wicked spirit had, in essence, brought her to the edge of her grave, it hadn't shoved her in. Miriam couldn't decide which was worse, actually being killed by an unseen power or living to tell about the experience. Either way she was trapped. Both seemed like an impossible choice. And yet, to tell the truth, choice was an indulgence she didn't have.

For the past nine months, Death had cast its shadow over Miriam, wherever she went and whatever she did. It had constructed a method for her to live a life of demise. Miriam expected and awaited its arrival at any time, as had Joseph while sitting in an abandoned pit where his brothers had thrown him. The waiting, that seemed endless, tormented her night after night. Every day felt like a year, and the moments when the Spirit of Death attacked her physically felt like they'd never end. By then hardly anyone would've recognized her. Dark circles surrounded her eyes, which looked as if they had been pushed back into her head. The bones in her face, as well as her body, stuck out unnaturally against her now pale, almost invisible, skin. Her lips and fingernails had turned the color of ashes, her hair looked as though it might suddenly fall out, and her arms and legs moved like they weren't connected properly. In other words, Miriam had taken on the appearance of the Spirit of Death without knowing it.

Though her body was still alive, her soul felt as if it had been claimed. Breathing but not really living, Miriam sat isolated in her own darkness. She staggered around alone, knowing that she'd never be able to escape the presence of the wicked spirit. Death, using the same intensity that it had for thousands of years, created a fortress of isolation so fierce that Miriam wondered how she could possibly go on existing.

Her life, in all honesty, had been reduced to pieces as small as the scales on a fish. She could try, of course, to pick them up and patch herself back together. Yet she wondered if it was possible, or worth the effort even, to make something out of nothing. Perhaps it was just easier to wait for Death's final deed against her. Then, at least, her misery would end.

To be sure, it was the spirit's responsibility to bring Miriam to the place from which she couldn't return, which is to say to the land of darkness—a land as dark as darkness itself, a place without order, where even the light resembled the darkness. After all, the only reason for the spirit to make an appearance in Miriam's life was to destroy and eventually kill. The spirit would not have come otherwise.

* * *

The Spirit of Death left Miriam's side and took a step toward the other six spirits. In typical fashion it exhaled intensity, sending fumes of fulfillment amid the group. With their eyes, each of them paid their respect to Death, for words weren't necessary. In return the spirit made it clear that the time had come to work together, all at once, now that each had taken a turn. Instead of one voice, all seven would speak freely. The kingdom of darkness would attack like never before.

9

AFTER A SHORT amount of time Miriam felt as if she had a beehive attached to her, with all of the constant buzzing. The seven cruel voices wouldn't leave her with even a moment of quiet. Combined with the fact that they kept stinging her with lies and threats, she reached a point of folly. And so, under the cover of darkness Miriam set out to escape what she could and could not see. She walked without direction or thought as to where she might end up. For hours she worked her way along the dark fields that lined the Galilean coast, until she arrived at a familiar sight. Without realizing it, Miriam stood near the place where it had all begun.

With familiar ease she made her way to the area on the hillside that she'd once found so comforting. It felt now like an old tunic that didn't quite fit right. Even still, the air was the same. Breathing in the sweet fragrances, Miriam sighed into the weight of the chains that bound her. Her hands skimmed along the top of the tall grass, bringing back an army of emotions, and her eyes scanned the area around her legs as if she might see something from her last visit there. But everything looked exactly as she remembered it. Miriam sat down and gazed out over the town and the calm waters of the sea, when an image of her as a young girl—laughing and carefree and full of energy—passed before her eyes. At first she laughed in response, but then she broke as easily as a clay jug, tears pouring out faster and faster.

I have nothing to live for... no one to love. All I have is pain and emptiness. I'm so lonely and hopeless. Everything I do is selfish; all of the temptations lead to a great hollow pit. What reason do I have to live? I walk the earth like a soul trapped between this world and the next. There is no life within me. I have sold all of myself to someone I cannot see. Nothing lives within me.

Seven

Miriam paused for a moment and a second wave of tears rose up like a tide. She surrendered to the overwhelming emotions in the same way that Naomi had when her husband and sons died. Her head pounded and her eyes burned, yet the voices seemed to have faded. For the first time in a while her own voice was the loudest one in her ears.

There isn't a person on this earth that knows me, who I really am or what I've become. So much has been lost compared to what has been gained. I feel destined to roam the earth alone. No one cares to know the deepest parts within me... the fears, the endless harassment...

As another tear dropped from her eye, she said, "There's nothing left."

Her face was flushed from weeping, and on her eyelids was the shadow of the seven spirits. Bound by afflictions and unseen irons, she breathed only because her body wouldn't stop on its own. Never, even at her most imaginative, would she have thought she'd be in this condition. So much had gone wrong, so much seemed unexplainable. While certain moments in the past ten years had seemed good, the truth was she felt that someone else had been leading without her permission, like a lamb led to be sacrificed. Forces beyond her control kept her in complete darkness just as Jonah had been inside the great fish. Worse yet, she didn't have the strength to challenge what she couldn't see. Question after question arose, as she sat there, but she had no answers. Instead, she was left only to stare into the darkness of the night as well as the darkness of her soul.

All around her the night displayed the glories of summer. Herbs and fragrances floated through the air, and breezes as sweet as a mother's touch stroked her face. The moon, high and bright, shone full above the water. Even the insects danced around in the warm air, making music as lovely as the song of *Devôrâh*, Deborah. It seemed to Miriam as if everything had been staged, yet she knew that nature, though sometimes harsh, was perfect in its own way. Once, Miriam would have adored such a wonderful night, but not now. Under the circumstances, everything reminded her of the things she didn't have, which is to say freedom, safety, and the comforts of a good life. Maybe, she thought, it was possible to start over now that she was back in the same place on the hillside. But the longer she sat overlooking the water with her memories, the more convinced she became that her situation was as set in stone as the commandments given to Moses.

Once again emptiness flooded over her, the tears unable to wash away the pain. Summer to summer, with ten years in between, had been a time of profound events, a time of continual struggle. Without warning the memory of the worst night of her childhood appeared as clear as the stars overhead. The horror and distress, almost as painful as it had been the first time, wounded her again. Miriam shut her eyes tightly as though she could squeeze the memory out of her mind. No matter how hard she tried she could still hear the voice of the nomadic man, haunting her a decade later, reminding her that her life was no longer hers to control. As his voice faded other thunderous voices rumbled through her head. These voices were more familiar and more persistent.

"You're right about one thing, no one loves you or cares about you," Rejection said.

"Everyone in your life has hurt you," said the Spirit of Bitterness. "Fight back! The only way to remain strong is through resentment."

"That's right. Even the god of your family has abandoned you," Rebellion added. "If not, you wouldn't be here now."

"So you must continue seeking acceptance and pleasure in other places," said the Spirit of Lust. "That's where you'll find contentment."

"As long as you keep your dark secret you'll be all right. You don't need anyone else," Pride said. "Really, you should keep going and find another town to settle into. This one isn't suitable for the things you need."

"Besides, if you stay here long enough the nomad might see you. He lives in town now," Fear said, "and not too far from your family. Your paths are bound to cross again."

"There's an easy way to avoid that. You want to die, don't you?" Death asked.

"*Ahhhhh!*" Miriam screamed, covering her ears.

All together the unclean spirits stopped talking and stared at her with eyes wide. Some wore the smiles of interest but the rest were serious and on their guard.

Miriam stood up and looked around as if she could see them. "Stop talking to me! Just *stop*! I can't listen anymore!"

Seven

And for a moment there was silence. Searching the night with her eyes, Miriam thought that perhaps she might have sent the voices away. But then the spirits, standing around her in a circle, broke the quietness. She heard a few low chuckles, which then grew and grew until cackles of laughter surrounded her. It sounded louder than any busy marketplace or harbor overflowing with fishermen. Shivers crawled over her skin and then burrowed inside her. In all honesty, she'd never heard anything as evil or as cruel as the laughter of the seven wicked spirits. All at once Miriam collapsed onto the ground and started weeping. Her enemy persecuted her soul, crushing her life to the ground, making her dwell in darkness like those who have been long dead. Her heart carried more distress than a camel full of water and her spirit cried out but to no one in particular. She was bereft of hope.

Unlike Job in his deepest grief, she didn't say: *Where is Yahweh my Maker, who gives songs in the night.* Instead, her enemies, like wild beasts destroying their prey, began mocking her.

"Impossible!"

"There's nothing you can do to get rid of us."

"This yolk is for life."

"It could always be worse..."

The voices seemed as if they'd never stop. In fact, Miriam assumed that they would keep her ears filled as long as she was alive. She couldn't imagine living that way year after year. Like dark shadows they would always be at her side. If the spirits had their way they'd keep her blind to the truth, forcing her to feel her way through life like a woman without eyes. Just as the tall grass brushed against her face again and again the answer, which lay right in front of her, kept coming at her. Once she took hold of it she knew what to do; her decision had been made. With a deep sigh Miriam rolled onto her back and looked up into the sky that was alive with the flickering of countless stars. She wanted to set that image in her mind before accomplishing her plan.

Then, as if she was a child walking in her sleep, she stood up and made her way toward the sea. Her last breath would be filled with water, that much was certain. The only thing left to determine was how to accomplish the task, yet Miriam knew that it would soon be as clear to her as the heavens above. At that point she noticed that the sky began growing lighter and the stars were bidding their farewell. She didn't have much time left. She too bade farewell: to her hometown, to a girl she once knew, and to her family. Pain seared her as she thought of them. She had made them suffer, but fortunately, suffering—both hers and theirs—had an end. With each step toward the shore, Miriam narrowed her list of options until only one way remained. It was the perfect choice.

What Miriam didn't discern, though, was that the spirits weren't finished with her. As a matter of fact, their plans were every bit as deep and engulfing as the waters awaiting her. And yet, what none of them expected, what they all thought impossible, was moving toward her with equal determination in the early hours of that morning.

PART TWO

10

As DAWN BROKE over the Sea of Galilee, colorful rays of light painted the morning sky. The purples, the reds, the yellows all swirled together, looking every bit as vibrant as a patterned headscarf. Hints of these majestic colors danced along the surface of the water. Subtle and delicate, they seemed to touch the sleeping body of water, as if gently waking a child, stirring the life underneath. Soon scores of vessels would be a-sail on its surfaces, bobbing along the waves like driftwood. Fresh as the springs running down from the mountains, the oval sea wore—like a multi-jeweled necklace—a shoreline of bustling cities: Capernaum, Genessaret, Hippos, and, of course, Tiberias and Magdala. Jews, Greeks, Herodians, and Romans had all built thriving communities around the beautiful bluish-green sea, all of which would be coming to life in the next few minutes. Miriam didn't have much time.

Considering her condition, the beauty of the placid water made Miriam envious. But soon that peacefulness and freedom would be hers as well. All of the harassing, incessant voices would finally disappear. As she moved toward the water Miriam thought about and yearned for the days of her youth every bit as much as the people in Noah's time longed to board the ark after the torrential rains began, which is to say a place of safety and comfort. All that remained now in her shell of a body was an emptiness larger than anything she'd ever felt. Nothing of hers, at that point, held any value. Not the fine-tailored clothes on her back, not the glittering jewelry adorning her arms and face, not the sultry city that she'd recently called home, not the Greek wisdom she'd soaked up, and certainly not the various forms of fornication that she'd practiced. Those things no longer enticed her, yet she knew that they all still held a primitive power over her. And there was only one way to be rid of them.

Just as she was closing the space between her and the sea, Miriam was suddenly attacked by a throbbing thirst. Moved as if by an unseen force, she changed direction and began walking into town. Even though she didn't want to be seen by a familiar face, her thirst—and something else, it seemed—demanded that she obey. She didn't have the same appearance she once had years ago, but she knew her eyes would give her away. The green one contrasting against the brown one made them memorable, regardless of time. And so, she determined to keep her head down, to swiftly draw some water from the nearest well, and then to put an end to the voices in her head.

Like a mouse in a pile of hay Miriam scurried through familiar roads to a house not too far from the one where her family lived, because she knew they kept their water jugs out back. *Here I am, stealing from old neighbors,* she thought as she picked up the jug, scampering away from the house. *People here would be mortified if they knew what has become of me.* Not allowing that thought to linger, Miriam sped over to the well and drew water up from its cool depths. She had beaten the crowd, but she knew she didn't have much time before the local women—her mother included—journeyed for their daily water. As soon as the water touched her lips she gulped it down, fighting against the rising anxiety within her. Miriam couldn't drink the liquid fast enough to quench her unspeakable thirst, and she gasped for air as she drank. Dribbling down her chin and onto her tunic, the water provided a pleasant though temporary relief. To tell the truth, it was her spirit that longed for the healing waters of deliverance. She had no idea, of course, that the rising of the sun would bring to her healing in its wings.

In that instant a peculiar thought approached her as if carried on the whispers of the wind. *Maybe you should go ask someone for help.* For a brief moment she considered it, but she felt, in all honesty, that there was no one to ask. She had left Magdala years ago without a word to anyone, severing all ties with her family and friends. She wouldn't let herself be the wayward child who returned home, tail between her legs. Miriam presumed that her family had progressed on with their lives, just as she had done. In addition, she'd separated herself from her Tiberian acquaintances, shunning them as a result of her undying pride. At that moment the familiar feelings of shame, pride, fear, guilt, and bitterness overwhelmed her once again. Over and over she heard the lies raining down on her head with the force of Sodom and Gomorrah's fiery hailstones. The seven spirits, each with their powers of deception, forced her to return to her mission at hand. And so, stopping only for a moment to whisper a final farewell to her family, Miriam turned toward the sea. Nothing, she thought, could stop her now.

* * *

He was walking through the same area of Magdala with a cluster of men when Miriam, carrying the small jug of water, came around the corner from the well. Hiding her face with her clothing to keep from being noticed, she saw the strangers out of the corner of her eye. Even with such a passing glance Miriam noticed one man in particular who seemed to be the core of the group. In an instant, she knew that there was something about Him as powerful as Elijah the prophet. A war immediately broke out within her between the seven screaming spirits and her own spirit, both tugging her in opposite directions with inhuman strength—the spirits telling her to run away and her own telling her to run to Him! As a result, she stood riveted in place, unable to move as she watched Him walk through town. Her thoughts no longer focused on being seen in Magdala or, more importantly, on her plan to drown herself. Instead, she focused on the fact that she felt pulled toward the strange man with more force than a team of oxen hauling a large plow.

The men that surrounded Him, all of them Jews, were engrossed in conversation about Torah, so none of them noticed as their leader looked at Miriam. They seemed to move in slow motion as if in a dream. Even the air around her seemed to stand still. After a few steps, the man looked sidelong to His left, making eye contact with her, and at once He saw into her. The sorrow, the pain, the lifelessness all stood before Him as bare as the Judean wilderness. Miriam felt His eyes pierce her like a sharp arrow. Opening her mouth slightly and inhaling a sharp breath, she knew He'd seen her for who she was, which is to say a young woman tortured by seven unclean spirits. From deep within, Miriam's spirit cried out to Him in spite of the wickedness that plagued her. The cry—silent yet thunderous—reached Him before she drew her next breath.

But the man looked away and returned to the conversation, at which point it seemed as if time resumed its normal pace. To her dismay, the group progressed farther and farther away. Just when it looked as if the stranger was about to leave that part of Magdala, the group of men slowly came to a stop as they watched their teacher walk over toward her.

Still unable to move, as if she'd been turned into a column of stone, Miriam never took her eyes off Him. Once the distance between them closed to a few arms' lengths, it seemed, again, that time slowed to a dream's pace, where the world became silent, even silent from the noises in her head. He appeared to be floating above the ground—His sandals barely skimming the dirt underfoot, sending small clouds of dust into the morning air. His piercing, luminous eyes focused on her with intensity, and although it was uncustomary for a woman to hold the gaze of a man in public, she locked onto them—calm and mysterious—and waited until He stopped in front of her. All of a sudden, the silence departed and she looked down at her feet in submission, becoming aware of her breath, since she seemed to be holding it at length.

She then waited for Him to speak.

To her surprise, however, before any words emerged He removed the veil from her head, took her face in both of His hands—hands that were rough to the touch yet tender to her skin—and looked deeply into her soul. In return, Miriam looked at the bold man with a mix of fear, longing, and confusion, wondering what He was doing and what He was about to say.

And then she heard the words that transformed her life.

"Miriam," He said, "you shall live in bondage no more."

Her eyes grew wide as she heard Him speak her name. *How does He know who I am?* Stunned, she allowed her mind to run through possible times or places she could've met Him before. But nothing came to her. As quickly as a ripe olive fell from a tree she refocused her attention on Him so as not to miss what He had to say.

Releasing His hands from her face, He said, "I know how your suffering began, how the nomad ignited the fires that consume you. The man was acting in evil, possessed by the same spirits that have been tormenting you."

What is going on?

How does He know everything about me?

Who is this man?

Her thoughts ran wild, bumping into one another with frenzy in her head.

Seven

She was certain she'd never seen Him before, much less spoken with Him. No one knew the secret she kept. Although the situation alarmed her, she couldn't pull herself away from His gentle, compelling force. Despite the fact that His hands no longer touched her, His words gripped her heart and mind.

"Whom the Son has set free is free indeed." His response to her thoughts startled her even more.

Then, the man—as authoritative as a member of the Sanhedrin—rebuked every spirit by name that controlled Miriam. He addressed each of the seven spirits and all of the lies, exposing them in entirety. After that, He sent them away, never to return. And in the place of the lies He offered truth, or in other words, principles that guaranteed life without bondage. These words—nothing explosive or theatrical—were simply pure and alive.

For fear He promised: "Yahweh does not give you a Spirit of Fear but of power and of love and of a sound mind."

For rejection He said: "You are fearfully and wonderfully made, and your inner beauty makes you desirable to love."

For bitterness He proclaimed: "Forgive, and you also will be forgiven."

One by one the invisible chains started falling off of her, piling up around her ankles. Miriam could feel the weight lifting. Enraptured by the change that was occurring, her eyes grew wider and wider. He was speaking *life* to her—words of life and not words of death! Miriam couldn't remember the last time someone had done that.

For rebellion He commanded: "Obedience brings freedom."

For lust He instructed: "Love comes from the Father—seek Him."

For pride He revealed: "Humble yourself before Yahweh and you will be lifted up."

And for death He explained: "I AM the way, the truth, and the life—follow Me."

In just a few moments' time, the mysterious man caused the enemies who had risen against Miriam to be defeated before her face. The spirits had come against her from one way, which is to say from the nomadic man, but were fleeing before her seven ways. With a simple command, each unclean spirit had been forced to remove its grip from her. Fear and Rebellion shrieked in fright, Bitterness and Rejection cursed loudly, Pride and Lust hissed and spat, and Death growled in aggravation, but they all submitted to what was, to be sure, the higher authority. Angry and spiteful, the spirits released their young victim with reluctance. Miriam heard the echoes of their piercing screams and violent, screeching protests. Yet in the end, they had no choice except to obey. And so, the voices disappeared—all seven of them.

As soon as she felt total freedom, the water jug that she'd been holding slipped from her hands and shattered on the earthen road. Water splashed on her feet and clothes, as well as on His, dissolving the broken chains.

In an instant everything changed. Miriam felt as if she had come out of a deep sleep, not unlike the child that Elisha resurrected through Yahweh's power. She felt alive and free! Realizing that the voices were gone, she heard only the sounds of peace. Both her body and spirit responded to the soothing stillness, returning home in a sense. It was, in fact, more wonderful than manna from heaven. Miriam considered her miracle to be as divine as Yahweh opening the barren wombs of Sarah, Rachel, and Hannah. And just as those women experienced Him in a personal, intimate manner, so did she. Her eyes and ears no longer held their coverings of lies, and her body no longer carried the poisons that destroyed her from within. Restoration had been accomplished. Now, a perfect peace resided in the spaces that had been occupied by the seven for the last ten years.

"Miriam," the man said, "it is the Spirit of Yahweh who gives life. The words that I speak to you are Spirit, and they are life. You have lived under a covering of deception and lies that has led you to obey your flesh. But obedience to the flesh profits nothing. The adversary of your soul is a liar, and a murderer, and a thief. The thief did not come to you except to steal, to kill, and to destroy you. I have come that you, Miriam, may have life, and that you may have it more abundantly."

Continuing, He explained, "All of the rights that were your proclamations are no longer valid. Through Yahweh, you now have different rights: the right to freedom, the right to grace, the right to forgiveness, to mercy, to joy, and to peace. Let not your heart be troubled, Miriam; nor let it be afraid."

She nodded her head, for words eluded her as rain hid from the desert sands of the wilderness.

"You have been delivered from the power of darkness and have been transferred into the kingdom of His love. Now you know the truth, and the truth shall make you free. These things I have spoken to you, that you may have peace. Peace I leave with you, Miriam; My peace I give to you. I do not give you the peace that the world gives; instead, I give a peace that passes all understanding, which will guard your heart and your mind."

Even though Miriam didn't understand all of what He was saying, she absorbed His words every bit as much as the water had sunk into the dirt underneath their feet. The man looked at the shattered water vessel on the ground in front of Him and then back up at her.

He said, "If anyone thirsts, let him come to Me and drink. If you believe in Me, you shall never thirst." He paused to look into her eyes, to connect with her spirit that was crying out for the Living Water, and pointed to the wet ground by their feet. "Whoever drinks of this water will thirst again, but whoever drinks of the water that I give him will never thirst. The water that I give will become a fountain, springing up into everlasting life."

Who is He?

What is He doing here?

How did He know my dark suffering?

She stared at Him in awe and struggled to understand what kind of person had the power to set her free from intangible spirits of the dark. Question after question inundated her mind, yet she was unable to address each one, much less answer them. Still, she knew the bondage had ended. Tears welled up in her eyes, and her chin began to tremble. With scarcely a breath, Miriam mouthed two simple words in return.

"Thank you."

And despite the group of men that had gathered around, only He was privy to that small yet passionate display of gratitude. In an understated way, the man smiled and then went on His way.

* * *

The tune began with a soft note. Then two or three additional notes joined in. Long and smooth, the notes gathered together, forming music. Instead of ignoring the music or pushing it back into a dark corner somewhere inside her, Miriam let it take flight. She enjoyed the way it felt in her spirit, which is to say boundless and bright. In essence, it felt like the wings of a humming-bird, where elegance and beauty moved together in graceful motion. Those first notes, quiet yet dynamic, created in her an awakening, or a resurrection perhaps. Either way, it was a spiritual response to the miracle that had just taken place.

During the ten years that the seven spirits had controlled Miriam's life, any semblances of music or singing had vanished, suffocated by the spirits. Looking back she remembered how she once sang, without a care in the world, songs that delighted every ear they touched. Now, Miriam under-stood that the spirits had removed that piece for almost half of her life. They had wanted full control.

But all of that was over now. She welcomed the fresh, pure music that wrapped around her spirit like a fragrant linen shawl. One by one little bumps covered her skin, and Miriam knew that something powerful was forming in the very depths of her, though she couldn't name it. She listened as these first few notes played with softness and delicacy. The musical nuances were not lost on Miriam; they spoke to her on a level that echoed the cries of her soul.

Miriam wondered if music was connected to the human spirit the way an arm or leg was to the body. She decided that it must be, that it must ex-ist within the human framework. Perhaps angels had played music when Yahweh formed Adam from the dust, forever to be a part of man—Jews and Gentiles alike. Music moved people in different ways, Miriam understood; yet everyone had within themselves an affection for it. Just as words or hugs acted as expressions, music was an expression. It lived as a response to the maker of heaven and earth, whether recognized or not, whether directed to-ward Yahweh or not. In essence, it vocalized the heart.

Although Miriam didn't know it, the music held between its notes a prophecy of sweetness. As she later learned, He too could hear the music playing within her, as could the angels that rejoiced with heavenly melodies of their own.

* * *

A bit in shock, a bit stupefied, Miriam watched the man who had healed and delivered her proceed on to another part of town. At first she hesitated to move, but then she remembered her freedom, and delight shot through her like lightning. Gathering her thoughts like a girded linen tunic, she ran to tell her family—and just about everyone else she knew in Magdala—that she'd been set free. The shattered jug lay on the ground as a visual symbol of what had broken internally.

11

Stretching the width of her face, Miriam's smile couldn't be contained. She beamed with joy the way the sun beams after a hard rain. As she approached the house of her childhood, she slowed down and walked the last few paces. Outside the back door Miriam stopped and looked in at her mother, who was weaving an elegant tapestry rich in hues as golden as the harvest moon. Miriam couldn't help but notice, as she stood in the same doorway through which she'd left many years ago, that time seemed to have stayed still after all. The anticipation of what would be said, what would be felt, was almost too much to bear. Truth be told, Miriam didn't know how her family would react, or if they would even recognize her anymore. Perhaps the past few years had changed her beyond what they could accept. Even though Miriam hoped that her return would be welcomed, she had to brace herself for the unexpected, despite her level of her excitement. In one quick move she stepped through the doorway and held her breath for what felt like an eternity.

Finally, after some moments their eyes met. Hannah immediately stood up from the loom, in as much shock as King Nebuchadnezzar when he saw *Shadrak, Mêyshak,* and *Ăbêd Nʼgôw*—Shadrach, Meshach, and Abed-Nego—alive and unburned in the blazing fire after they refused to bow down to the golden idol. Hannah gasped, not hiding her surprise and unbelief as Miriam stood the length of two men away that Friday morning. Face to face they stared at one another, time seeming to pause for their sake. Nothing else seemed to exist at that moment; even the air seemed to stop circulating in anticipation. It was just the two of them. To Miriam, it felt like the best dream she'd had in the last decade. The sunlight illuminated her from behind, and she knew that in her mother's eyes she must have seemed like an apparition. Miriam's heart beat with such fervency that she thought she might choke. When neither of them moved for some time, she began to have second thoughts about returning home. But at last, as if timed in unison, tears ran down both of their cheeks, greeting one another in silent emotion. And then, forgetting her weaving faster than *Kâlêb*, Caleb, drove out the Hebronites, Hannah walked over to her daughter, skeletal and soiled, and gathered her into her arms. Sounds of weeping filled the room from wall to wall.

"You're here... you're really here again," she cried in disbelief. Hannah held her daughter tighter than a linen shroud covers a body, not wanting to let her go. "My Miriam... my sweet Miriam. I thought you were gone forever," she whispered between sobs. Releasing the years of grief, Hannah wailed in relief mixed with confusion, alarming Miriam as well as the neighbors.

Though it was unspoken, forgiveness—or a measure of it—had been granted to Miriam. She didn't know what to say first, for in truth there was too much. An explanation of where she'd been or of why she'd returned— both as long as the descendants of *Châm*, *Shêm* and *Yepheth*, otherwise known as Ham, Shem and Japheth—seemed unfitting right then. While they stood locked together like a pair of yoked oxen, the air around them echoed the cries of two wounded hearts that had been touched by an unseen hand of grace.

Suddenly, their next-door neighbor burst through the door. "I heard you crying, Hannah—what's wrong?" Miriam turned around and smiled at the neighbor, who gasped and clutched her chest in amazement.

"Miriam?! Is that really you?"

"Go get Zebulun," Hannah said, sniffling loudly. "Quickly!"

"But... what has happened?"

"Now! Go, and I will tell you afterwards."

Hearing the footsteps of sandals fade into the distance, both Miriam and her mother looked at each other for a long while, letting the light of their smiles reflect off of the tears. Finally, the darkness had lifted.

"It's good to see you again, Ima," Miriam said with great excitement. "It's been such a long time..."

"We thought that you were dead, Miriam," she said, stroking her hair.

"For months and months your father and brothers searched for you all over Galilee. We had no proof but we just assumed... especially after a couple of years. We never thought that we'd see you again." Though Hannah didn't intend on sounding curt, her tone carried an edge of roughness, or perhaps it was just the voice of hurt.

Nodding her head slightly, Miriam acknowledged her mother's confession. "I can only imagine what you've been through. I'm sorry for hurting you, more than you know... but I have good news! It will make everything better."

"What are you talking about? What could be better than your return? And where exactly have you been all this time? Why did you just disappear? You nearly sent me to my grave early, not to mention your father."

Miriam looked toward the door, waiting with mixed emotions for her father's arrival. She then launched into an enthusiastic yet muddled explanation of the past six years. And the more she explained, the more Hannah grew confused. Unclean spirits and Gentiles and acts forbidden in the Torah—it was all too much for her to comprehend. To tell the truth, it was as if they were having two different conversations, Hannah with her own thoughts and Miriam with hers.

"I don't understand, Miriam, you're not making any sense. What's really going on? What are you wearing and what's all over your face? You look terrible, and yet you're glowing. Oh my goodness, are you...?"

Laughing, Miriam responded, "No, Ima, I'm not carrying a child. But something *more* amazing *has* happened to me! Just listen—"

But before she could say another word, Zebulun raced into the house, leaving a dust cloud to linger outside the entryway bigger than a sandstorm hanging over the desert dunes.

"It's true! You're back!"

"Abba," Miriam said softly when she saw him. A fresh batch of tears greeted him, just as they had her mother. She missed the warm embrace that only her father could give; it was wonderful to be there once again. Kissing the top of her head, Zebulun whispered to Yahweh a blessing of thanks. He held her a long while, swaying gently alongside the tide of emotions, and Miriam could hear the faint sounds of weeping as his lips pressed against her hair.

"Oh, Abba," she said with a repentant voice, "I didn't master the sin."

Through the tears he chuckled and held her tighter. When he released her Zebulun said, "I know. And yet somehow I love you more for it."

"I'm sorry about everything."

"I am too, Miriam. But we can deal with it all in due time," he said, referring to the law and commandments. Looking at her he said, "For now it looks like you need to get changed and cleaned up... I wouldn't have recognized you on the street with all of this extravagant clothing and jewelry on."

"Me either," Hannah said.

"Not quite how you're used to seeing me, I know."

"Hopefully that's all of the Gentile world you brought home with you."

"I think what she means to say," said Zebulun, "is that whatever sin you've committed, or committed yourself to, must remain outside until it can be purified."

"Don't worry; I met someone who delivered me from it all! That's what I've been trying to tell Ima."

"What?" he said, cocking his head to one side. "What are you talking about?" He looked at Hannah for an explanation, but she shook her head and shrugged.

"This man I met just a little while ago..."

"Who? What man?"

"Oh... I don't know His name... but that isn't as important as the fact that I've been set *free*," said Miriam. "Listen to me, please!"

"Maybe her head has gone mad—she isn't making any sense," Hannah whispered to her husband.

"Miriam—"

Maybe, she thought, a Torah reference would help. "I know none of this makes sense to either of you, but I'm telling you the truth. My life has been changed like the water that Moses turned to blood." Again she tried to explain what had happened to her, segmented though it was. But even as Miriam heard her own voice describing the past, she too realized that it seemed irrational.

"I think you're overheated. Come here and lay down," her father instructed.

Perhaps another approach. "Where are Levi and Benjamin?" They would understand; she just needed to talk with her brothers.

Her parents exchanged glances as if to say: *It really has been a long time, hasn't it?*

"Three years ago both of them married—Levi after the fall feasts and Benjamin before the spring ones," Zebulun said.

Miriam smiled as she imagined her older brothers as the heads of their own households. "They're still in Magdala?"

"Of course," said Hannah, "and not too far from here."

"Do they have children?"

"Levi and Zipporah lost their first child before it was born, but she's six months along with another one; and Bimah, Benjamin's wife, well..."

"Bimah seems to be having difficulty," her father explained, "but with Yahweh's help, she will conceive soon."

"I'm sorry to hear that." Miriam thought about her own body's ability to produce a baby. While she had been cautious about conceiving with any number of men in Tiberias, she certainly had been foolish on more than one occasion. During those days she was thankful that her body didn't create another life. Now, looking back, she saw the facts for what they were, which is to say that she was probably as barren as *Mânôwach's*, Manoah's, wife. But this knowledge, both bitter and sweet, didn't alter the newfound peace within her.

"Well, tonight is the Sabbath," Miriam stated. "Will they be coming here?"

"Of course," Hannah replied, "they join us every week for Sabbath. Sometimes we'll go to one of their homes, but mostly we have it here."

"Good," said Miriam.

"Your mother likes it that way," Zebulun said with cautious affection. "She'd always rather be the host than the guest. Isn't that right, Hannah?"

Miriam saw the look that her mother gave her father and smiled to herself. Some things, no matter how much time covered them with its footprints, did not change. In those few moments, she understood that she needed to tell her family everything from start to finish, not just the prominent events.

"Now, Miriam, you haven't really explained anything. Do you know how much pain and anguish you've put us through?" Hannah said, tears forming once again. "Since you disappeared, I've been trying to imagine why you would do such a thing."

"Ima, I am more contrite than I can convey."

"It doesn't seem like it," she sniffed. "You've been bubbling over with excitement to tell me something—though I still can't understand it all—just like you used to as a child; as if you never left."

"You're right. I do need to explain everything in a way that you can understand, but I think it's best to wait until Benjamin and Levi get here."

"But I can't wait that long—we have a handful of hours before then. Just tell me something that will help me."

"It's not as easy as that. I thought I could, but I have to start at the beginning; otherwise it only makes my story muddier."

"I don't think I'm asking too much, Miriam."

"Ima, as I've said, the last ten years have been—"

"Ten years? But you've been gone only six."

"It started long before I left, Ima."

"What are you talking about? Miriam, please—"

"I will, you have my word, but I want to wait and explain properly. No wonder you're so confused with all of my ramblings. It will all make sense, I promise."

Hannah looked at her with a tangle of emotions but held her tongue.

"For now," Miriam said with the sweetness of honey, "you can tell me about what's happened here in Magdala since I've been gone."

And so, Hannah talked and talked about every manner of subjects, some of great interest to Miriam and the rest not. And just as she had for years and years, Hannah gave Miriam a list of things to help prepare for the Sabbath. All day long they cooked and prepared the foods and decorations for the sacred family meal, all the while stealing glances at each other as if making sure it wasn't all a dream induced by a high fever. Zebulun decided to roast a goat for the occasion—a luxury reserved only for special circumstances of celebration. Mint sprigs and olive oil laced with garlic would serve to garnish the meat.

"Bimah will bring the olive bread, melons and dried apricots, as she always does."

"Is her olive bread as good as yours?" asked Miriam.

"Even better. Though she likes to keep her recipe a secret, unfortunately. And Zipporah will bring almonds, leeks, and tart apples covered with honey and cinnamon."

"My stomach is growling just thinking about them!"

"Then you should eat as much of them and everything else as you can," Hannah said, looking at Miriam. "I can almost see your bones through your skin, for the sake of heaven and all the angels!"

Miriam tried to avoid that direction in conversation. "What else can I do, Ima?"

"Do you remember where the Sabbath lamps are?"

"Yes, of course."

"Put those on the table, and then light the incense—let's use spikenard tonight."

At that moment a knock on the door sent Miriam's stomach into another lurch. All afternoon she'd been thinking about Levi and Benjamin and how they would react to seeing her again. Perhaps it wasn't the wisest decision, but Hannah and Zebulun didn't let them know in advance that she had returned. When Miriam opened the door their shock was as great as *Melek Dâr'yâvêsh's*, King Darius', when he saw Daniel sitting unharmed after a night in a den with hungry lions.

"Miriam?" Benjamin gasped as he lurched backward, almost knocking down his wife.

"Moses and all the prophets! That is you!" shouted Levi.

"Yes," she said, smiling, "it's me." Both of her brothers rushed in and hugged her with the force of wild bears. In all honesty, it took the breath right out of Miriam's lungs, but she didn't mind in the least. For the third time that day, tears streamed out of her eyes, running down her cheeks in fast currents.

"When did you come back?"

"Did you just arrive?"

"Since this morning," she said.

"What?!" Benjamin said. "You didn't come and get us?" The question, ringed with confusion and insult, was directed at Zebulun.

"Forgive us, sons, but we wanted some time alone with Miriam. You can surely understand."

"I suppose," said Levi with mock seriousness.

"For a few hours, perhaps, but not all day!" Benjamin retorted.

"Benjamin, it's all right," Miriam said.

Seven

"Where have you been?" Levi asked.

"Tiberias."

"We looked all over that city," said Benjamin.

"What has happened to you? You look so... different," said Levi, seeing her gaunt figure and gaudy accessories.

"A lot has happened, both bad and good—"

"Tell us!" Benjamin said, demanding answers.

"How about introducing me to your wives first?"

"Of course, Miriam, I'm sorry. This is my wife, Bimah."

"And this is my wife, Zipporah," said Levi, his smile beaming like a full moon. "As you can see, we're expecting a child."

"That's wonderful."

Miriam greeted the two women, embracing them in the proper manner, and drank them in from head to toe just as Lydia had taught her, which is to say in a sly and undetectable manner. Both of them were beautiful, yet they were as different as the kings of Judah and Israel. It was strange, of course, for Miriam to meet her sisters by marriage after they'd been part of the family for more than three years. But maybe in time, she thought, they could become friends.

Then, like a mother hen gathering her chicks, Hannah ushered them all into the main room of the house where the meal would take place. She explained that Miriam would divulge about her life after, or perhaps during, the meal. And even though Hannah was more eager than a bird to catch a worm, she didn't neglect the duties of the Sabbath.

For them all, Zebulun and Hannah, Benjamin, Levi and their wives, the Sabbath meal represented a time of refreshment and rejuvenation, or in other words a canopy of sanctified time. Sabbath—a period of one full day's rest— was the time that everyone followed Yahweh's lead and imitated His rest from work. They would all ponder the seven days of creation and offer silent adoration to the designer of life. Miriam, having renounced the ways of her ancestors, felt the same way that a Gentile would at their table, which is to say alone and out of place. But for the meantime, that remained between her and Yahweh.

The setting sun gave the signal for dinner to begin. The seven of them sat around the low table, with Zebulun at the head and his wife next to him. The others draped themselves around the table, Miriam the last to take her seat, and settled into the soft cushions made of goose feathers. When every-one had made themselves comfortable, Zebulun prayed, using words from the Psalms.

"Blessed be the Lord of Israel from everlasting to everlasting. Blessed be the Lord, who daily loads us with benefits—Yahweh, our salvation!"

Hannah lighted the lamps, one for each member of the family. Then melodious songs—songs of ascent written by the sons of *Qôrach*, or Ko-rah—filled the room. Their sweetness swirled around the candles, touching each person and illuminating the room even more. The mix of voices com-plimented one another, and before long their individual voices melded into one that soared through the roof and up into the heavens, caressing the ears of Yahweh.

As she mouthed the words to the songs, Miriam was overwhelmed by the familiar warmth of Jewish custom. She wondered how she could've rejected such a beautiful heritage. When the singing stopped and echoes of sweet voices remained, a moment of quiet allowed everyone to pray. With eyes and lips closed she released from her heart the incense of prayer to Yahweh, just as King David had after he committed the sin of murder.

Have mercy on me, O Yahweh, according to Your loving kind-ness; according to the multitude of Your tender mercies, blot out my transgressions. Wash me thoroughly from my iniquity, and cleanse me from my sin... Create in me a clean heart, O Yahweh.

Tears as silent as her words tumbled out. Remorse, regret, and embar-rassment all fought for center stage inside her. At that point, she inhaled a deep breath and released it a few moments later, ushering the three harmful emotions out as best she could.

When her father began speaking, she wiped her cheeks and looked up again. First he blessed the bread and then the wine. "Blessed are You, oh Lord, king of all the heavens, who brings forth bread from the earth. Blessed are You, oh Lord, king of all the heavens, who created the fruit of the vine."

As head of the household, Zebulun blessed his children by name, his sons first and then his daughter. He spent more time blessing Miriam for Yahweh had returned his daughter to him. While somewhat discomfited, she was grateful for the extra blessings spoken over her.

Last and most importantly, Hannah received Zebulun's blessing and praise for being a wife of extreme excellence, or as the Scriptures said, a crown upon his head. Reciting from memory a proverb written by *Melek L'mûw'êl*, King Lemuel—the man whose name Miriam's childhood friend had inherited—he said:

> *Who can find a virtuous wife? For her worth is far above rubies. The heart of her husband safely trusts her; so he will have no lack of gain. She does him good and not evil all the days of her life... Her children rise up and call her blessed; her husband also, and he praises her... Charm is deceitful and beauty is passing, but a woman who fears the Lord, she shall be praised.*

Miriam cherished the way that her father looked at her mother with caring, soft eyes, as found in blossoming love, while the blessing flowed forth from his soul. Deep inside, she yearned for someone to care for her that way. The devotion and adoration that Zebulun carried for Hannah put even the lover in Solomon's book of songs to shame. Closing her eyes, Hannah let the words wash over her and revitalize her for the coming week, for the praises of her husband gifted her like nothing else could.

At last, the formalities ended and the meal began. A toast rang out for Miriam's return, the wine soothing the years of damage that her disappearance had caused. They talked about the usual things: the weather, the olive grove, Zipporah's pregnancy. Once conversations slowed, eyes began turning toward her, and she knew the moment was rapidly approaching. To tell the truth, she felt jittery, so she forced herself to focus on the meal. The goat's meat, tender yet tangy, held little pouches of sweet citrus. Cucumbers combined with tomatoes and red onions, all covered with sweet vinegar and olive oil, complemented the meat. Miriam missed her family's cooking as much as *Yôwkebed*, Jochebed, missed her infant son when she put him afloat in a basket in order to save his life. For more reasons than that, of course, she was glad to be home again.

The time had suddenly arrived. Eating waned and pauses grew. Though nervous, Miriam was more enthusiastic to share the marvel of inner healing that she'd received than *Y'chizqîyâh*, or Hezekiah, when the Lord extended his life fifteen years. Surely, she thought, it would change their lives too!

Because she wanted to avoid exaggeration or embellishment, Miriam drank only a few sips of wine throughout the meal. She took a deep breath and embarked upon her story. She considered leaving out the unpleasant details of her life in Tiberias, by giving only vague hints of the depths of her sin, but she decided that the truth of those horrible events made her healing all the more significant. Miriam's family listened intently to the years of torment as well as the miracle that had transformed her life. She left virtually no detail unearthed, no spiritual factor masked. There was, at that point, nothing from which to hide. Omitting only the worst of the worst, Miriam watched as they all responded with a measure of shock combined with discomfort. In the end, Miriam emphasized again and again the goodness and glory of her deliverance; that, of course, was what she wanted them to remember.

All along Hannah wept quietly, her heart breaking at the lost innocence of her daughter. Her brothers stared with eyes wide, oddly speechless. Zebulun grew angry at her actions, rigid at her candor, and then defensive, for he'd been unable to protect his youngest child from such trauma. After a few moments he spoke, shattering the silence that had fallen upon them all.

"You should be stoned for... for so many things!"

"True, and if you choose to inform the Pharisees then I certainly will be. But if you can, focus on the fact that a *miracle* has happened! Doesn't being delivered from unclean, wicked spirits have the greatest meaning of all?"

"Maybe she's not truly at fault if she was possessed," Levi said.

"I doubt the authorities will care," Benjamin answered.

"Did you feel possessed?" Hannah asked with a weepy voice.

"Well, I had control over my body, for the most part, but in truth my thoughts and heart were afflicted with such wickedness from the endless stream of lies."

"So for ten years you endured seven unclean spirits and this morning, in the blink of an eye, they're all gone?" said Zebulun.

"Exactly! I know it seems impossible or unlikely, but it's true!"

"Who did you say the strange man was?" Levi asked.

"I don't know His name. I do know this though: He is Jewish, a Galilean, and He has the power to banish spirits with His words."

"So many false prophets are roaming around Galilee these days," said Hannah.

"I would hardly call Him a false prophet, Ima."

"What would you call Him then? A rabbi? A healer?"

"I don't know."

"Well, what *do* you know, Miriam? You've told us almost nothing about Him."

"You're right. He's calm yet commanding. His eyes are piercing yet they are embracing. He is gentle but rugged," Miriam explained. Unlike her family, she was the sole person that reacted from deliberate faith. Her family had yet to come to that place. "My encounter with Him is the closest I'll probably ever come to meeting an angel."

"Are you sure it wasn't just another spirit talking to you?" Zebulun asked.

"This man was no unclean spirit! He's flesh and blood. There were a dozen men talking with Him, like I explained."

"Did you recognize any of them?" Benjamin said.

"Some looked familiar. Fishermen, I think. But I couldn't tell you their names."

"There are rumors about men dropping their responsibilities, leaving their families, and following a complete stranger. I wonder if it's the same person," said Zebulun.

"Have you heard of Him?" Benjamin asked Levi in a lowered voice. Levi shook his head in reply.

"I'd like to meet this man," her father said. "I wonder if He's still in town."

"While I'd like to know too, I think we should focus on Miriam—that she has been brought back to us. That's all that really matters," Hannah said. Miriam, surprised at her mother's comment, smiled and nodded. Even if they didn't accept the truth of her healing that night, she would try again and again.

"Of course, but I want to know more about this man," Zebulun explained with growing concern. "I'll look into it." Giving his sons a distinct look, he signaled to them that they too were commissioned to find Him. Despite the fact that a stranger had restored his family, he couldn't will himself to extend blind faith. After all, he was a traditional orthodox Jew, so his faith limited him to the confines of Torah law and history—a history that didn't portray personal deliverance from wicked spirits. Zebulun teetered, like the two women who fought over the rightful ownership of a baby before King

Solomon, with his misgivings at one end and his daughter at the other.

Miriam smiled at everyone seated around the table. "I don't have all the answers," she reasoned with them, "but what I do have is complete peace and restoration. I can offer you only my past experiences and struggles to weigh against my current freedom. I am whole once again. I know it sounds unbelievable, but you have to believe me. It's the truth, Yahweh as my witness."

Silence filled the room once again, and Miriam knew that each one of them struggled with the truth of her story. She couldn't blame them, after all, because she'd probably feel as they did if the story had happened to someone else. They might never believe her, but Miriam had to leave that in Yahweh's hands. She hoped, actually, that it wouldn't divide their family like a double-edged sword.

"I believe you." Bimah's soft voice broke the quiet.

Miriam looked at her and smiled. "Thank you, Bimah."

"How could you?" Benjamin asked his wife. "It doesn't make any sense."

"Sure it does. Being released from unclean spirits isn't unusual—it happens more often than you think."

"Yes, by rabbis who are trained by Yahweh and who serve in the synagogues. Not by some nomad who claims to have power," he answered.

Miriam winced at the insensitive term. The hurt on her face displayed her displeasure.

"Sorry, wrong word. But, Miriam, we really don't know much about this man do we? He could be any number of things."

"You're right," said Miriam, "He could. But if you'd met Him, you'd know that His intentions are as clear as the water of a brook. I'm not sure how to explain it to you, but believe me when I say that He saw me and how I was suffering, even though I didn't say a word to Him. He never asked for money or shelter or anything else in return. In every sense, it's a miracle! As far as I'm concerned it's no different than believing that Elijah was taken up into heaven in a chariot of fire."

"Ach, now you're bordering on blasphemy!" Benjamin cried.

"This is getting worse by the minute," said Zebulun.

"Wait, wait! I have no intention of stirring you all up in anger. All I want to do is spread my honesty out before you like this wonderful meal. Everything that has happened to me is every bit as uncovered as Adam and Eve when their disobedience exposed them before Yahweh. Even if you don't believe anything I have told you, I ask one thing of you." Miriam paused and exhaled. "Please forgive me for disowning you and bringing shame upon you."

As the strange man had instructed, Miriam sought their forgiveness. Mimicking Yahweh's forgiveness that had been extended to her, she decided to forgive herself as well as others who'd hurt her or contributed to her downfall. Perhaps she would have to repeat the decision to forgive on a regular basis, yet she was willing to do so in order to keep her peace. She had no intention of ending up in the pit of despair again. After years and years of adversity, she committed herself to living with only one voice inside her head, which is to say her own.

"Thank you, Miriam, I choose to forgive you," Zebulun said, giving permission for others to follow.

"So do I," said Levi.

"Well, I don't believe you, but I do forgive you," Benjamin confessed.

"Thank you, Benjamin, I'm grateful for that."

"Indeed you have shamed us all, Miriam, but you are alive and back in our home. I forgive you as well," said Hannah.

"Thank you all, I know this isn't the most pleasant of situations, considering the choices I've made. I do believe that Yahweh will honor you in some way for it. I, of course, will honor you too."

"So what are we going to tell people when they ask?" Levi wondered aloud.

"We should just say the bare minimum," Hannah said. "That Miriam has returned after living in another Galilean town, and she's cleansed herself as is proper."

"No—I want people to know the truth! I don't have to tell the details, but they should know that I was afflicted by unclean spirits and that I've been healed of them," said Miriam with a determined voice.

"That will only bring the authorities out against you," Benjamin responded. "As father said, they have more than one cause to stone you to death. Is that what you want?"

"No, of course not, but I'm not going to lie. While I'm not proud of my disobedience to the law, I am committed to telling the truth. If I don't tell my story to others, how will they know that the man who heals is walking around Galilee? There are people out there—more than ten boats' worth—who need healing," said Miriam. "You all know that!"

"Yes, but—"

"For all we know, He could be the Messiah," Miriam cried.

"That's enough! Now you're blaspheming!" said Zebulun with a stern voice.

"Abba, I—"

"No more, Miriam."

"All right, I'm sorry."

"If you truly want to live to tell your story to others then I suggest you keep from saying such things. You're family will protect you, but our neighbors will not."

"Yes, Abba."

"Be wise about who you share information with," Hannah said, "for this town has ears everywhere, even when people aren't around." Miriam knew that her mother was right. Wagging tongues were virtually a pastime in Magdala.

"Telling people that you were roaming the hills possessed by seven demons is sure to stir up life here," Levi said, laughing. "That will make gossips out of the rocks!"

"Then I will pray about what to say and how to say it. I don't want to bring any more destruction to this house, you have my word."

"And you have my full blessing to return to your rightful place as my daughter. I will not hold your sins against you, as long as you cleanse yourself inside and out."

"Of course, Abba. Thank you."

Long after her brothers and their wives left, after her parents had gone to bed, Miriam sat outside in the courtyard behind the house, listening to the sounds of the summer night. It was almost frightening how similar that night was to the night of her physical attack ten years ago. Now, as back then, she couldn't sleep. But instead of dwelling upon the unpleasant events of her life, she thought of her encounter with the remarkable man earlier that day. He had defied all established custom to acknowledge her unspoken statements, to save her from destruction. Certainly, His mysteriousness made Him all the more enchanting, yet she knew by intuition that His character ran as deep as the well at Aram-Naharaim where *Ribqâh*, or Rebekah, met Abraham's servant, who was looking for a wife for Isaac. Miriam felt something stirring inside of her. It was peaceful and hopeful, though, not apprehensive and confusing, as it had been with the unclean spirits. She looked up into the dark night and thanked Yahweh again for restoring her health and bringing her back to her family.

Then, almost as an afterthought, Miriam said, "I wonder what the man is doing now."

The more she thought about Him, the more she wondered about the identity of her healer. Like her parents and brothers, Miriam had questions. At that moment, she made a decision. She knew she had to find out more.

12

It took Miriam a couple weeks to settle back into the old routines. Though she had switched to a Gentile lifestyle rather easily, she felt awkward picking up the Jewish mantle again so quickly. But each day became more comfortable than the one before. Miriam had to balance being respectful of her parents' wishes against the growing desire to pursue another encounter with her healer. Carefully, as she went about town, she made general inquiries.

The more people that Miriam spoke to in Magdala, the more she heard similar stories of miracles bestowed by the same man, upon both women and men alike. To tell the truth, there weren't many other Jewish men going from city to city in Galilee, healing the sick and aiding the poor. In fact, He seemed to be the only one who fit that description. Obtaining information about Him was every bit as easy as changing money at the Temple for sacrifices. His name, she had learned, was *Yêshûwa ben Nâzâret*, Yeshua of Nazareth.

Piece by piece, Miriam assembled the bits of information together, forming a coarse yet lengthy summary of the man who stilled remained a mystery to her. And with every new piece, her excitement grew. He was, she learned, the eldest son of a carpenter, which had been His trade until He left Nazareth to begin a different life. A group of twelve men traveled with Him, all from Galilee, and a few women had joined as well. Roughly thirty years of age, He challenged the synagogue teachers almost every Sabbath, no matter the town, no matter the rabbi. He never stayed in one city or town for too long, as people both young and old thronged to Him. He fed the hungry, gave sight to the blind, restored the legs of the crippled, and treated everyone He met with raw kindness.

But those were just the facts. There seemed to be as many opinions of Yeshua as there were stories. Some people saw Him as a prophet, some a teacher, others a miracle worker, but some considered Him a troublemaker or a fraud. Gossip ran through the streets of the towns as fast as hummingbirds moved from flower to flower. This, of course, motivated people to seek Him out for intentions both honorable and dishonorable. The common people—the ones most in need—embraced Him and His righteous deeds, while the rulers of the synagogues and local governments—the ones most critical—rejected Him as a threat.

Miriam thought of these things as she completed her daily chores at home. It was strange not to have Benjamin and Levi there, filling the rooms with gruff laughter and youthful scuffles. In their place a silence—uncomfortable yet expected—hung about. But even as she thought of this, Hannah filled the void with her singing. Miriam's heart ached at the first sounds of it, for she hadn't realized how deeply she had missed it. Her mother's voice softened the awkwardness that Miriam felt and eased her back into a secure and predictable life.

Still, Miriam was unable to stop thinking about the man who had set her free from the seven unclean spirits. It had been almost a month. While that amount of time seemed like an entire season, it also felt like mere moments. The joy that she'd been left holding that Friday morning led her around each day, as if it were His hand she was holding. Even the happiness of *Ăbîygayil*, Abigail, when her wicked husband *Nâbâl*, Nabal, died after a stroke, or Elisha when blessed with a double portion of Elijah's anointing didn't compare. At first she thought it was the host of unanswered questions that lured her mind back to Him, but as time passed something deeper surfaced over and over, telling her that it was a matter of the heart and not of the head. If only she could be in His presence once again, to feel the genuine kindness and peace that poured out of Him without effort. But Miriam assumed that was not possible.

Then one day as she allowed her old friend, the Sea of Galilee, to caress her feet in its refreshing and warm waves, she heard a familiar yet unexpected tune. It was, of course, the same tune she'd heard the morning of her encounter with Yeshua. Like a breeze rolling over the waves and onto shore, the music moved over her once more. It was unlike anything she had previously known. The melody was beautiful and rousing, soft and rhythmic. With her ankles in the water and her head covering swaying in the wind, Miriam stood alone—despite the clusters of fishermen—listening to the music inside of her. It sounded like something from her dreams. Before she knew it the melodies were flowing out of her mouth, her voice carrying out over the boats on the sea.

She knew with clear certainty that she was giving life to her feelings. Her spirit was expressing deep veneration, or in other words the kind of holy awe that the Israelites showed near the *b'rîyth ârôwn*, the Ark of the Covenant. Like Yeshua, the music had appeared without warning, arriving in a torrent from the depths of her being onto her lips. Staring out across the busy sea, Miriam sang as if she were calling to Him. She closed her eyes and imagined His face, His hands, His compassion. What came next was unexpected.

Tears of relief, of joy, of freedom filled her eyes. Miriam didn't try to control her voice, or emotions, for that matter. She allowed them to overtake her. Except for a small offering of thanks, she hadn't said anything in response to Him that day. Words had eluded her then. Now, though, they seemed to flow uninhibited, answering Yeshua, the voice of truth. Just as the inhabitants of *Tsîyôwn*, or Zion, sang out to Yahweh from the depths of their souls, this was Miriam's song.

* * *

Month after month passed, but the quiet restlessness inside her rose instead of fell. In the same way that the lamentations for Jerusalem consumed *Yirm'yâhûw*, or Jeremiah, her thoughts were consumed with Yeshua. More and more, Miriam wanted to join the group of people who traveled with Him, yet she knew that kind of life wouldn't be easy. He had rescued her from a life of perpetual torment, after all, and she longed to repay Him. The notion of leaving her family again and taking up a life of unknown hardship seemed unreasonable. But staying in Magdala and shadowing the life of her mother seemed equally unappealing. She had, in a sense, come to a crossroads.

One morning in the early fall of that year, Miriam awoke and knew with certainty what she had to do. She had dreamed that night about leaving her family and joining the followers of Yeshua. He had appeared to her again, and extended an invitation. "Come," He said, "follow Me." Miriam knew both in the dream and the following morning that she had been called. It was as definitive as the Lord calling to young Samuel. Sitting in her bed that morning, Miriam felt excited yet unsure. Could she really leave again? But how could she stay, feeling as she did? Closing her eyes, she exhaled a long breath.

In a voice a notch above a whisper she made a confession to Yeshua. "I don't want to do anything else but follow you, to devote my life to you—whatever that means, whatever form that takes. I am willing. You have given my life meaning and purpose, and I am eager to repay You."

At that point, the only thing left to decide was how to inform her family. Miriam knew, of course, that it was equally as scandalous for her to follow Yeshua as it had been for her to follow Dagon to Tiberias. At least Yeshua was Jewish, she reasoned, and had come from a devout family of acceptable trade. But her family, on the other hand, knew Yeshua as well as they knew Dagon, which is to say not at all. Distrust and resentment naturally ran as high and thick as the walls in Jerusalem. The following Sabbath evening Miriam attempted to explain to them her desire for the future. She told them about her dream.

"Are you serious?" Levi asked.

"Yes, I am."

"No. It's not an option," her father said.

"Again? You want to leave us *again*?" Hannah cried, her tone shaky and confused. "We lived through it once, but twice would surely put us in the ground!"

"Hannah, please," said Zebulun, trying to calm his wife.

"Ima—"

"Miriam, you are just responding to the fascinating encounter you had with this man. It does not merit changing your life," Benjamin said with disdain.

"Please don't talk to me that way, brother. I am perfectly clear-headed, and I know exactly what I am doing." Her voice, while firm, was gentle.

"You'll wind up doing the same things you did in Tiberias," Benjamin continued, "and bring more shame upon yourself and this family."

"I can promise you that I will not. That part of my life has been buried, so fear not about my temptation to sin."

"But isn't this just another form of rebellion?" said Levi. "You're defying our customs and traditions to follow a carpenter around Galilee, for the sake of all creation."

"It may seem that my decision is a rebellious one, but in truth it's the opposite. I am leaving out of a sense of duty."

"Your duty, daughter, is to work in this home, marry an honorable man, and have children," Zebulun said with authority. "It's what Yahweh commands of you."

At that moment Miriam noticed that her father's dark curly hair had turned gray around his ears and temples. He was aging into the latter years of his life, and he was eager to see his children have many children. Compassion filled her heart.

"It would be nice to have children, I agree, but it seems as though Yahweh has closed my womb." Her voice bore touches of sadness. "And who will marry me now, at twenty-two and with my history?"

After a shared pause, Levi said to Zebulun, "She's right. It may not be the wisest thing to keep her here."

"That's enough from you," Zebulun responded.

"It was just a dream," Hannah said.

"Yahweh spoke to Joseph in dreams," Miriam replied.

"Realistically, Miriam, what are you going *to do* with these people?" her mother asked.

"I am going to join the men and women who support Yeshua," she replied.

"But you will be ostracized from every Jewish community in Galilee and possibly labeled as a woman of indecency," explained Benjamin.

"Benjamin," she chuckled, "I *was* a woman of indecency. There is nothing that people can say about me that probably isn't true."

"Yes, but only our family knows that. It isn't common knowledge around Magdala. Or is it?" he inquired around the room.

"Not that I am aware of, no," Hannah answered.

"So you see? You'll be labeled in no time if you do this." His voice was tender and full of concern.

"I understand your concern, I really do, but that doesn't matter to me anymore. My life has been changed and the things of the past are exactly that. I am concentrating on the future, and I'm eager to help others, just as I was helped. There is a world of people out there who need love and attention."

"So let someone else go," her mother pleaded.

"Is this not part of our duty as children of Yahweh? To take care of the poor and needy?"

"For the sake of Israel and all its kings, Miriam, you can do that here in Magdala! You don't have to leave to find them," Hannah answered.

"This is different. Yeshua does not simply tend to them in their present condition. He tends to them by *changing* their condition. Can't you see how that makes all the difference in the world? Look at me—I am proof of that! Nothing else in my life will be as rewarding as this decision," she promised them.

"Having a husband and—" Hannah began to say, the hope in her voice as naked as the cloudless sky.

"I'm sorry, Ima," Miriam said. "I know you will be disappointed, that you all will be disappointed, and for that I am sorry. But I believe this is what I am being called to do by Yahweh. As He has served me, I will serve Him. Take comfort in that."

For a few minutes silence paraded around the room. Each of them thought about Miriam's words, either warming to them or shutting them out. At last, Levi broke the stillness.

"Whenever you travel through Magdala you must visit us." As always his smile was disarming.

Miriam vowed, "You have my word."

The next day, once her family had more or less conceded, Miriam had only two items to acquire prior leaving Magdala. And her father retained them both.

With momentum on her side, she boldly asked him for a portion of her dowry money. As she had expected, Zebulun refused her request at first, but after some coaxing on Miriam's part they reached a compromise. He agreed in the end to give her some money but less than what she'd hoped for. She didn't ask why, and he didn't offer an explanation. Regardless, Miriam thanked him and promised that the money would affect greater good for the poor and oppressed than for her as a spouse. With that, of course, he did not agree. But his consent stemmed from his understanding of Miriam's determination, inherited from his own bloodline. Zebulun—traditional yet willful—both admired and despised that determination. With the money in her hands, she hesitated before seeking her next request, drawing in a deep breath and letting it out in measures.

"Abba," Miriam said with meekness, "there is one more thing that I'd like from you before I go."

"What is it?" he asked warily.

"Your blessing."

He inhaled sharply and seemed to hold his breath. "Miriam, it's no secret that I believe you're making another huge mistake."

"I know. I wish that I could change your mind on that."

"We both seem to be unyielding in our outlook. Sadly, I know that your decision does not rest on me giving this blessing. You will go with or without it." Miriam nodded her head slowly, never once taking her eyes off his face. "When I look into your eyes I can see that something is different. You have the look of determination to do what you believe is right. As much as I am heartbroken to see you leave us again, I want us to part on agreeable conditions."

Miriam smiled and felt a thin layer of tears appear over her eyes. Pulling her to his chest, her father hooked one arm around her back and cupped his other hand on the back of her head. The tenderness melted both of their hearts. Inhaling and exhaling deeply, Zebulun offered her his blessing with reluctance yet sincerity, while fighting back tears of his own. The priestly Torah blessing was every bit as beautiful as the sun rising over the Galilean hills.

"May the Lord bless you and keep you; may the Lord make His face to shine upon you, and be gracious to you; may the Lord lift up His countenance upon you, and give you peace."

"Thank you, Abba," she whispered.

At that point, Miriam felt the freedom to depart in peace. Though sad to say goodbye, she surrendered those feelings as well as their outspoken disappointment. She rested in the knowledge that she was headed in the right direction.

Having decided in her heart that she wanted to yield her life to Yeshua of Nazareth, every thought and every action changed in response. This was the man who had delivered her from the depths of evil the likes of which most people would never know. No other human being could care for her like this. Nothing else mattered anymore.

13

ONCE MIRIAM HEARD that Yeshua and His followers were staying in the town of *Kinn'rôwth*, otherwise known as Gennersaret, just north of Magdala, she set out early one morning to find them. As her feet moved rhythmically over the short distance between the two cities her mind did as well. She thought of all the tribes of people who'd traversed the same path, as far back as the sons of Jacob. In fact, Magdala and Gennersaret were among nineteen cities—and their surrounding villages—that had been given as an inheritance to the families of the tribe of *Naphtâlîy*, or Naphtali. That, of course, hadn't happened until Joshua led the Israelites into the land of promise, fighting and killing all of the inhabitants of the northern kingdoms. She imagined the vast amount of bloodshed that had spilled on the very ground where she walked. She later learned that Yeshua too caused struggles—not with swords but with words—to occur between fathers and sons, mothers and daughters, just as He had within her own family.

As soon as she arrived in Gennersaret, she went to the center marketplace and immediately found what she was seeking. A large crowd had gathered with flocks of people moving like agitated sheep, trying to make their way to the center where she assumed He stood. While Miriam didn't push and shove her way toward Him, she did use openings in the crowd to move forward, listening to what people were saying. It seemed that Yeshua and the other men had anchored on shore after being out at sea. At once people had recognized Him. His fame, for better or worse, traveled faster than a famished lion after a gazelle. The people had run throughout the city and beyond, gathering up the sick—many bound to their mats—and bringing them to Him. Within minutes the streets had been littered with men, women, and children, some suffering from one ailment or another, others just witnessing the miracles.

In one ear Miriam heard the sick begging Him to touch them, and in the other ear she heard shouts of praise from those who'd been healed. Though assorted, every cry was passionate, causing bumps to rise all over her body. All at once the memories of her own healing rushed through her head, and she experienced again the elation of having an encounter with Yeshua. Miriam stood among the desperate and the curious, for what seemed like hours. She absorbed the scene as if she was a garment soaking up dyes of various colors. Slowly, the crowd thinned and she caught a glimpse of His face. It was, of course, exactly how she'd remembered, except perhaps that it looked wearier.

The multitude departed the marketplace one by one, and only a handful of people remained. Yeshua had taken a seat on a wooden box, His head resting in His hands. A dozen men were scattered about, some talking and some lounging in the shade. It was then that Miriam noticed the women moving around, tending to people and supplies. She assumed they were the ones dedicated to Yeshua's work. Like a lost animal, she stood in one place, looking around before determining her next step.

"I'm sorry but Yeshua has finished for now," one of the men said as he approached her.

Miriam jerked her head and met his eyes. She couldn't decide if he was being defensive or sincere. "No, I'm not here to be healed."

Hearing a familiar voice, Yeshua looked up. "Miriam," He said in a soft yet delightful tone.

"You know this woman?" a different said.

Ignoring the question, Yeshua asked Miriam, "Why have you come?"

Bowing out of respect, she said, "You said to follow the way, the truth, and the life. That's what I'm doing."

"Indeed, I did," said Yeshua. His tone had changed, she noticed. Rising, He moved toward her.

"Was I wrong? Am I not welcomed?"

He looked at her for a few long moments, causing her to question her decision even more. Everyone seemed to be staring at her. Then, He offered a smile more captivating than Levi's. "Please, join us."

Miriam breathed a heavy sigh of relief. At that same moment she heard someone ask, "But who is she?"

"She is the woman from Magdala who once carried seven unclean spirits," Yeshua answered. "And her name is Miriam."

A few of the disciples greeted her warmly, but the others seemed strangely hostile. In that moment, Miriam knew her place would be at the end of the line. After all, she'd just joined the group, so she had no ground on which to be troubled. Even though she'd been rebuffed by some she savored the fact that Yeshua had not only recognized her but had welcomed her as well. At that point, she couldn't have asked for more.

Before she noticed, a pair of women approached her, taking her eyes away from Yeshua. Miriam tensed a little, not knowing what to expect from them.

"My name is Susanna," the taller one said. Towering and thin, she looked like an Egyptian reed. Her eyes were as black as her shoulder-length hair, but her pale skin balanced them. Her striking appearance seemed like the dark and light sides of the moon. Miriam sensed that her personality would be just as dynamic.

"And I'm Joanna," the other woman said, her smile full of sweetness and light. She was short with honey-colored waves of hair that fell softly around her face. Long, delicate eyelashes framed her light brown eyes. "We're glad to have another woman among us."

"Maybe we'll form a group of twelve as well," said Susanna with a wry smile.

Pointing to the men scattered around, Joanna said, "These are the twelve men that Yeshua has chosen to follow Him."

"Just as the stink of fish follows the four of them," Susanna said, nodding toward a cluster close to Yeshua.

"Peter, Andrew, James, and John—two sets of brothers—used to be fishermen," explained Joanna. "Thaddeus, Thomas, and Judas are underneath the tree over there."

"Philip, Bartholomew, and Alphie are the quiet ones."

"Alphie?" Miriam said.

"His name is James, son of Alphaeus, but Susanna affectionately calls him Alphie. I think she may be enamored with him," Joanna teased.

"Ha! He's about as lively as one of Peter's gutted fish."

"But Simon on the other hand..." said Joanna, smiling.

Seven

Susanna laughed. "Simon—the group's zealot—spends more time talking about ridding the land of Romans than the Romans talk about their glorious empire, which is difficult to imagine. He thinks he's capable alone of ushering in the Messiah."

"It does make for some interesting conversations between them," Joanna replied.

"As you'll see, it's like traveling with twelve different constellation signs—each one with his own celestial nature," Susanna said.

"But that's only eleven," Miriam said. "Where's number twelve?"

The women looked around the empty marketplace; the mid-day sun had ushered almost everyone under one covering or another. "Ah, hiding in the bushes over there," said Susanna, "is the last one, the former money merchant."

"The who?"

"Matthew," Joanna answered. "He used to collect taxes. Oddly enough he resembles the image on Caesar's coins." Her whispery laugh made Miriam smile.

"Well, he may look like a Gentile, but he's as Jewish as a circumcised—"

"They all are, of course," said Joanna, cutting off Susanna. "Jewish, that is."

"His followers?"

"His *disciples*," Susanna replied.

Until then Miriam hadn't realized that the twelve men were Yeshua's disciples, for she had thought they were mere supporters. It was a practice as old as her religion itself. His instructed ones, or *Tâlmidîm* as they were known, received the personal teachings and training of their wise mentor. As tradition went, Yeshua had chosen specific men—men who had traded their families and professions for a life of intense educational learning—to follow Him. Though some disagreed, it was a privilege and an honor to be chosen for such a renowned lifestyle. The end goal, of course, was for the disciples to become like their learned teacher, or in other words to emulate, imitate, and replicate him, so that one day they too would become teachers and instruct others in the designated way.

"We, on the other hand, support them in whatever way we can," explained Joanna.

"Like the backbone of the group, so to speak," Susanna said. Looking

Miriam in the eyes, she added, "Are you prepared to give all that you have?"

Miriam learned more than she could've imagined within the first two months of joining the followers of Yeshua. Perhaps the most informative time, though, occurred one evening as the disciples sat with Him in a circle surrounding a small fire of coals over which they were cooking their dinner of fresh fish. The women sat in a smaller circle removed from the men but within hearing distance. Without looking in their direction Miriam listened to what Yeshua was disclosing to His chosen twelve.

She heard Him describe how the Spirit of the Lord rested upon Him, and how He carried an anointing to preach good tidings to the poor. He had been sent to heal the broken-hearted and to comfort all who mourn, giving them beauty for ashes and the garment of praise for the spirit of heaviness. As *Yeśha'yâhûw*, Isaiah, had prophesied hundreds of years beforehand, the Spirit of Wisdom and Understanding, the Spirit of Counsel and Might, the Spirit of Knowledge and of the Fear of the Lord all rested upon Him. The Spirit of the Lord was greater than those who were of the world—those that she'd known all too well. Miriam then heard Him say that prison doors would open before Him, releasing those who were bound, proclaiming liberty to the captives. At that she stopped eating and looked at Yeshua, thinking that He was speaking of her. But truth be told, all He meant was that He intended to give former captives—her included—the things that had been stolen from them. To restore the years that the swarming locust had eaten away, as the prophet Joel had said. A flash of humility and embarrassment coursed through her veins. Color flushed on her cheeks. Susanna and Joanna watched and smiled with understanding. As Miriam later learned, they too had experienced similar moments early on.

While finishing their meal, the three women talked, each asking questions, each forming opinions of one another. To Miriam, it seemed as if Susanna and Joanna were merchants and she their customer, exchanging information like goods at the market.

"Are you married?" Joanna asked Miriam.

"No," she replied with some confusion. If she were, she wouldn't— couldn't—have left her husband to follow Yeshua. "Are you?"

Seven

"Yes, I suppose I still am, though I left him a while ago. He hasn't demanded a divorce from me yet, but I suspect it will happen at some point."

"Chuza—that's her husband—does everything with Herod in mind. As one would expect of the ruler's business manager," Susanna said with some disdain.

"She's right, of course," said Joanna to Miriam, "he does seem hopeless in his devotion to Herod."

"More like hopeless in his addiction to power."

Joanna nodded and shrugged her shoulders. "Unfortunately, it's at the expense of others... like me." Susanna understood, but Miriam did not. "Chuza has a temper as violent as a raging sea, and even though he hides it well, those living with him experience the worst of it. He never touched strong drink, and for that I am grateful, for the beatings would have been much worse."

Miriam winced, imagining Joanna, delicate and small, enduring the physical wrath of her husband. Without warning tears pooled in her eyes, but Joanna touched Miriam on the arm and smiled.

"No need to cry, I've been saved from that life. I believe it's what brought me to meet Yeshua, so even the most awful days were worth it."

Miriam felt a pang of recognition in her statement. She'd never thought about it in that way, but she too felt as Joanna did. "How did *you* meet Yeshua?"

"Well, as I mentioned," Joanna replied, "life with Chuza was not good; it had gone from bad to worse, and I was plotting a way to escape. Even though he held tight control over me, he didn't know this. I hadn't even told Susanna, my handmaiden, as she would have been overly impatient to leave."

"He was a miserable man," said Susanna.

"At night I would lie awake and dream of a different life, but when daylight arrived I lost the nerve to follow through with anything. I lived in fear of what he might do—or have others do—to me."

Miriam knew that fear. "So how did you leave?"

"Truly, it was Yahweh's hand of mercy on me. I was wandering around Capernaum, avoiding our villa as much as I could, when I heard that a group of Jewish men were helping people in dire situations. So I gathered all the information I could from people in town and then planned to meet Yeshua the following day to seek refuge with them. Then I told Susanna."

"It was about time she left Herod, that worthless donkey."

"Well," Joanna said with a chuckle, "it took longer than planned, but finally we approached them—first some of the disciples and then Yeshua—and explained that we were desperate. Even though I didn't know how, I offered to cook and mend clothes, thinking that Susanna could help me. Now of course, I'm not too bad at it."

"Maybe cooking is your spiritual gift," Susanna said in jest.

Joanna rolled her eyes. "The way sarcasm is yours?"

"Precisely," she said in between bites.

"So what did your husband do?" Miriam asked.

"I hoped that Chuza would declare me insane for joining them and leave me alone. I was right about that, for he still thinks I'm unwell in the head. But as I've said before, he can think whatever he wants as long as he can't harm me."

"Swine," said Susanna under her breath.

"Susanna," Joanna responded in a reprimanding tone, "as you know, swine or otherwise, *somebody* has to occupy hell." At that the two women laughed until tears pooled in their eyes. But Miriam was taken aback; she didn't know how to respond. Seeing her surprise, Joanna said, "Don't worry, Miriam, I'm only making a joke."

"A pretty good one," replied Susanna, wiping the corners of her eyes.

"In truth, I pray every day for Chuza, that he would come to his senses and repent before Yahweh. If He can touch the heart of a tax collector—

"Swine of a different breed," Susanna said as she drank some diluted wine.

"—then He can reach Chuza." Joanna gave Susanna a look for her last comment. "As Yeshua says, we're no better than the worst of them, but unlike them we have chosen to leave the filth behind in order to pursue righteousness and peace."

They all nodded in agreement. After a few moments, Susanna broke into their quiet reflections. "Maybe Chuza will be trampled by a colony of lepers..."

All at once the three of them burst into laughter. Right then, Miriam knew she had found companionship unlike any she'd ever experienced. As different as they all were, she was delighted to discover that they all shared similar thoughts, even if unorthodox.

Seven

Before sunset that same evening, Miriam returned to the Sea of Galilee with a renewed spirit and a renewed mind. With the others close by, she walked to the shore with a mission: to rekindle her companionship with the comforting, familiar waters of her youth. With the past behind her and the recent days looming in her mind, she pined for the ease of an old friend. So much had transpired and yet so much lay ahead. The good and the bad, the horrors and the miracles—equally as influential, equally as life changing—seemed to stack up like the freewill offerings the Israelites brought for the Tabernacle.

Her mother always claimed that she was a water child. "You loved it as much as the fish," she used to say. And truly, Miriam loved the water. There was something about water that she couldn't enunciate—something intangible, like a good dream whose sweetness lingers for days. As she later learned, the sweetness was the hovering of the *Ruâch haKodesh*, Spirit of Yahweh, or the Holy Spirit. Just as the spirit had hovered over the face of the waters at the dawn of creation, it hovered now over the face of the placid Sea of Galilee.

Sitting on the end of a pier, Miriam dangled her feet into the cool water and lifted them up again, feeling it course between her toes, down the length of her feet, and off her heels back into the lake. It was a motion she repeated over and over in mindless fashion. Her mind was somewhere else, on some*one* else.

It was on the person of Yeshua.

Miriam saw the kindness and the love of Yahweh in the man who had saved her from her demonic demise. It was not by her works of righteousness or the fact that she had once been a good person; it was by His mercy that she had been saved. Miriam soaked up, like the sea into her skin, the abundance of grace that had been poured out on her. Grace was hers because she didn't deserve it. Grace was hers because she had the faith to believe.

* * *

As they traveled throughout Galilee, Miriam saw many towns. She enjoyed experiencing other places, like Bethsaida and Capernaum, which was the base of Yeshua's ministry. But none, she thought, felt as good as Magdala.

Miriam valued the company of the disciples and other women, yet the most important person to her was Yeshua. She essentially could do without the others but not without Him. He was her reason for living. Because of this, she got to know Him—watching, learning, and soaking up every ounce of detail as He ministered to the needy. And for the most part she observed in silence.

Town after town, Miriam watched Him with raw eagerness as He touched lives and cared for those in need. From the mildest violation of the law to the most devastating physical ailments and infirmities, His compassion for humanity—as vivid as a full moon and its accompanying stars—was breathtaking. He gave the same full, all-encompassing attention to Peter's fever-laden mother, a cripple, two blind men, and a group of lepers. Miracles seemed to be given out in the same way that visions were granted to Daniel, which is to say abundantly. There were miracles of demonstration, such as when a fierce storm over the Sea of Galilee vanished at the command of His voice; miracles of provision, where more than five thousand people were fed from two fish and five bread loaves; and miracles of healing, such as opening deaf ears and mute tongues speaking.

And when Yeshua wasn't ministering to people, He was teaching them. Walking under the mantle of anointing reserved for priests, kings and prophets, He taught His followers as well as critics to execute true justice, to show mercy and compassion, everyone to his brother. He instructed them to refrain from oppressing the widows and the fatherless, the strangers and the poor. Above all, He commanded them to hate evil and love righteousness. Miriam didn't need to hear that admonition twice, for she'd lived with evil nearly half of her life and had seen the results. Translated from the clutches of unclean spirits into the hands of Yahweh, Miriam had gone from one spiritual extreme to the other. For her, as well as for so many others, darkness, despair, and death had been turned into light, hope, and life. Miriam now lived in perfect peace because her mind stayed on Yeshua. Because she trusted Him.

Like Susanna and Joanna, Miriam supported Yeshua and His ministry through concrete physical provisions as well as intangible spiritual ones. She gave them facets of the world seen and unseen, or in other words, food for the body and prayer for the soul. Through the heat and arid parchment of summer, the cool days and nights of brief autumn, the rainy, cold, and gloomy months of winter, and the crisply fragrant weeks of the spring, she remained faithful. As rapidly as the seasons changed, Miriam matured in character and in spirit, emerging as brightly as the local wildflowers.

During the months that Miriam followed Yeshua—much to some disciples' skepticism and dismay—her heart grew more and more attached to Him. He did not, however, carry a comeliness or appearance to behold. When Miriam looked at Him, there was no beauty that aroused desire within her. It was not a physical attraction, but rather a spiritual one, which proved to possess chasms of wonder deeper than the well at *Mamrê*, Mamre. She loved every human and divine attribute that He demonstrated.

But Miriam sensed that there existed in this man a dynamic of loneliness. It seemed as if He had come from another country with no other friends or relatives, as if He daily pined to return to His original homeland. A sojourner of sorts.

In her moments of compassion, she tried to comfort Him, though He looked at her with the eyes of a father and of a person who loves more than the human mind can understand. He sympathized with her weakness, and was tempted in all ways as she. Yet He refrained from sin. His character did not include behavior that was common to sinful man—no lust or deceit or immoral actions. As much as Miriam was often tempted to pursue a closer relationship, she was just as often reminded of His eternal purposes.

One night after the evening meal they said their goodnights and embraced in a hug, as did all the other women. The stars radiated in the expanse of sky above them. She folded neatly into His arms, feeling their strength as well as the strength of His spirit. She held Him tightly. Miriam heard the beating of His heart and smelled the mix of sweat and sea air on His skin. Yeshua wrapped His arms around her with gentleness, the right hand embracing her back and the left hand cradling the back of her head. Her father had held her the same way while giving his blessing just months ago. The scene was, to tell the truth, a replica of the *Shûwlammîyth*, or Shulamite, woman and the shepherd as King Solomon had described in his love writings. Just as the shepherd in the story was the lover of the woman's soul, so Yeshua was the lover of Miriam's soul. His wide, sinewy hand encircled the shape of her head, giving her a sense of being shrouded by love.

Miriam at once felt her knees buckle, and she had to fight to stand up against the overwhelming warmth that emanated from His entire being. Although she wanted Him to know her blossoming feelings toward Him, she felt only friendship and fatherly protectiveness in His embrace, so she refrained. She wanted to stay in His arms all night, standing in the crisp twilight air, yet she knew it would not and could not happen.

Having experienced His ministry, Miriam understood that He, without question, had to be sent from Yahweh, the Holy One of Israel. So many were rejecting the notion that Yeshua was the awaited Messiah. She knew differently. Not a mere prophet, not just a teacher. But the One for whom all of Israel waited.

Fighting tears, Miriam recalled her youthful dream of a man holding her with such grace and reverence. The reality of it was almost too much to bear, so she pulled free. A foolish display of affection would only embarrass her. His was the touch of a father—strong, secure, compassionate, loving. Miriam understood the deep spiritual connection they shared, and that the importance of their spiritual intimacy far outweighed any physical intimacy. It was her human flesh that often confused the two, yearning for the lesser essential. Their unique bond would last forever, Miriam realized, even if the mountains crumbled into the sea.

14

ON A COOL, CLEAR evening Yeshua went up a mountain in between Magdala and Gennessaret. He remained all night, praying. All that time He had been alone. At daybreak He called the disciples, who had waited with Miriam and the other women at the bottom, up to Him.

After some time, they all descended the slopes of the dry and thirsty mountain. The disciples stood with Yeshua on a large, level area that looked ten shades of brown under the hot sun. Soon clusters of followers as well as curious on-lookers surrounded them. Miriam could hardly believe that people had traveled from all over Judea and Jerusalem as well as the coastal towns of Tyre and Sidon. Yeshua's fame had spread north, south, east, and west, leaving a blazed trail of healing and deliverance never before seen in the land of Israel.

For hours He ministered to the sick, as healing power went out from Him into everyone who touched Him. None walked away in the same condition. Miracles happened faster than the stars had come into existence at Yahweh's command. Miriam just stared at Yeshua in utter wonderment, mesmerized by His compassion and unending patience. Hand after hand reached out to Him, voice after voice called His name. He caught Miriam staring and smiled, as if to say, *Love conquers all*. She blushed and then turned her attention to the crowds, helping those in the worst conditions draw close to receive their breakthrough.

Some days Yeshua grew weary from the constant need thrust at Him, but not that day. When all had been cured from disease and set free from evil spirits, He began talking to the disciples. The crowd abruptly stopped chattering in order to hear what He was saying. Whether directed at them or not, they didn't want to miss the morsels of wisdom that He was doling out.

"Yahweh blesses you who are poor, for the kingdom of heaven is given to you. Yahweh blesses you who are hungry now, for you will be satisfied. Yahweh blesses you who weep now, for the time will come when you will laugh with joy. Yahweh blesses you who are hated and excluded and mocked and cursed because you are identified with Me, the Son of Man."

"Who *is* that? What does Son of Man mean?" a voice said behind Miriam. She turned around and saw Oreb, Dagon's friend from Tiberias. She was more surprised than *Y'chezqê'l*, Ezekiel, when he saw the dry bones coming back to life. She stood and waited for him to catch sight of her eyes.

"Miriam!" he said, throwing his arms wide and moving toward her. His embrace was prodigious, lifting her off her feet. She could feel the curious gaze of Susanna and Joanna on her.

"Oreb," Miriam said, "it's good to see you again. What are you doing in this part of Galilee?"

"Traveling, my dear," he answered, "visiting towns and admiring women from all over." His chuckle brought back torrents of memories. No need to ask if he was still pursuing a life of frivolity and lust. She could see the answer on his face, smell it on his clothes. Miriam hadn't noticed that her friends had moved closer, inquisitive yet silent.

"Speaking of," Oreb said. "Who are these lovely women?"

Miriam introduced Joanna and Susanna and watched him drink up every ounce of them. She knew he saw delicacy and a soft glow of beauty in Joanna. But the sharp contrast of Susanna's features—the juxtaposition of dark hair and light skin—appealed to him like sweet treats to a child.

"Such beauty has never met my eyes," he gushed.

"You must never go outside," Susanna retorted.

"On the contrary, my dear, I make it one of my duties to find women of rare beauty and charm."

"A noble undertaking," Susanna said with thick mockery.

He grinned and chortled. "I like her," he said to Miriam.

"How do you know Miriam?" Joanna asked.

"We met years ago in Tiberias," he replied, "through a friend. She looked different then, arrayed in expensive tunics and copious jewels that accentuated her beauty…"

"I surely dressed the part," Miriam said with remorse.

"I can hardly imagine," said Joanna.

"She was the envy of every man in Tiberias," Oreb said. "Including me."
Miriam flushed four shades of pink.

"Had Dagon not been a friend of mine…"

"Where *do* you find the time to woo all those women?" Susanna asked,
eyes ablaze with disdain.

Oreb gave Susanna his signature smile. "I *make* the time," he said smoothly. "Any chance I can interest you—"

"None," she said before he could finish. "I think maybe we'll get back to
more worthwhile things." She gave Miriam a look that rivaled Queen Jezebel
and ushered Joanna back toward the crowd listening to Yeshua.

"You've made nice friends in these parts, I see," Oreb said to Miriam. As
much as she disapproved of his underlying motives, she tolerated his playful
banter. "What on earth are you doing here, with this crowd?"

"Enjoying my new life," she said, "and pursuing a purpose that is greater
than myself."

"Hanging around with the poor and the outcasts? That hardly seems
fulfilling."

"It is far more fulfilling than anything I was doing in Tiberias. All of that
was a waste of time and completely selfish. Oreb, to be honest, I don't think
your lifestyle is accomplishing anything—"

"Ah, but on the contrary. It accomplishes much pleasure!" he said as he
eyed an exotic looking woman approaching the crowd.

"One day it will come to an end," she said. "It cannot—and will not—
last forever."

"When I left my father's house in Greece with the portion of my inheritance, I swore that I would never go back. He had my whole life planned out,
and I wanted nothing to do with it."

With that statement Miriam felt the unmistakable presence of the Spirit
of Rebellion. Oreb was operating hand in hand with that vile entity. She
had believed the same lies, followed the same path that turned her away from
family and security. Because he had partnered with the Spirit of Rebellion, he

gave permission for other spirits—namely Lust—to follow.

"What happens when your inheritance runs out?"

"My inheritance is large, my dear," he answered. "It has no end."

"Oreb," she said with sincerity, "I think you should go back to your father."

A stern reply smacked her in the face. "I will *not*!" He saw her flinch, and then softened again. "Miriam, I will hang on to my life of pleasure to the bitter end. It's all I have."

Miriam smiled sadly. "Like you, I ran from my family in rebellion against my father. That's how I ended up in Tiberias. And like you, I had years of enjoyment that I thought fulfilled me. But following rebellion into a life of pleasure doesn't last. I was brought down to a place of despair, Oreb. My friends had disowned me, my beauty had vanished, and I was left with nothing. Don't let that happen to you."

"Miriam," he said casually, "the kind of friends I have will never turn their backs on me." But even as he spoke the words, Miriam could see doubt run across his face.

"Just remember, it's never too late. Go back to your father and ask for forgiveness before you are completely broke. Before your friends shut the door on you. Before you find yourself staring into the eyes of starvation and abandonment."

He looked at her, unsure of what to say. Just as they paused in their conversation, Miriam and Oreb heard what Yeshua was saying. He looked in their direction.

"What sorrows await you who are rich, for you have your only happiness now. What sorrows await you who are satisfied and prosperous now, for a time of awful hunger is before you. What sorrows await you who laugh carelessly, for your laughing will turn to mourning and sorrow..."

Miriam couldn't believe her ears. Yeshua had just spoken a word of warning to Oreb, addressing the very issues of his heart. His face had suddenly turned ashen as if hearing his future told to him. Oreb looked at Miriam with suspicion and fear. She began to reach out to him, but he grabbed her hand.

"Goodbye, Miriam," he said. "My place is not here with these strange, deranged men." He kissed her hand gently, and escaped through the crowd.

She watched him move more quickly than a deer avoiding a hunter's bow.

Seven

Don't let him escape from You, Yahweh. Remind him what Yeshua said, and lead him back to his father's house. May he find grace and mercy there.

Miriam hungered for Yeshua's words. They dripped from His lips like sweet honey. There was nothing else like them—so powerful, so poignant, so pristine. Every time she tasted their sweetness her whole being felt infused with raw life. And with every taste she wanted another helping.

One week after seeing Oreb again she and Yeshua ended up in a private conversation. They were walking through an olive grove in late summer, the harvest rapidly approaching. The serene atmosphere would soon become one of hustle and bustle. Olives would rain down like manna from heaven, giving life and treasures of oil. The fragrances and sounds of the grove made her miss her family. She closed her eyes and pictured her parents and brothers organizing and preparing for the long days of harvest. Visions of herself as a little girl playing in the grove with Hadassah, Levi, and Benjamin flickered in her mind, echoes of their laughter reaching across the years. Miriam had loved when her brothers chased her around the trees, and when her father handed her clusters of ripened olives to nibble on. She remembered swinging from the long branches and using them for hammocks with a canopy of overgrown branches covering her. Truth be told, she missed her family. She had, in essence, traded them for a different kind—one of quirky men and dedicated women. Miriam loved both families, but knew that her new one, for now, replaced the old.

Afternoon shadows decorated the small grove. Walking in and out of them, Yeshua stopped in the shade of what appeared to be the largest tree planted squarely in the middle. The men each leaned against the centuries old trees. The women sat down for a brief rest. At that moment, Miriam seized the opportunity to approach Him.

"Yeshua, did you know that Oreb was in the crowd that day?"

He nodded. "His heart has been clouded by a Spirit of Rebellion."

"I realized that when I spoke to him," Miriam said. "I tried to make him see that, but he refused... and was even offended."

"Love doesn't force someone to choose the right direction. It can only present the opportunity and point the way. Everyone must choose for himself."

"His life has led him to love money and entertainment more than anything, it seems," she said.

"Evil infiltrates two ways. For Oreb it was through choice. He chose to leave his father and squander his inheritance."

"What's the other?"

"Circumstances," Yeshua answered. "Wounds bring a person to the presence of evil, but lies keep them enslaved."

Miriam nodded, thinking of her own past. Those two factors seemed to go hand in hand like tithes and offerings. As if reading her thoughts, He elaborated on this point.

"Choice and circumstance are often linked. The physical abuse you encountered as a child opened the door for the seven spirits; they were not a result of *your* sin. The nomad's choices—his sinful behavior—created the circumstance for your wounds."

This was only the second time that her past had been mentioned, the first being the day He had set her free. Miriam was not uncomfortable talking about it, truth be told. Part of her, in fact, had secretly desired to hear His thoughts. So she stood solemn and focused.

"Agreeing with the spirits and the lies they preached led to bondage," Yeshua continued. "You partnered with them when you took their word as truth, and that gave them power over you."

She didn't like to think of herself as partnering with evil. Though her spirit understood, her flesh bristled. "But I didn't know," Miriam replied. "I was so young, and I didn't know what was happening to me."

"True, Miriam, but the enemy of your soul does not care how he gains access, as long as he gains it—to steal, to kill and to destroy."

Reflecting, she said, "It wasn't fair."

"No, it wasn't."

"I didn't know what to do."

"By covering up the nomad's sin you chose to hide the truth. You chose not to seek Him who is higher and mightier. You chose to run from Yahweh instead of running toward Him."

His words were truth and they were light; her eyes moistened at the sound of them. Flashbacks of her proclamations served as reminders. *I don't want Yahweh's protection; I can't stand living by the law anymore.* A tinge of painful remorse rippled through her body. How could she have been so foolish to say those things? What had she been thinking? Miriam now knew whom she'd been listening to, and she hated the memories. Would they ever go away?

I did. I ran from good toward evil.

Yeshua placed His hand on her arm. Peace flooded her body, her mind. Miriam took a slow, deep breath, letting His *shâlôm*, or peace, penetrate her. She couldn't help but soak in the beauty around them, the bouquet of ripening olives filling her senses. Intuitively, she knew that the trip through the olive grove was intentional—planned out in true characteristic form. His motives were never devoid of purpose. *Not unlike the seven spirits,* she thought. *But His never have to be questioned or challenged.*

A warm wind blew through the grove. Miriam's gaze, following the flight of a nearby bird, landed back on Yeshua. Realizing that He had been watching her, she smiled with a touch of embarrassment and timidity. It was strange, she thought, to have someone who always listened to the thoughts and the intents of her heart.

"Of course you are right. I did run from Yahweh. I guess I didn't believe that running toward Him would help me. I'm not quite sure, exactly, what I believed," Miriam confessed.

"Them. You believed them," He replied gently. "And all of the lies that flowed from their lips. Wide is the gate and broad is the way that leads to destruction, and there are many who go in by it."

I was walking in such darkness. I was so deceived.

With tenderness Yeshua explained, "The more that you chose to believe the lies and deception, the more access and power the spirits had over you."

Miriam nodded her head.

"Giving them attention and interacting with them encouraged their presence as well as their stamina. Like feeding a fire until it becomes all consuming."

How sad, she thought. *And how easy it is to end up that way... for people like me to be sucked into such affliction unknowingly.*

"Unclean spirits are not a respecter of persons. They are ruthless—in mission, in practice, in determination. *Complete evil.*"

"I am glad to be rid of them forever," she answered with disgust.

"Don't be fooled. At any point the spirits are ready to re-enter your life and to bring more destruction. But you now hold the keys to your freedom. *Deny them entrance.* Otherwise, once they have been given a foothold in the doorway they occupy every room in your house," He explained.

"How do I do that?"

"After you have identified their presence, refuse to partner with them. Resist the spirits and they will flee from you, back to the kingdom of darkness. And worship Yahweh aloud," He said with a mischievous smile. "They hate hearing His name glorified."

Miriam thanked her infallible friend, who was continually sought after and descended upon, for taking the time to teach her spiritual lessons. Traditionally, only the disciples would be privy to the one-on-one teachings.

He spoke with tender conclusiveness. "My people perish from a lack of knowledge. Knowledge brings power, and power brings the ability to see beyond the natural."

With His words she could feel herself ripening in spirit like the olives on the swaying branches. Green ones were finally giving way to brown and black. And all the varying shades in between displayed the maturation process—a beautiful illustration of Yahweh's refining methods.

She could not have known that His reasons for cultivating her soul and her mind were, in fact, preparation for latter ministry. They looked at one another for a long moment, their eyes exchanging expressions of love. At that point James approached them, and Miriam turned toward the group of women.

Susanna and Joanna were sitting with others who had followed along that day—Salome, and the mothers of James and the Zebedees. On a brown wool blanket sat some dried figs and honey, olive bread, apples, sweet dates, and a small wineskin of diluted wine. Eating slowly and leisurely, the women fellowshipped with one another while talking and resting.

Miriam sat down and stretched out with her legs crossed. Tiny beads of sweat formed on her upper lip and beneath her arms and on her lower back, moistening their surfaces; only the occasional breezes of late summer wiped them away. As she hummed, her delicate voice filled the space around them and carried through the grove. Miriam didn't even notice that everyone—Yeshua, the disciples, the women—all halted their conversations to listen. The music flowing from her spirit captured every heart and pulled heaven to earth.

15

MIRIAM, JOANNA, AND SUSANNA waited one day, a cold overcast sky hanging over them like a *talīyt*, or prayer shawl, for Yeshua and the twelve to return. Not long after dawn they had journeyed, at His request, across the Sea of Galilee to the area of the Gerasenes. When they arrived back in Capernaum some eight hours later, the men were all a-chatter about storms and pigs.

"I couldn't believe it when they all ran off the cliff into the lake," Thomas said. "Thought the herdsman was going to push us off too, he was so mad."

Joanna jumped right in to their conversation. "Who?"

"The pigs," replied Philip.

"The what?"

"A herd of swine," he said.

"A legion, you mean," Thomas answered.

"See what happens when men go to degenerate Greek towns for the day," Susanna said to Miriam. "They come back lunatics."

"Peter, what happened?" Joanna asked.

"When we got to the other side—after almost dying in a storm, I might add—a naked, wild man came running toward us, shrieking and screaming."

Susanna smirked and nodded as if to say, *See?*

"He had so many demons that they called themselves 'legion'. They kept begging Yeshua to spare them—to send them into the herd of pigs nearby instead of everlasting torment."

"At least you had only seven," Susanna whispered to Miriam.

"You could see Him debating," Philip added.

"But He did it. He sent them into the pigs—" Peter said.

"Who ran squealing and grunting down the steep hill and plunged into the lake!" exclaimed Philip.

Miriam's eyes—and Susanna and Joanna's—were as big as full moons, mouths agape and stunned into silence. Who had ever heard of such an outrageous occurrence? To them it sounded more absurd than Balaam's talking donkey.

"It happened so fast," Philip continued, "and the herdsmen who saw the whole thing took off running into town, petrified."

"And the wild, naked man?" Susanna asked.

"Sat quietly at Yeshua's feet, completely sane and in his right mind."

Miriam smiled, knowing how dynamic the change had been for that man. One minute to the next, moving from torment to freedom, from chaos to peace. Only those afflicted with such agony could taste liberty sweeter than the richest honey.

"Then the herdsmen came back, along with the entire city, shocked at the deranged man now sane, afraid of Yeshua, and furious about the loss of the pigs!" Philip said. "They told us to go away and not return."

"I've never seen people so terrified," Thomas added. "They couldn't wait to get rid of us."

"But the man, he wanted to leave with us—begged us to take him, in fact," Peter said. "But Yeshua told him to stay and tell everyone in the entire area what had happened."

Miriam thought how thankful she was that Yeshua had allowed her to stay with Him and the disciples. He could have given her the same instructions that He gave the man across the lake. But He didn't, and for that her heart beat stronger for this mysterious man.

By the time Peter, Philip, and Thomas had finished telling the story, a sizeable crowd had gathered around Yeshua. Unlike the Greek Gerasenes, these local men and women received Him with open arms. When Miriam moved closer to Him she saw Jairus, the leader of Beth El synagogue, on his knees in front of Him. He was begging for help.

"Please! You must come! My daughter is about to die... she's so young... only twelve. Please come and place your hands on her; heal her so she can live!"

Full of compassion, Yeshua agreed, and they started for his house. The crowd, eager to witness another miracle, pressed in around Him with an intensity that reminded Miriam of olives being crushed at the mill. Miriam noticed a woman about the age of her mother move through the crowd until she was close enough to touch Him. Black circles rimmed her eyes and wisps of hair swung in front of her face. She was so thin Miriam could see her bones under her skin, which was as ashen as a corpse. Miriam knew that look of death, for she had worn it herself just months before. From behind Yeshua the woman stretched out her bony hand and embraced His garment, fingering the fringe that hung on the edges. Instantly, the woman sucked in her breath, and her eyes flickered a shock. She let go and stopped walking while the crowd continued forward. A second later Yeshua also stopped.

"Who touched Me?" He said.

Miriam looked from Yeshua to the woman but held her tongue. He looked at the faces surrounding Him, but didn't find the answer. The disciples looked at Him in utter confusion.

"Master, the whole crowd is pressing up against you," Peter said, as if Yeshua hadn't noticed.

"Someone deliberately touched Me, for I felt healing power go out from Me."

Making her way toward Him, the woman said, "I did." Trembling with fright and freedom, she fell at His feet. The jolt of healing still pulsed through her blood.

"It was I who touched you," she began, her voice quavering. "For more than twelve years I have been bleeding—a curse that has followed me day and night. I have spent all my money visiting every doctor in this region, but not a single one could cure me." She kept her eyes down while talking to Yeshua, as if explaining herself to His sandals. "I had given up hope completely and resigned to die... to slowly bleed to death. But then I heard rumors... about You, about people getting healed... and I knew I had to try."

Her long, bony fingers danced around her lap while she talked, as if replaying the moment they connected with the fringe. The crowd was strangely quiet, focused on her every word.

"As soon as I touched your garment I felt a rush of heat through my body, and the bleeding stopped. It happened before I blinked my eyes," she said. "No more blood, no more pain..."

"Daughter, your faith has made you well. Go in peace."

She looked up into His eyes and smiled. He met hers with unparalleled kindness, and she laughed in gratitude. Silently, Miriam rejoiced with this woman of suffering, who now radiated joy and sheer delight. Words, she knew, could scarcely describe the feeling.

At that moment, a messenger from Jairus' house arrived, forlorn and afraid. "There is no reason to trouble the Teacher now," he said. "Your daughter has died."

Sounds of sympathy moved through the crowd. But before Jairus could fall to the ground and bury his face in the dirt with agony, Yeshua addressed him.

"Do not be afraid; only believe, and she will be made well."

The crowd, led by Yeshua and the disciples, headed for the synagogue leader's house, where his deceased daughter waited. Miriam could feel the Spirit of Death in the atmosphere, showing its ugly face to the young and old alike. Thankfully, the woman had been set free from it before it was too late, but Miriam ached for Jairus that his daughter had not escaped. She wondered, as did everyone else in the crowd, what Yeshua had in mind as He walked with assurance toward the girl of twelve.

While the people moved on, Miriam stayed behind and approached the woman who had just been healed. She kneeled in the dirt with hands cupped together in thanksgiving toward heaven. Miriam could almost see her praises ascend like vapors at the hot springs. She knelt down beside the woman, touching her arm with tenderness.

"I never thought this would happen," the woman said. One tear, then two fell down her cheeks. Laughing and crying, she allowed her emotions to alternate back and forth the same way yarn shuttles on a loom. The frail woman—overwhelmed by the enormity of her miracle—leaned on Miriam, burying her head against the shoulder of a stranger.

Miriam wrapped her arms around the older woman. "You have been set free. It truly is a miracle of Yahweh."

"I thought I was going to die," she said hoarsely. "I could feel that death was near. And if I hadn't found Him..."

"Certainly the Spirit of Death was at your side—today and for many years."

"Yes," she said. Suddenly she sat upright and looked Miriam in the eyes.

"It won't come back? The bleeding? The presence?"

"No, it won't," Miriam reassured her.

"How are you certain?"

"I too was tormented by the Spirit of Death for many years. Like you, Yeshua set me free from affliction. I walk in freedom now."

"Are you one of His followers?"

"Yes, my name is Miriam of Magdala."

The woman smiled. "I am Sarah." Her gray hair, once a beautiful brown Miriam guessed, emerged from her head covering; her brown eyes flecked with bits of blue started coming alive.

"Sarah," Miriam said, "Death no longer has a hold on you."

She shook her head in amazement. "I can't believe that I am well... after so many years. I thought there was no answer, no cure."

"You believed lies from the Spirit of Death," Miriam explained.

"I believed I would always be sick and that hope was useless..."

"More lies."

"I just can't believe it," said Sarah.

"You must believe truth over lies. You must believe that Yahweh has healed you and blessed you with new life. You must believe that you will never have the issue of blood again. Truth brings freedom, Sarah. You have been given the Spirit of Life—hold onto that!"

Sarah grabbed Miriam's hands as if they had been lifelong friends. They exchanged tender smiles, awed by the wonderful works of grace.

"Thank you," Sarah said. "For your kindness and wisdom."

"Yahweh is with you. Go now and live in perfect health and peace. Declare the glory of the Lord to this generation and His mighty miracles to all who come after you."

The two women stood together and embraced. Like Abraham and Lot, Miriam and Sarah then parted ways. And Miriam watched her run—for the first time in twelve years.

While still in Capernaum, Miriam and Joanna and Susanna faithfully served Yeshua and the disciples, who faithfully served the hungry, the sick, and the oppressed. She felt, truth be told, more content and fulfilled than a child with a full belly. Miriam had traded her family for the opportunity to follow the person whom she considered to be the Messiah of Israel. As difficult as that had been, she knew with certainty she was being led and used of Yahweh.

These thoughts lingered in her mind one morning as Yeshua ministered to the people in that town. He had just finished laying His hands on and blessing a group of children who had been brought by their mothers. Though the disciples thought the children a nuisance, Yeshua embraced them with love and joy. He spoke to them and then laughed with them—the mirthful laughter of babes. It was the sweetest sound Miriam had ever heard.

No sooner had He finished than a young man—a religious leader by dress—approached Yeshua with focused intention. The man looked familiar to Miriam, but she couldn't remember where she'd seen him before. As soon as he spoke, however, all confusion vanished.

"Good Teacher," he said, "what should I do to get eternal life?"

Lemuel! It was Lemuel! Miriam couldn't believe her old childhood friend stood before her eyes, looking so different from her memories. All of his features had shed their soft edges. He seemed more refined, more chiseled now. Her heart began racing. She had more butterflies than Queen Esther had before approaching King Ahasuerus unannounced. Miriam tried to quiet her insides to hear what he was saying.

"Why do you call Me good?" Yeshua asked him. "Only Yahweh is truly good. But as for your question, you know the commandments: 'Do not commit adultery. Do not murder. Do not steal. Do not testify falsely. Honor you father and mother.'"

Lemuel replied, "I've obeyed all these commandments since I was a child."

Miriam looked from one to another, not missing a word. She could feel Lemuel's sincerity and Yeshua's genuine love for her friend as He looked at him.

"There is still one thing you lack," Yeshua said. "Sell all you have and give the money to the poor, and you will have treasure in heaven. Then come, follow Me."

Miriam's eyes grew wide. Yeshua had just invited Lemuel to join them. Their lives would be reunited, their friendship restored. It felt to Miriam that time stood still as she watched his face. But when Yeshua's words moved from Lemuel's ears to his heart, sinking in like olive oil on fresh bread, he became visibly sad. He then turned and slowly walked away.

Yeshua watched him go, and then said to His disciples, "How hard it is for a rich person to get into the kingdom of heaven! It is easier for a camel to go through the eye of a needle than for a rich person to enter the kingdom of heaven!"

"Then who in the world can be saved?" they asked.

He replied, "The things which are impossible with men are possible with Yahweh."

The disciples and Yeshua continued their conversation, but Miriam couldn't take her eyes off Lemuel. She could scarcely believe that he was now a wealthy religious leader much less that he had rejected Yeshua's invitation. Why had he left his father's pottery business? How long had he lived in Capernaum? Had he even noticed her there? Miriam's head spun with unanswered questions faster than the wheel in Ezekiel's vision. Standing nearby, Susanna and Joanna watched her as she watched Lemuel gradually disappear into town.

"Miriam, why are you staring at him?" Joanna asked.

"I know him."

"You do?" Joanna said. "Who is he?"

"His name is Lemuel. We grew up together in Magdala. He was one of my closest childhood friends."

"He's the best looking man in Galilee," Susanna commented.

"I was suppose to marry him," Miriam retorted.

"What!" Susanna replied.

"My father had arranged it. But I didn't want to, so I ran away."

"Foolish, foolish," said Susanna.

"Maybe you still can," Joanna said, as she looked at Miriam who still hadn't taken her eyes off Lemuel.

Miriam smiled but shook her head. She knew her destiny was alongside Yeshua. But she also knew that she needed to sew up some dangling threads. As soon as she began running toward him, Miriam yelled over her shoulder, "I'll be back."

When she caught up to Lemuel, her mouth went completely dry. What should she say? Would he even talk to her? Silently she offered a prayer of petition. *Help me to choose my words, how to reach him.*

She took a deep breath and then said, "Excuse me?"

He stopped, looking up from the ground where his gaze had been fixed, and saw two mismatched eyes staring at him. "Miriam!" he said in a whisper, as if he'd seen someone alive from the dead.

"Lemuel," she said, her voice full of compassion and warmth.

An unexpected presence of love seemed to wrap around her. Miriam looked at him as if seeing him for the first time. His straight, dark hair and crystal blue eyes, his long eyelashes and his ruddy cheeks. She felt surges of magnetism, one right after the others like the persistent waves of Galilee's sea. How had she seen him through a friend's eyes only? Unprepared for these sensations, her cheeks sprouted roses of color in hues of pink and red.

"What are you doing here?"

"I just saw you talking to Yeshua." He looked at her in confusion. "I have joined them—Yeshua and His disciples."

"What?" he replied. "When?"

"Only recently. He healed me, Lemuel. He delivered me and restored me!"

He paused, soaking up her words. "From what?"

"Seven unclean spirits."

"What?" he said again, incredulous.

"Do you remember the summer when your father helped my father fix the courtyard well?"

"Yes."

"Well, I was attacked that summer. By a nomad, late one night upon the hill. He tried to..." she said, not finishing. "He basically made me unclean."

She could see his eyes begin to moisten. Maybe his feelings and emotions were not as hardened as they appeared.

"He left me tainted, but also with seven evil spirits."

"I don't understand..."

Miriam nodded. "Fear, Rejection, Bitterness, Rebellion, Lust, Pride, Death."

He raised his eyebrows, unsure of how to respond.

"When we had our last conversation on the rooftop, I was operating under the influence of the Spirit of Rejection. I was irrational and convinced that everyone was against me. It consumed me, Lemuel, they all did."

"How?" he asked cautiously.

"With lies. They attacked me day and night with lies and evil thoughts. They tormented my mind and sometimes by body."

He stared at her, processing everything—their sudden reunion, her strange story.

"But one day Yahweh had mercy on me, and Yeshua set me free."

"Did He?" Lemuel replied. "How?"

"By rebuking the unclean spirits and forbidding them to return. Then He gave me truth and peace and a sound mind. It was like waking up from a dream, Lemuel. Suddenly, after ten years, I could think clearly. The harassment was gone. The voices were gone. I had been given a miracle."

After a moment he said, "I... I don't know what to say."

"I know. It probably seems that I'm weaving a story, but I'm telling you the truth."

"You did seem so erratic on that rooftop... not yourself..."

Miriam nodded.

"And then you just disappeared one day."

"I know."

"Your father had arranged our marriage, Miriam," he said with a measure of resentment.

She lowered her eyes, feeling his hurt and confusion.

"I was so happy that day. I knew something was wrong with you, but I figured that once we married everything would be all right."

"I know that I hurt you deeply," she said. "Lemuel, will you please forgive me?"

After a handful of moments that seemed to last longer than a gradual sunset, he answered her. "I would be an unjust religious leader if I withheld my forgiveness from you when I demand others to forgive."

Miriam looked up and softly smiled. "Did you marry?"

"How could I?" he answered. "It wouldn't be fair to my wife to always harbor feelings for you."

His eyes took on the same look they used to when children, which is to say, unveiled adoration. Truth be told, they both felt compelled to embrace, to melt away the years of pain and misunderstanding. But propriety held them back—a promise for another time, perhaps. They smiled, however, at one another they way only two people with an intricate history can.

Lemuel's voice then took on a tone of soft sadness. "I waited for you to come back, Miriam. For three years I waited. By then I knew you weren't coming home."

Miriam sighed deeply, picturing him watching Magdala's horizon for sight of her. While he was kept waiting, she pursued life of a different kind in Tiberias. Neither of them imagined that their paths would ever cross again.

"But now you're here," he said. "In Capernaum."

"How long have you been here, Lemuel?" Miriam asked, looking at his religious attire.

"After those three years I couldn't wait for you anymore. And I couldn't stay in Magdala. Every face, every part of town reminded me of you. So I decided to come here. To start a new life."

"You gave up your father's business?"

"Yes. They were disappointed, but they understood. Deep down, Miriam, I had always felt a strong connection with Yahweh. It was an open door for me to make a living tending to His people."

"A good living, I can see," she said, noticing his fine linens and sandals.

"Yes, I have become far wealthier here than I ever could have in Magdala. And I have to say, it has been an enormous consolation to me."

"Does it make you happy?"

He sighed. "I have worked hard for many years, earning the respect and support of the religious leaders and teachers in this town. They value me highly. They look to me for many answers."

Miriam could feel a familiar presence. In an instant she could hear the distinguishing tone of the Spirit of Pride. She winced, not wanting to believe it had found her friend also.

"Lemuel, truly you have been a righteous man, serving the Lord. You have kept all of Yahweh's commandments, as you said. But can't you see that pride is keeping you in pursuit of earning more?"

He looked at her quizzically. "What are you saying?"

"Back there, Yeshua told you to sell everything you own and give it to the poor. And then to follow Him. But your face showed huge disappointment."

"I can't, Miriam. I can't sell it all. I have poured myself into this life, working very hard to earn a sound reputation. I earned my wealth honestly. My possessions are all I have."

"But don't you see? They have *you*! Don't give in to the Spirit of Pride's lies—"

"I am *not* possessed by an unclean spirit, Miriam!" he said, cutting her off.

Rebuffed, she replied, "No, Lemuel, I didn't say that. I don't believe that you are. I do believe, though, that arrogance has you extremely proud of your wealth."

"There's nothing wrong with that," he said defensively.

"When it takes up prominence in your heart, there is. Even Yeshua—a discerning man of Yahweh—determined where your heart lies, which is why He told you to give it away. You came to Him, seeking an answer to your heart's question."

"I didn't like His answer."

"Resist pride, Lemuel," Miriam urged. "It's force is strong yet subtle. Remember that it caused even Yahweh's most beautiful angel to fall."

Lemuel looked at her with surprise. Not too long ago he had used that same analogy on a local businessman at the synagogue. Never had he thought of himself as vulnerable to the Spirit of Pride. She could see his countenance softening like fallow ground saturated by rain.

"Resist pride," she said again. "Don't let who you are or what you own be the most important things in life. I can tell you from my unpleasant experience with the Spirit of Pride that it is powerful and all consuming. It has a way of blinding you to the truth and making you disagreeable."

He watched her, amazed at her calm assurance, her strong conviction. She had become, in his eyes, a woman outgrown of her youthful confinements. Her beauty had not diminished over the years but had, in fact, become more elegant and cultivated. He felt an inherent duel nature—both calm and strong—in her eyes.

"Your importance lies in who Yahweh says you are, not what man does. Yahweh gives grace to the humble, but He resists the proud. If He resists pride, Lemuel, then you should too."

He thought for a while, the space between them growing more and more charged. He exhaled slowly, the weight of his future resting in the next few words. She could sense the Spirit of Pride whispering seductive lies in his ear.

"I'm sorry, Miriam. I just can't. I won't give up everything. Not now. Not after all that's happened."

She felt her heart squeeze with an aching pain. Truth be told, she had let her mind imagine Lemuel giving his possessions to the poor and following Yeshua. The thought of him traveling throughout Galilee ministering to the needy alongside them had caused her heart to dance around in her chest. But now she felt only defeat and disappointment. Here they would leave their friendship. Here they would part ways once again.

"Maybe one day, then," she answered. She looked into the heavens and then back at him. "It was good to see you again, Lemuel." Miriam touched his arm tenderly, both of them feeling a surge of heat at the connection.

"Are you going back?" he asked, referring to the followers of Yeshua.

"Yes. My place is with them."

He sighed deeply. "Goodbye then, Miriam."

"Goodbye, Lemuel."

Their eyes held onto one another a few moments longer, expressing what their bodies could not. Miriam let Lemuel walk away first—she couldn't commit the same mistake twice. As he moved toward the lavish synagogue, she prayed. *Yahweh, open his eyes to see the Spirit of Pride pursuing him. Bless him to make the right decision for his life. Bless him with the knowledge and conviction to honor You.*

She then turned her face toward the west, to resume her position next to Yeshua. As she walked back, her thoughts galloping faster than a team of horses, she realized that Yahweh had set up the two encounters with Sarah and Lemuel. Miriam had come face to face with the Spirit of Death and the Spirit of Pride once again, though from a different position. Now she was able to discern them. Now she was able to guide others—her friends and strangers alike—away from lies and toward truth. Each would have to make a choice in the end, but she had the opportunity to minister from her place of victory. What she had freely been given, she would now freely give.

16

ONE SABBATH DAY, Yeshua and the twelve disciples camped out at the synagogue known as Beth Kiddush. From early morning they had been inside praying and fellowshipping. A steady stream of men and women drifted in and out like wispy clouds under the temperate influence of wind. Yeshua began teaching on the kingdom of heaven—His favorite, and just about only, topic, to tell the truth.

Miriam, Joanna, and Susanna sat listening and watching that morning. They too were wrapped up in the glories of resting on the Sabbath, quieting their minds, feeding their souls. They had been there for a few hours, but the time seemed to pass more quickly than sand shifts in the desert.

Just before the noon hour an old woman shuffled in slowly, one foot sliding in front of the other as she made her way into the sanctuary. Her long white hair was braided neatly under her head covering. Her face looked drier than the wilderness of Judea, its brown skin covered with deep lines and grooves in crisscross fashion. She walked with a cane, bent over at the waist with a large hump sitting atop her back like a child perched on a pillow. Crippled, she made her way to the offering box with coins in hand, ready to make her deposit. To Miriam, she looked as if she was locked in a position of pain. She couldn't take her eyes off the woman. The sound of her sandals scraping against the floor seemed to groan in agony while her lips remained silent.

When Yeshua noticed her, He stopped His discourse. Miriam recognized the look He gave the woman, for it was the same sort He had given to her the day her demons fled. There was an unmistakable twinkle in His eye. Miriam knew that Yeshua had seen into the woman's heart, into her soul. She smiled as she sensed His compassion fill the synagogue.

"Woman," He said gently, "come here."

She looked at Him from the tops of her eyes, her head unable to lift itself upright. He nodded in response to her unspoken question—*Me?*—that seemed to hold as much meaning as a psalm of *Âçâph*, Asaph. Gradually, she made her way over to Him, the attention of everyone resting on her. A distended pause filled the air, and then Yeshua broke out in a huge smile.

"Woman, you are loosed from your infirmity."

The same way a mother knows when her child has lied, He knew the old woman had been living under the oppression of an evil spirit. Yeshua laid His hands on her, one touching her back, the other touching her head. Immediately, the bones in her back rippled with noise, cracking and popping, and then she stood up straight! The woman yelped in surprise. The crowd gasped.

"I can stand up! I can stand up!"

Sounds of astonishment and wonder leapt from her mouth as she stood straighter than she ever had. She began shouting and praising and thanking Yahweh, tears springing from her eyes in unexpected joy. Applause gushed from around the room, enlarging her rather robust display of gratitude even more. Her cane hit the floor with a thud after she raised her hands to heaven. She waved her arms; she jumped and clapped; she gloried in her healing and deliverance!

Miriam clapped and praised Yahweh as well. Truth be told, she felt as if her heart couldn't hold all the goodness that Yeshua delivered. But while the majority of the people rejoiced with the old woman, the synagogue rulers—the leader in particular—did not.

"There are six days of the week for working," he said to the crowd. "Come on those days to be healed, not on the Sabbath." The synagogue leader's indignation for Yeshua healing the woman on this day of rest rang louder than the noon bells.

But He replied, "You hypocrite! You work on the Sabbath day! Don't you untie your ox or your donkey from their stalls on the Sabbath and lead them out for water? Wasn't it necessary for me, even on the Sabbath day, to free this woman, a daughter of Abraham, from the bondage in which Satan has held her for eighteen years?"

Miriam expected the leader to offer a retort, to defend his authority.

But to her surprise and satisfaction, he said nothing. Yeshua's words had put His adversaries to shame, shutting down their lofty expositions, discrediting their stances. A second eruption of applause filled the sanctuary. The multitude rejoiced for all the glorious things that had been done by Yeshua. An atmosphere of praise, as electric as lightning, flooded each heart and every corner of the synagogue. Miriam could sense the fiery and glorious presence of angels. She closed her eyes and imagined feeling the wind from their wings caressing her face. Surely the kingdom of heaven was at hand.

When the crowd quieted down again, Miriam and others went over to the former cripple, offering their personal sentiments. Embraces and smiles enveloped her, and the woman accepted them all like gifts given a queen. She exulted in the commendations and the miracle that had changed her life. Miriam waited for the opportunity to talk with her once the overjoyed group dissipated. Susanna and Joanna joined her.

"The Lord be praised!" Miriam said. "He has healed you!"

"Blessed be the name of the Lord!" the woman answered. "It's a miracle!"

"An amazing miracle from heaven!"

"I was just coming to the synagogue to offer my tithe this morning... and then I heard Him call me."

"What is your name?" Miriam asked.

"Tirzah," she answered.

"He saw into you, Tirzah. Yeshua perceived your oppression, desiring to deliver you."

"Eighteen years!" she exclaimed. "For eighteen years I have been bent over, unable to move freely."

"How did it happen?" Joanna asked.

"It started after my husband divorced me. He had grown tired of me and found another to fulfill his happiness. I reminded him that Mosaic law forbade divorce unless I had been unfaithful, which I had not. So he spun a web of iniquity, and fabricated a story with evidence to support it. I denied everything to the priests, but they always take a man's word over that of his wife. Within days I was branded an adulteress. Worst of all, he poisoned my sons against me in the process." She spoke with a measure of disdain, which Miriam sensed right away as a familiar voice. "Suddenly, I was alone. They no longer spoke to me. They no longer cared."

Susanna shook her head, and Joanna put her hands on her heart to show sympathy. Miriam acknowledged her story and identified with Tirzah, feeling her past pain, her past trauma.

"Not long after that my back started to bend. I thought he had put a curse on me for trying to stop him."

"Tirzah, were you angry at your husband and sons?" Miriam asked.

"Of course I was! They had ruined my life."

"Did you let your anger turn to bitterness?"

Tirzah paused to think, then nodded.

"The evil spirit that afflicted you for eighteen years was a Spirit of Bitterness," Miriam explained.

Tirzah looked at her quizzically. "How do you know? Did the man who healed me tell you that?"

"He didn't have to. I carried around the same spirit for almost a decade."

"Is that true?"

"Yes. Like you, I experienced a terrible event that altered my life. After some time, I turned bitter and allowed the person who hurt me to inflict more pain by withholding my forgiveness." Miriam waited a moment before asking, "Did you ever forgive your husband for divorcing you?"

"No," she said softly, "I did not. I felt that he didn't deserve forgiveness—mine or Yahweh's."

Miriam smiled at the recognizable lies. She didn't want to focus on that today, however, but on freedom instead. Freely the woman had been released from Satan's grip, and likewise she would need to release her husband.

"Tirzah, Yeshua set you free today from a Spirit of Bitterness in your body. Your back has been restored," Miriam said. "Make sure your heart has been too. Don't let bitterness seduce you anymore. Forgive them, forgive them all, and let Yahweh address their sins."

The old woman nodded and the other two did as well. Smiles were passed around like fine wine at a banquet.

"And rejoice!" Miriam said. "The enemy of your soul has been defeated. Tell of all the good things Yahweh has done for you today!"

Laughter erupted among the women and praises to Yahweh again filled the atmosphere. Tirzah then took her hands—a map of past experiences—and cupped Miriam's face. Even fully upright she was shorter than her young advocate. "Daughter," she said, "Thank you for your wisdom. May you be blessed." Miriam grinned. "To Yahweh be the glory."

At that moment, Tirzah began to sing the songs of David, the hymns of the sons of Korah. Arms stretched to heaven, she walked from the dimmed sanctuary into the bright daylight, from living under oppression to living under the banner of freedom. The limitless sky of grace shone over her the same way it had after the great flood, which is to say full of promise and redemption.

Joanna said to Miriam and Susanna, "I love when Yeshua heals the cripples. There's nothing like seeing that kind of miracle with your own two eyes."

"Truly He is the Son of Yahweh," Miriam answered.

"The more we experience His ministry, the more interesting it gets," Susanna added. She noticed the synagogue leaders huddled and whispering in the far corner. "He certainly isn't making friends in the religious community."

"He always does what's right," Miriam said. "The Lord will protect Him."

From the time Yeshua began His ministry in the region of Galilee, every city and village had heard the good news of the kingdom of heaven announced. He moved from town to town, from the seaside to the hills, preaching and teaching and changing the land of the Jews, one encounter at a time. Miriam could hardly believe the miracles that accompanied Him, much less the signs and wonders. They seemed to appear alongside Him just as the hovering cloud and pillar of fire had appeared to the Israelites in the wilderness.

Many seasons had passed and Miriam realized with a measure of surprise that she had been traveling with Yeshua and His followers for more than a year and a half. The events she shared in and the miracles she witnessed far exceeded her loftiest expectations. With every experience, she understood more and more the realities of heaven at her fingertips.

One day, in the afternoon hours of late autumn, a Pharisee of Bethsaida invited Yeshua to dine with him at his house. Yeshua gladly accepted and brought along, as usual, His dedicated pupils. Once they entered Simon the Pharisee's home, the men took their places around the low table for the evening meal. The women—Miriam, Susanna, and Joanna—helped his servants with preparations and cooking. The large house had many rooms arranged in a maze-like form. Miriam knew it served the purpose of impressing everyone who entered, but she thought it a nuisance traveling so far between the areas of cooking and dining. She knew also that this Pharisee carried his own atmosphere governed by unseen spirits—she could feel the power of religiosity hovering throughout the house.

Truth be told, Simon loved to hear himself talk, and Miriam's ears filled with his religious discourse every time she crossed into the room where they ate. She tried to focus her attention on Yeshua and His needs, as well as those of the twelve, instead of listening to the host. As quickly as she came, she left.

"He can talk the jots and tittles off a Torah scroll," Susanna said in the back room.

"I think he's just trying to impress Yeshua with his learned knowledge and stature as a Pharisee," Joanna added.

"We know *that* won't work," Miriam added.

"Do you think he's going to let anyone else talk tonight? Or is it just a conversation for one?" Susanna asked.

"Well, it is his house," Joanna answered. "And we have all entered his arena."

"I don't think I can bear any more talk of Pharisaical law," Miriam said.

"I caught James and Albie dozing off, so I accidentally stepped on his toe," said Susanna with a sly grin. "Wouldn't want him to miss anything."

The women laughed the mirth of cohorts. Their friendship had become as interwoven as the rope *Râchâb*, Rahab, used to lower Joshua's spies in Jericho. When they finished filling the pitchers with water and baking the small loaves of bread, the women went to serve the men. Deep in discussion, they hardly noticed Miriam, Joanna, and Susanna, as they poured water into each cup and dotted the table with baskets of bread and bowls of olives. Only Yeshua gave each woman a silent nod of appreciation.

From the far side of the room a beautiful woman suddenly appeared, carrying a small wooden box. Without a sound she made her way over to Yeshua, hesitant at first but resolved in her mission. Her clothes made of fine linen and her copious jewelry made of precious metals seemed to announce her occupation as much as her presence. An excess of kohl around her eyes and lips stained the color of blood identified her as a woman of ill repute, which is to say, a prostitute. Miriam could feel disdain in the air. The men looked at her with contempt for her livelihood and annoyance at the interruption of their meal.

Within seconds the woman, who looked to Miriam a few years younger than herself, reached Yeshua's side. The emotions she had been holding back suddenly surged out, the weeping causing a prick of tears among the other women. Even before she broke the gift she was carrying, something shattered from deep within her. She all at once collapsed at His feet, as if unable to stand in His presence. With a thud she landed on her knees beside Him, her tears falling on His feet, making lines in the dirt that covered them and running onto the floor. The room was filled with the sounds of her tears only, the strength of repentance echoing from wall to wall. To Miriam it looked like His feet had been washed with water, such were the number of tears that fell. Her long hair that hung freely to her waist served as a towel to clean them. Gently and full of adoration, she wiped them as if she were wiping away her own sin. Though the woman never spoke, Miriam knew she was tormented by unclean spirits, the same as she had been. She remembered the overwhelming feelings and empathized at the sight of stains left by immoral behavior. But more than that, Miriam understood that this woman would not leave His presence unchanged.

After bathing His feet, she began kissing them with the tenderness of a lover. This, of course, made the men at the table—the host in particular—severely uncomfortable. The Pharisee stared at her, and spoke in a low whisper.

"This man, if He were a prophet, would know who and what manner of woman this is who is touching Him. She is a *sinner*!"

When she had covered His feet completely with her caresses, she took the small wooden box and opened it. Inside was an alabaster jar made with the smoothest, milkiest stone. Without warning she broke the jar, and unleashed a fragrance into the house that smelled of priests and royalty. The sight of the alabaster jar and the aroma pouring out of it jolted Miriam—it was the precious fragrant oils that her family sold in Magdala! She started to move toward the woman, but stopped herself. The unmistakable smell reminded her of Zebulun and Hannah, Levi and Benjamin. A flood of emotions rose up in her faster than the waters of the Jordan under a downpour. And she wished once again that her family would embrace Yeshua the way the prostitute did, which is to say, without shame or uncertainty.

Suddenly, Yeshua broke the silence and said to the host, "Simon, I have something to say to you."

And he said, "Teacher, say it."

"There was a certain creditor who had two debtors. One owed five hundred denarii, and the other fifty. And when they had nothing with which to repay, he freely forgave them both. Tell Me, therefore, which of them will love him more?"

Simon answered, "I suppose the one whom he forgave more."

And Yeshua replied, "You have rightly judged." Then He looked at the woman by His feet and said, "Simon, do you see this woman? I entered your house and you gave Me no water for My feet, but she has washed My feet with her tears and wiped them with the hair of her head. You gave Me no kiss, but this woman has not ceased to kiss My feet since the time I came in. You did not anoint My head with oil, but this woman has anointed My feet with fragrant oil. Therefore I say to you, her sins—which are many—are forgiven, for she loved much. But to whom little is forgiven, the same loves little."

Yeshua gazed at the woman with such love that it permeated the room. Gently, He brushed the hair from her face and ran His fingers down the side of her tear-streaked cheeks. The tenderness displayed gripped Miriam's heart, and from the look on their faces, that of His companions as well.

Then He said to her, "Your sins are forgiven."

All at once, the table of men started whispering to themselves and each other. Miriam heard all manner of questions floating around like agitated flies.

"Who can forgive sin besides Yahweh?"

"Who is this man?"

"What authority does He have?"

Ignoring them, Yeshua said to the woman, "Your faith has saved you. Go in peace."

She smiled up at Him, knowing the weight of sin had been lifted from her. No amount of kisses could express her gratitude, her delight, her veneration. She started to gather up the fragmented pieces of alabaster, and Miriam quickly joined her. Truth be told, she loved being close to Yeshua. And while her motives were to help the woman clean the floor, she also selfishly wanted His attention to fall on her too. There was nothing like being caught in the circle of Yeshua's love.

Meanwhile, the conversation among the men picked up, their voices growing, their expressions becoming animated. Miriam followed the woman to the door, where Susanna and Joanna met them with food wrapped in cloth. The three friends looked at the young woman and offered sustenance for her stomach and her soul.

"My name is Miriam," she said to the woman.

"I am called Scarlett," she replied meekly, "But my real name is Bahar."

"Well, Bahar, you are lovely," said Miriam.

The woman lowered her eyes, feeling pangs of shame. "What a gift that He forgave my sins," she said. "I never would have dreamed it possible."

"Yeshua is so gracious, and He wants us to turn from our sins," Joanna answered.

"But mine were so many," Bahar said, thinking of the cluster of men with whom she had shared a bed.

"There are never too many that He cannot forgive," Miriam said.

"Like He said to Simon," Susanna added, "the greater the amount of sin, the greater the amount of forgiveness."

"I was so unsure of what He would do with my gift... of how He would respond to me."

At first, Miriam thought Bahar was living under the influence of the Spirit of Lust, but something inside allowed her to identify a different spirit.

"Where did you get the fragrant oil?" Miriam asked, wondering if she had bought it from one of her brothers or, perhaps, her mother.

She answered, "A man paid me with it a few weeks ago. I think he bought it in Magdala. Said it was worth more than my life."

"Bahar," Miriam said with a smile, "you are unaware of how valuable you are."

Again, the young woman looked down, her eyes unable to meet Miriam's. Her self-reproach spoke louder than the stigma attached to her name.

"You are so young," Miriam said. "How did you end up in this condition?"

Bahar took a deep breath. "My mother died giving birth to me, and my father has despised me ever since. Not only was I not his long awaited son, but I also took his wife from him." She began to cry silent tears. "He always told me that I ruined his life and that I was not worth anything."

Miriam wrapped her arm around Bahar's thin shoulders. "Those were lies," she whispered to her tenderly. "You have believed lies, and they have tormented you."

Bahar's shoulders shook with grief and the memory of so much pain. But Miriam held fast to her, knowing that the root of her identity was at the surface.

"Bahar, a Spirit of Rejection has been escorting you all your life. Your father blamed you, but it was never your fault. He was wrong. And through his cruel lies he ushered in an unclean spirit. You didn't understand that your father's rejection could not be made right in the arms of men, that you would never find your value in them."

She looked up at Miriam then and nodded, "Not once did I ever feel accepted. I tried and I tried, but they all treated me the same in the end. Like the prostitute that I am."

"That you were," Miriam corrected. "Your sins have been forgiven. There is no need to return to that life. You are precious, you are important, and you are beyond any price. Yahweh accepts you! His love has been poured out on you, just the way you poured out the fragrant oil on Yeshua's feet."

"But where am I going to go? What am I going to do now?"

Miriam and Susanna and Joanna looked at one another in wordless agreement. "You can stay with us."

"But I don't have anything to offer."

"Of course you do. You can help gather materials and prepare food."

Bahar smiled, incapable of expressing her gratitude. Truth be told, she was overwhelmed by the unparalleled love shown to her that day. Miriam nodded in return, knowing that Bahar would not stay with the group forever, but would spread her wings to fly in a different direction once she replaced lies with truth. The process of undoing the damage accumulated by the Spirit of Rejection would take time. But just as her sins had been eliminated by Yeshua, so would the lies of the enemy.

"Go and get your things," Miriam said.

Bahar hugged the three women and opened the door. Within a moment she was gone and out into the night.

* * *

During those months, Miriam and Yeshua connected several times in the absence of words. Despite the presence of others, as the sizable group traveled through vineyards or wheat fields or olive groves, eye contact was enough of a communicator between the two of them. Yeshua had the ability to read her eyes, her inflections, her body language like no one else. Just being in His presence satisfied her. No words were necessary. No embraces, no exchanges. Mere fellowship was enough. In those times, Miriam felt that she was truly dwelling in the secret place of the Most High, abiding under the shadow of the Almighty.

She wondered during those days if He could read her thoughts.

There is nothing that I want more than You. There is nothing more that I need. You are the completeness that my soul craves. My surrender to You is all encompassing—there remains no part of me that is withheld. My purpose and destiny can be fulfilled only through You. What else is there besides You? More than anything or anyone else could know me, You do. You never disappoint, go back on Your word, or decrease Your love for me. It's unimaginable. Living without You would equate to living with the seven. Never again.

In the same way, Yeshua rejoiced over Miriam with gladness. He delighted over her with anthems of joy—heavenly, resolute, compelling. And He quieted her with His love. In that quietness and confidence Miriam found her strength. A time of refreshing, that would carry her in future days, had come from being in the presence of the Lord.

17

JUST WHEN LIFE seemed to be perfect for Miriam, everything came to a crashing halt in one day. Two and a half years after their first meeting, Yeshua took her aside from the group of followers early one spring morning. They had been enjoying the beauties of Yahweh's creation among the blossoming hills of Galilee. The scenery boasted a template of color—red, yellow, and white flowers intermingled with vivid green grasses, where goats and sheep grazed in the plush distant fields. He smiled to Himself, but she didn't understand, at that point, that He too was a lamb, lowly and submissive. But His smile quickly disappeared. What He said next bored into her heart and seared on her mind.

"Miriam," He said, "a day is coming when I will give up My life as a sacrifice for mankind, making My soul an offering for sin."

She froze in mid step. Confusion flashed across her face as she felt her heart sink. "I don't understand. What do you mean, 'sacrifice'?"

"This has been the plan all along," said Yeshua. "Just as lambs are used as sacrifices for atonement of the Hebrew people, I am the Lamb that will be the atonement for all of humanity."

"Quit teasing me, Yeshua." She playfully nudged Him with her elbow. Despite the fact that she knew He could not lie, her will and her emotions refused to accept such a fate for this man.

"I honestly would like to be, Miriam," He said. "Trust me; I am always seeking the Father to make sure that there is no other course of action... no other way."

Pausing, they both pondered the implications of His words. After what seemed an interminable amount of time, Miriam broke the silence. "I don't understand, is someone going to tie you up and place you upon the altar?" Images of Abraham and Isaac flashed through her mind.

"Sort of... but it won't be the type of sacrifice that you are accustomed to seeing. It will be worse."

Trying to figure out exactly what Yeshua was saying, Miriam probed further. "What other type of sacrifice is there? What could be worse than dying by the knife upon an altar?"

"Crucifixion."

"What?! You mean to tell me that you are going to voluntarily allow yourself to be killed in the name of atonement?"

"Yes."

"*Crucified?*"

"Yes."

"Have you gone insane?" She started shaking; her eyes darted all over. "You must not be feeling well... you're not making any sense."

Yeshua paused and uttered a brief prayer under His breath. He then presented the entire plan out before her like a map showing the route from Egypt to Israel.

"As you know, Miriam, there must be atonement for sin, it is the ordained way that began through Moses. The Torah says, 'For the life of the flesh is in the blood, and I have given it to you upon the altar to make atonement for your souls; for it is the blood that makes atonement for the soul.' However, that sacrificial system will be used no longer, for I am to replace it—one time, for all eternity. Blood must be spilled for atonement, and I am offering mine so that every man can possess atonement, whether a Hebrew or not."

Yeshua waited a moment to confirm that she was following along. "Just as the prophets in the Scriptures foretold of My arrival and ministry, they foretell of My sacrificial death. So really, this is no secret."

Miriam was stricken, unable to move from her state of shock. She squinted her eyes to concentrate on His words, which made little sense. What was He talking about? How could a sacrificial death be possible? Her skin drained itself of color and her lips pressed together with visible tension.

"The events will happen rather quickly, though they will be agonizing. I will be despised, hated without a cause, rejected, and sentenced to crucifixion by Hebrews and Romans—rulers and ordinary men alike—though *all* of them know not what they are about to do." He paused, inhaling deeply.

"Mankind will esteem Me as stricken by Yahweh, and afflicted, thus giving merit to their cry for My death. But, in fact, the opposite is true: I will be wounded and pierced for their transgressions, I will be bruised and crushed for their iniquities; the chastisement for their peace will be upon Me, and by My stripes they will be healed," He said. The words confirmed the ancient prophesy of Isaiah.

"But that shall not be the end, Miriam," He reassured her. "I have work to do even during the time of my physical death—to ransom people from the power of the grave, redeeming them from death— and I will return after conquering the grave, so that this work of my Father will be complete through Me." Yeshua let some moments pass before adding, "Just remember, no man takes My life—I give it up freely."

When she realized that He was finished, she looked deeply into His eyes, and knew with clear finality that He was not goading her. The world suddenly seemed unsteady, and she did not even bother to stop the tears that broke forth as His words pierced her heart. Miriam was devastated by this news from her friend. She wanted to be sick and scream at the same time. Dread gripped her and adrenaline threw the beating of her heart into overdrive. Her words emerged rapidly, shaky, and incredulous.

"This cannot happen," she cried.

"It *must* happen," He replied tenderly.

"I'm going to lose you?" She couldn't imagine what was worse: having just been informed that her reason for living had been killed or knowing that death was impending. Either way it was too much to grasp.

"My sacrifice will be the best thing that has ever occurred on the face of this earth. Everything else has been simply leading up to this point. It just gets better from here! When I pour out My soul unto death, you and every man, woman, and child will be able to access the heavenly throne of grace—so you can come boldly, Miriam, to obtain mercy and find grace in time of need."

Yeshua's heart gushed love and compassion. He said, "Miriam, I know that this is painful and difficult for you to understand, but I have come to make all things new for mankind, just as I did for you many years ago. Despite how you feel now, you will rejoice one day soon, remembering this day."

Miriam knew that she couldn't fight Him. She understood that He was explaining prophetic events, yet she refused to accept what it truly meant. Nothing would ever be the same. She was about to lose the best thing in her life—the person who knew her past and future, the person who enjoyed her company, the person who understood her emotions, the person who loved her beyond words, the person who loved to make her laugh.

Life will never be the same, she thought. *I should be grateful that I knew Him for a few years... I am grateful... but I'm hungry for more. What am I going to do without Him? He's all that I have now...*

She pulled her mind back to Him. "How long?"

"Not long."

She looked at Him expectantly.

"The spring feast," He finally answered.

Before she was able to utter the words that had formed on her lips, He nodded His head. With His eyes of love, He confirmed the brevity of time that they shared on earth together. Passover was a mere two weeks away.

18

THE TIME HAD arrived and Yeshua set His face to go to Jerusalem. His disciples and faithful supporters joined Him on the long three-day journey to the City of David. Though He had foretold them of the events awaiting Him there, only Miriam seemed more focused on the foreboding factors than on the festive celebration of Passover.

With its combination of the old generations and the foreign Roman control, Jerusalem contained the past, present, and future. Behind the high city walls, peoples and tribes from the north, south, east, and west collected densely to make the ancient city of Yahweh a coat of many colors. Narrow, hilly stone streets with marketplaces and prevailing Roman palaces with modern feats pushed against one another, each trying to proclaim their importance to the history and the makeup of the world renowned city. It was cosmopolitan yet aged, innovative yet traditional. So many fervent ideologies and philosophies intermingled inside the towering walls, creating a setting that challenged the possibility of peace. It was a place of chronicles, a place of hostility, and a place of destiny.

Jerusalem had a different feel to Miriam. It shared commonalities with the Galilean cities of Magdala and Tiberias, such as the golden-toned limestone homes and buildings; the crowded marketplaces brimming with voices, merchandise, and aromas; and the devout religious families carrying on with their traditions. But something unidentifiable about this city in particular stood out in her mind. Maybe it was the sounds of uneasiness and the tension that seemed to ooze from everyone, teetering on the edge of violence. Maybe it was the smells that accompanied the organism of a larger city. Maybe it was the sight of the enormous Temple that centralized the focus of activities for the week. Or maybe it was simply because the city represented the end of the remarkable life of following alongside Yeshua's footsteps. Regardless, Miriam did not share in the others' excitement to be in the holy city for Passover.

* * *

Early morning on the fourth day after entering Jerusalem, Yeshua made His way amid the soft air of dawn from the Mount of Olives to the Temple. Overhead the sky hung low with rain clouds, though they had not yet begun to drop their moisture. He began praying, or to tell the truth, talking to Yahweh like a trusted friend. It wasn't long before a crowd of worshippers—religious leaders and common folk alike—gathered there. Seeing an opportunity to teach on the kingdom of Yahweh, Yeshua sat down among the crowd and gave the spiritually hungry a feast.

A few minutes later Miriam heard a commotion to the west. She looked over to identify the noise—muffled yet fervent—but couldn't find the source. She then noticed a cluster of five men walking toward the Temple at a hurried pace, dragging a woman with them. It was her voice crying out, her pleas filling the space around them that captured Miriam's attention.

"Stop! You can't do this!" she pleaded and pulled against them. "I don't want to die!"

The men spoke harshly to her, yanking harder, then threw her down in front of the crowd. Her long golden hair looked tousled from sleep and her body wore only a small, thin tunic that revealed her equally golden skin. She was shivering from cold, shaking from fear. The sound of her whimpering reminded Miriam of the time she saw a sick dog kicked by a drunken man. Miriam's heart ached with compassion for the woman who clearly had broken the law in some manner. Why else would the Pharisees and religious teachers drag her kicking and protesting to the Temple first thing in the morning? Yeshua stood up and glared at the men.

"Teacher," the oldest Pharisee said to Him, "this woman was caught in the very act of adultery."

Gasps bounced around the crowd and heads shook everywhere. She undoubtedly had been wrenched out of bed, the aroma of lust still fresh on her skin.

"The law of Moses says to stone her," he continued. "What do You say?"

Susanna leaned in to Miriam and whispered, "Where is the man?" Miriam shrugged, nodding in agreement with her friend. "The law requires *both* the man and the woman be stoned for adultery," she said under her breath.

The crowd stood silent, waiting in anticipation for the verdict. Miriam sensed these five religious men were trying to trap Yeshua into saying something they could use against Him. But, instead of answering them right away, He stooped down and began writing in the dirt with His finger. For a few moments everyone watched, wondering what He was doing. Miriam knew He was answering them without using words.

The Pharisees were irritated by His silence and again demanded an answer. Following suit, the crowd began murmuring, then shouting, then chanting. The noise grew like the cloud Elijah prayed into existence—small as a fist at first, then expanding into a huge rain cloud. *Stone her! Stone her!* The woman tried to cover herself with her tattered tunic, mortified to be on trial for her life in front of such a large group of people. Giant tears rolled down her face as she rocked back and forth, muttering to herself. Yeshua looked at her, acknowledging her sin, feeling her shame.

"Teacher!"

"What is Your answer?"

"We are waiting!"

Yeshua stood up again and raised His hands to quiet the crowd. "All right, stone her. But let those who have never sinned throw the first stones!"

He looked at every set of eyes challenging Him. There was more tension in the air than when Cain killed Abel—these men were crying out for blood! The woman's eyes were shut tightly, her body frozen in place. Murmurs ran through the crowd, and the religious teachers grunted in frustration at their thwarted plan. Yeshua kneeled down a second time and wrote again in the dirt. One by one they slipped away, the oldest Pharisee first, followed by the rest. When all of her accusers had disappeared, she was left face to face with Yeshua in the dust. She looked at Him, amazed at His influence with the religious powers of Jerusalem.

He stood, eyes fixed on the adulterous woman. With sincerity and love He said, "Where are your accusers? Didn't even one of them condemn you?"

Shaking her head, she replied, "No."

And Yeshua answered, "Neither do I. Go and sin no more."

The atmosphere—fully charged just moments before—now stood diffused and calm. He turned back toward the crowd and began teaching once more, the occasion ripe for revelation and truth. The woman watched Him move the onlookers toward the Temple steps, giving her the opportunity to walk home with a handful of dignity. But before standing up, she looked at the dirt where He had traced some words. With a gasp she saw her name staring back at her.

Nevaeh.

She reached out to touch the inscription, but a pair of sandals appeared next to it, and she withdrew her hand. Miriam crouched down in front of her.

"Hmm," she said curiously, "*Heaven.* I wonder why He wrote that..."

The woman looked at Miriam. "It doesn't say 'heaven,'" she explained in a whisper, "it says my name." She gently traced the letters that were backwards to Miriam. "Nevaeh."

Miriam stared at her for a minute, feeling the nudges of something inside. Then she spoke with tender confidence. "It's not just your name. It's also your destiny."

Nevaeh looked at Miriam and then said, "I don't belong in heaven. Not after what I've done."

"But you do," Miriam answered as she lifted her from the dirt. She took off her head covering and put it around Nevaeh's shoulders. "Where do you live?" Nevaeh pointed toward the north, and Miriam led them in that direction. She wrapped her arms around the woman, offering the warmth of touch.

"Why are you helping me?" she asked.

"Because I have made mistakes as well. And Yeshua gave me grace, just as He gave it to you."

Nevaeh shook her head and brushed her hair from her face. "Who is that man? Why did the Pharisees listen to Him?"

"He is sent from heaven, from the very presence of Yahweh," Miriam replied, smiling at the connection with the woman's name. "I believe He is the Messiah, though most people aren't as convinced."

"What makes you so sure?"

"Nothing rattles Him. Not leprosy, not unclean spirits, not adultery. He carries power to override all those things... and more."

"How do you know Him so well?"

"I have been traveling with Him for more than two years now, helping as He feeds the poor and heals the sick. Before that, I had an encounter with Him, like you."

"What happened?" Nevaeh asked.

"He delivered me from seven unclean spirits."

Nevaeh's eyes grew wide. She looked at Miriam in disbelief, but Miriam assured her of the truth. She briefly explained what had happened, how she came to live under the influences of the seven spirits, and how they shaped her life.

"I struggled with lust for many years," Miriam told Nevaeh. "That spirit led me in a downward spiral of sin against my body. I had many experiences with men, both married and not."

"You did?" she replied.

Miriam nodded. "It was easy to be lured into doing something that I knew was wrong. The passions were so strong, the opportunities so abundant."

"I know," Nevaeh agreed, "for me too. I never had any intention of committing adultery...it just happened. And after that, it was easier and easier."

"Are you married?"

"Yes," she answered. "My husband sells papyrus papers and inks, and he travels to many different countries... he is gone many weeks at a time."

Miriam thought of Brutus and his collection of writings on Egyptian papyrus. Maybe he had crossed paths with Nevaeh's husband. Then she thought of Dagon who also traveled extensively, and understood that unclean spirits will use any situation for the advancement of evil.

"One day as I was in the marketplace, I met a man I'd never seen before. The moment I saw him something inside me came alive. It felt like true love. My marriage was arranged, and I have grown to respect my husband, but I have never loved him with anything more than duty." Miriam remained quiet to allow Nevaeh to finish her confession. They continued walking toward her home at a reasonable pace. "You can imagine my surprise when I looked into the eyes of another man and felt heat for the first time. For days we did nothing but talk. I enjoyed his company and we discovered that we had many things in common. Against my wishes, he consumed my thoughts day and night. And then..."

Miriam nodded. She and the woman shared, it seemed, more than a few things in common. Her experience with the Spirit of Lust allowed her to guide Nevaeh back onto the right path.

"Nevaeh," Miriam said delicately, "you need to end the relationship with the man who isn't your husband."

She sighed deeply. "I know the prophet said to 'sin no more', but I doubt my ability to walk away. I know it's a sin but..."

"Sin is fun for a season, my father would say," Miriam said, "but it always leads to destruction. Nevaeh, do not let your lust and passion for this man control you. Remember that you made a covenant before Yahweh to remain faithful to your husband, and every thought, every action should honor the Lord."

She could see Nevaeh wrestling with her thoughts. Her hands fumbled with her tunic, bunching it and wringing it, until Miriam put her hands on top to still the woman's. "You were almost killed today!" she said in a strong whisper. "That should be the only thing you need to convince you of the seriousness of your actions."

"I know," she said, "I am distressed more than you can see."

"It's not worth being in this situation a second time. The Pharisees might not give you another chance, unlike Yeshua."

"I still cannot believe they walked away from me..."

"Believe in Yahweh's goodness to you. Believe that a Spirit of Lust wants you to defy everyone and keep living in sin."

She looked at Miriam with a measure of doubt and uncertainty. Nevaeh agreed that she was partnering with sin, yes, but a spirit didn't possess her. Miriam seemed to read her thoughts.

"Do you hear voices telling you, 'Go ahead, nobody will know'?" Nevaeh stopped walking. "How about 'Your husband will never find out' or 'You deserve to be with someone you truly love' or 'Adultery really isn't wrong'?"

Nevaeh's eyes were wide, her mouth agape. "How did you know?" she asked sheepishly.

Seven

"Because that's what the Spirit of Lust says to get you to sin against your body and against Yahweh," said Miriam. "Those are lies, Nevaeh. And the more you listen to them, the easier it becomes. The lure of lust is stronger than most of us are prepared to handle. But it is not impossible! With Yahweh, you can turn from sin and never go back."

"But how? How do I change after all this time?"

"You first need to repent before Yahweh, and thank Him for the grace that Yeshua bestowed upon you today. Then, you tell the man that it's not worth risking your life to be with him." Miriam watched her for a few moments. "And whenever you hear voices telling you to obey your flesh, tell them to go back to hell."

Rain started to dripping from the dark clouds; the women moved along faster. Once at Nevaeh's house, she turned to Miriam and embraced her. She slipped off Miriam's head covering and then slipped inside the door. Before shutting it completely, she offered her a parting promise.

"I will be strong," Nevaeh said. "And thank you."

Miriam smiled at her, and bade her goodbye. When the door stood firmly between them, Miriam placed her hands on it and whispered a blessing over her life, her body, and her decisions. To tell the truth, she felt blessed to be able to minister to other women who experienced the same struggles she once knew. Helping them identify lies and embrace truth—to reject sin and follow righteousness—gave her untold satisfaction. It was, in small measure, exactly what Yeshua had been doing all along.

* * *

Astride a donkey the day after Sabbath, Yeshua entered Jerusalem from the Mount of Olives. Miriam understood that the final moments of His life were set in motion. She fought the urge to try and change what she knew was coming, imagining scenarios in which her devotion to Him would provide her with the power to stop His death. Yet she could hear whispers of her redeemer saying: *This is the will of my Father who sent me; although there is much pain and agony to bear, I will overcome.* He had also said that through death He would destroy the one who had the power of death, that is, Satan, and release those who through fear of death were all their lifetime subject to bondage. The purposes for His death seemed more numerous than the stars that Yahweh had asked Abraham to count.

Five days later as the Passover week drew to a close, the festival meal was held at the house of a local man, as Yeshua had ordained. He and the twelve dined in a large, furnished and prepared upper room, while Miriam, Johanna, Susanna, and other women ate in the lower level with the master of the house and his household. They celebrated, along with the entire nation of Israel, Yahweh's goodness and provision with the Passover lamb. The duality of the sacrifice—both animal and human—seemed lost on all but one.

Because Yahweh had given them freedom from Egyptian bondage, the Jewish people commemorated annually. It was a time of remembering their slavery and honoring their independence. Downstairs, the master led his family and the guests through the rituals that had been handed down generation after generation. But Miriam could hardly keep her mind focused; she wanted to be in the upstairs room. She was supposed to be concentrating on the story of the exodus from Egypt, putting herself in the shoes of her ancestors in order to properly give thanks for Yahweh's goodness to the Israelites. Yet all she could do was imagine what was happening in the room above. Though she told no one, not even the other women, Miriam envied the twelve disciples of their closeness to Yeshua. In her mind, she appreciated and loved Him more than the twelve of them combined. As Yeshua had said, he who has been forgiven much loves much. She had been forgiven much, perhaps the most of them all. Therefore she loved Him much, and that love led her to observe and absorb every morsel of nourishment that He offered. She wondered how the twelve could be so obtuse at times. They seemed to need a drawn-out explanation of just about everything He said in symbolic form. Not that she understood it all perfectly, but Miriam felt that she didn't need a translation of His metaphors and parables. No doubt, had she been in the same room, she would have intuitively picked up on the symbolic references that He would make throughout the Passover meal. But it was not to be.

It wasn't until much later that Miriam learned of the events that night in the upper portion of the house. She learned from John that Yeshua told the story of their ancestors to His disciples, as was customary the night of the meal. The twelve listened in awe, for Yeshua narrated the story with passion and grace, making it truly come alive. Never had they heard such an intense, powerful rendition of the Passover chronicle. As if He were reliving the original event, Yeshua spoke with authority quoting the passage from the book of Šemot, Exodus, just as Yahweh had spoken to Moses:

On the tenth of this month every man shall take for himself a lamb, according to the house of his father, a lamb for a household... Your lamb shall be without blemish, a male of the first year... Now you shall keep it until the fourteenth day of the same month. Then the whole assembly of the congregation of Israel shall kill it at twilight. And they shall take some of the blood and put it on the two door-posts and on the lintel of the houses where they eat it. Then they shall eat the flesh on that night; roasted in fire, with unleavened bread and with bitter herbs they shall eat it... And thus you shall eat it: with a belt on your waist, your sandals on your feet, and your staff in your hand. So shall you eat it in haste. It is the Lord's Passover.

For I will pass through the land of Egypt on that night, and will strike all the firstborn in the land of Egypt, both man and beast; and against all the gods of Egypt I will execute judgment: I AM the Lord. Now the blood shall be a sign for you on the houses where you are. And when I see the blood, I will pass over you; and the plague shall not be on you to destroy you when I strike the land of Egypt. So this day shall be to you a memorial; and you shall keep it as a feast to the Lord throughout your generations.

Familiar with the story of Passover, the twelve disciples failed to see the connection between the version that happened thousands of years prior and the version that was happening before their eyes. Symbolism ran through every part the story, yet it would be some days before any of them connected the two seemingly incongruous accounts.

Yeshua then said to them, "With fervent desire I have desired to eat this Passover with you before I suffer; for I say to you, I will no longer eat of it until it is fulfilled in the kingdom of Yahweh." Taking the unleavened bread, He broke it and gave it to them. Symbolically, Yeshua was handing over Himself—the bread of life without sin. He then recited the Hebraic blessing over the bread. The disciples expected that. What they did not expect was His next statement.

"This is My body which is given for you; eat this in remembrance of Me." Remembrance! The language equaled that of the Exodus story. But they wondered what He meant. If they were to remember Him, then He had to be leaving. Surely He wasn't going to leave them—He was the long-awaited Messiah, the one who had come to free the Jews from Roman rule. And He had to be present for that to happen. No one voiced the universal questions that ran through each of their minds. Instead, the disciples remained wide-eyed and apprehensive of the words and meanings that their beloved master spoke.

Dinner commenced with four cups of warm, red wine. Each symbolized a specific aspect of the Passover experience, and each one had a corresponding prayer to be recited over it. The first cup symbolized the *bringing out* of the Israelites from the land of Egypt. The second signified the *deliverance* from the oppression of the Egyptians. The third cup represented the Israelites *redemption* at the hand of Yahweh, and the fourth cup indicated that they *belonged* to the Creator of heaven and earth.

Following this, a prayer of sanctification was spoken. Roasted lamb, unleavened bread, bitter herbs, and *chârosêth* lined the table. The bread symbolized the Jewish expediency of salvation from bondage; the herbs were a reminder of the bitterness of slavery; and the charoseth—a mixture of apples, wine, nuts, and honey—represented the mud-like consistency of the mortar that Israelites had used to make bricks for the Egyptians. Each aspect of the Passover meal connected the Jews with their ancestors, who had walked the earth hundreds of years prior. And with each generation, thousands more joined that unique birthright. Truly, no other culture contained such a cherished connection—linking the distant past with the present—throughout each century.

Yeshua then raised His cup of wine and confused the twelve further.

"This cup," He said, "is the new covenant in My blood, which is shed for many for the remission of sins. Assuredly, I say to you, I will no longer drink of the fruit of the vine until that day when I drink it new in the kingdom of Yahweh." Again the disciples were mystified. New covenant? Why did He speak of a new covenant? Were they supposed to disregard the old covenant of Moses? Surely not, they reasoned. What they could not see was the fact the Yeshua was their cup of redemption—their present slavery being sin.

Seven

In closing they sang a customary hymn. A psalm of David, it praised Yahweh for His everlasting mercy. The eloquent psalm opened and closed by saying: *Oh, give thanks to the Lord, for He is good! For His mercy endures forever.* Yeshua and His disciples began singing, their deep voices reverberating through the floors and walls. Miriam and the others below glanced up at the ceiling, and one by one they joined the chorus of male voices singing praise to Yahweh. She would remember that moment for days to come.

⟦ 19 ⟧

THE FATEFUL DAY that Miriam was dreading arrived. She could no more stop it than the trees could stop their leaves from changing and dropping. Struggling against the reality of the unfolding events, Miriam remained as close to Yeshua as possible, though her place in line was behind the flock of disciples. Miriam considered the betrayal of Yeshua as a slap in the face, and she wanted to find *Y'hûwdâh Ish Kiriyôt*, Judas Iscariot, to rip the backstabbing tongue out of his mouth with her bare hands. She wanted to defend her friend against all that was happening. But she realized, painfully, that even her best efforts would not and could not save Him. Even so, Miriam desper-ately wanted to try, even if it meant sacrificing her own life. *No greater love has a man than to lay down his life for a friend.* Yeshua had said that, hadn't He? If only that were the solution to prevent His death, Miriam reasoned. As she later learned, she had it backwards. The entire process of His personal sacrifice had to take place in order for *Him* to save *her*. Although Miriam loved Yeshua with abandon, she knew that His love for her was not the same. It was love of a different kind. His love toward her was reserved, gentle, separated. He loved her like a father, yet He treated her as an equal. Once she had accepted her role in His life, she embraced the beauty of it in the same way that the birds embrace the dawn. Selfishly, she wanted to be the most important person to Him—the one He held most dear. But on the other hand, she didn't want to alter their personal relationship for the sake of a bruised pride. She had given that up for the promise of new life.

Miriam would not leave the presence of Yeshua that day. She would stay close, whatever the cost. Even though His disciples were disappearing left and right—a fact that greatly disappointed and infuriated her—she remained faithful and steadfast through the events that led up to His death. Where else was she going to go? Her place had been carved out along side of Yeshua just as His future tomb was carved out of rock. To abandon her post at that hour would have been tantamount to personal as well as spiritual treason. Miriam was not willing to deny Him or her faith in Him before men, a principle that carried eternal ramifications either way. No matter the situation, she would not change her position of surrender to Him. No matter the bleak outlook, no matter the future consequences, no matter whatsoever.

* * *

On the small plot of land referred to as Golgotha—the place of the skull— that stood outside of the city walls, Miriam stood with the other women who also devoted their lives to His ministry. She could do nothing but stare at Him, physically destroyed. There she remained motionless, almost without breath, at the shock of watching her friend slip away. Total numbness encased her limbs.

Nothing at all compared to Him—to knowing Him, to loving Him. Everything else was meaningless, insignificant, temporal. The agony of watching Yeshua die the slow death of crucifixion hit her full force, leaving her with the feeling that someone had thwacked the breath from her lungs.

Silent words emerged through quivering lips. Abundant amounts of joy had surrounded and filled Miriam throughout her days with Yeshua—the kind of joy that did not depend on circumstances or seasons, the kind of joy that walked hand in hand with life. But at that moment, joy was nowhere to be found.

All at once, she remembered the events that had led her to the exact spot where she stood. Miriam saw the scenes of her life: her childhood, the seven spirits, her deliverance, her days of ministry, the experiences with Yeshua, the preceding Passover week, the trial, the scourging, the mockery, and the elevation of the cross. Flashbacks of the past few hours emerged, as she watched Him progress in pain and suffering. The harshness of the memories gave way to the harshness of the present scene that unfolded before her, the way a bad dream transitions from the subconscious to the conscious.

Staring blankly, trancelike, a single tear crawled down her face and touched her lips, igniting a sensation that slapped her back into reality, bringing her back into awareness of Golgotha. Though she seemed to others to be in a different reality, she felt deep love rising up from her belly, flooding her mind and heart once again.

Right then torrents of tears emerged. As if pulled down by weights, Miriam collapsed and screamed. *If He dies, I die!* She felt as if every breath that agonized Him was equally agonizing her. *How can the one man who loved me so openly and purely be ripped out of my life so violently?* Knowing that He would die soon, she sobbed.

Watching, waiting for death to come and claim Him, Miriam shuttered with a cold remembrance of her own near-death experience. She had witnessed Him raising people from the dead, so how could He now be powerless against it? Why didn't He come down from the cross and show the mockers that taunted Him that He indeed was the Son of Yahweh? How could He surrender to death? It just wasn't right for Him to die! He had contributed so much to so many—physically and spiritually. One man had affected more good for the Israelites and Gentile people than all of the Hebrew prophets combined.

Everything that had made sense previously, suddenly did not. Yeshua had explained the plan—death, then resurrection—but right then, it felt like chaos. Miriam couldn't get past the reality of death to look three days into the future.

If He had to die, then He deserved better than a Roman death on a cross. *Cursed is anyone who hangs on a tree*, the book of Isaiah proclaimed. What Miriam could not see that day was the fact that Yeshua had become the curse for all humanity. Past, present, and future curses stopped at the cross: generational curses, genetic curses, cultural curses—any curse, any source. Curses, therefore, had been rendered null and void through the power of the cross. Through His affliction humanity gained freedom. It was only a matter of placing the cross between a person and the ravages of sin. Of course, Miriam would come to understand that in due time. But as she stared at Him, all she could comprehend was the gruesome reality that lay bare before her.

Starting at the sound of His voice, Miriam held her breath to hear Him. He struggled to speak, the slow suffocation making Him pant. "Yahweh, Yahweh, why have You forsaken Me?" He managed to cry out with a passionate voice. The distress laced in His tone screamed of severe mental anguish.

Seven

Miriam reeled against that one word. Forsaken. Deserted, abandoned, and left to die a miserable death alone... the implications were too overwhelming to comprehend. How could the Father forsake the Son, she wondered. Why would that even be a possibility much less a reality? Miriam had no answers. Chills scampered all over her body. She had known the horrors of isolation and the angst it brought. Hope dissipated under its weight, comfort departed at its ferocity.

Remembering the isolation that consumed her, Miriam shuttered. It had belied its penetrating strength, just like the seven spirits. Under a different guise, isolation had seemed to be an advantageous condition, as if it were a partner to independence. But time had proven otherwise—isolation had been no friend. It had ravaged Miriam mentally and emotionally. It had controlled her physically and relationally. It had destroyed her morally and spiritually. She empathized with His cry of desperation and despair. It was a feeling and an experience so powerful that it shook the very foundations of the soul. Isolation was no respecter of persons; everyone who encountered it stood helpless and powerless in opposition. Miriam had cried out against it, the same way Yeshua was crying out now. Almost three years prior, He had heard the voice of her cry and had freed her from the forces of spirits and the forces of isolation. She desperately wanted to be able to do the same for Him. Yet she saw with unveiled clarity the impossibility of her desire.

Alone, Yeshua hung there, crushed beneath the forces of abandonment. Miriam couldn't stand that He—her redeemer, her friend—felt forsaken by Yahweh. Her inability to remedy that or to help Him in any way merely added to her unbearable grief.

Then, all at once, Yeshua surrendered Himself up. "Father, into Your hands I commit My spirit."

The fight was over. The end had arrived. Miriam's world suddenly came to a screeching halt. Everything she had and everything she did revolved around Yeshua. Now that He was gone, what would she do? Her purpose and mission in life disappeared before her eyes. Who was she without Him?

In all honesty, she felt it wasn't fair. She had spent ten long years suffering the vices of unclean spirits, and only three years nurturing her soul with the Son of Yahweh. If only they had been given more time! The gratifying mission of following Yeshua had ended so abruptly, so unexpectedly. Even with His warnings, Miriam had been unable to prepare herself for this day. How could she have? She realized that no amount of preparation could come close to easing the pain she was experiencing. Nothing could reach her pain, except for Him. But He was gone.

When Yeshua breathed His last, the agony in her heart magnified itself one hundred fold. As His head hung down on His chest, the guards waited to ensure the finality of His death, piercing His side for confirmation. Despite the thunder and the succeeding earthquake, Miriam heard nothing save her heart that begged to die with Him. Without warning, Miriam let out a wail that shook everyone within fifty feet. Face down, belly to the earth, her tears mixed with the dirt and encrusted her face. The pain of a broken heart and a broken spirit were more than she could have ever imagined. How long she lay there she didn't know, or care.

* * *

All was silent. During those few days when Yeshua fought the powers of death everything became deathly quiet to Miriam. What she perceived to be an abrupt end of life—of hers figuratively, His literally—turned out to be but a moment in time. Looking back, she would compare it to a caterpillar that dies in its cocoon in order to become a butterfly. But at that time, the music of her life ceased to play and the world ceased to have meaning. Nothing but silence pervaded her being. Her heart and her mind both were silent, just as His grave was silent.

20

AFTER HAVING RESTED on the Sabbath, as much as she could following the events of the days before, Miriam rose early that third day and prepared to go to the tomb. Her mission that morning, which is to say adding fragrant oils and spices to the linen-shrouded corpse, reached back to early customs of her heritage. She vaguely remembered the soldiers removing Yeshua from the cross and *Yôwçêph ha Râmâthea*, Joseph of Arimathea, taking Him away for burial. Motivated by memories, Miriam set out to attend His grave and pay respect to His body.

In the pre-dawn light the core group of women, including Susanna, Joanna, Salome, and the mother of Yeshua, gathered together and made its way over to the garden tomb. Not having much to say, Miriam led the short journey through Jerusalem, wondering whom they would get to move the stone from the grave entrance. As they approached the garden area, the orange and pink rays of the sun broke through the darkness, proclaiming the promise of a new day. In all honesty, the women had no conception of how prophetic the rising sun would be that morning.

At last they arrived at their destination. The garden that housed the tomb sat outside the city walls, near to the place of crucifixion. Pathways made from flat stones meandered through the garden, some leading to a cistern, some leading to small open areas, and some leading down to the lower level where a tomb had been carved out of a large rock wall. Following the paths, the women walked under canopies of trees and foliage. The dark greens and browns of the vegetation contrasted against the light colored stones, giving the façade a raw yet refined feel.

That morning the garden felt quiet yet quenched, the way the earth smells after it rains. There was something strangely familiar about the place, Miriam realized. It smelled, mysteriously, like the fragrant oil that her family produced in Magdala. After entering from the far side of the garden, she distinctly noticed the olive trees and an old olive press. Miriam had a momentary flashback of her conversation with Yeshua that took place in the olive groves of Galilee. *Olive grove!* The correlation all at once staggered her—He had been pressed like the olives.

Miriam knew that ripened olives were bruised and crushed and hung to drip, in order to retrieve the precious oil within. *I will be bruised and crushed for their iniquities*, He had said. She remembered that the night before His crucifixion He had gone with the disciples to pray in the garden of Gethsemane. At the time the name didn't mean anything to her, but suddenly she recalled that the word Gethsemane meant *oil press*. Yeshua, of course, had understood the prophetic symbolism all along. *I will pour out My soul unto death*, were His words to her. How beautiful it all was! Just as oil poured out of the presses, His love had been poured out upon the earth, lubricating the souls of all who would dare to believe.

That astonishing revelation coated the surface of Miriam's spirit. For a moment she felt a certain, temporary happiness. But then she remembered the reason for her presence at the garden tomb. As promptly as it had appeared, the joy vanished. Pain and longing still throbbed underneath it all. Deep within her, she ached. She was there to tend to the bruised, crushed, and pressed body of the entombed Yeshua. The reality of that grinded against her heart.

Approaching the small tomb entryway, Miriam noticed that something was amiss. Picking up her pace, she skipped a few steps as she drew nearer to His resting place. And then her heart felt as if it had fallen straight through her torso landing with a crash in her abdomen.

The stone had already been rolled away!

Alarm set in and Miriam began to sweat and become panicky. As soon as she looked into the tomb, her worst fear became a reality, and she gasped while clutching the stone wall.

"He's gone! What happened? Where did His body go?" she yelled aloud, not directing the question to anyone in particular. Miriam feared it had been stolen.

Even though two men robed in white sat on either end of the short stone table—a niche on the right hand side of the tomb, where the body of Yeshua once laid—Miriam did not notice them until the first one spoke.

"Why do you seek the living among the dead?"

Almost jumping out of her skin, she stared at the radiant man as he spoke.

"Woman," the angel said, "the man you seek is no longer here. Remember how He spoke to you when He was still in Galilee, saying, 'The Son of Man must be delivered into the hands of sinful men, and be crucified, and the third day rise again.' Go and tell everyone that He is risen!"

More panic. *What?! What did he just say?*

Distressed by the whole encounter, Miriam turned as she heard someone just outside the tomb. She pushed passed the others and abruptly approached Him, feeling the familiar inundation of tears.

The man said, "Woman, why are you weeping?"

"Sir, if you have carried Him away, tell me where you have laid Him, and I will take Him away," she pleaded with urgency. Her voice crumbled as the words unfolded.

Miriam didn't wait for the man to answer, but just kept rambling on about how important it was for her to find the body. Her trembling voice increased in speed with every emitted word; she thought the sooner she got answers to her questions, the sooner she could locate His body. Thanks to the blood pounding through her body, her words were somewhat incoherent and jumbled. Her hands were speaking just as fast as her mouth, flapping about, pointing this way and that. Miriam kept looking around the garden for some sign of the shrouded body, which prevented her from noticing the familiarity of the man to whom she spoke.

The man, whom she assumed to be the gardener, spoke again. "Who is it that you seek?"

In that instant, the music that she had felt in her soul while ministering with Yeshua throughout Galilee erupted, once again, into song! Miriam's spirit knew something that her mind did not, but she was too shaken up and confused to realize what was happening. Her spirit shouted that He had done it—He had conquered the grave! Her mind, however, continued to scream something altogether different: *I need to find you!*

Looking for the former Yeshua, bruised and broken, Miriam did not rec-ognize Him, new and resurrected. The conqueror. He no longer fit the old, expected mold. She would not have paid any attention to this man in the garden; she would gladly have left Him there in pursuit of her master, as He wasn't answering her questions. But an image of Adam in the Garden of Eden flashed through her mind, leaving her with a sensation that this moment was directly connected to the beginning of mankind. That it was part of an or-dained plan. A second beginning of sorts.

It was not that Yeshua was unaware of her desire; He just needed to hear it from her own lips. Forcing her to pronounce aloud this desperate plea of heart, Yeshua enabled Miriam to enter into a new dimension of faith and relationship.

Forever faithful to her, He heard the voice of her cry. And He answered it.

After a momentary pause where the faintest smile pulled at the corners of His mouth, the risen Messiah gently said, "Miriam."

It was the tone that got her. The way that He spoke her name was like the soothing sounds of water lapping at the shore. Whipping her head around to face Him again, Miriam nearly fainted upon recognizing Yeshua, standing alive before her, and in one piece!

"Rabboni!" she shrieked. Her shock and excitement echoed throughout the garden.

Her mind was always the last to catch up. Her spirit and soul were al-ready singing with exclamation, but her mind had been frantic. Controlled by her powerful emotions, Miriam ran over to Yeshua and fell on Him, not caring what anyone else thought. She wrapped her arms around Him and literally fell into Him, causing Him to stagger backward a few steps. The tears poured out of her, soaking the front of His tunic.

"I can hardly believe that You are alive—but You are!" she cried. "I never thought that I would see You again!"

She had found Him. Honoring her desperation to seek Him out, Yeshua gladly embraced Miriam. She marveled and sighed at the familiar warmth that radiated out of Him; she smelled the aroma of fragrant oil emanating from His skin. Now she understood why her soul was singing and rejoicing! He was alive! Miriam was incredulous yet elated, stunned yet revived. To tell

Seven

the truth, she felt that her heart had been resurrected alongside Him.

After letting her possess those few brief moments, Yeshua grasped her arms to loosen her grip, and spoke with the utmost tenderness. "Miriam, do not cling to me." Greeting His mother and the other women, who had been standing a few feet away with their mouths agape, Yeshua quickly gave them instructions—Miriam in particular—to go and spread the good news that He had conquered the grave! Having to focus her attention, Yeshua once again took Miriam's head in His hands—though now pierced—in order to hold her still. Her heart was bursting with adoration and exhilaration. She had to concentrate to hear Him over the music playing inside her.

"Because you are so important to me and to the kingdom of heaven," He explained as He looked deeply into her mismatched eyes, "I want you to be the one who tells My disciples. I am trusting you with this good news. Will you do that?"

She nodded while smiling tearfully. She was amazed and honored that He would ask of her such a request! Miriam was overwhelmed with excitement and energy. Laughing from sheer glee, Miriam took off running to share the miracle of all miracles—the resurrection of Yeshua of Nazareth!

Running as fast as she could, her feet kept up with the momentum of the music playing within her. The music ran through her body as she ran along Jerusalem's winding walls. He had just given her—a woman—a task of infinite importance. He trusted her and needed her and counted on her to be faithful to Him. Miriam's feet hardly touched the ground as she sprinted to announce the news to His disciples, her laughter keeping pace as well. Rushing through the crowded streets, Miriam realized that her own misgivings had been conquered in the same way. The time during which Yeshua lay in the tomb had been a time of hopelessness for her heart. But now she could tangibly feel eternal hope thrusting through her veins.

Miriam was a firsthand witness to the fact that one man had changed the world dramatically and eternally. And she knew that man, loved that man with all of her heart, with all of her strength, with all of her mind.

Minutes later, after telling the disciples and watching them run toward the empty tomb, Miriam stood and waited, reflecting and processing the incredible events that had just taken place in rapid succession. She smiled, envisioning the risen Yeshua, and embraced the music that echoed within, filling her heart.

21

DAYS LATER, MIRIAM found herself wondering how she had been granted the privilege of time and place, and involvement with the kingdom of heaven. She was still giddy from Yeshua's glorious and miraculous resurrection. How amazing that morning had been! In the weeks following, He spoke of strange things such as the promise of the Father and waterless baptisms.

One evening Miriam and the other women overheard Yeshua talking to His disciples. "In My Father's house there are many mansions," He said, "if it were not so, I would have told you. I go to prepare a place for you. And if I go and prepare a place for you, I will come again and receive you to Myself; that where I am, there you may be also."

"What? He's leaving again?" Miriam said, her heart sinking.

"Why all the coming and going?" Susanna said. "He's here, He's dead; He's back, He's going..."

"I'm not sure," Joanna answered. "Seems confusing to me as well. And why did He use a bridegroom allusion—'going to prepare a place'?"

"That's just plain strange," replied Susanna. "Who's His bride? The disciples?"

Joanna laughed. "Sometimes I cannot keep up with all the parables and prophesies."

"And the mansions?" Susanna added.

"I know," said Joanna.

"The twelve would get lost in anything bigger than a fishing boat."

"Maybe they will all share just one."

The women chuckled at the amusing image. They stood and watched the disciples for a few minutes.

"I wonder how long before He leaves again," Miriam said.

"Faster than we want Him to," Joanna replied.

"Well," Susanna said, "until then, we won't let Him out of our sight."

"Agreed," they chimed.

* * *

Forty days after that, Miriam, alongside the other women who also loved Yeshua, watched from a distance as the man who had changed her entire being—body, soul, and spirit—mysteriously ascended into the heavens. He had blessed His followers with out-stretched hands, and subsequently disappeared as fast as the Babylonians had destroyed the first temple.

The reason He needed to leave the earth, as they learned, was to usher in another entity. They were all instructed to remain in Jerusalem until Yahweh sent His promise, or His Spirit. And so they waited, just as a pack mule awaits to be loaded with goods before a journey. Day after day they waited; day after day they prayed. No one was sure what the arrival would look like. But ten days later on *Shâvuôt*, the Feast of Weeks, the promise arrived.

No one had expected it that day. Not the twelve disciples—who had recently replaced Judas Iscariot with Matthias—not the brethren of new followers, and certainly not the women who had journeyed alongside Yeshua. They had all been celebrating and giving thanks to Yahweh for the ingathering of first fruits, an annual Jewish custom since the days of Moses. They had transitioned into the summer harvest from Passover. Remembering their freedom from slavery, the Israelites had rejoiced in Yahweh's ultimate deliverance for them. As they later understood, through the death and resurrection of Christ, Yahweh had delivered them once again from bondage. Not from slavery to people but from slavery to sin.

On that day, everyone had gathered together in one house. Without warning a violent windstorm filled the skies and sent them looking out the windows. The noise and force of the wind was such that men and women alike thought the house would collapse. Then all of a sudden, it blew into the house from the east to the west. Miriam clung to Susanna and Joanna as she watched tunics and head coverings fly through the air. She could see fear on the faces of half the disciples. Joanna shut her eyes tightly, and Susanna shielded her face with her arm. But Miriam watched it all with eyes gaping. To tell the truth, it sounded like the roar of a crowd, and for a moment Miriam wondered if the Jews that hated Yeshua and His followers were storming the house.

But within minutes the wind vanished. Though the windows remained closed that morning, it traveled through them as if they sat wide open. What it left in its wake, no one would have imagined. As eyes opened and people looked around, what they saw shocked them more than the abrupt windstorm. Over each head stood a small flame that looked like fire. The flames flickered and moved as if alive. At that point, no one dared move. The tiny tongues of fire were strangely beautiful. Colors of gold more vibrant than the Israelites' golden calf mesmerized Miriam. Silence filled the house until one lone voice spoke softly.

"What *is* that?"

Heat began to permeate the room. All at once, the hovering flames came to rest upon each head, disappearing into hair and head coverings alike. Warmth plunged from their heads down throughout their bodies. But the heat didn't feel like traditional fire, Miriam realized. To her, it seemed more like a burning from within. The Spirit of Yahweh, the Holy Spirit, quite literally took up residence within each of them.

One voice, then two began talking. But Aramaic or Hebrew it was not. Heads turned and expressions showed confusion as languages from surrounding areas and countries emerged from every mouth. Peter spoke in the tongue of the Egyptians, James in the Elamites', Simon of the Cappadocians', and Thomas—skeptical as always—in that of the Arabians. Miriam heard Joanna speaking a Latin dialect from Rome and Susanna uttering Greek. Amazement filled the house, the languages flowing back and forth between His followers with growing enthusiasm. Then Miriam discovered that her language given by the Spirit of Yahweh was one that she had never heard. In fact, it didn't sound like a traditional language at all. At first this confused her, but she quickly welcomed her new tongue. No doubt she would discover its derivation sooner or later.

From the far side of the house, Miriam heard laughter erupt. The combination of strange heat pulsating through their bodies and the fact that uneducated men from Galilee were speaking foreign languages with fluency seemed absurd. What was happening? Was there more coming? The laughter caught on, and joy spread from one person to the next as fast as the fire had spread through their bodies. When it reached Miriam, the joy hit her squarely in the gut. At the exact same time, she began laughing with Joanna and Susanna. The three of them laughed harder and harder until Miriam was bent over and Joanna was rolling on the floor. Tears couldn't be stopped. It was, truth be told, the most perplexing yet wonderful thing she had ever experienced.

After some minutes of giggling and cackling, men began spilling out of the house and into the street. They fell atop one another, stumbling again and again, all the while laughing with supernatural joy. A joy so strong human legs could not bear the weight. They looked, of course, completely drunk. And to those who came across them in the street, the followers of Yeshua seemed more bizarre to the Jews than the plagues did to Pharaoh. But as people listened to what the disciples were saying, they heard the spectrum of languages being spoken. And they heard them giving praise and glory to Yahweh. Soon people from all nations were running to see and hear what was rumored to be an unusual miracle.

"How can this be?" a voice asked.

"These people are all from Galilee," another said, "and yet we hear them speaking our languages!"

"What can this mean?"

"That they're drunk!" a Pharisee shouted.

"What a disgrace!" another said.

"These men are disciples of Yeshua, are they not?" a man asked.

"Yes, yes!"

"See what shameful behavior they display?" he mocked. "They are making fools of themselves."

"But they are talking about the wonderful things Yahweh has done!" another replied.

The onlookers stood there amazed and bewildered. As the laughter quieted down, Peter—led by the Holy Spirit—stepped forward to explain. The other eleven followed.

"Listen carefully, all of you, fellow Jews and residents of Jerusalem! Make no mistake about this. Some of you are saying we are drunk. It isn't true! It's only the third hour of the day and too early for that. No, what you see this morning was told to you centuries ago by the prophet Joel."

He then quoted the ancient man of Yahweh as recorded in the Scriptures, where Yahweh said He would pour out His Spirit on all flesh. Both young and old would prophesy and dream dreams; they would see wonders in the heavens above and signs on the earth below. Exactly what was happening before their very eyes.

Miriam looked at her friends, witnessing prophecy being fulfilled yet again. She, like them, couldn't believe what had just happened. And for once, the three of them were speechless.

* * *

Toward the end of that week, Miriam heard a voice. Her heart accelerated twofold and her breath caught in her throat. She immediately recognized that it was not her own, but neither was it a voice from her past.

"Miriam," it whispered.

She glanced around, wondering if anyone else heard it. No one seemed to notice. In all honesty, Miriam bristled against the idea of hearing a voice other than her own again. For ten years she heard seven voices. For the three years following that, she heard only hers. But now, an unknown voice appeared unexpectedly.

"Miriam, you were once an enemy in your own mind, but you have been reconciled through the death and resurrection of Yeshua. Now, you are presented as holy and blameless in Yahweh's sight. Continue to walk in the faith, grounded and steadfast, so that you are not moved away from the hope of the gospel—the good news—which you have witnessed and heard," the Holy Spirit said.

Miriam guessed that the voice belonged to the Lord, the same one that blew through the house and deposited an unknown language within her. But she wasn't completely sure. With some hesitation she asked, "Who are you?"

"I AM..." the voice answered. "I AM the Spirit of Yahweh."

Whereas the voices of the other spirits boomed with voracity, the voice of the Holy Spirit was much quieter. Miriam grew to love that voice of great peace. All at once she understood her father's explanation on the art of hearing Yahweh. He had always quoted a passage from the book of Kings that described Elijah's encounter:

> *And behold, the Lord passed by, and a great strong wind tore into the mountains and broke the rocks in pieces before the Lord, but the Lord was not in the wind; and after the wind an earthquake, but the Lord was not in the earthquake; and after the earthquake a fire, but the Lord was not in the fire; and after the fire a still small voice.*

A delicate whispering voice. So simple, yet so powerful.

"Be aware, Miriam, and do not let your guard down," the Holy Spirit said. "The enemy is persistent and relentless in pulling people downward, especially those who eyes have been opened to the truth. To those who believe in Yeshua."

"I certainly don't want to fall back into the arms of the seven spirits," Miriam replied, "or any other evil spirit, for that matter." Immediately she uttered a simple, heartfelt prayer. *Teach me to do Your will, for You are my Lord. Your Spirit is good. Set a guard over my mouth; keep watch over the door of my lips. Do not incline my heart to any evil thing. Lead me in the way of righteousness.*

"The voices of evil will surely come to you again."

Miriam tensed and her mind began to race with harmful thoughts.

"Do not be afraid! They no longer have power over you, for you have Me, the Holy Spirit, inside you now. As Yeshua said, resist them. Do not let their thoughts become your thoughts. They give lies and false doctrines, but I give you the mind of Christ in all things."

Miriam thought for some moments. She asked, "How can I be sure if the voice talking to me is evil? Unclean spirits are masters of deception, as I know so well."

"When you hear a voice say something that does not replicate Scripture and the instruction of Yeshua, it is not from above but from below."

"Of course," she said softly.

"I will not give you commands that are contrary to Yahweh's word. The spoken word and the written word will always come together to edify, to strengthen, and to give life."

Seven

Miriam embraced that truth as a mother embraces a young child. And though she didn't acknowledge it aloud, she felt the new language stirring within.

"Remember the things that Yeshua said while He was with you on earth," the Spirit instructed.

"I hope that I can recall it all... He said so much!"

"Do not fret. I will bring back to your remembrance all that He taught you. I will be your teacher and your guide, to keep you on track as you press ahead in obedience to what He is calling you to do."

Miriam sighed deeply. "Thank you, for I surely would not be able to do it on my own."

"Truly, it will not be by your might nor by your power, but by My Spirit. Listen to your spirit within you, Miriam, to the new language," said the Holy Spirit. "I will always communicate truth to your spirit and to your heart. It is not man's language. It is My language. Listen to hear My voice; tune your ears to recognize when I am speaking."

"I will do my best," Miriam promised.

Such conversations gave Miriam the strength of confidence. Day in and day out, she was consistently amazed that while Yeshua was absent, the essence of who He was remained with her. It was as if He were right next to her, only invisible. Slowly but surely, Miriam began to appreciate the wisdom and blessing of relying on the delicate voice of the Holy Spirit. It was the only spiritual voice that she now entertained. It was the only spirit worth knowing.

Soon the Holy Spirit began to draw spiritual parallels for Miriam to understand. For example, the Spirit reminded Miriam of the recent Passover where Yeshua had been crucified. But instead of thinking about the horrific details of His death, her mind was drawn higher. She remembered the day when the priests led the flock of spotless lambs into Jerusalem. Hundreds of them bleating and bumping against one another. Men, women, and children shouted *hôšâ-na!*, hosanna!, and used palm fronds to guide the lambs down the streets to the Temple. "Save us! Save us!" they shouted at the unblemished sacrifices. All the activity and drama of that Jewish ritual clouded her eyes to connect the fact that Yeshua, atop a young donkey, entered the city on the same path a few minutes behind the lambs.

Suddenly, the words came back to her. Yeshua had said: *I am the Lamb that will be the atonement for all humanity.* And like a thunderbolt, it hit her. It was not a figurative statement. He was the pure, sinless sacrifice! During the event Miriam had not made the correlation. But now, thoughts too numerous to count rushed into her head, leaving her feeling dizzy with the excitement of revelation. Had anyone else realized this at the time? The disciples? Her female companions? Had anyone made the connection? The enormity of it weighed upon her, overwhelming her more than the inhabited promised land did for Joshua and the Israelites.

Gently, the Helper guided her into truth. "What man has done for centuries with millions of perfect lambs, Yahweh has done once in the form of one perfect human being. Whereas the Passover lamb covers the sins of a household for one year, the true Passover Lamb covers the sins of all humanity, for all time."

"Of course!" Miriam exclaimed.

"Just as the blood of the lambs on the doorposts of the Israelites' homes forced the angel of death to pass over the families, the blood of Yeshua on the souls of human beings forces the powers of hell to pass over them for eternity. Back then, blood was applied to the doorposts and lintels of the houses in Egypt; now, blood is applied to the doorposts and lintels of the heart for men and women."

Miriam couldn't wait to explain what she had learned to Joanna, Susanna, and the other women. She knew they, like her, would rejoice with this truth. In all honesty, she was more excited to receive this revelation from the Holy Spirit than *Malkâh Shebâ*, or the Queen of Sheba, was to witness the wealth and wisdom of King Solomon. Silently, Miriam cried out for more.

* * *

One night, as spring gave way to summer, Miriam dreamed of Yeshua.

"Miriam," He said to her, "for years you have followed Me and offered yourself as a supporter and follower of the Way. Now it is time to reverse our roles— you will teach others about the kingdom of heaven, and *I* will support *you*."

Seven

Though she wanted to respond, her mouth was unable to form words. She stood calmly, eyes set on Him.

"You have the ability to see the natural and the supernatural clearly," said Yeshua. "Your eyes mirror that. One brown, the other green. It is a gift, Miriam. The world may see it as a mark of imperfection, but it is a mark of greatness."

She felt her eyes brighten and instinctively put her hands to face. Yeshua reached out and grasped them. Heat and power poured into her, rippling over and over.

"In my name, preach repentance and the remission of sins, for you are a witness of these things. All authority in heaven and on earth has been given to Me, and I, in turn, am giving it to you. Teach those who will believe to observe all the things that I have commanded you. The harvest is ripe. Now is the time. *Go.* And behold, I am with you always, even unto the end of the age."

Miriam opened her eyes, the dream gone. She had the strangest feeling, though, that it had not been a dream. For all she knew, He could have been there. The dark room was silent as usual. But the air around her smelled of Him, that fragrant aroma of crushed olives—musty yet sweet—with hints of myrrh and frankincense. Miriam breathed deeply and rolled over, falling back into sleep with a smile on her lips.

Several times over the course of the following days, Miriam thought of her dream. Once she recognized it as her official commission, she determined in her heart to return to Galilee. Miriam could feel the soft nudging of the Holy Spirit telling her to prepare to leave Jerusalem, the way a mother bird nudges her young from the nest in order to fly. On the one hand, she brimmed with eagerness to share all that had happened in the city of David, but on the other, she hesitated leaving the fellowship of believers there. Her mixed feelings were as entangled as *Yôwthâm's*, or Jotham's, parable about kings and trees, yet she could sense the time approaching for her to go.

Despite the fact that everything in Jerusalem reminded her of Yeshua, when she closed her eyes she pictured Him in Galilee. Truth be told, she pictured herself there as well. It was her home. The sights, the sounds all appealed to her there. Jerusalem, though fascinating and significant, could not compare. She had stayed because Yeshua commanded them to. She had stayed even longer after the Holy Spirit began using the followers of the Way, as they had become known, to shake up the city. But all along, she wondered if Yahweh would ever bring her back north. The dream, of course, had answered that.

"When should I leave?" Miriam asked the Holy Spirit.

"Soon."

"Whom should I go with? I cannot go alone…"

"I will show you," the Holy Spirit said.

"How will I know it's time?"

"Just be prepared. And follow My lead."

22

As the number of believers increased daily, they pooled their money and possessions together to share. People sold houses and land and brought the proceeds to the disciples to distribute among themselves as well as to others in need. One man called Barnabas, from the island of Cyprus, sold a field he owned and contributed all the money. Another man named Ananias also sold some property, but he and his wife, Sapphira, kept a portion of the profit for themselves. This would not have caused an issue except for the fact that they tried to deceive the disciples, and, in essence, lie to the Holy Spirit. They both fell to the floor and died within three hours of each other, as a result.

"There are some crazy things going on right now," Susanna said to Miriam. "First the arrival of the Holy Spirit with wind and fire, then Peter—once a coward—healing the cripple and preaching before the Council, then Ananias and Sapphira dropping dead..."

"I know," Miriam replied.

"What next?"

"I'm not sure, but my guess is it won't be good. The rulers of this city are clearly not happy with us."

"It's the most commotion they've seen since the trial and crucifixion of Yeshua."

Joanna added, "Threats against the disciples for preaching boldly have been increasing for days now."

"You're right," Susanna said, "it won't be long before they put action to their words."

"It's exactly what they did to Yeshua," said Miriam.

"Should we do something?" Joanna asked.

"For now we just need to wait and listen to the Holy Spirit," Miriam answered. "We will know what to do when the time comes."

That night as Miriam was trying to fall asleep, she thought about the sin that Sapphira and her husband had committed earlier. She remembered her own sin from living with the voices of the seven spirits, and felt twinges of regret, guilt, and disgrace. Suddenly, she heard the soft voice of the Holy Spirit.

"There is no condemnation for those who believe in Yeshua," the Spirit explained to Miriam. "If you are faithful to confess your sin before the Lord, then He is faithful and just to forgive you, and to cleanse you from all unrighteousness."

"I have confessed all of my sin before Yahweh, but I sometimes feel regret over things I have done or have said."

"You must choose to surrender any feelings of guilt, and you must choose to forgive yourself. Otherwise you will become weakened and ineffective, unable to fulfill the purposes that Yahweh has called you to accomplish."

Pausing to *Çelâh*, or ponder, Miriam reflected intensely.

"You see, Miriam, guilt comes from the enemy; he wants you to remain convinced that Yahweh has not truly forgiven you, thereby keeping you in bondage to the past. Can you see that?"

"Yes," Miriam whispered. "I can."

"Unlike guilt, conviction of sin has an end—it leads to repentance. It has a purpose, which is reconciliation to Yahweh. It also leaves no shame. Guilt over sin is a tactic of the enemy, but conviction of sin is a gift from Me... as long as you accomplish the will of Yahweh by turning away from sin and turning toward Him."

"One way creates captivity and the other freedom."

"Yes. One destroys, the other heals."

As her teacher and guide, the Holy Spirit reminded her of Yahweh's word. "The Scriptures declare that Yahweh casts your sins behind His back, that He buries them in the deepest sea. The Scriptures also say in the Psalms that as far as the east is from the west, so far has He removed your transgressions from you. For as the heavens are high above the earth, so great is His mercy toward those who fear Him."

"Yes, I remember now," Miriam said.

"When Yahweh says that He remembers your sins no more, it is more than the mental act of remembering—Yahweh will no longer take action on the sin. The debt owed is gone. The blood of the Lamb covers it, and so you are cleansed from unrighteousness before Yahweh. Even more, you are seen as holy in His eyes."

"Truly, Your ways are higher than my ways, and Your thoughts higher than my thoughts. I feel so unworthy."

"Through Yeshua you are abundantly loved and *worthy* to receive all of Yahweh's blessings. Every morning His mercies are new; every day His compassions cover the earth."

Miriam silently thanked and praised Yahweh. *Great is Your faithfulness.*

"The love of your heavenly Father knows no bounds," the Holy Spirit assured her. "He desires to have a right relationship with you, which is why you must follow His lead and surrender the yoke of guilt and penance. That yoke is not from Yahweh. The yoke that Yeshua gives you is easy and light. It shackles together forgiveness and humility. So take His yoke upon you and learn from Him."

Once again, Miriam chose to surrender her own misgivings and embrace the Lord's words to her. Then succumbing to drowsiness, she closed her eyes.

"Miriam," the Holy Spirit whispered, "freedom is yours to keep."

When sleep finally overtook her, Miriam dreamed deeply. She saw herself walking home to Magdala with a group of others. They stopped at a caravansary for the night in Samaria, where the strangest thing happened. One by one, her family walked in; then Lemuel; then Dagon, Lydia, and Brutus; then the widow. Lastly, the nomad entered. Everyone in the room turned and looked at him, but his gaze was fixed on Miriam. Then at the same time, everyone looked back at her. And she woke up.

* * *

Toward the end of summer, persecution began against the followers of Yeshua, just as Miriam had predicted. In the same way that the temperatures were rising in Jerusalem, the animosity related to the new faction escalated tenfold. Had they remained quiet and not proclaimed the good news of the

Messiah, the authorities would have left them alone. But the Holy Spirit gave them such boldness they couldn't contain themselves. Truth be told, they did more preaching than *Ts'phanyâh* and *Chaggay*, Zephaniah and Haggai, did to the wayward residents of Zion. That only angered the high priest, Pharisees, and Sadducees. So, after repeated warnings to Peter, John, and the others, the Council in Jerusalem unleashed a measure of wrath.

One Pharisee, known as Saul, willingly took the reins. His offense at hearing Yeshua proclaimed as Messiah rang out as loud as the shofar in a heated battle. Fire burned in his eyes, fury emerged from his lips. With permission from the Sanhedrin and direction from Satan, Saul spearheaded the persecution. He made it his mission to squash the blasphemous rebellion, to rid his holy city and the Jewish faith of the contagious heresy.

First, Saul had the men whipped and flogged. But when the apostles continued to praise Yahweh—rejoicing, in fact, to be treated the same as Yeshua—Saul threw them in prison. There, he thought, the men would have time to contemplate their disobedience to the authorities while writhing in pain in a cell that resembled hell. They emerged the next day after angels of the Lord opened the prison doors. The apostles, much to Saul's indignation, marched straight to the Temple and spoke as the Holy Spirit gave them direction. To make matters worse, they encouraged others to do the same.

Saul, at that point, decided in his heart to have them all murdered. As it turned out, he didn't have to search far to find his first victim. Stephen, full of faith and power, was performing great wonders and signs among the people. This got the attention of the Council, who disputed with him and ultimately conspired against him. Accusations arose and multiplied minute by minute. The high priest asked Stephen if he indeed had spoken against Moses and the law. And despite the fact that everyone who sat on the Council saw his face shinning like an angel's, they proceeded to interrogate him callously. But Stephen answered them all with truth deposited from heaven.

When he blamed the Jewish authorities for killing Yeshua, the righteous Messiah, they shook their fists in rage and hurled curses at him. In that instant, Stephen gazed upward to heaven and saw Yahweh's glory with Yeshua standing in the place of honor at His right hand. As soon as he excitedly told this to the Council, they put their hands over their ears, drowning out his voice with their shouts. They began rushing at him with the same passion for blood that the Egyptians pursued the departing Israelites. Saul immediately ordered for Stephen to be dragged away and stoned to death.

A band of unmerciful Sadducees dropped Stephen in an open square nearby, picked up their stones, and rained down their rage upon him. Miriam, Susanna, and Joanna watched from a distance, shocked that the persecution had intensified so quickly. They clung to one another, hearts racing and eyes darting around. Would the Council also condemn them? They certainly were associated with the followers of Yeshua. That was no secret. Miriam noticed Saul standing on the sidelines, grinning with sick pleasure at his apparent victory. She could sense, even from a distance, a group of evil spirits surrounding him and fueling him with demonic passion.

As soon as it was finished, the Sadducees and Pharisees fled the scene, leaving Stephen's body alone and covered in blood. But the women couldn't just leave him there. They had to risk removing him from the open place. Many minutes later, when no one else remained, Miriam and her companions hurried over to him and used their head coverings to wrap his body. Had they left Stephen there, vultures and mangy dogs would have begun feasting, just as had happened to Queen Jezebel. Other believers arrived to help clean his body and prepare it for burial. The city was a-cry with vengeance and sorrow. At that point, Susanna pulled Miriam and Joanna aside.

"I think we need to leave Jerusalem."

"It's time," Joanna agreed, weeping for Stephen.

Miriam wiped tears from her eyes and nodded. Though torn between staying with the growing group of believers and departing the city, she knew Susanna had confirmed what the Holy Spirit had been telling her.

The next day, the women packed up their belongings at the house. As they were formulating a plan of departure, Philip, Matthew, and Andrew, rushed in and hastily shut the door behind them. Miriam looked at them, seeing fear in their eyes.

"What is it?" she asked.

"Saul," Philip answered.

"He's on a rampage of terror," said Andrew.

"What has happened?" Susanna said.

"He is systematically ridding Jerusalem of believers."

"All of them?" Miriam said, her voice shaky.

"Yes," Philip said, "men and women alike. He is going from house to house, dragging them out like dogs and throwing them into jail."

Susanna gave Miriam a look of urgency. Outwardly, she appeared calm, but her insides swelled with apprehension.

"We are going to go to Samaria," Philip said in hushed tones.

"When?"

"Today," Andrew answered. He noticed that the women had gathered together a few small satchels. "Come with us."

The women looked at each other. Samaria was a good distance away, but maybe they should go farther.

"We were talking of going back to Galilee," Miriam said.

"Let us make it to Samaria first, then we'll see where the Holy Spirit takes us," Philip said to everyone. They all nodded.

"Meet in one hour by the Jaffa Gate."

* * *

The atmosphere inside the city of Jerusalem had shifted dramatically in the last few months. It seemed charged with abundant forces from the kingdom of darkness. But as soon as Miriam and the convoy left the area, she could feel the air change, or in other words feel more normal. The farther away they traveled, the more she relaxed. Her thoughts eventually shifted from the persecuted group of believers to the Samaritans who had yet to hear news of resurrection power and Holy Spirit fire. Even though Philip had his sights set only on *Shôm'rown*, or Samaria, Miriam knew she was being led back to Galilee. She didn't know how long they would stay in Samaria, but she wasn't concerned. The Holy Spirit, liberally giving wisdom and discernment, would guide her.

Walking along the road, Miriam reflected on the last three and a half years of her life. The presence of Yeshua and the indwelling of the Holy Spirit had changed her completely. Like the disciples, she had relied upon Yeshua's presence to touch lives, one by one, in a miraculous way. He had led; they had followed. But when He departed the world forty days following His resurrection, the disciples and followers became the leaders. And so they needed the same power that Yeshua had carried, which is to say the power of the Holy Spirit. Whereas before, the physical hand of Yeshua had touched people one at a time, bringing healing and salvation, now the invisible hand of the Holy Spirit was touching scores of people at the same time, bringing power and boldness. Yahweh, in essence, had made them all replicas of the original model; the apostles and followers of Yeshua were now the ones out preaching, teaching, and healing.

The road to Samaria was long. Miriam thought the day felt hotter than the furnace used by King Nebuchadnezzar to punish defiant citizens. Sweat dripped down her body, offering small amounts of cool on her swelling skin. She was eager to find a place of shelter for the night, but none loomed on the horizon. The caravan could not travel much farther. The animals struggled under the freight and the heat. The sky would begin to grow dark before the full moon rose out of the east. Miriam loved the full moon. As soon as she imagined its warm, glowing face, she heard the soft voice of the Holy Spirit.

"Call to Me, and I will answer you, and show you great and mighty things that you do not know."

She whispered, "Holy Spirit, what do you want to show me?"

Immediately, the words Yeshua had said before His ascension came to her mind. *But you shall receive power when the Holy Spirit has come upon you; and you shall be witnesses to Me in Jerusalem, and in all Judea and Samaria, and to the end of the earth.*

She meditated on this for a few minutes, knowing that the Holy Spirit wanted to impart revelation. "Give me wisdom," Miriam said, "and understanding."

"The Scriptures say, 'Blow the trumpet at the time of the new moon, at the full moon, on our solemn feast day.'"

All at once, she understood. She was to announce—*to trumpet*—the grace of Yahweh through Yeshua during full moons, new moons, and feasts. The upcoming feast, *Yom HaTeruah*, otherwise known as the Feast of Trumpets, was a fall festival symbolizing Yahweh's reign as king of all creation. He had instructed Moses in the Torah that, "In the seventh month, on the first day of the month, you shall observe a day of solemn rest, a memorial pro-claimed with the blasts of trumpets, a holy convocation." And so, every year the Jews celebrated with the sound of trumpets. The feast had expanded over the centuries to represent the coming of the long-awaited Messiah. With a blast of the trumpet, He would arrive and establish peace throughout the world. Bringing physical and spiritual liberty to all of the earth's inhabitants, the expected Messiah would redeem the lost and gather all unto Himself.

Unlike the majority of Jews, Miriam believed with her whole heart that the Messiah had already come, and that He had indeed brought liberty to hu-manity. To her it seemed as obvious as the imminent full moon. But Yeshua did not have the appearance or demeanor of a king; He did not act as they expected their king to act. So few people had seen Him as the redemption of Israel; so many kept on waiting.

With each step she took toward Samaria, Miriam understood that she was to bridge the gap between the Jewish festivals and their fulfillment through Yeshua. Not only was she to announce the good news of Yeshua to the lost and dying—*Those who are well have no need of a physician, but those who are sick*, He had said—she was to reach those who embraced Yahweh but rejected His son. Nothing had been more important to Yeshua than the fo-cus of His ministry, the object of His attention, which is to say the mosaic of humanity. He had treated each soul as important to the whole mosaic. After all, without the individual life—the individual tiles—what would humanity be? Yeshua had made His mark on the world, forever changing how mankind would relate to one another as well as to Yahweh.

Autumn was rapidly approaching. The mission before her seemed daunt-ing. Even so, she believed the Holy Spirit would steer her in the right direc-tion and enable her to walk in grace overflowing. Just as she once worked to bring in the harvest of ripened olives at the grove, Miriam now would labor to bring in the harvest of ripened hearts. She laughed at the imagery.

Miriam began singing to help pass the time. The song, captivating and emotional, echoed her past and dreamed of her future. Her voice swirled around the caravan of men and women in raw elegance. Even the animals acknowledged the expressive, melodic sound. The road they walked seemed paved with voices. Everything had led her to this moment, this place. Miriam

Seven

turned her head, looking back at the past few years. So much had happened. The journey behind her was greater than anything she could have ever imagined. But the journey ahead would rival everything she had experienced so far. And she couldn't wait to get there.

EPILOGUE

LIGHT IS ABOUT to break the darkness. The soft glow of the descending full moon touches the corner of Miriam's eye, and she turns her head. She has talked through the night without realizing it. Looking over her right shoulder, she sees Joanna still asleep but Susanna stirring on her mat. When she looks back at the broken man, unmoving on the bed, Miriam notices something odd.

The side of his face is wet, a single line running from his eye down to his neck, as if a tear has fallen. The light from the oil lamp reflects against his skin. Miriam moves toward him to wipe his cheek when a small teardrop rolls out. As soon as her hand touches his face, he catches her arm. She sucks in a shock of surprise. Her gasp wakes Susanna, who sits up abruptly.

"He's not dead," she says.

"No," Miriam whispers, staring at the man.

"You didn't wake me."

"I never got tired..."

Slowly, the man opens his eyes, taking in his surroundings. Pain courses through his body, but he keeps that to himself. He blinks away the moisture and squints to focus on her face. She notices that his rough hand feels abrasive against her skin. He sees her looking at her arm, then immediately lets go. His hands gradually clutch and un-clutch themselves, and his lips move but no sound emerges. Watching him with patient curiosity, Miriam waits for his words.

"I am sorry," he says at last, his voice coarse and low.

"That's all right," she answers. She rubs her arm unconsciously. A moment of silence passes.

"No, you do not understand."

The distant accent that is familiar causes her breath to catch in her chest. She looks at him as if seeing a spirit from the past. Shadows dance against the wall.

"I am sorry for what I have done," he says. "To you."

Miriam goes cold. Susanna inches her way closer, not making a sound. Neither of them can believe what is happening. It is an inconceivable recurrence.

When Miriam doesn't respond, he asks, "You are the woman in the story, are you not?"

Taken aback, she exhales cautiously. "I am."

"And I am the man who attacked you more than twelve years ago," he confesses.

She stares, thunderstruck.

"Your eyes..."

Miriam turns her face away. He looks nothing like he did back then. She never would have recognized him, had he remained silent. Without warning, feelings of rage and bitterness and revenge pounce upon her. The throbbing in her ears and head is so loud that she can hear nothing else. Her whole body trembles. She feels like she's drowning in conflicting emotions—she wants to run out of fear but her flesh wants to strangle him. It would be so easy. She would have closure in her life. Miriam rivets her eyes on the wall, trying to determine what to do. The room is silent for some minutes.

The man angles his head toward the sky. Without looking at her, he says, "I remember that night. It was a full moon, just like tonight."

Miriam looks at the moon and marvels that the same face that had watched them collide years ago, watches them reunite now. It seems like the face of God Himself, ever-present and full of light. She exhales a long breath, escorting the murderous inclinations out. She knows with abrupt clarity that He has brought them together again for a specific purpose, and that His purpose will not go unfulfilled. Relying on the Holy Spirit to guide the situation, Miriam settles herself and waits.

"I had never done anything like that in my life," the man continues. "Many bad decisions, and worse outcomes... I am not an innocent man." He then faces Miriam again. "But I was not in control of myself that night—I knew it then just as I know it now." The initial guardedness gone, he speaks with complete openness.

Miriam agrees with a nod of her head. It is apparent to her that the Lord does not see as man sees; for man looks at the outward appearance, but the Lord looks at the heart. The sacrifices of God are a broken and a contrite heart. Compassion overwhelms Miriam's heart, surprising even her. She places a shaky hand atop his. "I know."

He stares at her with eyes wide. "Why did you take care of me?" he asks. "You could have let me die here. Should have."

"I didn't know it was you..."

His eyes bored into hers. "Now that you know, go ahead and kill me. I am powerless against you." His breath, raspy and confrontational, sounds like unseen voices.

"I cannot. I *will* not," Miriam says quietly.

"Why not?"

"Because in my heart I have already forgiven you the evil that you rendered against me many years ago."

"You have?" he asks warily. "Why?"

"There is no peace in holding onto resentment," she answers. Her body begins to feel the peace of the Holy Spirit; the quavering trickles away.

He shakes his head slightly. "It does not make sense."

"The things that are wise in God's eyes seem foolish to men. My heart was deeply wounded, but the Lord in His infinite mercy reached out and healed it. The ways of the supernatural—the ways of God—often make no sense. But this I know: His ways are higher than our ways and His thoughts are higher than our thoughts."

He gives her a confused look.

Miriam explains, "In the natural, it seems impossible to be healed and restored of deep emotional wounds. But with God, the supernatural overcomes the natural and the wounds heal, leaving no pain to dwell beneath the surface."

The man looks at her skeptically. "But what about the scars? There are always scars."

"Ah, yes. Scars then go from being reminders of pain to being reminders that God miraculously takes away the pain. The memories remain but behind them lie only goodness—feelings of experiencing God's grace, His unmerited favor."

The man closes his eyes, processing everything Miriam has said. It appears after some moments as if he's fallen back to sleep. Sounds of snoring filter into the air, but it comes from Joanna instead. Susanna creeps to the end of the bed and sits behind Miriam. She puts a warm hand on her back. They watch the man, whose chest barely rises and falls. Maybe he will die in spite of everything. But minutes later, to their surprise, his eyes pop open.

"They are powerful," the man hisses, "the spirits."

Suddenly, Miriam feels the fingers of Fear, as if the spirits have stepped out of the shadows. She gets up and walks away, standing in the doorway for some fresh air. One deep breath follows another. Even with her back turned, she can sense the presence of the seven spirits. They have returned.

"They are, indeed," she says.

She hears them taunting and mocking her, proclaiming that she had never really been set free. Miriam notices her hands shaking. She tucks them into her tunic and presses against her stomach. With great intention, she forces out the apprehension and focuses on the greater power of peace.

"Like you, I knew the spirits were there," says Miriam. "It was easier for me in the beginning to pretend nothing was happening, in spite of the fact that I knew things weren't right. Later, their thoughts became my thoughts, and I fell into step with their agenda. At the very end, I felt as I had at the beginning, where I literally was not in control. They made my life miserable. Regardless of whether I struggled against them or cooperated with them."

The man listens to her every word. He is amazed the same spirits assaulted both of them. He wonders if she knows that they are in the room. That after the calamitous night he has never lived without spirits of his own.

"I have seen many people possessed by evil spirits—you see a lot when you travel the roadways," he says. "I never thought it would happen to me."

"Inflicting pain and bondage is their mission. The more they bind up a person the better, keeping them from anything that resembles freedom or love. They serve Satan, the Father of Lies, which is why lies are their primary weapon. They are armed with an endless supply of strategies, and they will bring the kingdom of darkness to earth every chance they get."

"So," the man says, grimacing, "it was not by chance after all."

Shaking her head, she walks back over to him. Miriam replies, "No, it never is. There is always an agenda."

She can see the thoughts running through his head, the voices giving him chase. Agony crosses his face. The pain of a bruised body matches the torment of the spirits. He hates the reality that he's caught up in—one of constant wrestling with life, one lacking peace. But he knows no other way. The spirits, however torturous, have become companions. Miriam sees a shadow hovering over the man. His body jerks and he squeezes his eyes shut. Another tear falls out.

"Do you want them to go away?" she whispers.

The air in the room is quiet; moths can be heard fluttering. But the unseen world around them is in a battle, the seven spirits raging with all their might, the Holy Spirit filling the room like a swollen river. While he weighs his options, Miriam prays in the language the Holy Spirit has given her.

Slowly, he shakes his head. "It won't work."

Miriam identifies the lie. She knows the spirits are filling his ears, reminding him of his past, declaring his fettered future. He cannot see beyond the chains.

"It is impossible," he states.

The Spirit of Fear poisons the atmosphere. They both feel it, seeping into their skin. It would be so easy for her to give in again. The unclean spirit would enjoy nothing more. But Miriam pushes through.

"With God, all things are possible," she replies. "But you need to crave freedom. It has to come from here," Miriam says, placing her hand on her chest. She doesn't take her eyes off his. She can see with intense clarity what is transpiring in the natural as well as the supernatural. Pain consumes him and his body recoils. Miriam feels the Holy Spirit urging her forward, giving her words.

She lifts a cup of water to his mouth. "Let the thirsty ones come—anyone who wants to," she says prophetically. "Let them come and drink the water of life without charge."

The man feels the cool liquid traveling down his throat and resting in his belly. It is a salve—for his body, for his spirit. With a jolt he sits up. Miriam and Susanna instinctively brace themselves.

He leans toward Miriam and moans. "Yes..."

She looks at him, hoping he will continue.

"I want them to go away..."

Miriam takes his hand. In a tone overflowing with confidence and authority, she speaks to the seven spirits. "I see you unclean spirits," she says, looking at the shadows. "Spirits of Fear, Rejection, Bitterness, Rebellion, Lust, Pride, Death, and any others... I know that you are here. And I break all agreement with you. We no longer partner with you, and you no longer have power over us. You must leave. *Right now.* Go back where you came from."

With a great suction of air, the spirits vanish from the room. Miriam's hair blows across her face, Susanna's tunic pulls across her body. All three of them look at the doorway, seeing the shadows fly out into the last minutes of night. The force of their departure leaves the atmosphere feeling frenzied. But a few seconds later the air regains tranquility. The room is brighter.

Miriam, Susanna, and the nomad stare at the doorway. Susanna starts laughing at what just took place; Miriam smiles gently and faces the man. He takes the cup from her hand, drinking the rest of the water. Peace floods his body, and he lies back down. His face reflects freedom. Tired, he slips quietly into sleep. This time, his soul echoes a calm disposition as his body releases years of suffering.

"Just when we thought we left all the unusual events behind us in Jerusalem..." Susanna says.

"I have a feeling that 'unusual' is becoming normal," Miriam replies.

"Did you know who he was?"

"No... I was quite surprised."

"I can hardly believe that your lives crossed paths again, in Samaria of all places."

"God has a way," Miriam says. "Had it not been for the Holy Spirit, I would have run out of this place faster than the Gentiles make false idols."

"Me too," Susanna confessed.

"The Spirit of Fear is so strong... but God is greater," she says with thanksgiving.

They both observe the nomad sleeping.

"Now what?"

"For now, pray," Miriam answers. "When he has rested for a while I will tell him of the good news. His heart must be filled with the Holy Spirit, lest the seven return with others more wicked than themselves."

Susanna nods. "Think we've encountered enough demons tonight."

Miriam prays for the nomad, thinking of what she will tell him when he wakes. That Jesus, though Jewish, never ignored the Gentiles. That God is not a respecter of persons. That God loved people first so that they could love Him in return. She plans on explaining that while He loves everyone, He does not love sin and wickedness. That sin keeps a person at arm's length because He is a just God, full of righteousness. But that the sacrifice Jesus made atones for all sin through His blood. She will say that His shed blood gives life—a better life on earth as well as an eternal life with Him. And that everything necessary to obtain this life is through faith that God raised Jesus from the dead. Then a confession by mouth; after that, salvation is secure. It's His promise. Surely the nomad wouldn't turn down that offer.

Though Miriam has not slept, she feels invigorated and full of God's presence. Affected by the evening's events, she praises God for His hand of goodness that has brought her and the nomad together again. She marvels that such an incredible divine appointment has taken place so soon after leaving Jerusalem. And she delights at the thought of more awaiting her in Galilee.

The courtyard rouses with the first rays of dawn. Animals look for water, people for food. The innkeeper emerges from around the corner and enters the room.

"How's he doing?" he asks Miriam.

"Better," she replies. "He is coherent but sleeping now, though I imagine he's in a lot of pain."

"I can find him something for that."

"He will need a few more days to recover."

"Fine," he says. "How long are you staying?"

Miriam and Susanna look at each other. "As long as it takes."

The innkeeper leaves, and Joanna awakens on her mat. She pushes sleep from her eyes, stretches, and walks over to her companions. She looks at the nomad for a moment and then at Miriam and Susanna. She sees volumes written on their faces.

With a cheerful voice she asks, "What did I miss?"

Questions For Discussion

1. Do you identify with Miriam or any part of her life, whether it is a traumatic experience or a life-changing miracle?

2. Are you concealing a secret(s) or event(s) that might have changed the course of your life?

3. What lies, if any, do you believe about yourself right now? If you hear something that sounds like a lie, ask yourself, "Would God agree with that statement?" Ask God to reveal the truth to you.

4. Are there certain spirits mentioned in this story that resonate with you more than others? Perhaps you have felt the effect of them in your life, either now or at some point? Can you see how allowing one might invite others?

5. Are you currently harboring un-forgiveness or offense at anyone, at yourself, or at God?

6. Do you believe God can set you free from lies and bondage (mental, emotional, physical)?

7. Do you consider Miriam to be strong or weak?

8. How do you think Miriam's life and the seven spirits would have played out if she had gone ahead with the arranged marriage?

9. Are there aspects of societal life in Tiberius that remind you of our culture today?

10. When you hear an unfamiliar voice, how do you respond? When you hear God's voice, how do you respond?

Glossary

Aaron – Ahărôwn

Abednego – Ăbêd N'gôw

Abigail – Ăbîygayil

Abimelech – Ăbîymelek

Abel – Hebel

Abraham – Avrâhâm

Adam – Âdâm

Ahab – Ach'âb

Ahasueras – Ăchashvêrôwsh

Amnon – Amnôwn

Amos – Âmôwç

Ahithophel – Ăchîythôphel

Aram-naharaim – Ăram Nahărayim

Ark of the Covenant - b'rîyth ârôwn

Asaph – Âçâph

Athaliah – Ăthalyâh

Babylon - Bâbêl

Balaam – Bil'âm

bath – mikvêh

Bathsheeba – Bath-Sheba

Beersheba - Be'êr Sheba

Benjamin – Binyâmîyn

Bilhah - Bilhâh

Boaz – Bô'az

Cain – Qayin

Caleb – Kâlêb

Capernaum – Kefâr Nâchûm

Daniel – Dânîyê'l

Darius -- Dâr'yâvêsh's

David – Dâvîd

Deborah – Devôrâh

Delilah – Delîylâh

Dinah – Dîynâh

Eli – Êlîy

Elijah – Êlîyâhûw

Elisha – Ĕlîyshâ

Endor – Êyn-Dô'r

Esau – Êsâv

Esther – Eçtêr

Exodus - Šemot

Eve – Chavvâh

Ezekiel – Y'chezqê'l

Ezra – Ezrâ

Disciples – Tâlmidîm

foreigner – gêyr

Galilee – Gâlîyl

Garden of Eden – Gan Êden

Gennesaret - Kinn'rôwth

Gentiles – Gôyim

Gibeon – Gib'ôwn

Gideon – Gîd'ôwn

God – Yâhwêh

Goliath – Golyath

Gomer – Gômer

Gomorrah – Ămôrâh

Grave / Dead – sh'ôl

Hadassah – Hădaççâh

Hagar – Hâgâr

Seven

Haggai - Chaggay
Ham – Châm
Haman – Hâmân
Hannah – Channâh
Hezekiah - Y'chizqîyâh
Holy Spirit – Ruâch haKôdêsh
horn / trupmet – shôphâr
hosanna - hôšâ-na
Hosea – Hôwshëä
Isaac – Yitschâq
Isaiah – Yešha'yâhûw
Ishamel - Yishmâ'êl
Israel – Yisrâ'êl
Jacob – Ya'âqôv
Jael - Yâ'êl
Japheth – Yepheth
Jeremiah – Yirm'yâhûw
Jericho – Y'rîychôw
Jeroboam - Yârob'âm
Jerusalem – Y'rûwshâlayim
Jesus – Yêshûwa
Jew – Y'hûwdîy
Jezebel – Îyzebel
Jochebed – Yôwkebed
Job – Îyôv
Joel – Yôw'êl
Jonah – Yôwnâh
Jordan - Yardên
Joseph – Yôwçêph
Joshua – Y'hôwshû'a
Jotham - Yôwthâm
Judah/s – Y'hûwdâh
Proverbs – Mishlê
Psalms – Tehillîm

King – Melek
Korah – Qôrach
Laban – Lâbân
Lemuel - L'mûw'êl
Levi – Lêvîy
Lot – Lôwt
Magdala – Migdâl
Malachi - Mal'âkîy
manna – mân
Manoah - Mânôwach
Meshach – Mêyshak
Messiah – Mâshîyach
Micah – Mîykâh
Michal – Mîykâl
Miriam – Miryâm
Moses – Môsheh
Mount Arbel – Har Ârvêl
Naaman – Na'âmân
Nabal – Nâbâl
Naboth – Nâbôwth
Nahum - Nachûwm
Naomi – No'ômîy
Naphtali - Naphtâlîy
Nazareth – Nâzâret
Nehemiah – N'chemyâh
Ninevah – Nîyn'vêh
Noah – Nôach
Obadiah - Ôbadyâh
Passover – Peçach
peace - shâlôm
Pharaoh – Par'ôh
Pharisees – P'rûshîm
Potiphar – Pôwtîyphar
prayer shawl - talîyt

Queen of Sheba - Malkâh Shebâ
Rachel – Râchêl
Rahab – Râchâb
Rebekah – Ribqâh
Rephidim - Rephîydîym
Reuben - R'ûwbên
Ruth – Rûwth
Sabbath – Shabbât
Samaria – Shôm'rown
Samson – Shimshôwn
Samuel – Sh'mûw'êl
Sarah – Sârâh
Satan – ha-Sâtân
Saul – Shâ'ûwl
Sea of Galilee – Yâm Gâlîyl
Selah - Çelâh
Seth – Shêth
Shadrach – Shadrak
Shechem – Sh'kem

Shekinah - Shêkinâh
Shem – Shêm
Shulamtie - Shûwlammîyth
Sisera - Çîyçerâ
Sodom – Ç'dôm
Solomon – Sh'lômôh
Tamar – Tâmâr
Tarshish – Tarshîysh
Tiberias – Tvêryâ
Torah – Tôrâh
Uriah – Ûwrîyâhûw
Uzziah - Uzzîyâhûw
Zadok – Tsâdôwq
Zarepeth – Tsârephath
Zebulun – Zevûwlûn
Zephaniah – Ts'phanyâh
Zion - Tsîyôwn
Zipporah – Tsippôrâh

The New Strong's Exhaustive Concordance of the Bible , © 1995, 1996 Thomas Nelson Publishers

Acknowledgments

I WOULD LIKE to thank my Heavenly Father, who whispered the hints of a novel into my ear one day; the Holy Spirit for inspiration and direction; and the Son, who gave it the stamp of approval.

My husband, Tyler, has supported me unconditionally for the last twelve years as I ventured, on and off, into this new territory. Thank you for your encouragement, feedback, reading, and re-reading. To my precious daughters, Madalene and Hannah, you are my delight.

Thanks to my parents and sisters for godly love and marathon excitement.

Thank you to my numerous readers on both coasts. Special thanks to Ellyn Davis at Double Portion Publishing, whom it was a pleasure working with; to Michelle Ryan for your editorial work and spiritual insights; and to Karen Yonally for your enthusiasm, suggestions, and use of your olive grove, Amici del Padre.

About the Author

Tristan Kenworthy Hodges has been involved in Christian ministry for more than twenty years through Young Life, Elijah House, and Believing Women. She holds fine arts degrees from Pepperdine University and Brooks Institute of Photography. This is her first novel.

Follow her blog at www.OneFootOnTheWater.wordpress.com.

Please visit AbbaOil.com or Amazon.com for purchase. Also available in e-book format on Amazon.com.

Biblically Inspired Products
for Anointed Living

Abba Anointing & Prayer Oils
from the Holy Land in 12 fragrances

Abba Fragrant Candles
Pillars, Containers, Tins

abba
jerusalem

Abba Bath & Spa
Lotion, Shower Gel, Bath/Soaking Salts

ABBA'S ANCIENT BIBLICAL FRAGRANCES
& THEIR SPIRITUAL SIGNIFICANCE

CASSIA- *humility, servanthood, consecration*

CEDARS OF LEBANON- *strength, permenance, restoration*

FRANKINCENSE & MYRRH - *intercession, healing, deliverance*

HENNA - *repentance, spiritual tenderness to the Lord*

HYSSOP- *cleansing, purification, refining fire*

KETUBAH - *marriage covenant, blend of 4 fragrances*

KING'S GARMENTS - *glory, splendor, majesty of coming King*

LILY OF THE VALLEY - *purity of heart, honor, devotion*

MYRRH - *preparation, purification, dying to self*

POMEGRANATE - *blessings & favor, fruitfulness*

ROSE OF SHARON- *inward beauty, prized treasure of the Lord*

SPIKENARD - *intimacy, extravagant worship with no regard to cost*

8850 Windfern Rd #5, Houston, TX 77064

<u>www.abbaoil.com</u>